M000240264

THE
HOLLOW
GODS

A. J. VRANA

PARLIAMENT HOUSE PRESS

Copyright © 2023 by A. J. Vrana. All rights reserved.

First published in July 2020.

No part of this book may be reproduced in any form or by any electronic or mechanical means, including information storage and retrieval systems, without written permission from the author, except for the use of brief quotations in a book review.

ISBN: 978-1-9561365-6-2

Parliament House Press

www.parliamenthousepress.com

Cover Art by: Monika Palosz

Edited by Malorie Nilson, Emily Peters, & Megan Hultberg

Note: This is a work of fiction. Names, Characters, Places and Events are products of the author's imagination, and are used factitiously. These are not to be construed or associated otherwise. Any resemblance to actual locations, incidents, organizations, or people (living or deceased) is entirely coincidental.

PRAISE FOR A. J. VRANA'S THE CHAOS CYCLE DUOLOGY

THE HOLLOW GODS

Vrana's dark, folklore-infused debut, the first of a duology, introduces readers to the residents of Black Hollow, who hold their daughters close and their twisted secrets closer...Vrana crafts a unique local mythology and draws from existing lore to create a sense of creeping dread. Vrana is off to a strong start with this solid, suspenseful tale.

  – *Publishers Weekly*

This dazzling debut pulls you in with its compelling characters and horrifying mystery and keeps you in its thrall until the final page. The writing sizzles with menace, and the dark mythology A. J. Vrana weaves from dreams and nightmares is unlike any I've ever encountered, in and out of books. A perfect story for contemporary fantasy readers who love their narratives razor-sharp and their secrets dark and deadly.

  – Katya de Becerra, author of *OASIS* and *WHAT THE WOODS KEEP*

A. J. Vrana's debut The Hollow Gods is an exciting contemporary horror-fantasy that shines when it declines to play frights, which are easy, and instead explores dread, collective and generational grief, trauma, and historical responsibility...The fragmented, surgically precise narrative builds from the utterly, painfully ordinary to the absurd and fantastic.

  – *Three Crows Magazine*

PRAISE FOR A. J. VRANA'S THE CHAOS CYCLE DUOLOGY

Grounded in secrets, myth, fantasy, and alternate reality, Vrana's debut installment in The Chaos Cycle series is a fast-paced, deeply intriguing urban fantasy. Prepped with intriguing details, the narrative is both engrossing and vivid, the writing assured, and the pacing perfect. Exploring varied themes of grief, depression, trauma, and collective guilt, Vrana hooks the reader from the very start, leaving them anxious for the next installment.

    – The Prairies Book Review

THE ECHOED REALM

Good vs. evil is cleverly turned on its head as Vrana pulls readers down the rabbit hole into her strange, folkloric world.

    – Publishers Weekly

The Echoed Realm cleverly expands Vrana's wholly original Dreamwalker mythology beyond the town of Black Hollow, with blood-chilling consequences. Gods are more powerful, possibilities are endless, and threats are more sinister than ever. Miya and Kai are haunted by the past, literally, while the lines between dreams and reality, lore and fact, and obsession and possession are paper thin.

    – Katya de Becerra, author of *OASIS* and *WHAT THE WOODS KEEP*

The Echoed Realm is the perfect sequel to Vrana's stunning and original debut, *The Hollow Gods*. Brimming with sharp edges, dark nightmares, and menacing villains, this book will haunt you in all the best ways. Compulsively readable, with complicated characters and expansive world-building, this is an epic, macabre folktale for a new generation. Vrana's lyrical writing is a mix of poetry, chaos, violence, and energy, blending to create a wild and wonderful potion, and I can't wait to read more from this rich new voice in contemporary fantasy.

    – Kim Smejkal, author of *INK IN THE BLOOD* and *CURSE OF THE DIVINE*

The Echoed Realm pulls no punches and offers a masterfully crafted supernatural horror that's not afraid to face the hard truths and imagine a different kind of world. *The Echoed Realm* leaves an aftertaste of a promise, of something bigger and better, deeper and even bolder than this. Look out for A. J. Vrana in NY Times bestselling lists in the next couple of years.

    – Three Crows Magazine

PRAISE FOR A. J. VRANA'S THE CHAOS CYCLE DUOLOGY

Everything about this book has a dark and spellbinding edge...an emerging threat in your peripheral vision, a creeping dread. Horror, supernatural, and fantasy push the threads of realism to its very edges.
  – *The Coy Caterpillar Reads Book Reviews*

For my parents, whose belief in me runs as deep as the roots of the world.

Stories aren't told to convey the facts. They're told to convey the truth.

— ANNABELLE,
owner of Black Hollow's best bed & breakfast

CHAPTER
ONE

MIYA

Miya had always been obsessed with the hidden. What lurked beneath the veneer of a perfect smile or the façade of Stepford contentment? What cracks hid under the polish, threatening to topple the entire structure?

But behind the gloss of the University of British Columbia logo printed on the envelope in her hand, Miya knew exactly what she'd find. She tore it open, not caring that whatever was inside became collateral damage. Piecing it back together, she forced her eyes to scan over the page.

Dear Miss Emiliya Delathorne,

After careful review of your academic performance, the Faculty of Liberal Arts and Social Sciences regrets to inform you that you have been placed on academic probation for failing to meet the Satisfactory Progress Policy requirements outlined below.

Sweat pooled at the back of her neck as her eyes tripped over every word.

No notation will appear on your official university transcript. You can review the Satisfactory Progress Policy on our registrar's website—

Miya tossed the letter aside, uninterested in the rest. *How the hell did it get this bad?* she thought, her stomach knotting with guilt. Her parents would be gutted. They'd agreed to pay for the semester, and they expected results. Distance learning was intensive, so they'd hoped to lessen the pressure to find gigs, allowing her more time to study. But scraping rent money together was still on Miya's shoulders. She was late again this month, and her ostentatious landlady, Patricia, was running dry on charity.

Digging a shallow grave in the sand with her shoe, Miya kicked the letter in and ground it into the dirt. She shifted on the swing and gripped the rusted chains at her sides, staring across the hazy white field where vendors would set up the market in a few hours. Her audience, an endless blanket of towering trees, loomed from the perimeters of the meadow only a few paces from where she sat.

For as long as Miya had lived in Black Hollow—an insignificant dent in British Columbia's temperate rainforests—the market was next to the abandoned playground on the edge of the misty black woods for which the town was named. Whenever fog descended on Black Hollow, the surrounding forest's emerald lustre seemed to darken. For twelve years, Miya had been returning to the old swing by that viridescent sea—especially on nights like this. She could find it blindfolded.

Don't lose your way, she heard the wind hiss an ominous spell, *or there'll be hell to pay.*

Feathers kissed the back of Miya's neck and she shuddered, jumping from the swing and spinning towards the forest. Some said the playground was haunted, and it wasn't unusual to hear voices in the wind, beckoning innocent bystanders to approach—or sometimes, to run away.

But Miya wasn't one to shy away from the unknown. "I'm not lost," she called to the darkness. "I know exactly where I am."

The declaration was met with silence. Miya sighed and reached down for her bag when the nearby shrubs rustled. A raven swooped down to the swing and cawed, his wings flapping as he steadied himself.

Miya squinted at the bird—barely visible in the dim blue light before dawn. "Tough luck. I'm going home," she told him and turned to leave, but a flurry of feathers and the scrape of talons on the back of her skull stopped her.

"Jesus!" She flailed her arms over her head and turned back towards the swing, only to find the raven still perched there. It was like he hadn't moved at all.

He canted his head and chortled.

"How did you—"

Before she could finish, the rustling from the woods grew louder, more persistent. There was someone there.

"H...Help."

It was a faint murmur, barely audible in the open air. Dropping her bag, Miya rushed towards the trees. As she kicked past the shrubs, she reared back when she saw a young woman clinging to a nearby branch for support. In the pale glow of sunrise stretching across the sky, Miya caught a glimpse of her face and recognized her immediately.

"Elle!" she gasped, rushing to catch the swooning girl. Although she was slight, Elle crashed onto Miya's shoulder like deadweight. She was barely conscious, her skin cold as ice, and her teeth chattered as she grasped weakly at Miya's clothes.

They didn't know each other personally, but it was hard to go a day without hearing Elle's name. She'd been missing for almost a week.

After struggling to pull her from the woods, Miya combed her over for injuries, but aside from a few scratches and shadows clinging to the hollows of her eyes, she appeared unharmed. Miya stripped off her jacket and wrapped it around Elle's trembling frame, then pulled her phone from her back pocket and dialed the police.

"I've found Elle Robinson," she blurted out when the operator answered. The voice on the other end perked up.

"Yes, she's alive, but I think she needs medical attention."

After hanging up, Miya sat down next to the huddled teenager and rubbed her shoulders, awkwardly attempting to warm her up. Her knee-length nightgown was fraying near the hem, the ivory satin soiled from tumbling through the woods. She was fiddling with the thin gold chain around her neck when she looked up. Who—or what—could have done this to her?

"You," Elle trailed off, wide eyes trained on Miya. "You told me to stay away from Black Hollow."

Miya dropped her hands from the young woman's shoulders. "I think you might be confused," she replied. "We've never met."

She must have been a bit loopy from dehydration.

Miya burned to ask where she'd been, what had happened to her, but it felt ill-timed. When the police arrived, they took Miya's statement as the ambulance carted Elle off to the hospital.

"Think it was the Dreamwalker?" she caught one of the officers whispering, only to be hushed by the lead detective.

"We don't deal with boogeymen, only criminals," he chided. He turned to Miya and shook her hand, smiling brightly.

"It's a miracle you were here," Detective Brandon Hughes told her. "You saved her life, Emiliya."

"Fateful timing, I guess." Miya revelled in the praise. Detective Hughes offered her a ride home, and she happily accepted. He didn't ask what she'd been doing out before dawn and seemed perfectly content to dole out kind words.

Miya ate them up like all-you-can-eat sundaes. Her heart swelled, the memory of the probation letter already fading. She'd done something amazing—even if by accident—and it was enough to momentarily abate the existential dread.

Perhaps even the shallowest grave was deep enough to bury failures.

MIYA WAS RIOTOUS WITH MOTIVATION. She wrote a statement to her university, acknowledging full responsibility for her shortcomings and imploring the administration for a second chance. The letter teemed with vulnerability, heart-felt apologies, and promises to get back on track. Without even waiting for a response, Miya began preparing for her triumphant return.

But when the article on Elle Robinson's disappearance came out, Miya's chest tightened as she scanned the story. There was no mention of her contribution. Still, she snipped the news piece from the diner's free paper when no one was looking and kept it as a memento—a reminder of how good it felt to do something right.

As the days blurred together, so did the print in Miya's textbooks. A week later, her bank statement arrived with a number stamped at the top: $41.52. Her gut clenched and, with a defeated sigh, she let the letter drift into the trash can. Miya had saved ten times that by her final year of high school.

Now she was fast approaching her twenty-first birthday, but there would be little reason to celebrate.

Rolling off the futon wedged between her sticker-covered dresser and dull, grey-blue walls, Miya stumbled out of her room. The final rays of orange and red were disappearing from the tiny window nestled in the corner by the door. After a few nights of no sleep, time whirled by like a high-speed train. Insomnia was that clingy, unwelcome guest who couldn't take a hint when they weren't wanted anymore.

It didn't help that Miya's browser was littered with tab after tab of job listings she didn't have the courage to respond to. If she got an interview and went dressed as a semi-mature twenty-something-year-old, she'd be found out for what she really was: an imposter. They'd realize she was only pretending to give a damn about their campy mission statement and it would all be over. Capitalism would be done with her, and she'd be forced to join a commune somewhere in the mountains where taxes couldn't find her.

Going somewhere *no one* could find her, on the other hand, didn't sound bad.

Miya got dressed and dragged herself to the door, but as her hand touched the knob, she glimpsed something darting across the room from the corner of her eye. She whirled around and came face-to-face with the wall—blank as a canvas save for the shadows cast by furniture.

Just my imagination playing tricks on me again.

Turning away from the mosaic of shadows, she left her basement studio with the playground burning in her mind.

After so many years, the walk was automatic. Miya knew that she was close when the buildings grew sparse and the sidewalk turned to gravel. At the intersection with the town's faded green welcome sign and the crooked maple, she ambled up the hill and through the field where the farmer's market operated on weekends.

The swings were still coppery with rust and weeds protruded from the wooden curb framing the playground. Miya caught the corner of her probation letter poking out from the sand, so she scooped some up and piled it on top for good measure.

The world had gone dark, and the sound of cicadas filled the air like an orchestra in an amphitheatre. Miya looked towards the forest and fixed her gaze on a spot between the trees near where she'd found Elle. It wasn't the first time she'd seen something unusual there.

She remembered being eight years old and swinging towards the sky when a swift movement in her periphery pulled her attention from the clouds. Digging her foot into the sand like an anchor, she scanned the edge of the clearing. A shadow slithered somewhere behind the trees. Breath held, Miya listened to the foliage rustle as the shape moved closer to the light. Moments later, an animal emerged—a wolf. Ears erect, posture stiff and alert, it watched her with uncanny attention as she in turn watched it. She was too enthralled to remember the ominous stories townsfolk whispered about wolves. She even forgot they were dangerous predators.

Every time Miya excavated this memory, she imagined locking eyes with the wolf. She didn't remember the colour of the animal's coat, but those eyes remained clear in her mind—large, curious, and full of life. Seconds later her name was called, the sound of it lashing through the air and striking her from her fixation. By the time she looked back, the wolf was gone.

Miya never told anyone what she'd seen that day. How could she in a town where people were frightened of a myth?

The Dreamwalker and her wolf.

Every child had heard the story a thousand times, and like some rite of passage into adulthood, they were constantly reminded of how important it was to the town's history and culture. People in Black Hollow believed in fairy tales. And while Miya loved the idea of fables hidden beneath the veil of the mundane, she'd yet to unearth anything truly spellbinding. After all, the wolf didn't spirit her away into the Dreamwalker's arms.

Still, she kept returning to the playground, hoping to see the wolf some-day. It was her sanctuary from everything she didn't want to face. Maybe it was childish, but Miya lamented that reality wasn't a fairy tale she could rewrite with the power of her imagination. Reality wasn't timeless or enchanting; it was finite and perilous.

There was no forever-after in Black Hollow or anywhere else. Eventually, Miya would have to rip herself free from this inertia and moving away seemed a seductive option. What did she have to lose? She could go to a new city, shed all self-imposed expectations and start over. Eventually, she'd make enough to pay back her family. All she'd leave behind would be a good friend and a sea of false hope.

Miya's bones pulsed with excitement; she could finally get a clean start. Tomorrow, she'd pull a blindfold over her eyes and drop a pin on the map. Wherever gravity wedged it, she'd make her new home.

The moon hung low in the clear night sky, and several stars glimmered over the pitch-black field. Sitting on the swing, Miya clutched the chains on either side of her and bent over backwards until her hair touched the sand. As she stared off into the meadow, she saw shadows shapeshifting like those on her wall. But one of them wasn't wavering like the others. It was solid, a figure she couldn't quite make out. Rather than waxing and waning, it slowly but surely moved closer. Miya realized the shape belonged to a person—a man tall enough to be intimidating in the dead of night.

She thought back to Elle, left with no memory of what happened, and stories of other girls who'd come before her.

Maybe it wasn't a spirit.

Maybe it was a person.

Miya sat up and gathered her things. As she threw on her shoulder bag, the man paused as though he'd caught sight of her. They both froze, like two animals meeting by chance in territory they'd each claimed. The hairs on the back of Miya's neck stood on end, and before the man could take another step, the headline of her memento came back to her.

Another missing girl found at Old Market Playground.

Miya bolted through the field, leaving her memories behind her.

CHAPTER
TWO

KAI

HE DIDN'T KNOW where he was, or how he'd gotten there. He only knew that it was a hot summer night and that every breathing fibre was searing with hellish pain.

It was the same dance every time, and it always ended like this: with a kick to the nuts. An angry snarl rose in his throat as he clutched the dirt between his fingers, rolled over, and pressed his back against the ground to rub his burning skin into the soil. That's right, it was August—the worst month of the damn year. Scorching hot surfaces, screaming children on summer vacay, smog, heatstroke, and everything that belonged in hell. August was a bitch even the devil wouldn't want to fuck.

His fingers clawed deeper until the ground turned cool. Grabbing a fistful in each hand, he smeared the dark soil over his face, desperate to make the itching stop. His scalp was crawling under the thick, dishevelled mess of black hair. He could smell blood under his fingernails, so he picked out the tiny clots while waiting for his vision to adjust. These eyes saw colour. The psychedelic effect of reds, blues, and greens bleeding into the world took a few moments to stop. Above him were shapes swaying through the air, and behind them loomed a dark expanse he assumed was the sky. Long, thin wisps slowly came into focus: willow tree branches.

Kai took a deep breath as the familiarity of this place flooded him. He'd woken up under the giant willow many times before, but he could never find it when he wanted to. Instead, it always found him.

Under the earthy scent of bark and dirt, he detected the faint undertone of death hanging in the air, tugging his eyes towards the unmoving heap several feet away. It was a woman—a dead one to be sure—her eyes wide and her blue lips parted in an expression that was both vacant and surprised. A thin, gold chain encircled her bruised neck, its imprint etched in her flesh.

Kai tried to remember where he'd last been, but nothing came back to him. It wasn't the first or even the second time he'd woken up to a dead body, but it remained an unwelcome surprise. Either way, Kai was *pretty* sure he hadn't done it. Strangulation wasn't his style, and there wasn't any blood.

Regardless, he had no intention of hanging out with a corpse. His clothes and what little money he'd had were lost, and now he had two choices: ravage the donation bin outside the local second-hand store or beat someone up and rob them.

Pulling himself up, he cracked his neck, rolled his shoulders, then dragged his feet, one in front of the other. Gradually, he picked up his pace, grateful that it was at least after dark.

Once out of the forest, he heard the swings from the playground—and they sure as hell weren't swaying from the wind. Some weirdo was there, staring at the moon. Normally, Kai would have skipped around them, but it was difficult to go unseen in an open field. He really wasn't in the mood for crawling, so he kept on his path without much concern. It was likely some dumb teenager. They'd be scared off soon enough.

The swinging came to a stop, and the person—a girl, he discovered—fixed her gaze on him. Her posture was rigid, and no sooner had he sensed her unease than she was dashing away like a frightened rabbit. Kai shrugged and continued on his way. He hadn't seen her face, and he was sure she hadn't seen his, either.

Only one road led into the downtown core of Black Hollow, but Kai knew the woods better than he knew the lines of his own face, and that opened up other options. Once he settled into his body, jumping wired fences and stalking through private property wasn't even light exercise. The streets were empty, with only the occasional passing car warranting some evasion. For the most part, there wasn't much to be wary of.

As Kai approached a local sports bar, the smell of alcohol, marijuana, and cigarette smoke hit him in a dizzying wave. On a better night, he would've been inside, racking up a tab before betting it on a game he couldn't lose.

But tonight, he wasn't looking for cheap thrills. He was hunting for prey.

Up ahead, several men were gathered around a pickup truck under a flickering neon sign, laughing loudly and taking swigs of beer. A faint orange glow emanated from the bar's greasy windows. Dark shapes danced across the pavement around the truck, distorted by the murky tapestry of thick, cracked glass. The light passed briefly over the men's faces as people walked by inside, illuminating their features just long enough for Kai to discern which of them was the most intoxicated. He watched from the shadows as one split off from the herd and headed into an adjacent alleyway.

Slipping around the parked cars, Kai sneaked after the man into the narrow passage. It was darker there, well out of the shine of fluorescent lights. His target was standing by a garbage dumpster with his legs apart, rocking back and forth while holding his pecker in both hands. The scent of urine mingling with rotting trash wafted through the air. Kai wrinkled his nose in disgust. Couldn't this asshole take a leak on something that didn't already stink?

Soundlessly strolling up to the stranger, Kai reached out and tapped him on the shoulder. The man whirled around, yelping in surprise.

"What the hell?" He stumbled back as he looked Kai's naked form up and down.

Kai grumbled and pointed at the man's jeans. "I need those." He took stock of the buffoon, still holding his dick for dear life. "Try not to soil them," he added dryly, taking a step forward.

He grabbed the man by the throat and lifted him off the ground in one smooth motion, feet dangling. Slamming him into the wall, Kai heard a hefty thwack as the man's head hit the bricks, his brain rattling around inside his skull before shutting off. Kai released the dead weight—who was lucky to have a pulse—and watched him crumple to the ground with a thump. Crouching down, he checked every pocket, disappointed when he found only a measly twenty-dollar bill. It pissed him off. So much so, he felt his hand curling around the man's throat without his say-so, his fingertips digging into the soft flesh around the jugular vein.

Hey there, monster.

Kai's every muscle turned to stone. It was that thing again—the voice of his nemesis—egging him on as he held the fragile life of this moronic human between his fingers.

Do it. Tear his throat out with your teeth. Relish in the taste of his life on your tongue.

Kai snarled at the empty air, and had it not been for the frantic voices calling for their missing friend, he may very well have gone for the kill.

"Hey! Get away from him!" a large, lumbering man shouted as he closed in.

Kai straightened, not bothering to turn as the air moved behind him. He side-stepped to avoid the incoming swing, and his attacker tumbled forward onto his knees. Kai kicked him in the stomach, leaving him lurching before his two companions arrived at the scene.

Their drunken flails were clumsier than a toddler trying to catch a butterfly. Kai evaded each one before his counterattack hit them twice as hard—one in the jaw, the other in the kidneys. It was like playing piñata without the blindfold.

The alpha managed to find his feet again and pulled a hunting knife from a sheath clipped to his belt. He lunged at Kai, stabbing erratically. Backed into a wall, Kai blocked one of the blows that came down towards his shoulder. The blade nicked his forearm, but he pried it away with brute force. Turning the knife around, he drove it into the man's side, then headbutted him in the face, revelling in the satisfying crunch of a fracturing nose. Blood gushed down the man's face, and Kai shoved him away as he screamed, the sound vibrating painfully in his ears. He wanted to fold them shut, but his anatomy didn't allow it, so he kicked his attacker in the head.

Kai sneered as the man crumpled to the pavement. "Goodnight, you glass-faced fuck."

The other two were already scrambling away, abandoning their wounded friends. Kai watched them flee, and some part of him took pleasure in their terror. He flexed his fingers around the knife handle sticky with blood from his hands. Red trickled down his jaw, dripping from his chin onto his toes. He caught the droplets on the back of his hand, then sucked the blood off his thumb. A slow, wicked smile spread across his face at the sight of the retreating figures, his shoulders starting to shake as he tried to suppress the laugh rumbling in his chest.

You enjoy watching them run.

"They're pathetic."

That's why you should have killed them.

"Not worth the bloodstains."

You're no hunter, the voice mocked. **Just a coward who likes playing sadist.**

"You taught me well, you whimpering bitch," Kai growled back. "Now teach me how to get rid of you."

Get rid of me? Raucous laughter thundered in Kai's ears. **There'll be more blood before you earn your release.**

As if Kai would spill blood for the monster's entertainment.

Poor little Elle. Didn't know the Big Bad Wolf lived under the willow.

"I *know* I didn't do that."

But do you remember?

No, he didn't. Sometimes, Kai wondered if he was crazy, but he'd seen crazy and knew this wasn't it. No, this was something else. This *thing* wasn't part of who he was. It followed him, but it sure as hell wasn't coming from inside him.

There *had* to be a way to break free of it.

Kai returned to his original target and stripped away his clothes. After throwing on jeans and a hooded jacket, he looted whatever money and valuables he could find on the two men left behind: a few bills, a wristwatch, and a Zippo lighter. He hung on to the knife, swiping the sheath from the leader's belt. By the time he finished, the voice had quieted, leaving him in peace for the time being.

Kai quickly deserted the scene. Whipping the hood up and shoving his hands into his pockets, he strode out of the alleyway. His stomach growled. He slowed as he passed a local grocer, reaching out and testing the knob. It was locked. Normally, he didn't have money when he went into stores. Now, he had money, but the stores were all closed.

"Fuck this." He kicked the bottom of the door before addressing his stomach. "And you too, you goddamn black hole."

He wondered what Alice would think if she was still around. Would she feel sad that he'd sunk to this? Ashamed, maybe?

Kai slumped his shoulders and sighed, trudging towards the forest from where he came. He reminded himself that Alice wouldn't—or rather, couldn't—care.

The dead had nothing to be concerned about.

CHAPTER
THREE

MASON

IT WAS JUST after sunset when Dr. Mason Evans drove into Black Hollow—several hundred kilometres northwest of Vancouver. At the end of the gravel road was a quaint old farmhouse that looked to have at least four bedrooms on the second floor. There were no signs and, had it not been for gas station employees who gave him directions, he never would have known this was the bed and breakfast he was looking for. The maps on his smartphone were of little use here, and this pleased Mason because it reinforced the idea that he'd gone somewhere no one could find him. He was finally free. He had six months to restore his mental health, and he knew that it wouldn't happen in the city where he'd spent his entire life.

Mason recalled the conversation with the head of oncology at Vancouver General Hospital. A week had passed, but it was still fresh in his mind:

"Are you sure about this?" Dr. Lindman had asked. He'd peered over his glasses at the younger man, his thin, greying hair slicked back against his skull.

"I'm sure," Mason remembered smiling uncomfortably. "I'm obviously not well-equipped to deal with the stress. I need some time."

"You got a recommendation from the psych department," Lindman had called him out. "You shouldn't blame yourself. There is nothing you could have done. Amanda would have died anyway—the leukaemia was one of the most aggressive I've ever seen—"

"If I hadn't put her through experimental treatment, she'd still be alive. She'd have more time. I made the wrong call." Mason hated being pitied. Lindman had disapproved of his decisions through every step of the way. Now he was trying to comfort him. Mason was a thirty-two-year-old man for Christ's sake. Did he really seem that pathetic?

"Yes," Lindman had nodded. "You made the wrong call. And you'll do it again."

Those words still haunted Mason.

Remembering the exchange left him ill as he pulled his beat-up Honda Accord in front of the rustic inn. He didn't want to end up like Lindman—a man too jaded to believe in miracles. This was the last year of Mason's residency, but it didn't matter that he was almost finished. After that conversation, he needed time away from oncology, and Black Hollow had called to him through a friend's Facebook page. Jazlyn, an old colleague from med school who'd dropped out and settled for nursing, was now working at a local hospital and routinely uploaded photos of the town and its surrounding landscape.

Now that he was there, Mason knew Jazlyn wasn't just a talented photographer. The bed and breakfast was as idyllic as a picture book. The window trims could have used a fresh coat of paint, but the grey brick chimney and pale wood panelling were reminiscent of a Victorian farmhouse. The porch was hidden snugly behind white posts that arched to form a sturdy gate leading to the front door. All around were expanses of forests and clear water lakes left untainted by urban life. It was the opposite of the big city: the constant rush, the noise, the depersonalized bubbles everyone existed in. For a while, Mason's job was the only tether he had to other people. He still wanted that connection, but without the impermanence and heartbreak.

The lady who ran the little inn had given him an irresistible deal; compared to Vancouver, his living expenses would be minimal. Sooner or later, he'd probably want to call his family and let them know where he'd gone—but not now. He'd left without a word, only notifying his landlord that he was moving out, and giving the Dean of Medicine a printed statement. Mason had disappeared off the face of the civilized world in hopes of leaving his mistakes buried in the dust behind him. Where he'd gone, he was certain they couldn't follow.

He strolled up the creaky porch steps. Nabbing a grimy newspaper on the way, Mason read the headline. It was just over a week old.

Elle Robinson, 19, Stumbles out of Woods after Five-Day Search—Fears of Supernatural Kidnapping Run High.

How odd, Mason thought, scanning the article.

Over the years...missing girls of similar age...all appear to have no memory...why they ventured into the forest...no idea how long they'd been missing...

Surely, they were just runaways who returned on their own, likely too embarrassed to confess their motives.

Fearing more kidnappings, citizens anticipate the Dreamwalker's return...Concern for Miss Robinson's life inspires pressure on local government to intensify wolf cull.
    "She can't kidnap our girls without her wolves," said the Robinsons' neighbour. "They're the ones luring girls away. We need to stop them."

Mason raised both eyebrows. He definitely wasn't in the city anymore. These rural folks were quite precious, he decided. He dropped the paper in the garbage bin and dusted off his hands. The welcome sign on the door was beckoning him inside.

Barrelling in, he stopped only to absorb the interior décor: floral patterns, lace framing almost every piece of fabric, antique wooden furniture, and a grandfather clock behind a makeshift reception desk crowding the narrow entry hall. The accoutrement added to the charm of the lodgings.

The house was silent save for the ticking of the giant clock. As the hand struck half-past eight and the bell chimed, a woman seemed to float into the room. She looked about fifty, wearing comfortable-looking jeans and a loose, chequered blouse. Her auburn hair was tied up in a messy bun, and she tucked the loose strands behind her ears after freeing her hand from an oven mitt. She flashed Mason a bright, dimpled smile that spread wide across her heavily freckled face.

"Gooood evening!" she greeted cheerily, and a little out of breath. "Welcome to Annabelle's Bed and Breakfast. I'm Annabelle!"

"Oh—is that what it's called?" Mason joked, extending a hand, "Mason Evans, a pleasure."

"That's right! Apologies for the lack of signs. Bad storm took out the last one." She squeezed his hand, then opened a three-ringed binder and flipped through the pages. "Mr. Evans, yes? I believe we exchanged a few emails just the other day. You were interested in renting a room on a weekly basis, if I recall?" She glanced up at him for confirmation.

"Yes, ma'am, that's right," he replied, wondering if she could smell the city on him.

"Please, call me Annabelle." She waved him off with a chuckle. "No need for formality here."

"Right. Sure. Got it." He paused before continuing, "You mentioned there was no need for a reservation?"

"Yes, that's right!" she remembered suddenly, shutting the binder before groping around the desk for her glasses. "Well, you're in luck! It's slow this time of the year, so you're the only one around. You can have our best room! Bathroom's fully loaded with a brand-new toilet and showerhead we just installed, and there's a memory foam mattress we threw on the bed just last week." She winked.

"Sounds great, ma'—Annabelle."

"Oh! And there's a TV, too. Nothin' fancy, but it's got basic cable if you like watching the news. There's also this nifty little phone cable that you just plug into your laptop for the Internet!"

"A LAN cable?"

"Oh, is that what it's called?" She smiled with a hint of mischief, returning his jest from earlier.

Mason smiled back, feeling more at ease.

"We've also got a laundry room you can use any day except Sunday when I do the linens," Annabelle gestured down the corridor, then pulled out a brass key attached to a tag with the number four on it. "Let me show you to your room."

Mason followed her through the entrance hall and up the stairs. The room was larger than he'd expected, with a broad window facing the forest. There was also a connecting bathroom, just as Annabelle had said.

"That reminds me!" She clapped her hands together. "If you're interested in learning more about the town, my son Mathias had an online blog about this area. He absolutely loved Black Hollow and was an avid photographer. Might be more interesting than visiting one of those dreary tourist centres."

Loved? Did he not care for the town anymore? Not wanting to be rude, Mason took down the blog's URL, and the lady of the house left him to his own devices.

He didn't have much to unpack: enough clothing so that he'd only have to do laundry once a week, toiletries, a novel he'd intended to read for years, his passport, and a laptop. Once everything was where he wanted it, Mason stripped off his belt and the beige khakis it held in place. He'd lost nearly fifteen pounds during his residency, the long hours melting the meat right off his bones. Once an avid frequenter of the varsity gym, his career had demanded more paperwork and fewer squats—a trade he'd happily made. As Mason undid his pinstriped shirt, one of the buttons caught on his hair, making him yelp as he yanked it free. His blonde curls were getting fluffy and in need of a trim. After changing into flannel pants and a t-shirt, he pulled out his laptop and plugged in the LAN cable poking out from behind the bed. To avoid the temptation of checking his email, he instead went straight to Mathias's blog.

The contents were vast, ranging from articles about the town's history to ethnographic research Mathias himself had conducted. Some of the posts were critical, while others raised questions about folklore in the study of history. There was plenty of lore on wolves, and several times he referenced a specific legend about a figure known as the Dreamwalker. The whole thing felt very *National Geographic*. The legend had a long history and held remarkable sway over the villagers' customs and beliefs. Mason skimmed the posts for some kind of summary of the story but found nothing. He figured the blog was mostly intended for locals—people who already knew this Dreamwalker myth.

However, he discovered that the legend also featured an ancient willow tree nestled somewhere in the forests surrounding Black Hollow—a tree which people claimed could not be found at will. Yet many residents reported having seen the tree when they least expected it. The willow was allegedly the real-life site of the legend, and as proof of its existence, those who did encounter it often took pictures. Somehow, though, its exact location remained a mystery.

At the bottom of the page was a scanned photo of Mathias with his hand resting on the willow's trunk. Who had taken the picture? Mason surmised this was the willow from the story in question. Was it truly impossible to find at will? The claim struck him as a challenge—perhaps a ploy to give tourists something to do. According to the sources on the blog, the tree was somewhere in the woods near the local farmer's market. The market itself looked interesting, so it wasn't difficult for Mason to decide where he would head first.

With his room in order, Mason wandered out to explore Annabelle's farmhouse. As he traipsed down the stairs, he saw her seated in the living area. She looked up from her book and smiled.

"This is my lounge, as I like to call it. Feel free to come down any time for a chat, or if you just want to hang out."

It was a decent-sized room with high ceilings and a brass chandelier above a wooden coffee table. There were two leather armchairs and a suede, burgundy couch, and each was adorned with pillows swathed in knitted covers. Separating the living area and the kitchen was a thick brick wall with a fireplace that looked well-worn.

Mason noticed a photo collage mounted on the wall above the hearth. A portrait of a young man in his mid-to-late twenties hung at the top. He had Annabelle's mischievous eyes, catlike as he smiled. With his reddish-blonde hair, button nose, and fully freckled face, the resemblance to her was striking.

Under the portrait was a collection of pictures. In each, he either posed alone or with Annabelle. In some, he was a child running through a sprinkler or eating cupcakes, and she a young woman—perhaps in her twenties. In one candid shot, he looked to be in his late teens, tinkering with an old Buick and smiling to himself, like he knew the photographer was lurking nearby. He was stout but athletic, like he might have been a starter on his college rugby team. One photo in particular caught Mason's eye; it was the one from the blog—of Mathias standing next to a magnificent old willow tree with his hand resting on the trunk. His smile was serene, perhaps a little sad, his muscular body visibly thinner and his face gaunt and pale.

"Your son?" Mason asked, engrossed in the little shrine.

"Yes, my son, Mathias," she said quietly. "He was a good kid. Grew up to be a wonderful man."

"Where is he now?"

Annabelle's shoulders dropped. "He passed away several months ago. A long battle with leukaemia. He struggled with it for nearly eight years, since his university days."

"I'm so sorry for your loss," Mason fumbled. His face was hot with embarrassment, but underneath his flustered exterior, he felt chilled to the bone. Was this a cosmic joke? Amanda had been nineteen years old, in her second year of university. After losing nearly twenty pounds and visiting clinics for a series of unusual infections, weeks of fatigue, and unexplainable bruises, she was brought into the hospital for testing. It was Mason who had diagnosed her with Acute Myeloid Leukaemia, and the prognosis was poor, just as it must have been for Annabelle's son.

But there were so many people with cancer. Statistically, this was nothing to be surprised about. He tried imagining how the doctors might have broken the news to Annabelle and how she might have coped. Mason remembered Amanda's parents tumbling through four of the five stages of grief during her treatment: denial, anger, bargaining, then back to denial before the depression set in. He wasn't sure if they ever reached the final stage: acceptance. He certainly hadn't.

"Do you have any help here?" Mason quickly changed the topic, banishing the memory of Amanda's lifeless face.

Annabelle shook her head. "I'm afraid not since Mathias. It's always been just the two of us. Still in the habit of saying *we*, even though he's gone. This whole business was his idea, really."

Mason's heart sank. How could life take a good son from his mother? Especially when he was the only one she had. Mason didn't know what to say, so he just stared at the photos, trying to keep himself together.

The relief he'd felt running from Amanda's death faded as doubts tugged at the corners of his mind. How long would it be before his family started to worry? Would he really be okay to go back to work after six months?

You don't have a choice, something in him chastised. *You haven't come this far for nothing.*

He bit down on his resolve and swept away the doubts; there could be no failure. Staring down Mathias and the willow tree, Mason seared the image into his mind. Soon, he would be his old self again. Whether it was overcoming grief or debunking small-town superstitions, there was no problem Mason Evans couldn't solve, no mystery he couldn't unravel. And tomorrow, he was starting with that willow.

CHAPTER
FOUR

CLUSTERED around the main road of Black Hollow were boutique shops, pubs, indie cafés, and independent grocers. Thick-chimneyed Edwardian homes, a quaint Anglican church with white-rimmed windows and a pointed black roof, and a red-brick firehouse flaunting a giant brass bell framed the central square. More recent buildings peppered the sidewalks, but nothing past the 1970s, with painted wooden panels and large, colourful signs that exuded quintessential country flare. It was all quite charming, with large maple trees lining both sides of the tarmac and open patios accompanying the eateries.

Upon arriving at the farmer's market, Mason was astonished to see how crowded it was. Lines of vendors selling fresh produce, antiques, artwork, and handmade crafts were spread across a large, open field bordered by endless forest. Mason resolved to take his time and examine every trinket, but something tugged at him. He wanted to know more about the mythology he'd read. This was his chance to ask about the infamous willow. He stopped by an empty stall and pulled out his map from the large pocket in his beige khakis.

"Excuse me," he unfolded the glossy sheet, "I was wondering if you could tell me where I might find your famous willow tree."

"The what?" the vendor barked, crossing his arms over his chest and eyeing Mason up and down.

"I...I heard this town is known for an ancient willow. I was wondering if you might know where it is?"

"No idea what you're talking about, kid." The vendor waved him off.

Mason withdrew from the table, the map still resting in his palm. Wasn't this supposed to be the town's selling point? The stuff that drew in tourists? But this pattern continued. No matter who he asked, the answer was always the same. No one knew where the tree was. Mason wondered if they were lying, which dispelled his earlier notion that the willow was a ploy. On the contrary, the townsfolk appeared rather protective of something.

"Shush," he heard a woman whisper to her nagging teenage daughter. They exchanged a foreboding glance, and the girl quickly backed down. Their secrecy spurred his curiosity, and the rationalist in him burned for an explanation.

As he made his way across the market, he noticed a playground at the edge of the woods where a girl sat alone on the swing. She looked about twenty with warm, olive skin and dark, ash-brown hair flowing past her collar bone. She stretched her long, coltish legs and fixed her eyes on him, her expression mostly bored save for a spark of inquisitiveness that shone through even at a distance. He wondered if she recognized him but knew that wasn't possible. He'd only been in Black Hollow for a day.

As Mason strained to get a closer look, he collided with another shopper. Several potatoes cascaded to the ground.

"I-I'm so sorry," Mason stuttered as the shopper grunted, clearly annoyed. Scrambling to pick up the loose produce, he forgot all about the spectre on the swing, his heartache taking a back seat as embarrassment took the wheel.

He returned the potatoes and scuttled to the nearest vendor, drawn in by the sprawling white doily draped over a large oak table with filigreed corners and smooth curves carved into its aging legs. Mason poked around the stall, inspecting the wares: crystals, amulets made of bronze and amber, wooden carvings, and a large, purple, iridescent rock shaped like a fang. Speckles of gold and meadow-green bled into the purply hues as tiny black veins streaked across the stone's surface. Never having seen anything like it, he lingered on the shimmering gem, holding it up to the sunlight and tilting it left and right, admiring the deep violet and emerald lustre.

"That's a labradorite," the vendor said, watching Mason play with the stone. "Beautiful piece, ain't she?"

"She?" Mason lowered the rock and looked at the seller, a tubby, middle-aged man with a hand-carved pipe and a Russian ushanka on his head.

"That's right, she," he nodded, chewing on the end of the pipe. "All labradorites are women—sorceresses and shamans."

Mason's eyebrows shot up, his mouth twisting. "It's a rock," he tried to suppress a laugh, but the vendor burst into a pirate-like cackle in his stead.

"It's also a metaphor," he shot back. "They call it the dream stone. Separates the waking world from...hidden realms."

Mason believed in only one realm: the one called reality. It was an objective, physical fact. Only people's personal perceptions made things murky. He turned the rock over in his hand. When it didn't catch the light, it looked pale and grey. "Any relation to the Dreamwalker?"

The vendor's face darkened, his teeth clamping around the edge of his pipe as he regarded Mason. "Tell you what. I'll give it to you for a special price. Fifteen bucks. And if you're lucky, you may just find out yourself."

In other words, the answer was yes. Mason frowned, but this was more than he'd pulled out of anyone else. Nodding, he dug through his back pocket and paid the man.

"She liked labradorites," the vendor remarked just as Mason turned to leave with his rock. "Helped her find her way." His lips pulled back and revealed a wide, toothy smile. Sliding the pipe from his mouth, he tapped it against a stone ashtray on the table—once, twice, and finally a third time. The chimes hung in the air, stark against the noise of the bustling market.

Helped her find her way? The heck was that supposed to mean? Mason smiled in acknowledgement and turned away, eyeing the rock in his palm and angling it so he could admire the fiery gleam.

"Ah, a detective."

The raspy whisper came from behind, so close Mason could feel the breath against his neck. He spun around, only to find a man who looked to be in his seventies with slicked, silvery-black hair and pallid skin. Oddly, he was nowhere close enough to have breathed down Mason's neck. Standing several feet away, he held a rigid posture, yet his shoulders hunched forward. He canted his head to one side, and it appeared to list as though he was jointed only at the neck.

"A detective," the man repeated in a flat voice. His eyes were eerily pale, set so deep in his skull they almost appeared to glow. Short in stature, he was lanky with long, slender fingers.

"Excuse me?"

The man didn't respond, his lips drawing back.

"Sir?" Unnerved, Mason stepped to the right, checking to see if the old man's eyes would follow.

His pupils flared. "I see you," he intoned in a raucous voice.

"T-that's good, sir," Mason stammered, thumbing the labradorite in his fist.

"I know what you seek, detective."

"You know what I'm looking for?" asked Mason.

"That which finds but cannot be found," the man rasped under his breath, a faint gurgling accompanying the words like there was something stuck in his throat. "I can take you to it."

Although his response was arcane, Mason was certain he was referring to the willow. He was tempted to take the bait, but his rational mind screamed that this man was mentally ill and would only lead him in circles. Mason smiled politely and shook his head. "I'm fine, thank you."

The old man's grin didn't falter. He pointed a bony finger at Mason's hand closed around the dream stone. "Come when you have the courage to seek the way."

The stone hummed to life against Mason's palm. Clenching his fist tighter, he watched as the old man walked towards the forest.

Only when the trees swallowed him up did the stone go still in Mason's grip.

CHAPTER
FIVE

MIYA

DURING THE DAY, it was difficult to believe this was where the missing girls reappeared. Miya could see the entire market from her place on the swing, watching people flood from one stall to the next. One guy in particular screamed *tourist* with a lost city-boy look to him. She could tell he was searching for something but wasn't having any luck. As he turned to leave a disgruntled vendor, he noticed her and stared back across the field, ogling until he collided with someone carrying a basket of potatoes. His previous swagger shattered as a few of the spuds toppled out and rolled off. Miya watched, amused, as he chased them down and was swallowed up by the crowd.

"What's up!" It was Hannah, pulling Miya from her field study. She sat on the other swing and wiggled her butt into place.

"Hey, not much." The edges of Miya's lips tugged into a smile as she greeted her friend, taking in the platinum streaks in her dark tresses. "Looks good."

"Thanks!" she accepted the compliment with ease—a feat Miya admired. "Got it done at work yesterday."

The two had been friends since childhood, but life had taken them on diverging paths. Hannah left home at seventeen to pursue a dance career—headstrong and unrelenting in her ambitions. But after a devastating knee injury, she was forced to abandon her dream. Miya reckoned that if anyone had a right to be pissed at life, it was Hannah, but she kept her chin up and went on to beauty school. *Tougher than I could ever hope to be*, Miya thought.

"Aren't you creeped out?" Hannah asked, glancing towards the forest.

"Why would I be?" feigned Miya.

"You know what this spot is."

"Yeah." She shrugged, "And?"

Hannah threw her head back and huffed at the sky. "I don't get how you can be so blasé about it. You *found* Elle Robinson here. What if it happens again?"

Miya's chest tightened as she remembered her encounter, but she knew telling Hannah would be like dangling bait over shark-infested water. "Next time someone stumbles out of the woods, I'm directing them to the nearest bar."

Hannah snorted and waved her off. "You're an asshole. But," she grinned ear-to-ear, "want to do me a favour?"

Miya pressed her lips together and shrunk back. "What might that be?"

Hannah flashed a beaming smile. "A reading, of course. You're always crazy accurate."

"A reading?"

"Right now!"

"You're so demanding," Miya joked, then reached into her backpack and pulled out playing cards.

"Guess that's why all the boys left the yard." Hannah flipped her hair over her shoulder.

"Women and their need for reciprocity!"

Miya's scoff was followed by an eruption of laughter between the two girls.

"Seriously though, how are you?" Hannah prodded as she shuffled the cards.

Miya had called her here to tell her she was moving away, but the words got caught in her throat. "Well, I'm broke."

"I know that part. Hard time getting gigs?"

Miya hesitated, one of the cards folding against the rest and popping out of her hands. "I've been...I don't know. I can't sleep. My thoughts are all over the place. Just feels like something's not right. Only there's nothing to feel wrong about. I can't explain it."

Hannah crossed her legs, her brow creasing. "I mean, that would mess with anyone."

Miya picked the stray card out of the sand—the king of spades. "It's been hard meeting deadlines for school. And every time I try to get my shit together, the anxiety hits harder, just to remind me I can't."

Using her overturned backpack as a make-shift table, she began laying out the cards in pairs. *Ace of hearts.*

"Have you talked to your family?" Hannah suggested.

"They'd worry too much, and I feel like a shitbag for wasting their money." *Jack of Hearts.*

"How about therapy?"

"I looked into it. Psychologists are way too expensive, and student insurance just doesn't cover it. I checked out student counselling too, but the wait times are insane. Seems like everyone's fucked up, only no one looks it from the outside." *Nine of diamonds.*

"You're pretty good at hiding it, too," she pointed out.

"Doesn't feel that way." *King of clubs.*

"I'm here for you, you know."

Miya looked over the card spread. It was obvious that Hannah had good things going for her, and there was no need to dampen that with personal problems. "You're my friend, Hannah. You can't be my therapist too."

"Why not?" she chuckled. "I don't cost a dime."

"Because being a therapist means saying things the other person might not want to hear from a friend. If friends made good therapists, psychologists wouldn't charge two hundred dollars an hour."

"Well, *fine* then." Hannah rolled her eyes and then nodded to the cards. "So, what's it say? I see hearts. Hearts are good, yeah?"

"Usually." Miya stared down at the pairs. She ran the cards' individual meanings through her mind, but she knew that wasn't how readings worked. Meaning had to be put together. The whole was greater than the sum of its parts.

"Well..."

Miya looked up at her and smiled coyly. "You're dating again, aren't you?"

"What!" Hannah shrieked, eyes widening. "How'd you know that!"

Miya tapped the first card. "Ace of hearts. New relationship." Then she tapped the second. "Jack of hearts—a message about love or, in more common terms, being asked out."

"Well, damn." Hannah leaned back and almost tumbled from the swing. "I *am* seeing someone new, but it's nothing serious. Not yet, anyway. What about the next two?"

"You'll have to tell me about him," Miya offered, but she knew Hannah wouldn't divulge until she was sure he was worth the breath. "The nine of diamonds is an improvement in your financial situation, and the king of clubs represents practical power. Might be a new job offer, or a promotion."

"Sweet!" She sounded more pleased with this than the dating part. "I've been applying for jobs. Had a few interviews and an offer in Burnaby." She hesitated. "I know it's super short notice, but I'll be moving in a few weeks. I found a really nice place and couldn't pass it up, and the pay will be way better, too."

Even for someone working full time, making ends meet could be tough. And if Hannah was struggling, Miya dreaded what that meant for her.

"Oh..." she trailed off, swallowing back the bitter taste. "But hey, looks like life is on the up and up for you." She tried sounding cheerful, but a deep, desperate fear clawed at her from inside. What did it matter where Miya went? Her problems would follow. What if she couldn't get a job quickly enough? How would she afford to live?

Leaving Black Hollow wouldn't solve her problems.

Hannah traced the edge of the ace of hearts, smiling contently. "You're really good at this, you know. You should try making some money with it."

"What? Be a fortune-teller?" Miya snorted at the idea, though not without secretly relishing the compliment. "I don't think I'd make enough to pay rent."

"Better than nothing! I bet you could really make bank with some Dreamwalker predictions." Hannah extended her hand. "Here, give me the cards. I want to do a reading for you."

"Oh no, no way am I taking part in that. Do you have any idea how many Dreamwalker fortune-telling scams there are? They scare the shit out of people." Miya gathered up the pairs and handed over the deck. "And weren't *you* the one freaking out about the Dreamwalker kidnappings two minutes ago? Now you want me to profit off them?"

"Someone might be next." Hannah shuffled the cards like they were trying to flee her fingers. "And we all know what could happen now that Elle's back."

"I'd rather not think about it," Miya mumbled.

Seven of hearts, five of spades. Ace of spades, king of spades.

Him again, Miya thought, eyes lingering on the king.

"Yikes—that's a lot of spades," Hannah remarked with a cringe. "I must be doing it wrong. Spades are bad, right?"

"Usually," Miya repeated, her gaze trained on the ace.

"You got one heart though," the eternal optimist offered.

"Sevens are about troubles." Miya fought to smile. "A seven of hearts is about troubled emotions."

"Oh..."

"Five of spades is disease. And the ace of spades," she picked the card up, "is death."

"Shit, it's totally wrong then." Hannah plucked away the card. "You're *not* going to die."

Miya flopped over the swing and let her eyes roll back. Slackening her jaw and letting her tongue hang, she released a shuddering gurgle. The display sent Hannah into a fit of giggles, and Miya savoured making someone laugh despite her mental fog.

She failed to mention that the ace of spades didn't always mean a literal death; it was the force that mediated the material and the spiritual worlds. If anything, the card signalled a spiritual death—an end to things as they were currently understood.

"Maybe I'll slip on some pigeon shit and crack my head open on the sidewalk!" Miya pulled herself up by the chain, laughing away the lump in her throat.

"I don't think pigeon shit is slippery." Hannah squinted. "What about the last card?"

"The king of spades?" He had come to her twice. "A powerful man. Or a spirit. Could also be fate. It's hard to say."

"That's because I can't do readings!" Hannah threw her arms up. "See, you're the psychic here."

"I'm totally not psychic. But thanks."

Hannah checked the time on her phone and announced that she would be late for work. After hugging goodbye, Miya remained on the swing, swaying gently as the wind tickled her face. She peered into the darkness between the trees, wondering what it would be like to live there. So much of her imagination was captivated by this spot, and all because of a momentary encounter with an animal that was probably dead. She was sure she'd never see the wolf again, but hoping ensnared her in something greater than herself, greater than her own mind.

After reluctantly returning home, Miya launched a fruitless job hunt. She applied for anything entry-level and wound up agreeing to a weekend of petsitting, but the month's rent couldn't be scrounged up walking poodles and scooping litter. Waiting to toll the bell, Patricia reminded her that time was running out.

Worn down by solitude, Miya mustered the courage to tell her family about the academic probation over the phone.

"I had no idea you were struggling so much," came her mother's sympathetic voice on the other end, but Miya could detect the thick layer of disappointment beneath the concern.

Her parents had moved to Calgary for her father's work—a temporary move, he'd promised—but Miya knew that *temporary* didn't mean *short term*. In theory, everything was temporary. She'd lost count of how many times the promise of a visit was fulfilled only by absence and a cheque in the mail.

"I'm sorry. I guess I didn't realize how bad it had gotten."

"Oh, Miya," she sighed. "You've always been so strong-willed. I'm sure you'll figure it out."

Will I, though? she questioned.

"Do you need money?" her mother asked.

"Huh? No, no, I'm fine," Miya lied. She wouldn't stoop to taking more freebies from them. "How's Dad?"

She was relieved when her mother changed the subject and began whining about his clutter in the storage room. Eventually, she ran out of complaints, and the conversation fizzled out until awkward farewells were in order.

Her loneliness unabated, Miya called the centre for mental health at school but ended up shuffled from one automated system to the next. After having her sanity whittled away by the holding queue, she decided whatever advice they had wasn't worth enduring the tinny, unyielding tune she'd been subjected to for the past forty-five minutes. She hung up and tried Google instead. The sheer volume of information was overwhelming. Unable to retain any of it, research devolved into distraction.

Miya remembered being taught that if she set goals and worked hard, life would repay her in kind. She'd wanted to go into investigative journalism, to uncover unspoken truths, to excavate what lay hidden beneath the surface. She worked her ass off for the perfect grades, enrolled in the perfect program, and then she realized how hollow it was. Journalism turned out to be as formulaic as everything else in life. There was a template for how to hit all the right notes, to invoke the lowest common denominator. Most didn't want nuance and complexity; they wanted a good soundbite.

"Keep it simple," her professor had said. "No one cares about the truth as much as they think they do. They just want easy answers."

As the program went on, Miya went through the motions, but she couldn't quell her disappointment. The knowledge presented to her was shallow. There had to be something more, something deeper. That was when she started losing sleep, suffering anxiety, and failing classes. Nothing held her interest. It was a frightening, muted existence that offered no promise of more. What *more* meant, however, was elusive as the wind.

Miya reckoned that plans were little more than pleas to the god of time, but the future was always ruthless in its uncertainty. Setting goals was like arranging a grandiose party for an unconfirmed visitor; it was self-sabotage, a setup for failure.

Slamming her laptop shut, Miya collapsed onto her back and closed her eyes. She reconsidered her mom's offer for financial help. It wasn't like she had siblings for her parents to splurge on. But if she asked for help, she'd have to deliver results—results she wasn't sure she could pull off.

What she wanted was adventure, not obligations. She'd hoped running away would give her a welcome taste of chaos, but it was a foolhardy whim. If she wanted something to sink her teeth into, she'd have to hunt it herself.

All the times she'd caroused near the woods in a private dare to the spirits within yielded nothing. She flirted with the possibility of investigating them, like a ghost hunter on some bad reality show, but she never found the courage.

Perhaps Hannah was right. Perhaps it was time to use what she had. She could take up cartomancy to find proof of the Dreamwalker—if only for herself.

First, she needed to know more about the last abduction. Miya whipped out her phone to research the details, only to be confronted with a grizzly headline.

Elle Robinson, 19, found dead in woods one week after reappearance. Father charged with first-degree murder.

"What!" Miya scanned through the article, posted barely an hour ago. The police had Gene Robinson in custody; his wife had turned him in after he'd come home in the dead of night and confessed to dragging their daughter into the woods and strangling her to death with her own necklace.

A shudder wormed up Miya's spine until she pulled the duvet over her shoulders. She was the one who'd found Elle. She'd touched her, felt the goosebumps on her trembling arms just over a week ago. She was alive, and now...

Maybe this was the wrong adventure for Miya.

"You should be careful," her father had said one year. "There are predictions going around about the Dreamwalker coming back. Young women will go missing."

The disappearances only happened once or twice every few years, usually in autumn and late summer. Miya thought the stories were exaggerated and the murders a product of sheer insanity. Yet they were always committed by those who knew the victims best.

"Girls have disappeared in the woods before," her mother said when she was too young to stay out late. "It's not just legend; it's been documented."

"Spirited away by the Dreamwalker."

The warnings rippled through Miya as she dropped her phone, wrapped herself in the covers, and squeezed her eyes shut. Perhaps it wasn't so bad that Hannah was leaving. Black Hollow was no place to make a life.

"It happens when the wolf populations grow. And you know what they say about wolves."

Fear mongering. The villagers warned that any girl could be *the* girl. They wanted them all to be afraid.

Are you afraid? a voice echoed.

Do you believe?

Miya started with a gasp, the question a low murmur in her ear. She sat up, her eyes darting around the room until they passed over a shadow in the corner. A single, violet wisp lashed out into the dim amber lamplight as if reaching for Miya. The edge billowed and splintered into a spine, then plumped into a pulpy, vapour-like feather. It broke away from the tendril and wafted slowly to the floor, vanishing like mist.

The spell broken, Miya's gaze drifted back to the corner. She heard a soft chuckle—a woman's voice. A delicate hand lifted from the dark silhouette and pointed a single finger at Miya, the gesture clear:

You're next.

Her voice was sickly-sweet, her words chiming through the deathly air of Miya's bedroom.

Time to lose your way, she trilled.

The Hollow's still got hell to pay.

CHAPTER
SIX

MASON

SEVERAL DAYS PASSED after Mason's adventure at the market. He still had the stone he'd bought, keeping it by his bedside as though it were a lucky totem. He enjoyed the way it glistened, and every so often, he'd hold it up to the light to admire how the green, gold, and purple shimmers melted into one another, the hues changing with the angle. Just as the stone could appear grey with one glance and suddenly a myriad of colours with another, life really was all about perspective.

It wasn't what he'd expected from Black Hollow, but between leisurely hikes, outdoor reading, and gorging on local fare, Mason immersed himself in the town lore, if for no other reason than to play Sherlock Holmes. The legends scratched at the walls of his rational worldview, planting a dark seed in his mind. With every passing moment he spent researching Mathias' blog and scoffing at its claims, the seed burrowed deeper, soaking up the rains of doubt until something thorny began to grow. His fixation intensified as he fancied himself a seeker of truth, determined to fortify his doctrine.

Nothing in Mathias' blog provided the answers Mason wanted. The villagers believed the Dreamwalker would return one day, but the myth about her and the willow remained a mystery. There was one blog entry he thought compelling—a critique of the town's enthusiastic support for a recent government initiative to slow the decline of caribou populations: a wolf cull. Mathias found the town's beliefs overbearing, if not ridiculous. He also referenced the history of conflict with wolves in Black Hollow—and one that was particularly bloody:

> *Based on our town's history, we tend not to view violent initiatives against the wolf population as a necessity for ecological balance, but rather, as a necessity for our own survival. Mythology is indeed a powerful shaper of sociocultural thought. However, I find it troubling that the people of Black Hollow, who pride themselves at maintaining our local history and culture, would turn a blind eye to the unyielding repetition—the endless resurrection of violence—that has always come from believing too firmly in a fable.*

Unyielding repetition? Endless resurrection of violence? Could something like that truly be credited to a fable? Mason removed his glasses and pinched the bridge of his nose. He didn't understand how a fairy tale could inspire violence. What exactly *was* this violence, anyway? It wasn't as though Black Hollow regularly made headlines.

Library archives were the only place he'd find reliable information. None in town were large enough to hold the kind of data Mason wanted, but a quick drive to a nearby university would solve that. And while he couldn't borrow anything, nothing was stopping him from reading in-house and using the photocopy machine.

"I'm heading out for the afternoon," he called to Annabelle from the lounge.

Poking her head out from the kitchen, she flashed him a bright smile. "You have yourself a good one, Mason!" she called back as she waltzed around the oven.

"Sure thing!" He saluted her with a lopsided grin and headed out the door.

MASON KNEW WELL that searching the archives was no easy task. They were organized by place of origin and date—not by their subject matter. Looking for a specific kind of document meant guessing who was most likely to have produced it. If the issue was violence, the best candidates were journalists and government officials.

It took Mason two hours to compile enough sources to sift through. Newspaper articles, police reports, town council blueprints clipped to damage reports—several of them going back to the 1860s. The town was no stranger to catastrophe, suffering from riots and man-made disasters that often led to property and habitat destruction. Among the violent crimes spattered throughout the last century, Mason noticed a troubling pattern: local women being murdered by close family at far higher rates than what would have been typical for such a small town.

As Mason tore through the documents, he grew frustrated at how poorly the older texts were preserved; hardly any of them were legible anymore. It didn't help that the archives room was barely lit. The smell of dust and the ceiling light's incessant flickering contributed to a skull-crushing headache.

As Mason sat on the floor, surrounded by paper, one thing became clear: The town had witnessed recurring eruptions of hysteria over abductions allegedly carried out by the Dreamwalker and her wolves. Several articles mentioned a trial that occurred in conjunction with a mass wolf cull in 1868. Accompanying the reports were written testimonies by citizens who lived through the event. Mason wasted no time photocopying them before filing them away in his backpack for safekeeping. He would look at those later.

But aside from the trial, there was little to go on. The available reports were vague, with not a word about the people involved—no mention of mayors, church officials, or authority figures. Mason flipped through the pages with growing impatience, until something seized him—an image clipped to one of the police reports from the trial of 1868. There was no caption at the bottom of the illustration—no credit to the artist responsible —but it must have been important to be included in an official report.

It was a grotesque depiction of a massive black wolf with a broad, spiky tail and hackles that shot up like daggers. Its jaws were open wide—nearly unhinged—tongue hanging out over long, tainted fangs. The claws were stylized as sharp, curved blades emerging from the wolf's paws. The eyes were bright, crimson red—unlike anything in the natural world. In the background, three women hung from crosses, flames at their feet as they looked towards the sky with agonized expressions. Mason leaned in close and examined them; they were all young, all dressed in plain clothes and drawn with the same face. Were they predecessors to the more recent murder victims? His gaze shifted to the wolf's eyes, the red paint raised from the page like dried blood. The way its jaw sliced open gave the impression of a wicked grin—a malevolent promise soon to be fulfilled.

Then, from somewhere in the room, the voice of the old man from the market echoed like a call from a distant land.

"In the flames, their daughters burned, traitorous daughters, against them they turned. Lost in the forests where they lay with darkness, their souls devoured and their bodies in her likeness. To exorcise the demons and to banish her from this world, they set them alight, they lay out the lure. Oh, cleansing flames, may this lay her to rest, may

this cleanse our shame. May we send her back to the realm of dreams, may we absolve our sins, whatever the means. But oh! How they were fooled. Oh! How they were wrong; the wolves cried in despair, haunting all with their song. Their blood now soaks the earth, awakening the forest as we approach her rebirth."

As the words reverberated through the air, ink slowly bled into the page beneath the monstrous image of the wolf. Each letter emerged with slow, deliberate revelation, as if the old man himself were engraving them as he spoke.

Mason's entire body went numb; his teeth chattered as he watched the ominous rhyme write itself into the page. His vision blurred, a chill seeping into his bones as his heart hammered and his chest began to hurt. The light flickered more erratically, shadows dancing on the floor with a life of their own. He released the file as though it was on fire, then felt a distinct hum against his thigh. His hand crept into his pocket, feeling around each of the three, smooth edges.

The dream stone was with him.

CHAPTER
SEVEN

AFTER THE ALARMING discovery of the dream stone, Mason shoved the photocopied documents into his bag and left the library in a cold sweat. He was shaken. So shaken, it took him over a week to gather the courage to seek out the old man. He'd pushed the incident out of his mind for as long as he could, distracting himself with menial tasks: helping Annabelle around the farm, experimenting with new recipes, indulging at bohemian cafes and a craft brewery. After dodging calls and emails from friends and family back in Vancouver, he finally responded with more than a pithy text message. They were more understanding than he anticipated. *Take as long as you need*, they'd said. Still, he grew increasingly irritable and found himself going on long walks that inevitably led him back to the same spot: the edge of the forest. He was burning to understand what happened to him in the library.

Come when you have the courage to seek the way, the old man had said.

Mason wasn't sure if it was courage or desperation, but he was willing to give it a shot. He'd torn through every psych lecture and mental health seminar from his post-secondary education in search of an explanation. The old man's harrowing voice could have been a simple trick of the mind; perception was a funny thing, and with anxiety and lack of sleep, it wasn't unheard of for people to twist their surroundings. But that didn't explain the words that had bled onto the page.

No, he hadn't hallucinated that. Something had happened to him, and he didn't want to settle on an easy but ill-fitting explanation. He needed the truth.

Having exhausted his own resources, Mason ventured into the woods. He took out the dream stone and stared it down, wondering if the old man would magically appear behind him. Of course, no such thing happened. Turning it over in his hands, he angled his palm so the rock caught the sunlight, watching the wave of purples, greens, and golds shimmer over the surface. Unable to tear his eyes away, Mason wandered as though hypnotized until he lost all sense of his surroundings and tripped, the rock flying out of his hand and landing several feet away.

Scrambling to his feet, a flicker of violet alerted him to its location. He picked up the fang-like stone and wiped the dirt away with his thumb. It was humming softly. Mason turned in place, waiting for the song to strengthen. When he felt the stone sing, he began to walk.

He was headed uphill, stepping over moss-covered tree roots that protruded from the ground and slithered through the soil like hardened snakes. As minutes passed, Mason thought himself crazy for following a stone, until he noticed he was on a path weaving through a maze of oak trees. Veiny boughs towered over him and twisted inwards, forming an imposing gate-like structure overhead. Eerily deformed, leafless and haggard, the long, crooked limbs entwined with one another and all but blotted out the sky.

Up ahead, Mason spotted a small round hut that looked half-devoured by an ancient redwood. The back wall and roof merged with the massive trunk. Leaves and pines scattered around the door like a bird's nest. The tree was colossal in both height and girth, forcing Mason to crane his neck as he peered skyward in search of its peak. It was like a tunnel leading to the sun, the base serving as a roost of some kind.

When Mason finally reached the redwood, the hut's door swung open and the old man from the market stood in the shadowy entrance. Without a word of greeting, he turned and walked back into the darkness as if expecting Mason to follow. The doorway was too small for a fully-grown adult. Crouching down, Mason followed him into his tiny world.

A single room extended into the hollow of the redwood. On one side, a hole was burrowed into the trunk like someone had hacked through with an axe. About the size of a carving pumpkin, it was just large enough to serve as a window. Save for the gap and the sunlight that peeked through the cracks, the room was dark. Above them, deer antlers and knife handles protruded from the walls like perches. How they'd gotten there was a mystery. Tied to the ends were webs of string that stretched across the interior of the trunk, glassworks and sparkling Christmas ornaments hanging from the delicate white threads.

The old man went about his business, moving around the dark space with unexpected ease; there was no groping of walls, no stumbling about. He lit a lantern—mostly for Mason's benefit—that revealed an impressive hoard of shining baubles. In the centre of the disorder was a small table with a deck of cards and several wax candles.

"Sit," the old man instructed as he glided in close. Mason was alarmed by how pallid his eyes were—like a cloudy sky with a sliver of ice blue dancing around his irises.

"You are curious about Black Hollow," he said.

"How did you—"

"There is someone you seek."

"Someone...?"

The sound of flapping wings by the window caught Mason's attention. Glancing over, he saw a large raven perched on the jagged edge. The bird cocked its head, its eyes like obsidian beads narrowing in on the new guest. Mason squirmed and turned back to the old man, but the person sitting before him suddenly appeared different. The air of death about him was gone. It was as though the vitality of youth had returned, and he was now ageless: His posture was upright, and his eyes—ghostly pale moments earlier—were now a deep, coal-black. His once grey, thinning hair now mirrored the colour of his gaze, the newly enriched strands glistening sapphire and obsidian like the plumage of his feathered friend. His bony frame had strengthened with long, wiry muscles, flowing gracefully as he extended his arms and breathed in deeply.

"Look with different eyes," he said cryptically.

Mason's head swam as the room turned hazy.

"If you do...Inversion. Revelation," he hissed. His thin lips quirked sharply, cutting across his face like a knife. He flipped one of the cards on the table—an ace of spades.

The raven cackled—the sound almost human—then flew away.

As the air grew lighter, Mason turned his attention back to the man. His eyes were colourless again as if he'd shed something of himself with the raven's flight.

"You never told me your name," Mason ventured.

"Ga-vran," the old man croaked.

"Gavran?" Mason repeated.

He smiled in response, a warmth in his expression that hadn't been there before. "She says I'm Gavran."

"Who's *she*?"

"The one you've come to ask about."

"The Dreamwalker." Mason had no clue if this Gavran had a lick of sense to him, but at least he was willing to talk about the town's fabled character. "Do you know the Dreamwalker?"

The old man grinned toothily. "All my life."

Gavran said nothing more, the eerie silence starting to weigh on the lopsided conversation.

"I-I'm Mason."

"I know who you are," Gavran chided, his grin warping his features into something alien. "Sit and ask your questions."

Mason finally obliged and helped himself to a folded quilt on the floor, clearing his throat. "Did you call me here?"

"You asked to be called."

The old man's response didn't make sense, and yet it did. He'd nearly gone mad looking for this place; didn't he himself do the calling? "But how did I get here?" Mason asked.

"The forest brought you."

"But why *me*?" Mason insisted.

"Grief reverberates, shaking things from their slumber."

Mason's heart nearly stopped. How did the old man know he was grieving?

"You're making noise." Gavran flattened his palm against the wall. As if disjointed at the knuckles, his fingers drew up in a grotesque display of flexibility, then splayed over the surface. He scratched at the wood with elongated nails. "The forest hears you, just as it heard *her*."

"*Her*?"

"There was once a woman. A Dreamwalker. In the woods, she was lost, and there she found him. Deep under the willow." White, sightless eyes locked onto Mason's.

Their blood now soaks the earth, awakening the forest as we approach her rebirth.

The words echoed in Mason's mind. "Found who?"

Gavran cackled at the question. "Who will you find?"

Mason wondered if he was being spoken to in riddles, but perhaps Gavran could tell him what the villagers wouldn't. What exactly was the relationship between this fable and all the violence that came after it? Why the monstrous depiction of the black wolf in the historical record? Why the murdered women?

"I heard your voice in the library," Mason continued. "And I saw..." he trailed off, unsure of how to articulate it. "Were you there? Did you follow me?"

Gavran's head teetered to the side, his eyes shifting to the window where the raven had been. Maybe the old man had no clue what he was being asked. Mason unfolded the paper with the illustration of the wolf and the burning women, then placed it in front of Gavran. He hadn't noticed before, but the words beneath the image had vanished.

"What does this mean?" Mason asked. Tapping his finger on one of the women, he tried to meet the old man's gaze. "Is this because of the Dreamwalker? Is she responsible for setting wolves on the town...for all the violence that's happened here?"

Gavran rocked forward, his eyes widening as he fixated on the wolf. "Each time they say she steals one...each time the stolen one burns."

Mason frowned. "The stolen one?" He remembered reading on Mathias' blog about the villagers' belief that the Dreamwalker kidnapped girls from Black Hollow. Then, he glanced down at the anguished faces of the burning women. "Why would the villagers kill the girls they were trying to save from being abducted?"

"Round and round and round it goes," the old man whispered, his pupils losing focus.

This was insane. Mason could hardly understand what was driving him—why he was pursuing explanations for historical events by interrogating a crazy hermit in the woods. But when he thought of getting up and leaving, of going back to Annabelle's and realizing he had nothing to do, something tugged at him to stay. His heart deflated at the thought of being alone with Mathias' ghost. *This is better*, a tiny voice said, kindling his growing desire to learn about this fable—to debunk it, and to expose this skewed telling of local history.

Accompanying this was a morbid curiosity; had these women truly been killed because of superstition? The idea was medieval—outrageous enough that a self-righteous air inflated the young doctor's chest. The prospect of enlightening the village eased the burden of his own mistakes.

Mason was about to demand elaboration when a female voice cut off his incoming question.

"Gavran, are you in there?" she called from outside, a light knock sounding at the door. The raps were echoed by the raven's beak, pecking at the window's jagged contours as he returned from his brief adventure.

"Are *you* out there?" Gavran replied before opening the door to reveal an elegant woman standing in the entrance.

Mason took immediate notice of her gorgeous amber eyes, framed by long, thick tresses that were white as snow despite her youth. She wasn't very tall, but her presence filled the redwood like sunlight spilling into a darkened room. A navy leather jacket fit her waist like a second skin, complemented by a long taupe skirt that split at the front to reveal black leather boots hugging her legs just below the knees. She was carrying a shoulder bag, the seams stretched from the heavy load. Observing Mason briefly, she returned her attention to the man she came to see.

"I brought you these," she told him, swinging the bag off her shoulder and laying its contents out on the table one by one: a chrome Chevy hub cap, a stainless steel toaster, silver collectors' spoons, what appeared to be a diamond engagement ring, and a handful of coins and colourful bottle caps.

Gavran wasted no time inspecting the eclectic items, possessively grasping each of the coins between his bony fingers as he searched for the perfect throne.

The woman calmly watched his manic hopping with a twinkle in her eye. "I found him, Gavran."

Mason winced as Gavran dropped the toaster with a loud clank and bounced back to the table to settle his new pieces into their proper places. Once he was satisfied, his peculiar dance brought him to a stop in front of his guest.

"Keep an eye on him. Make sure he's not late this time." He glanced up at the raven and grinned. "Take my eyes, too."

She inclined her head as if showing reverence, and Gavran patted her hair like one would a favoured child. Then, as if guided by ritual, she turned to leave without another word, the raven following close behind.

"Wait," Mason interrupted her exit. "Are you a friend of Gavran's?"

She stopped just outside the doorway, speaking to him over her shoulder, "My name is Ama. We will meet again, I'm sure."

Mason turned to Gavran after she ambled away. "How would she know that?"

The old man clapped his hands together and pranced about in delight. "Light the torch of your grief," he cackled. "Follow it deep into the woods."

"I don't understand."

Gavran reached out and placed a knobby hand on the young doctor's chest. "When night falls, only flames reveal the road ahead."

CHAPTER
EIGHT

KAI

DURING THE DAY, Black Hollow was a different world from the pitiful cesspool Kai used as hunting grounds when the moon was out. The main road was busy with commuters and pedestrians, shops were open and welcoming, and the urge to hide pressed in on him with the throng.

Unaccustomed to being so exposed, he fumbled with both curiosity and unease, leaning away from people when they got too close—fighting the instinct to snarl when someone bumped into him from behind. He had no trouble hurting people or indulging his vices in the safety of a seedy dive bar; he was comfortable there, acclimated to the shadows and din that disguised misery and desire alike. But in broad daylight, there was nowhere to retreat, and the slightest human contact, the most innocent of glances, felt utterly debilitating.

The demand for social propriety wasn't the only thing plaguing Kai. His ghostly menace had been awfully quiet these last few days, and Kai knew better than to believe the peace would last. Something was coming. Every time the dickish phantom disappeared, it was because he was squirrelling away his energy. Maybe he would hurl some moose shit at Kai's face? Derail a train and have him mauled? The possibilities were endless, and Kai lamented that his imagination wasn't wicked enough to conjure anything that could prepare him. The worst part was not knowing—not knowing when, where, how, or around whom the attacks would happen.

But Kai was a spiteful son-of-a-bitch. The more his antagonist pushed him, the more stubborn he became. An eye for an eye. A nut for a nut. Kai didn't care if he had to reach into the fifth dimension and castrate the motherfucker barehanded. He swore he'd one day be rid of this curse—even if it killed him. He just had to figure out *how*.

Turning a corner, he abandoned the main road in favour of a quieter route where his senses didn't feel like they were being chopped in a blender. He was only here to pawn that damn watch. Several blocks away, a bus idled as passengers stepped off. Kai's eyes narrowed at those mammoth, rumbling wheels that stunk like tar. He *loathed* buses. The way they looked. The sounds they made. The way they smelled. Not to mention that every time he got on one, he felt nauseous and dizzy.

Kai picked up an empty soda can and crunched it between his fingers. He whipped it as hard as he could, satisfied by the crumpled aluminum ricocheting off the window. The monster spewed more noxious gas as it made its escape, and a confused passenger stuck their cheek to the glass to look around.

Licking the sugary residue off his fingers, Kai turned and headed the other way in a stubborn refusal to take the same path as the bus. Meanwhile, the elderly man who'd just gotten off at his stop stared at Kai like he was a lunatic, muttering something about young people and communism.

After successfully pawning the watch for a hundred dollars, Kai was eager to get the fuck out of Pleasantville. As he pushed the cash into his leather wallet, he retrieved a piece of an old lilac birthday card he always kept with him, his name scrawled on the back in dark blue ink.

Happy Birthday, Kai Donovan.

It was barely legible. He knew how hard it had been for old Alice to hold a pen, but she tried anyway.

Kai zigzagged through the smaller alleys, feeling more comfortable in the narrow corridors behind the main roads. It was quiet, and although it smelled like shit, it wasn't disorienting like the crowded downtown streets where everything from cheap perfume and mystery meat to used tampons and acrylic paint bombarded his nostrils.

He couldn't wait to return to his den—a tiny cabin nestled in a grove of pines and cedars. It was used by miners and forestry workers before the sudden insurgence of wolves a few years back and had long since been abandoned. The outside panelling was falling apart, and there were several holes in the roof that needed repairing. The windows were cracked, and it wasn't unusual to find a fox or a raccoon scavenging inside. Still, it was home.

As he stalked past the chain-link fence behind the buildings, a heavy shadow followed. Kai slowed, hesitating until he felt the darkness nipping at his heels. Something cold slithered up his neck, then reached around his throat and squeezed. The chill spilled down his collar bone and cut into his chest, twisting through his heart.

The air fled his lungs, and his ribcage tightened as the phantom blade splintered. The ridges on his spine sundered, grinding back and forth like spider legs trying to break free. Something was inside of him, moving, shrieking, biting. It was a parasite, injected into his core by a cold, spectral hand.

"S-stop..." Kai knew it was his antagonist. He gasped as his insides constricted, his desperate attempt to breathe yielding only a pathetic wheeze. His vision was growing dark, white noise drowning his ears as he fought to move his feet, but it was like someone had welded them to the ground. Squeezing his eyes shut, Kai cursed loudly when he heard a distinct laugh from somewhere within the frequencies.

"What the fuck are you!"

From all directions came the low, rumbling reply.

Abaddon.

"Aba...ddon," Kai strained. "Fuck...off!"

He managed to force out the words, the verbal outburst freeing him just enough to push one stride forward. Kai focused on the street ahead, the light of the main road drawing him like a moth to a flame. Gritting his teeth, he drove a fist into his leg until it moved. He didn't dare look back where the shadow followed him step by step, inch by inch. But there was no way in hell he'd let himself collapse here, even if it meant tearing his own heart out along with whatever phantom vermin was crawling around inside him.

Grains of mortar bit into his palm as he grabbed at the wall for support. He turned the corner and stumbled out of the alleyway and into the open, the world around him spiralling into blinding white chaos. Unable to see or smell, he staggered waywardly, his every capacity crippled.

The last thing Kai remembered was the stench of carbon monoxide and the booming horn of a goddamn bus, hollering at him to get the fuck out of the way.

CHAPTER
NINE

MASON

THE IDYLLIC LITTLE town Mason had been hell-bent on escaping to wasn't providing much respite, even when he spent his time lounging in local joints, reading books on the farmhouse rooftop, and soaking up Annabelle's stories about the '70s. While he was distracted from his grief over Amanda, there were other, fresher thorns pricking Mason's overactive mind. He'd been sucked into a black hole of events that clung to no rational explanation. He was a stranger in a world too unfamiliar to navigate.

Exhausted by the constant reeling in his mind, Mason decided what he really needed was a distraction—a distraction from *this* distraction. He found himself drawn to the familiarity of the very place he'd run away from, browsing social media and catching up with family. They were surprisingly nonchalant about his disappearance, to the point that he wondered if he was even missed. His sense of loss seemed to go over their heads as they spouted rote platitudes.

Time heals all wounds, his sweet but somewhat vacant mother had said.

Then he remembered that Jazlyn, his old friend from medical school, was working at a hospital somewhere in the vicinity. Pulling up her profile, he sent her a message, hoping she wasn't too busy to respond.

Mason stared at the screen in anticipation. When nothing came after several minutes, he shut his laptop and flopped back onto the bed, the textured white surface above him rippling with the after-images of the giant redwood and its ghostly inhabitant. He thought back to the woman—Ama —and the way she looked at him when she said they'd meet again. It was as though she knew, better than Mason did, that he was already far too tangled in the spider's web. There was no hope of escape.

A ping sounded from the laptop, and Mason rolled over to push the lid up. It was Jazlyn, responding with enthusiasm that exuded from the letters on the screen. She said she was busy working double shifts the entire week but would be happy to make time for him *at* the hospital. Mason read on, his heart sinking as he fixated on the last sentence.

Why not stop by the hospital today? You'll fit right in!

Oh, if only she knew. The last place Mason wanted to go was the hospital. The sight of those grey, sanitary halls, the smell of cheap burnt coffee and latex gloves, the sound of heart monitors and the pop of syringes—it was all still too fresh. And then there were the blood-stained sheets, stubborn blemishes, the essence of life and death mingling under the scrutinizing lens of a microscope. He heard the heart monitor again, the steady beeps slowing until the intervals were long enough for him to hold his breath and choke. Then there was the flat line, ringing in his ears. The deafening silence that followed. The taste of sorrow creeping onto his tongue.

He wasn't prepared to go back.

But the other side of the coin remained. If he succumbed to his fear, would the phantoms of Black Hollow devour his mind? Was this the universe's way of testing him? The prospect of seeing a familiar face motivated him to have faith. Maybe he was ready. Maybe after all the strangeness he'd seen in this town, he'd be ready to return to the medical community— even if it was as a mere spectator. He was not a practising physician, he reminded himself. It would be all right.

Mason and Jazlyn agreed to meet at the Tim Horton's on the ground floor of Ashgrove & District General Hospital for a late lunch. After agonizing over his wardrobe for several minutes, he settled for a semi-casual look, reaching for his best jeans and a white dress shirt. It was a quick drive, though it felt like a hundred years. By the time the red cross on the side of the facility was visible, he'd begun questioning the wisdom of his decision. His hands were so clammy with sweat that they nearly slipped off the steering wheel as he pulled into the parking lot.

Mason stuttered through the main entrance, his eyes scanning the area for the coffee shop logo. It was easy to spot; Ashgrove's hospital was a fraction of the size of any one of Vancouver's major health centres. There were several people gathered around the dingy beige tables, nibbling on bagels and sipping hot drinks. Some had dark circles under their eyes and were likely waiting for loved ones in care. Seeing that Jazlyn hadn't arrived yet, Mason ordered himself a peppermint tea.

Just as he was slipping his wallet back into his trousers, he felt a light tap on his shoulder. Turning, he was startled by the empty space in front of him. Nobody was there.

"What in the..." he muttered, looking around when he heard a giggle from his periphery.

"Over here!" a feminine voice called.

Spinning with a touch of panic, Mason came face-to-face with a young woman of elfin stature. She was a good head shorter than him and grinning like a Cheshire cat. Her strawberry blond locks were tucked behind her ears, and he reflexively sought out the familiar brown freckle in one of her blue eyes.

"You look like you've seen a ghost, Cap!"

Indeed, Mason felt like he'd seen one too many of those in recent days.

"Christ, Jaz, you scared the shit out of me." He let out his breath before returning her smile. "How've you been?"

"Yeah, you always were a pussy," she snorted. "And I'm great!" She threw her noodly arms out for emphasis then gave him a hug. "Grab your tea, grandpa, we're goin' for a walk."

Mason lifted his paper cup in a toast to her crassness, following her as she led him away. For a cute, blue-eyed blonde that was petite enough to squeeze through the bars of a jail cell, she had a pretty nasty mouth on her. But at least it was an honest mouth.

"How am I a grandpa?" he asked.

"Because you're drinking peppermint tea—I can smell it. That and you being a whole three years older than me."

"Gee, I may as well retire then."

"Isn't that why you're here?" she jabbed him in the ribs before calling the elevator. "Last I checked, newbies don't get much vacation time."

"I'm not here on vacation," he mumbled, the glumness in his tone surprising them both.

Jazlyn raised an eyebrow. "What did you do? Kill someone?"

Mason's choked on his tea, his eyes darting to her face as his lips pursed. The elevator doors drew open with a light ding, the people inside looking perplexed as Mason and Jazlyn stood frozen to the tiles, unmoving as their silent exchange conveyed all that needed to be known.

"Oh..." she trailed off, then turned and walked into the elevator.

"Yeah," he sighed once they were side-by-side again. "I'm on leave. Need some time to myself."

"Right."

"Yeah."

Jazlyn shifted her weight, her posture stiff as she cleared her throat. "How are you holding up?" she asked once they stepped off.

"I'm all right," he lied. "Just been trying to get away. I thought this town might be a good place to escape to when I saw how peaceful it looked. Saw it on your profile."

"Hah!" she burst out, then quickly backpedaled. "I mean, sure, it's pretty and all, but um, I'm sure you've noticed...if you've been here long enough that is."

It was Mason's turn to raise an eyebrow. "Noticed what?" He looked up and took note of the signs on the walls. They were headed towards one of the hematology labs.

"The people here," she hissed under her breath while faking a polite smile at a passing doctor. "They're all freakin' nut jobs. Weirdos, the lot of them."

Mason straightened up. "You mean the legends. They really believe, don't they?"

"Shhhhhhhhh!"

"What?" He frowned as they walked through a pair of swinging doors. "Are outsiders not allowed to talk about it or something?"

"Didn't you hear?" she grumbled. "Some psycho killed his daughter because he thought she'd been kidnapped by the Dreamwalker. Gene Robinson. Took this supernatural stuff way too seriously."

Mason grabbed her shoulder to keep from tripping. "What did you just say?" he gasped.

"You didn't hear?" She reached out to steady him. "Her name was Elle Robinson. It's all anyone's been talking about."

He shook his head. "My hostess didn't say anything." And why hadn't she?

"Normally I don't pay attention." Jazlyn shrugged and pulled some files from a cabinet once he released her arm. "I mean, I've heard stuff here and there. Mostly from teenagers who end up in the ER after doing something stupid. You know, like going into the woods in the dead of night looking for that old willow—you must've heard about it—then getting lost or falling into a ravine. Parents here are super vigilant, too. Soon as someone goes missing for like, forty-five minutes, they call the cops. Then again, can't say I blame 'em. We had a girl go missing last year. She ended up on IV antibiotics for two weeks because she'd been barefoot in the woods for almost five days. She nearly lost three toes! How the hell does that even happen!" She threw her arms up, exasperated.

"I don't know," Mason responded, his mind reeling.

"Anyway," she sighed, shutting the cabinet and leading him out while fanning herself with the Kraft folders. "Her fiancé was arrested a week later for her murder. It's just like Elle's story."

The articles from the archives flashed through Mason's head as he followed her. "Why does this happen so much here? Why are these people killing their loved ones after they've been found?"

"Capgras syndrome is the official story," said Jazlyn. "I don't know why there's so much of it here, but if you're feeling morbid, someone leaked a video of the interrogation with the dad—sick bastard. The police are scrambling to take it down, but once on the internet, always on the internet." She started down the hall. "Come on, I need to get these to a doctor. You want to come with? Hospital staff is pretty easygoing, small town and all."

"Right." Mason wanted to know more, but Elle Robinson would have to wait. The immediacy of introducing himself as a visiting physician made his stomach swim.

It felt dishonest. He wondered what it was like for Jazlyn, working under people who would have been her professional equals had she graduated as an M.D. Was she happy like this? He couldn't imagine quitting, taking a lower-paying and less-respected job, especially when it was just as much work. "Hey, why'd you decide to become a nurse? Why didn't you just tough it out till the end of med school?"

She slowed as she considered this. "I realized I didn't want to be responsible for making life-changing decisions for anyone."

Mason gulped down the last of his tea and threw out the cup. "What do you mean?"

As they waited by the elevators again, she shook her head like she was remembering something unpleasant. "I spent my whole life taking care of people. Being a parent to my own parents. Dad had a gambling problem; Mom couldn't grow a backbone to kick him to the curb. That left me stuck in the middle, picking up the pieces. I remember being sixteen and thinking they were *my* responsibility, not the other way around. And that's kind of messed up."

"Wow." Mason sucked in a breath, not expecting to hear something so candid and weighty. "I'm sorry, Jaz, I really didn't know it was so rough for you."

"Naw, it's cool," she waved him off. "I don't think it affected me that deeply to be honest. That's why I didn't talk about it. It wasn't important."

"Really?" He raised an eyebrow. "You weren't just embarrassed or, you know, being secretive?"

"Nope," she shook her head again. "It was just life. I never even thought to question it."

Mason chewed over this, struggling to accept her mentality. She sounded so damn tough, like she could take life's blows and come out stronger than before. He imagined she would have made a much better doctor than him.

"Anyway," she continued when he didn't respond, "I did my MCAT after undergrad, and at the time I thought I *wanted* the responsibility because it was all I knew. I was used to it. Then, halfway through our program, I realized that I was sick of it all. I didn't want anyone to turn around one day and say it was my fault that someone died or didn't get better."

She turned to him and smiled. "I don't think I could live with that for the rest of my life." The elevator doors pulled open, the hallway mercifully empty this time. "My mom, my dad, my little brother," she counted them on her fingers, "I felt like I failed them all. I don't need the guilt of a complete stranger added onto it. So I decided to quit and go to nursing school instead. Not that nurses are free of responsibility, but at least we're not making life-or-death treatment decisions. As a nurse, I still feed my pathological need to take care of people. I can advocate for my patients, but I won't always be in a position to make a bad call and end up accountable for someone's life."

Her frankness was a breath of fresh air. For the near-five years he'd been in residency, Mason couldn't remember the last time someone spoke about the realities of their profession with such bare-bones honesty. Most people went on about how empowering it was—how rewarding it felt to help others and earn their gratitude. And he was one of those people. But no one ever mentioned the flip side—the guilt of failing, the resentment of letting someone down. It was the dark underbelly that went unnoticed behind the blinding shine of the medical community's pride.

"I've honestly never thought about it that way," he admitted. "For me, it was just—"

"Yeah, yeah, I know, Cap. I still remember that stupid t-shirt with the Captain America shield on it." She gave him a sympathetic glance. "You just wanted to save somebody."

Staring at his shoes, Mason shoved his hands into his pockets and slumped his shoulders. "Never thought about the dark side much."

Jazlyn snorted, elbowing him playfully as they walked out of the elevators and back onto the main floor. "You don't belong on the dark side, Mason. People like you just wouldn't survive there."

He flinched as his side was hit, blinking after her as she sauntered off. "I'm already floundering, Sith Lord."

"Then go on get home!" she said in a southern accent and pointed towards the doors. "Pick up your pretty blue lightsaber and give Steve Rogers a kiss!"

"You're getting your universes mixed up," he whined. "George Lucas and Marvel? Just...no, Jaz! No! You can't do that!"

"Screw you, I'm writing a crossover!"

Mason spent the next hour following Jazlyn through the ER and introducing himself to her colleagues, his mind flitting back to Gene Robinson every now and again. Despite the overwhelming urge to excuse himself and find the interrogation video, he was quite at ease with the hospital staff. His earlier anxieties dissipated with the friendly smiles and curious inquiries regarding work-life in Vancouver. The atmosphere in Ashgrove was utterly different from what he was used to. He noticed none of the competition that marked the relationships between physicians and nursing staff in metropolitan hospitals. For the first time, Mason wondered just how deeply the negative emotions of patients and staff at his resident hospital affected him. So sharp was the contrast that he began to hope again—maybe he was cut out for this. Maybe he just needed a different work environment.

As Mason helped change the sheets on one of the beds, the wail of sirens cut the thread of his dreamy escape. At the alarm, doctors and nurses quickly assembled towards the designated ambulance area, isolated near the back of the ER.

"What's going on?" he asked Jazlyn as she flew past him after speaking to a colleague.

"Patch phone went off a few minutes ago," she told him while putting together a new file.

He finished throwing the used sheets in the laundry bin. "Yeah, I heard. What did EMS say?"

"We've got a John Doe, no ID, was struck by a bus at high speed."

"What's the damage?" Mason's tone was hushed, but he couldn't stop years of medical training from kicking in.

Jazlyn's fingers paused on the drawer handle, her eyes narrowing at him in silent assessment before she answered. "He's sustained multisystem trauma, including a skull fracture, bilateral femur fracture, heavy internal bleeding, and flail chest." She met his gaze, addressing him as though he were a physician on the trauma medical team. "EMS intubated him, ventilating at a rate of ten with good airway compliance. He's on IV to sustain blood pressure and has tachycardia at 165 beats per minute."

"Jesus." Mason breathed out. "He's probably not going to make it..."

"No," she shook her head, "but you never know. Miracles do happen. You should wait here. They're bringing him in now."

She rushed past him and joined the rest of the team in the trauma bay. Despite being an oncologist, Mason had done an ER rotation for his program's requirements. No one liked doing the rounds, but it was part of the job and a rewarding experience. He'd been assigned to watch over several patients in critical condition but was fortunate enough to never encounter anyone so close to death. Regardless, he suddenly felt left out; he wanted to be with the others, running next to the stretcher, giving orders, or at least taking them.

Unsure of what to do with himself, he paced back and forth with his eyes lowered to the floor. People died in the ER all the time, he told himself, so why was he so nervous? Why did this one stranger's life carry so much weight? Mason rationalized it was the first time since Amanda that he was in such close proximity to death. Even though his position was that of a bystander, the feeling of powerlessness that came with being adjacent to that dimming life tickled him with unpleasant familiarity. And without Jazlyn to act as his buffer, he felt vulnerable against the onslaught of cruel reminders, the uncertainty creeping back in from the corners of his mind.

When it became too much, Mason parked himself in a hallway chair. He pulled out his phone and searched for the only thing he knew would occupy his attention: the murder of Elle Robinson, the girl last stolen by the Dreamwalker.

CHAPTER
TEN

IT DIDN'T TAKE LONG to find the video. It was grainy and muffled, but clear enough to make out once Mason plugged in the earbuds he kept tucked in his pocket. He clenched the edges of his phone as he hit play.

"You killed your daughter," said the detective, leaning over and looking the suspect in the eye.

Gene Robinson, an unremarkable-looking man in his fifties, glanced up, startled. His hands trembled on the table in the blank-white interrogation room. "I didn't kill my daughter," he insisted. "I didn't do *anything* wrong."

"You're denying killing anyone?" the detective choked back a laugh. "Your own wife turned you in."

"What I killed..." Gene trailed off, hiding his face in his hands as his voice broke. He sucked in a breath and straightened up. "The thing I killed was not Elle—not my girl. What I killed was a thrall of the Dreamwalker. The wolves lured my Elle away," he sobbed, "and she's lost to those woods forever. She's never coming back."

"You're damn right she's not," scoffed the detective. "Someone get this guy a psych eval."

"You don't get how this works!" Gene Robinson slammed his fist down on the table, his eyes wide, tears streaming down his face as his composure crumbled. "All that returns is a shell. The girl goes into the forest but—but something else comes out."

Mason was at a loss. How could this man have killed his own daughter? Gene Robinson appeared utterly grief-stricken, still going on about how smart, beautiful, kind, and dignified his baby girl had been. Mason knew of Capgras, or imposter syndrome, but most cases were so rare and outlandish, it was difficult to believe they happened outside of psychology textbooks.

"She started withdrawing," Gene whispered, his face hidden again. "That's how you know. They get depressed, moody, want to be alone all the time. They're just...not themselves. You try to get your happy little girl back, but they just...they just pull further away. Then they disappear."

They're teenage girls! Mason wanted to scream at the video. How could this man be so stupid? Withdrawal could have signalled just about anything—stress, trauma, mental health concerns. How could he think normal adolescent behaviour was a tell-tale sign that his daughter had been abducted and replaced? It was terrifying.

"When she came back, she told my wife that someone had warned her to stay away from Black Hollow," he added after a pause, "but she wouldn't say who."

"Let me guess," the detective drawled. "The Dreamwalker?"

"Yes!" Gene's hand struck the table. "Who else could it have been?"

Part of Mason wished he'd never watched the video, wished he could wipe it from existence. But both Mason and the people of Black Hollow were spellbound by the mystery of the Dreamwalker—even if for entirely different reasons. To the townsfolk, the Dreamwalker was fact, but Mason desperately needed her to be fiction.

Nearly an hour passed until Jazlyn finally returned. Her expression was forlorn, her lips downturned as she appeared rooted in thought.

Mason yanked out his earbuds and pushed himself to his feet. "What happened?" he asked as she stopped in front of him.

"Doctors rushed him into surgery," she began, planting a hand on her hip, "suited up in less than two minutes, but by the time they got inside..."

Mason's heart sank. She didn't finish her sentence, but she didn't have to. "He didn't make it, did he?" Mason asked quietly, a sharp pain cutting through his chest. How could this happen again so soon? He'd worked so hard to get away from the traumatic death of his young patient. And yet, the day he returned to a hospital to see a friend, the day he finally began feeling capable of being a physician again, he was struck with yet another death. A distant one, yes—but it was still a cruel reminder of how ill-equipped he was to deal with life's finale.

"Huh?" Jazlyn blinked, looking up at him as if noticing he was there for the first time. "Oh—naw, Cap. You got it all wrong. John Doe ain't dead."

"What?" His head snapped up. "Then what was with that morbid look on your face? If he's not dead, then what is he?"

"That's just it!" she exclaimed, throwing her arms out to the side. "By the time Dr. Callahan got the CT scan, X-rays—well," she hesitated, stumbling on her words. It was a rarity for the girl he knew as a spitfire.

"Yes?" he beckoned her to continue.

A mystified Jazlyn swallowed hard, looking him straight in the eye. "There was nothing to operate on."

Mason squinted at his old friend as if she had turned into someone else. "What do you mean there was nothing to operate on? Wait—how did they find time to run tests on a guy just barely hanging on?"

She nodded quickly. "Exactly! He would have been lucky not to die on the operating table! But when the surgical team looked at him, a lot of the damage EMS reported wasn't even there! Not only that, but his vitals were completely stable!" She sighed, shaking her arms out. "Callahan ordered the scans afterwards."

"How the..." Mason mouthed the words and crossed his arms over his chest. He stared at the wall as he processed this information, then turned back to a befuddled Jazlyn. "Are you sure the report on the patch phone wasn't a mistake? Could it have been someone else? Did the surgical team get the right patient?"

She was already shaking her head by the time he asked his first question. She seemed to have forgotten about her obligations as she worked through the shock. "Nope. It's definitely him. Asked Terry and three other EMS personnel. All say the same thing—that's the guy they picked up. And yes, we checked the file three times over."

"Did they report the trauma wrong, then?"

"No!" Jazlyn sounded frustrated. "Terry said he was mangled and bleeding out when they got there! There was no mistake!"

"And now? Where is he now?"

"In the ICU. He's still in a coma, but stable. A few broken bones, but nothing we can really do for him. We don't know his blood type, so Callahan ordered tests. I can't tell if he healed or if it just...never happened."

"Hold up—he's drawing blood from a patient who almost died?" Mason looked at her as though this Callahan was plotting murder.

"Duh! What would you do?" she shot back, exasperated.

"Just give him O negative!" Mason sputtered. "How can he have enough blood for sampling?"

"*That's* how much he's recovered!" she huffed. "They want him prepped for a transfusion just in case. But either way, wouldn't you want this dude's freaky blood on file? Pretty sure that's why Callahan wants it drawn!"

"I guess..."

Mason paced the cramped hallway for the umpteenth time, then forced out a breathy laugh from his already-tight chest. "Jaz," he suddenly stepped forward, gripping her by the shoulders. "I know this is totally against protocol, but could you let me see this guy?"

"What!" she leaned back as he grabbed her, eyes widening. "Are you nuts? Do you have any idea how much trouble I'd be in if I let non-medical personnel see a patient who just got out of surgery?"

"Come on," he pleaded in a harsh whisper. He knew it was a bizarre request, unfair even, but what if the doctors miscalculated? What if Mason left the hospital thinking all was well, only to find out John Doe had actually died? And if John Doe was as Jazlyn claimed, *how* did he manage to heal so quickly? Mason couldn't fathom leaving without a glance. "You know me. And technically, I am medical personnel. I'm a licensed doctor—a specialist at that! And you've been showing me around all day, so I'm sure it's fine. Please, Jaz, I need to see this guy for myself. After what I've been through, this could really mean something. This could *help* me."

His tone was desperate, sorrowful even, his eyes brimming with tears as he gulped down the emotions. How he yearned for something to take him back to his old self—the hopeful young med student who was ready to conquer the world.

"Fine," she sighed after a drawn-out pause, then jerked out of his grasp to raise a finger to his nose. "But only for a minute. If they catch us, I could lose my job."

"You got it," he nodded like a puppy. "Only a minute."

She nodded back stiffly, then turned around and waved for him to follow. The intensive care unit was only a short walk away. Jazlyn turned abruptly at the end of the hall, opening one of the rooms and poking her head in to ensure no one else was inside.

"Coast is clear," she hissed back to him before holding the door open. "One. Freaking. Minute," she warned. "I'll stand guard."

"Thank you. So much," he replied emphatically, his eyes shining.

Rushing inside, he looked back at his stone-faced partner as she pulled the door shut, leaving him alone in the quiet. Over on the bed was the patient, lying perfectly still with a heart monitor and an IV bag hooked to his left hand. He had a chest tube between his ribs—treatment for a partially-collapsed lung. How could he have been well enough to bypass surgery and only need the tube? Walking over, Mason examined the young man he'd wanted to see badly enough to risk his friend's career.

His face was bruised and lacerated, and there were bits of red on the sheets—clear signs that he was still quite hurt. Yet Mason felt uneasy, as though this man was somehow aware despite being unconscious. A scowl marked his harsh features like he was struggling through an unpleasant dream, fighting his way back to the land of the living.

Fumbling around the drawer for a penlight, Mason quickly inspected his target's pupils. Indeed, everything looked normal. While the left side of his body was black and blue from soft tissue damage, nothing appeared severely broken, just as Jazlyn had said. Could this stranger have really been hit by a bus moving at high speed? If so, he should have been wholly mangled, if not dead.

How could a person recover so rapidly from being ground into the pavement by a *bus*? Curiosity burning, Mason rushed over to the chair where the patient's torn, bloody clothes and personal items were left in a plastic bag. Rummaging through, he gripped something leathery and solid—a wallet. Emptying its contents, he found nothing but some cash and a small, lilac piece of paper with a name scrawled across in chicken scratch.

Happy Birthday, Kai Donovan.

A knock sounded against the door, followed by Jazlyn's voice.

"Are you done yet? I'm freaking out over here!" she hissed through the crack.

"C-Coming!" he jerked back, returning the penlight to the drawer and stuffing the wallet's contents away before throwing it into the plastic bag. He rushed out of the room, giving the strange young man a parting glance as he closed the door behind him.

"Thank God," Jazlyn huffed. "I thought you'd never come out."

He smiled sheepishly. "You said one minute."

"Yeah, and you were in there for at least two!"

Mason ducked his head as she glared at him. "Sorry—couldn't help myself."

"Of course not." She rolled her eyes, taking him by the elbow and dragging him away. "Now let's get out of here."

Mason didn't fight her as she yanked him along. He was still in a daze, confused but enthralled. He thought he'd be staring death in the eye again, but the universe was proving capable of mercy, after all.

When they turned the corner, the fast-paced squeaks of rubber soles against the beige tiles drew their attention as someone called out to Jazlyn. It was one of the other nurses, rushing towards them with a frantic expression.

"Jazlyn!" she cried out again when they noticed her. Her dark hair was tied back in a low ponytail, the light blue scrubs hugging her rounded hips.

"What is it?" Jazlyn asked as they walked further down the hall, a good distance from the room with the miracle patient.

"It's his blood tests—John Doe's, I mean. Something isn't right." Her cheeks were flushed, her hands gripping the folder until it bent.

"What do you mean?" Mason asked in concern, momentarily forgetting himself, only to be reminded by Jazlyn's elbow in his side.

"Jazlyn! Amy!" It was another nurse, calling to them as she flew around the corridor from where they'd just been. "We've got a code yellow!"

Jazlyn's jaw dropped, and Mason's face turned borderline purple as he held his breath, sweat breaking out over his hairline.

"Seriously!" Jazlyn all but shrieked. "What is up with today? How—"

"I just went to check on the patient!" she explained, her voice wobbling as she tapped the folder Amy had in her hands. Visibly trying to calm down, she recited her every action in a slow, measured tone. "I went into his room...thought I'd got it wrong...checked my records...double-checked the room number...but I was definitely in John Doe's room!"

Mason swallowed the lump in his throat as he considered if his day could possibly get any stranger. He had just been there. He had just been in John Doe's room. The man was in a coma.

Horror, wonder, and an undeniable sense of excitement crept up his spine. This had to be some kind of joke. Or a dream. But it most definitely couldn't be real. Although he'd told himself not to speak—not to get involved—he couldn't stop the words from forming on his lips, his voice sounding meek and foreign as he said aloud what everyone already knew,

"He's gone."

CHAPTER
ELEVEN
THE CROSSING

MIYA

W HEN M IYA OPENED HER EYES, *she was looking towards the sky. It was sunset—the last specs of orange and red bleeding into the horizon, leaving a luminous, ephemeral streak under the darkening blanket of night. This wasn't the sky of the waking world.*

She stood at the foot of a mountain covered in forest. It was peaceful and intimate, her senses gifting her a sharp awareness of her surroundings. She felt more in control here than in the outside world.

A cobblestone path up ahead led into the hilly woods, so she began to follow it. Only after travelling a fair distance did Miya realize there was something familiar about this place, something resembling a memory. She continued walking uphill, the oak trees framing the tiny road twisting as she passed them. The massive boughs curved overhead as though she had disturbed their endless slumber, watching her move through their land. Their leaves turned red, then brown, withering and succumbing to the pull of gravity. Seasons changed before Miya's eyes, the cycles moving at a pace befitting the perception of an immortal spirit—one who had witnessed them a thousand times over. By the time she reached the end of the path, the trees were all dead.

Where the passage ended, there was a colossal redwood towering so high it reached through the clouds and disappeared somewhere beyond. Miya could hear it breathing, pushing and pulling life in and out of the soil. A small figure stood near the base of the massive trunk, his back turned as he appeared to speak with someone. Miya could tell that he was old—very, very old. She wanted to reach out to him, unexpected longing coiling around her heart. She was about to call out, but he burst into a thousand ravens, rushing skyward with an eruption that shook the earth. The world disappeared beneath her, and she fell into the darkness.

Miya was back at the forest's edge, a small village behind her. Her peripheral vision was blocked by something dark and soft; she was wearing a cloak with the hood drawn over her head. Without rhyme or reason, she walked into the woods, this time finding no path to guide her. Ducking under branches and stepping over tree roots, she had no idea where she was going or why. Something was pulling her, but the call was too faint for her to grasp. She was lost, the sun still sinking towards the horizon.

She continued to wander, weaving through the trees until she found herself in a glade encasing an eerie, old willow tree. Like the redwood from before, it seemed alive, its roots pulsating just beneath the earth. The old guardian's branches were like a long, fluid curtain, separating her from whatever resided behind them. As the breeze parted the willow's arms, Miya caught a glimpse of a shadow—a mass of dark fur lying under the protection of the swaying wisps. She felt the pull once more, the wind at her back pushing her forward until she passed into the darkened space.

There, under the willow, Miya found a black wolf. He was unmoving, his eyes closed despite her presence. It dawned on her that he was dying, his thick coat matted and sticky with blood. She crouched down to examine him, though the stoop left her feeling vulnerable, apprehensive. And yet it wasn't the wolf that frightened her.

Something hovered behind Miya with intent she couldn't place. She perceived curiosity, amusement, and perhaps something more insidious. She didn't dare turn around for fear of what she might see, but the presence was distinctly female. It drew closer and closer until Miya felt breath on her ear—dark, feather-like shadows caressing the ground around her. Miya's eyes fell on the wolf; she was paralyzed in anticipation of the apparition's voice—her message to the intruder.

"Don't lose your way," she hissed an ominous spell, "or there'll be hell to pay."

Then, a horn blared in the distance, the sound bellowing as the last specs of sunlight burrowed deep into the earth. Miya's time here was up.

Gasping for air, Miya's eyes shot open, wet strands of hair clinging to her face and neck as she tried to remember where she was. The windowless grey walls and the sight of her beloved red panda on the wobbly dresser dizzied her with relief as she finally recognized her own bedroom. Taking a deep breath, Miya flopped back against the pillow and exhaled, pulling her hair from her hot, irritated skin. She'd always had pretty wild dreams, but nothing like *that* before—and never about the fable of Black Hollow. She thought about her earlier resolution to hunt the Dreamwalker, and the shadowy woman who'd visited her bedroom with a message. The tables had turned. The Dreamwalker had come to her.

No, she was coming *for* her.

Miya's pulse thundered in her ears, the afterimages of the place she'd returned from fresh like a wet painting. Squeezing her eyes shut, she tried to preserve the impressions, willing herself to record every minute detail. But the dream slipped away like vapour. The paint bled off the canvas, leaving her with nothing but the residue of disquiet.

Yet the dream wasn't the only thing that disappeared. The fable too was gone, as though it had been wiped from her psyche. But how could that be? She'd heard the legends a thousand times. Miya strained to remember the lore she'd been taught by the school librarian, the warnings her father lectured her with in high school. But it had all vanished. She only knew there was a Dreamwalker that spirited young women away. The details, however, were a fast-fading ripple in an ocean of memories.

She checked the time on her cell phone and realized it was evening; she'd been out for over twelve hours, and yet still felt exhausted. Usually, after a long bout of insomnia, she'd collapse into a day-long coma that left her drowsy and lethargic. But this was different—like she'd gone somewhere during the night. Miya's head rattled like a battered punching bag. Disgruntled, she sat up and threw the covers off, rubbing her eyes until she regained the coordination to stand.

Something was...wrong. Her skin crawled and her eyes watered. The hairs on her neck stood on end. She kept glancing over her shoulder as though someone was following her, hugging the shadows in every corner. The compulsion to check burned the peripheries of her awareness until there was nothing but an urge to flee. Every cell in her body screamed.

Wild, Miya grabbed her keys and ran out of the apartment. Out the door and into the darkness, she didn't dare look back, sprinting until sound fell into a vacuum and silence enveloped her.

She didn't stop until she could barely see buildings flickering past her—until traffic lights grew sparse, sidewalks disappeared, and the road narrowed into a single lane of cracked pavement. She moved fast towards the black mass in the horizon—the forest. But before she reached the fields, Miya's chest caved in, and she collapsed into a squat, heaving in an effort to catch her breath. She had nothing with her—no wallet, no jacket, no cell phone. Groping around her back pocket, she fished out a five-dollar bill.

She wanted to go to the playground, but in her frenzy she'd taken a wrong turn and veered off the usual path. It didn't help that she hadn't eaten all day, but grocery stores and fast food were well out of the way. She ventured towards a lone gas station at the edge of the road and bought some beef jerky and a can of pop with the measly bill. After tax, Miya was short a few cents, but the clerk let it slide. Grateful for the pass, she thanked him with a barely audible mumble and scuttled back outside, afraid he might change his mind.

She reached the crooked maple some fifteen minutes later. As she approached the meadow, the air grew thick and misty. It was quite something—how different the fields looked at night. Without the stalls and vendors embellishing every inch of open space during the market hours, Miya felt like she was passing through a different world. Everything felt more expansive, disorienting, and precarious. By day, it was a space of congregation and community for the people of Black Hollow. By night, it had a life of its own without the presence of humans—one that didn't *want* to belong to them. It made Miya wonder if *she* would be accepted.

She found her swing set despite the blinding vapour. As she settled in, the mist began to lift, allowing a few meters of visibility. Miya pulled out her snacks and popped open the can, raising it in a toast to her sanctuary.

"Cheers," she whispered and took an obligatory sip. Now out of the basement, she felt lighter. It was odd, but in silence, Miya was least alone. She could finally look at what she wanted to see and not worry about what others were seeing in her. Elated, she reached for the jerky and tore open the bag, the crinkling plastic alerting her to how eerily quiet her surroundings were. With the settled storm came the awareness of how chilling it was to be alone in a blanket of fog. But Miya was mesmerized, her blood rushing with new life; she was the only one here, and it made her feel powerful—the air full of lingering potential.

Her emboldened state, however, was short-lived. She heard a rustle in the nearby bushes and froze, jolted out of her daydream.

I must be hearing things, she thought until the snapping of twigs followed the momentary silence. Whatever was back there must've had some weight to it, but Miya didn't know of any missing girls since Elle Robinson. Her heartbeat picked up as she scanned the area.

Don't worry, she reassured herself. *Whatever it is, it's probably more scared of you than you are of it.*

With the moon barely penetrating the haze, it was almost impossible to see, but the crackling directed her attention until a shape began to emerge from the shadows.

A large, black wolf limped towards Miya from the cover of the forest, his dark form parting the white mist like a slow-moving bullet aimed straight at her chest. The soles of her shoes melded into the sand; she was paralyzed as her fondest memory stepped closer. Miya never thought a memory could waltz out of the past and into the present—transcend the déjà vu and become something more. But perhaps that was the point of repetition. Perhaps it was a fight to rupture the bounds of time.

Miya considered whether her marbles had rolled away as she leapt over the canyon of logic and expected to land safely on the other side. But she did. She couldn't fathom why else this wolf would be there in the exact same spot, why he would be as unafraid as she was unless they already knew one another.

He reached the edge of the playground and stopped, his lustrous, jet-black fur gleaming in the moonlight. Even in the dimness of night, Miya could make out the mahogany-red in his eyes—the faintest of glints that left her haunted. The sound of his breath thundered through the open air, echoing in her ears like a heartbeat. Wonder flooded her from the ground up, her entire framework of reality giving way to something utterly foreign. She was looking at a wolf, but every fiber of her soul was asking one insane question:

Who are you?

A cold chill ran through her, an undeniable air of danger emanating from him and rushing down her spine.

How do we know each other? The question relentlessly pounded through her head.

Miya wanted to reel back and run. This was ludicrous—a wolf without fear of humans was dangerous. She knew this from years of living in a town surrounded by them. Wolves were shy animals. Without a natural avoidance of humans, a wolf might well attack.

Or maybe he's here to kidnap you, a tiny voice whispered in the back of her mind. *Maybe it's your turn to go missing.*

But the sight of him limping severed Miya from her questions. His head hung low as he hobbled to the left, then looked up and met her gaze. She grew distant from common sense; he was hurt, and she couldn't just ignore that. What if he died? To leave him in this state seemed cruel, though she realized she had no means of helping him. Miya looked anxiously into his eyes. She was powerless, and if she approached, she could get mauled.

"I—I have nothing on me to help you with," she told him, distressed by the situation and her apparent expectation that the wolf would comprehend her. But she figured if he hadn't lunged at her yet, talking to him wouldn't hurt. "I don't know what to do."

He appeared unfazed and, as if understanding her, eased himself carefully onto the ground. The desire to go to him welled up in her chest—a deranged notion, she was sure, but the urge was too compelling to ignore. Her fear melted away as she grappled with different possibilities in a frantic search for the best course of action.

"I've got beef jerky?" she proffered, realizing how harebrained it sounded as she lifted the bag she'd been snacking out of. Animals rarely refused free food, and she hoped this one wouldn't attack the idiotic biped offering it. "You can have it if you'd like."

The wolf continued to watch Miya, perhaps wondering what the strange noises coming out of her mouth were. But seeing that he wasn't growling or trying to back away, she gathered enough courage to approach with fidgety half-steps until she was close enough to crouch down and reach out.

His ears twitched as she rustled through the bag and withdrew a strip of jerky, hesitantly extending it to him. He leaned forward for a cautious sniff before snatching it with his teeth, pulling his head back and out of reach as he promptly devoured the treat. Encouraged, she fished out more and offered it piece by piece until the bag was empty. With each turn, he grew bolder in accepting the food, allowing himself to linger for a moment of contact. Miya relished the feeling of his wet nose and tongue against her palm, relaxing her fingers against his soft muzzle.

"I'm sorry, that's all I got," she said with a sheepish smile as he looked up at her expectantly. "You probably need ten times more than that." The wolf canted his head as he held her gaze, inspiring her to persist in her mad rambling. "I would have gotten you a whole chicken if there was a grocery store nearby."

With the words out of her mouth, Miya started to worry that maybe she *was* losing her grip on reality. A strange sensation rose in her chest and curled around her heart as she watched him intently—a crushing vulnerability, conjured by the surreal appearance of this wolf. A lump lodged itself in her throat like a piece of hot coal, and she bit her bottom lip to keep from crying.

As she fought the tears, her companion inched forward, leaning his head down and licking her hand. Miya figured it was salty from all the meat, so she lifted her palm to his nose and laughed between shaky breaths. "I guess all you really care about is food, huh?"

He regarded her momentarily, then drew back like he'd realized he'd gotten too close, too friendly. Even if he didn't understand words, Miya considered that maybe he still understood—a kind of empathy. His tail swooped down as he lowered his nose to the ground, then turned and silently disappeared into the forest from where he came.

Miya sat on the edge of the playground and stared into the darkness beyond the trees. Only when her heart began to pound did she realize she'd been holding her breath, waiting in vain. She considered following him into the labyrinth, the darkness luring her in. She could hear the invitation in the wind, daring her to venture through the gate, tempting her to cross the threshold and lose herself on the other side.

Maybe the insomnia had finally gotten to her. Maybe she'd accepted that a life of drudgery punctuated by moments of wonder was all one could hope for. Whatever the case, it took a good deal of restraint not to fall for the dare. Wandering the woods wouldn't pay the rent, and last she checked, she preferred a mattress to the forest floor. Forcing herself back to earth, Miya pulled her wary body off the ground. Eventually, everyone had to go home.

CHAPTER

TWELVE

KAI

DURING HIS SHORT LIFE, Kai had grown accustomed to hunger; he'd learned as a child that food was a luxury as much as it was a necessity. He remembered seeing a kid ask their dad for a cheeseburger and poutine off a food truck on the street. But when Kai asked Alice, she told him he could have a peanut butter sandwich when they got home. She didn't have the money for fries and gravy, let alone half a pound of beef. That was fifteen years ago. His time with Alice had been short, but it had left its mark; without her, he wouldn't have survived among humans.

Before Alice, his earliest lesson was that sustaining life meant taking life —that to live was to devour. This logic wasn't unique to the animal world. The rich thrived at the expense of the poor; industry thrived at the expense of nature. Those who held the best cards won the game, and that left everyone else with little choice but to cheat. The game was rigged anyway.

As he lay under the willow tree, his eyes barely open while every fibre in his mangled body ached and bled, he still found the strength to be annoyed. He was angry at her—the girl—for approaching him, for disarming him to the point that he'd let her hand-feed him like some tame pup.

Don't kid yourself.

Ignore it, Kai told himself. He closed his eyes and thumped his head back against the tree. Wrapping an arm around his abdomen, he palpated the area with his fingertips. His ribs were still cracked.

You lured her out.

"Did not," Kai grumbled aloud, his head lulling against the bark as he fought to stay conscious. "Just...stumbled out, after you tried to kill me with that fucking bus."

Kill you? the voice laughed, empty and humourless. **Who do you think healed you?**

Kai's blood turned cold. He knew he was a lot tougher than the average human, so he'd assumed his quick recovery was just a biological advantage. "They would have turned me into a goddamn lab rat," he snarled, refusing to give the entity even a lick of credit. "Don't screw with me—I know you want me dead."

And what would I do without you? Abaddon feigned sweetness.

Wishing he'd stolen some morphine from the hospital, Kai forced himself to his feet. He grit his teeth as pain shot up his left side and straight into his skull. Fuck Abaddon. He'd already gotten too much of Kai's attention.

Instead, he thought of the girl. What was she doing there? Most of the roaches steered clear of the fields at night, but this chick had a danger fetish.

What were *you* doing there? You're just as guilty as she is.

Kai's jaw clenched so tight it began to ache. "Shut up," he ground out. Even he couldn't make sense of it—why hadn't he just stayed put when he'd sniffed her out? The beef jerky didn't smell *that* good.

Aw, is it love? It's too bad you won't save her. You're always too late.

"Shut up!" Kai drove his fist into a tree with everything he had left. "You're the reason I never make it on time! You stop me from helping, then try to convince me I killed them!" He felt his knuckles break, the skin tearing clean off, but at least the voice of Abaddon finally quieted. Wincing, he pulled his arm back and sucked on the bloodied knobs on his hand.

After what happened in the alleys of Black Hollow, he was sure Abaddon was to blame for his meet-cutes with dead bodies. Why else would Kai black out whenever he tried to help the missing girls?

And now, Abaddon had detected his weakness for this one.

Love. How he hated that word. The mere mention of those four letters strung together in the right order set him off like a nest of hornets. He didn't understand love—what it was or how it was supposed to function. He didn't understand why it was so important, or if it was even real. From what he could tell, sex and loyalty weren't enough, not even when companionship and affection were part of the deal. No, there was something else—some invisible quality to love that only humans believed in. Whether or not they actually knew what that quality was remained a mystery. In all likelihood, their brains were melting out of their asses, because from what Kai had seen, the line between love and hate for the human species was paper-thin.

Limping, Kai struggled back home, the familiar scents and sounds guiding the way. He knew not to rely on his vision; the forest liked to play tricks on people who did. Following the sun didn't work either because time made no sense here. It seemed arbitrary—slowing, expanding, or stopping altogether sometimes, and he often didn't have a good grasp of it. Time, in general, was a tricky concept for Kai. It was mechanical and empty, but when he found himself immersed in his senses like this, it was as though time didn't even exist. He hadn't an inkling of how long it would take him to find the cabin, but it was never any trouble, either. It was simply a matter of trust. He knew his instincts would take him there.

While his life wasn't at risk, the injuries would cause him grief for at least a week or two. He wouldn't be able to move easily, let alone hunt. Even now, he had to stop frequently. His lung was still partially collapsed, and the back of his head pounded like a hammer slamming through concrete. At one point, he doubled over and puked his insides out from the pain, his central nervous system screaming at him to stop pushing so hard. But he wanted shelter—a hole to nestle in where he could feel safe.

It took almost all night, but he managed to claw his way back into familiar territory by the time light peaked over the horizon. As he leaned against a large, red maple, he heard a distinct cry from above, accompanied by the scent of someone unfamiliar. They—she, rather—was inside his cabin, waiting for him. He squinted up at the treetops in search of the fat raven.

As the sun hid behind a passing cloud, he spotted the bird perched on a branch—a little black blob with three-pronged talons curled around the bony wooden limb. He was watching Kai; his beady little eyes gleamed as he trembled in delight.

"What are you looking at?" Kai frowned as the bird tilted his head and chortled lightly. He knew how smart ravens were, and this one had been nesting close by for a while. They were playful birds, often plucking at wolves' tails to inspire a game of *Catch Me If You Can*. But Kai had no tail to be plucked, and the last few days had left him with a short fuse.

"Get out of here!" he barked, satisfied when the raven jumped.

Kai's throat was parched worse than a desert. That beef jerky had been packed with enough salt to dehydrate an elephant. He growled, doing his best to march into the clearing and towards the cabin. It hurt like hell, but he cussed through it until he reached the door and punched it open.

Kai hated how it smelled in the cabin—like musty, rotten wood and dust. He had no cleaning supplies, no means of making it liveable. His bathroom resembled a murder scene. The mirror was cracked, the tiles stained with all manner of bodily fluids, and the toilet—well, the toilet was a dimension of its own. The tub looked like a dilapidated, porcelain lifeboat that had survived an apocalypse. There was a hose coming through a hole in the wall with a shower nozzle attached; while Kai appreciated having a tub, the water pressure from the showerhead was like a pissing rat.

Kai stood at the threshold of the tiny main room furnished with an old wooden table in the centre, taking up most of the available space. A plywood countertop was plastered along the back wall with a cracked sink haphazardly plunked inside and a portable, electric element tucked away in the corner. A woman sat on the edge of his futon near the adjacent wall—garbage he'd collected after someone had thrown it out, but a good scrub with some stolen bleach had made it useable again. Her legs were crossed, and her palms pressed down against the blankets on either side of her hips. As he walked in, her mouth quirked like she'd known the exact moment he would return. She was probably in her early thirties, with luxurious, silvery-white hair that fell over her shoulders and bright, amber eyes that looked like they could sear through iron. Her earthy scent and unusual hair colour gave her away. She was the first of his kind that he'd seen in sixteen years—a fact he didn't rejoice while territoriality ran high.

They both stood frozen until Kai began to circle her from one end of the room to the other, trying to hide his limp. He trained his eyes on her, but she didn't move, instead watching with a placid smile as he stalked like a nervous predator. Neither of them spoke. All that needed to be said was conveyed through the slightest frown, a twitch of the brow, a momentary slouch. It was a power dynamic being worked out—a battle for status that could be derailed with the tiniest hesitation. For some time, Kai refused to approach her. Fear prickled his skin as aggression rose into his throat; to sit on his sleeping area was not just bold, it was insulting—like pissing on his favourite tree stump.

"I wouldn't try anything stupid," she spoke, at last, raising an eyebrow when he bared his teeth at her. "You're hurt. I'll tear your throat out faster than you can blink."

Kai hated threats. He hated them even more when delivered cold from his own bed—but there was nothing he could do in his current state. Defeated, he pulled a chair from the table and turned away so she couldn't see him cringe as he sat down.

"Good. I suppose you're not as stupid as your temper."

"You want something from me?" He looked up, shoulders pulled back and fists clenched.

Her smile widened, making her eyes appear cat-like. "Relax. There's no need to get all alpha male on me. Especially when you're half-dead." Uncrossing her legs, she leaned back on her palms and tilted her head. "I'm not here to steal your turf."

Kai's shoulders sank as he gave himself to the pain, hunching over and resting his elbows on his knees. "What do you want then?" he asked, his breath laboured.

"My name is Ama," she replied. "A friend called me here."

The raven from earlier swooped down from outside and landed on the windowsill.

Kai glanced at the bird. "Didn't realize anyone was looking for me."

Ama absently scratched the tip of her button nose. "For some time now, yes."

"How long?" he snapped, his muscles tensing as he gripped the edge of the chair.

"Longer than you've been alive," she answered cryptically. "Since before the beginning."

Kai looked back at the raven who was now hopping about, inspecting the walls around the window frame. "That sounds like horseshit."

Ama chuckled. "I suppose it's just a bit complicated for you right now." She looked around the cabin while he seethed. "It's a bit early to explain, but all will be clear soon enough."

"And who's this adoring fan of mine?" His lips curled up in a cold smile. "Did they send a bird to keep the monsters under the bed away?"

To his surprise, she burst out into a hearty laugh. "On the contrary, *you* are the monster under the bed as far as fairy tales are concerned." She leaned forward, resting her chin in the palm of her hand.

"I don't know what the fuck you're talking about," Kai hissed, his teeth clenched.

The hair rose on his arms as she narrowed her eyes and watched him. He shifted uncomfortably, pretending to be more interested in the walls than her.

"Let's bring him out then," she murmured, rising from the bed with a creak.

The movement seized Kai's attention. He turned back to her, eyes wide. "What?"

He leaned away as she grabbed his chin between her thumb and forefinger. She tilted his head back, and as he tried jerking away, a bolt of pain shot down his spine. Whiplash was a remarkably unyielding asshole.

As he struggled to raise a broken arm and tear her hand away, she quickly intercepted it, smacking it down like an annoying fly. Kai bit down a scream, his shattered bones blighting him with more agony. The limb fell limply to his side, and before he could muster the strength for another attempt to free himself, her eyes locked on his. Their warm, orangey hue brightened as everything around them began to fade out. It was like she was inside of him, her irises growing brighter as the life in him waned until he could no longer sit up or stay conscious. His every muscle wilted, and he tumbled to the floor with a thud.

Stepping away from the unconscious figure, Ama listened to his heart-beat and breathing to ensure he was out for the count. Once she was satis-fied, she crouched down and hooked an arm around his back, lifting him up and dragging him to the bed where she dropped him like a duffle bag. The raven looked on from the windowsill.

"He's built like a tank," she huffed, rolling her shoulders out. The bird tilted his head and responded with a low croak. She smiled at her feathered friend, then sauntered over to the chair and sat down, resuming her cross-legged position.

A light groan sounded from the bed as Kai broke out into a cold sweat, his face contorting. The raven dipped his beak to watch while Ama grew still and vigilant. Holding her breath, she tightened her jaw and swallowed hard.

"It's begun."

CHAPTER
THIRTEEN
THE REUNION

KAI FOUND *himself standing barefoot in the woods. The faint smell of smoke wafted from somewhere nearby, voices shouting, closing in. Crimson blood soaked the mud and snow around him. Gradually, Kai realized he was surrounded by death. Animal limbs and entrails were strewn across the tainted earth. Alongside them lay mangled wolves, maimed and disfigured, the hinges of their jaws ripped open in grotesque snarls of agony. As he walked amidst the carnage, the smoke grew stronger, cinders rising to the sky as the smog thickened in his lungs.*

The bloody trail led into a village. It smelled of Black Hollow, but there were no roads or cars, no buildings made of brick, and no alleyways to hide in. Houses were aflame, roofs collapsing as wood turned to ash. At the mouth of the tiny settlement was a pyre, ropes encircling a black, charred mass. It was shaped like a human, the outline of the skull still visible amidst the blaze, her mouth agape—frozen in a silent, eternal cry of terror.

A shrill call drew him back towards the red-soaked earth. A raven crawled, his wing broken and his leg writhing, towards the body of a dead child. The boy was pristine—midnight hair stark against his waxy skin, parted grey lips and glassy, lifeless eyes giving him the appearance of a porcelain doll. The raven bobbed his head as he curled his talon around the boy's swollen fingers—that one, pearl black eye gleaming before he plunged his beak into the corpse's abdomen, tunnelling his way inside. A satisfied rattle echoed from the scavenger's bubbling throat as he devoured all he found, his slick form gradually disappearing as he burrowed into the hollowed cadaver.

The boy's chest wall swelled, bulges pulsating under the flesh. His head lulled to the side, his jaw slackening with each undulating distention. The convulsions faded out, an eerie stillness following the possession before an arm jerked, a leg twitched—and finally, an aberrant gasp for air ripped through the boy. As if pulled by puppet strings, he flowed upright in one smooth motion, his hand twisting as the puppeteer grappled for control. Grasping the boy by his chin, the hand snapped the jaw back into place, teeth clamping together with a click...click...click. His neck jerked this way and that, snapping in and out of place before it grew accustomed to the new range of motion. Slowly, the head turned towards Kai, tilting to a near right angle—wide, pitch-black eyes boring into his soul.

The horror invaded Kai's body, waves of nausea rocking every cell. From the pit of his stomach, a sound emerged, tearing into a scorching scream that rent the air. Little by little, he became aware of another presence. Kai looked up, but he was no longer in the village.

A tall figure stood in the shadow of a rocky wall, cutting off Kai's escape. It was a man, his imposing height and broad shoulders slicing through the shade of the stone structure. Dried blood crusted his hands and tattered black hair, and the expanse of his back was marred with scars that traced around his chest as he turned.

The air stilled, thick and suffocating as Kai found himself unable to breathe; the man wore Kai's face, but his gold eyes gleamed with malicious intent.

Kai was certain he knew him.

CHAPTER

FOURTEEN

WITH A VIOLENT PULL, Kai was wrenched from his nightmare, gasping as cold sweat poured down his burning skin. He was shaking uncontrollably, and for at least a minute he couldn't see a damn thing—that hateful sneer and the mangled corpses still dancing in front of his eyes. The stench of fumes and rotting flesh made him lurch forward, coughing until he nearly threw up. Fire smouldered every inch of his skin, searing into the back of his skull. He clenched his knees to his chest, regressing in both body and mind, desperate to grab hold of something real.

"Kai."

It was Ama's voice, breaking through the fog. A hand was on his shoulder, fingertips squeezing him until he jerked back. The first thing he saw was the golden amber of her eyes—warmer and darker than the cold gleam from the figure in his nightmare.

"What the fuck did you do to me?" he growled, swooning as he swatted her hand away. He was still injured, still in pain, and now thoroughly scrambled in the head. "How do you know my name?"

"He told me," she said, canting her head towards the window where the raven still sat.

Kai glanced at the bird, the image of the boy's corpse flashing through his mind. Feeling his stomach churn, he reeled forward onto his knees. He clenched his teeth and bit back the bile. It wasn't the gore that made him feel sick, but the disorienting whirlwind of sensations that flooded him as he grappled with the memories. "What did you do to me?" he demanded a second time, his voice crossing over into something feral.

Ama stepped away and sat in the chair. "I called *him* here."

Kai was about to bark at her to stop being cryptic when his doppelganger flitted before his eyes. He knew exactly who she was talking about.

"Why?"

She considered him carefully, absorbing his reactions. "I wanted to see how bad it was. I got my answer."

"Why!" he snapped again.

"I told you," she sighed as if speaking to a child. "I'm here on behalf of someone who's been looking for you."

Before he could lunge at her with another question, she lifted a finger, cutting him off with a sharp look. "This entity that's been haunting you— does it have a name?"

Kai swallowed as he watched the raven, wondering *what* it was, and why it had crawled into that boy's corpse. He still didn't trust Ama. If that was the kind of monster she was working with, he wanted to run for the fucking hills. Why was she even here?

"Well?" she coaxed, arching an eyebrow as he paled again.

"Calls himself Abaddon," Kai said after a pause. "No idea why."

Ama's eyes widened, her lips pursing. "Well, that's dark, if not a tad poetic. I'm guessing you don't know what Abaddon means."

"Don't really give a shit either."

"Biblical angel, or demon." She ignored his disinterest. "Depends on the version you're reading, but the book of Revelation portrays him as a destroyer—the angel of the abyss, the king of plague. Some scholars consider him to be the antichrist. Others believe he's the devil himself. A few, however, say he's doing God's work."

Kai blinked at her, his brain unable to process her holy drivel. He was too exhausted to deal with information. He'd spent all night crawling back to the cabin. He'd just barely finished screaming, thrashing, and crying like a diva. Hell, he might have even shat his pants a little—and now, while he sat in a pool of his own sweat, she wanted to give him a bible lesson?

"I don't give a rat's ass about the name," Kai shot back, his patience wearing thin.

"Oh?" She tsked. "You should. After all, he picked it for a reason."

Kai shifted to a dry spot on the bed, stripping off his shirt and wiping his arms and chest with the sheets as he crossed his legs and settled back against the wall. He refused to look at her, the gesture thinly veiling his embarrassment for being caught in such a state. Instead, he reached for a whisky bottle he kept tucked behind the mattress.

"Whatever." He popped the cork and took a swig. "How exactly do you lure out dickish spirits?"

She watched as he threw the soaked shirt to the floor. "I've got an all-access pass...to the then, the now, and the wherever."

He gave her a withering look. "That doesn't tell me shit."

She wagged a finger at him in deliberate condescension. "Yes, you're right. It's not supposed to tell you anything."

"Right." Kai huffed. "And now that you've had your kicks, would you kindly fuck off and leave me alone?" If he hadn't been half-broken, he would've torn her head off and whipped it at the damn raven. *It could be just like bowling*, he sneered to himself.

But she was undeterred by his threat. She rose from the bed and strolled over, her knees touching his as she peered directly into his eyes—a bold move. "Don't you want to know what Abaddon is?"

Of course he did; he pined for an answer, but his response was flippant as he curled a lip at her, loathing her display of dominance. "Evil spirit. Angry douche-turd. Invisible dick dipped in cow shit."

"That would make him quite flammable."

Kai snorted, unable to help cracking a smile. "I wish."

"I don't think he's just an evil spirit," she told him more seriously, slowly circling the room. "He's too self-aware. Giving himself a name—a biblical name at that—seems rather symbolic, don't you think?"

Kai followed her movements, waiting for her to get to the point. He fought to keep himself sealed off, but her steadiness melted away his indignation.

"I used to think I was crazy," he confessed after a long gulp of whisky. "But even the shrink eventually realized something didn't fit. Just never thought it'd be a ghost with a holy stick up his ass."

"You spent enough time with humans to let them take you to a thera-pist?" She sounded surprised. "Let me guess—schizophrenia?"

"I was a kid when they found me. Didn't have much choice." Kai shook his head. "PTSD and conduct disorder. Said I was hearing things because of repressed trauma."

"Oh? What happened?"

"You've gotten enough backstory." Kai glowered, catching himself. He wondered how lonely he'd become to divulge his past to a home invader. "Now how about you tell me what's wrong with me?"

Ama drummed her fingernails against the wooden table. "The notion of linear time is a brilliant illusion, isn't it? You're born, you progress through life, and then you die. But your understanding of death depends on how you understand time. If you eliminate the construct of time from the equation, there's no saying what death really is."

"I don't think about time or death," he told her. "I'm too busy trying not to get fucked sideways every day."

"I don't think about it either." She smiled. "We're animals. Time has a different meaning to us because we're constantly engaged in the immediacy of our instincts. Still, we *are* aware of human constructs. Maybe we're even becoming human."

Kai flopped back on the mattress with a sigh and corked his whisky. If getting clocked by a bus didn't kill him, Ama's yapping would. "This doesn't sound like it has jack shit to do with Abaddon."

"It does," she said, "because if you want to understand Abaddon, you're going to have to move past the present moment. You'll have to think about death." She walked around the table, her finger tracing the edge until she'd drawn a large circle. "Humans are afraid of death because it's so final. At least, based on their idea of time. We can say that time is an illusion, but death certainly isn't. It's very real, and yet the experience of death is more than just an end. Ironically, the end *is* endless."

"Ama," he said tightly as he rolled up, lip twitching. "I'm not a fucking poet. Get to the damn point or get the fuck out."

He caught the edge of a smile. She was toying with him, shredding his brain with riddles.

"Blow me," he snapped. "You don't know anything except that he's here to make me scream for my dead mommy."

Ama shook her head. "Not today, I'm afraid."

Kai stood up and began to pace, predatory and anxious all at once. "Why's he stuck on me? What the hell did I ever do to him?"

"I don't know," she replied, "but obviously something binds you together. Seems he wants to punish you."

He was trying to remember his dream—trying desperately to summon those grotesque visions, but the effort grew vainer by the second.

"Why can't I remember?" he growled, reaching up and ruffling his hair. "It just keeps slipping away!" There was a drawn-out pause before he slumped his shoulders in defeat.

"That's quite normal," Ama reassured him. "To be left only with the feelings and none of the images."

Kai seethed at her, squeezing his fist so hard his nails cut into the pads of his hand. He felt used, manipulated, one-upped, and powerless. "So your *friend* sent you here to get into my head and mess with me but didn't tell you *what* that whimpering bitch is? Or why he hates me?"

Ama tilted her head and smiled. "Sounds like you and Abaddon bicker quite often. And no, my friend isn't someone I can get hold of on a whim. He reveals only what he wants, when he wants. And I was only told to come find you and keep an eye on things. I'm sure he's already seen what he needed to."

"Your friend sounds like some of his brains have been pecked out."

"He's not all there sometimes," Ama admitted. "But I'm curious as well. What kind of spirit names itself? And why?" She lowered her gaze, speaking to no one in particular. "You were counting on my curiosity, weren't you?" Then, she turned to the raven with slit eyes.

"You're fucking insane."

"Maybe!" She laughed, walking to the door. With her hand on the knob, she glanced over her shoulder and smiled coyly. "But what does that make you?"

Kai watched as she saw herself out without a single shit given for his response, her footsteps fading into the distance. What was the point of that? She'd waltzed into his home, mind-fucked him, then waltzed right back out. And he couldn't do a damn thing about it.

He kicked the wall next to the doorframe and stalked back to his bed, tearing off the covers and chucking them in the corner. He couldn't lie in her scent. He refused to. Throwing himself down, Kai closed his eyes and sighed as his body let go. Sleep was finally creeping up on him. Sleep—without any hope of rest.

checking John Doe's vitals while he was still comatose—of seeing, feeling, and hearing with his own faculties the impossibility of the young man's recovery. Sure, he was banged up, but he was nowhere near death like the paramedics stated in their original report. Jazlyn confirmed they hadn't reported it wrong, so what was it? Some kind of rare, undocumented healing ability? If so, John Doe's blood would have the answers. The other nurse, Amy, had mentioned there being something off about it, but when the code yellow hit, everyone dispersed. Neither he nor Jazlyn got a chance to ask Amy what the deal was with John Doe's blood.

He knew he was jumping ahead, but Doctor Mason Evans couldn't stop himself from imagining the possibilities. If this was some kind of mutant healing ability, John Doe's strange blood could hold the key to astounding medical breakthroughs. It could give terminal patients a better chance. It could give doctors a second chance.

So much for Occam's razor.

As his imagination got away from him, Mason barely registered the sound of double-doors swinging open and the click-clack of shoes against the beige vinyl floor. The staff meeting was over, a sea of white coats and scrubs rushing the halls. Among them was Jazlyn, winding around her colleagues. She stopped in front of Mason. Her eyes were downcast as she chewed viciously on her lower lip, nose wrinkling intermittently and fists clenching at her sides.

"Well?" Mason broke the unbearable silence. She didn't seem surprised that he was still at the hospital, her apparent stupor so intense she didn't ask about his presence.

"I know why Amy was so freaked out," she replied, finally looking up at him. "John Doe's blood—it's not human, Cap."

Mason blinked furiously, batting away the confusion. "What do you mean his blood isn't human?"

"I mean, the son-of-a-bitch doesn't have a blood type!" she exclaimed. "Lab techs couldn't identify it! But we don't have the technology here to figure out what it *could* be."

Mason questioned the Universe; was it truly possible that John Doe's blood had no sign of ABO antigens? He wondered if this was a bizarre mistake or an elaborate prank orchestrated by...by whom? Who would joke about such a thing?

"Y-You need to take it to a university lab," he stammered. "Get a more powerful microscope."

Was this the first case of an unknown, fifth blood type? A new antigen? Was that the secret to John Doe's superhuman healing? It certainly seemed more believable to Mason than some ridiculous theory about being possessed by wolves.

Jazlyn frowned. "What? Why? The hospital doesn't have that kind of time. His blood will be trashed in the biohazard bin with the rest of the samples at the end of the week."

Mason's mouth popped open; he meant to protest but stopped short. Composing himself, he tried again. "Jaz," he said evenly, "don't you think that's kind of a waste? I mean, aren't you curious about what this might be?"

"Well, sure..." she trailed off. "I'm curious, but what can we really do if the doctors here don't care to pursue it?"

"Salvage the blood sample," Mason urged. "If it's getting thrown out anyway, let's swipe it and take it to a better lab."

The mystery of John Doe was growing more and more enticing by the second. With evidence of a scientific anomaly at his fingertips, Mason knew he wouldn't be able to step away. But there was only so much he could do alone, and the matter of DNA was out of his field of expertise. To take this further, he'd need the help of a geneticist.

"You want me to swipe the vial?" Jazlyn looked aghast, and with good reason. This was the kind of thing that got people fired, or worse...arrested.

"I'll do it," Mason offered with a casual shrug. "I know where the lab here is. I can do it."

"Mason—that's *stealing*. You can't just steal hospital property!"

"I...I know it's against the rules. This isn't something I'd normally do." He ruffled his curls and looked at her, eyes pleading. "The sample's getting tossed. It'll be gone, and I'll wonder forever what this was about. I'll take the risk if it means finding the answers, Jaz."

"It's still crazy," she argued. "What about the cameras?"

"Useless deterrent," he scoffed. "They get overwritten every forty-eight hours, and the footage is too grainy to actually catch anyone. Besides, they're only checked if an incident is reported, and I'm sure police have already confiscated the tapes from today to check for John Doe. I won't be in them."

She seemed annoyed that he actually remembered his hospital security training, shifting her weight and grumbling under her breath. "Fine," she conceded after a long pause. "But I won't help you. I just...won't report it."

"Thanks, Jaz." He exhaled, dangling his arms to his knees. Some part of him wondered if he was being unfair, or if he was endangering her career just by telling her his plans—but the thought was fleeting. This mystery was bigger than the both of them. "You have no idea how much it means to have your support."

"Oh, I'm not supporting you," she corrected. "I'm just tolerating your bullshit until you get your head screwed back on. But if you get arrested, I'm not backing your ass up."

"Still," he smiled, "thank you."

Shoving her hands in her pockets, she glanced around the halls. "You're nuts," she hissed then turned back to him. "What exactly are you going to do once you figure this out? It's not like you can *find* John Doe."

Mason pulled out his phone and showed her the note he'd typed. "I'm going to check public records for a Kai Donovan. Found it written on a scrap of paper in John Doe's wallet."

She crinkled her nose at him, pushing the phone away. "Seriously, dude, that's pretty damn stalkerish."

"Hey, you asked!"

"And I'm regretting it!"

"But just imagine the possibilities if he's—I don't know—special!" Mason beamed at her, his eyes lighting up as his dirty blonde curls seemed to bounce around his head.

Jazlyn didn't respond, shooting him a cutting look instead. Seeing she was unimpressed, Mason gave her a quick squeeze. He thanked her again, then zipped away before she could try to change his mind. The lab was waiting for him.

"You won't regret this!" he called back, yelping as he nearly slammed into a revolving door. He was fine. Everything was fine. His every vein was pulsing with renewed life. Now he had something substantial—something potentially groundbreaking to pursue. It was exactly what he needed.

CHAPTER
SIXTEEN

STEALING a blood sample was surprisingly easy. During his time as a doctor, Mason often saw trays of them laid out in the hall for anyone to take. But why would they? Blood theft wasn't expected. Not to mention, nurses were overworked, and hospitals understaffed, so it wasn't uncommon to find labs empty and accessible. Small-town hospitals like Ashgrove's didn't even require ID tags to get inside. All Mason had to do was stroll in when no one was looking, check the previous day's collections for a John Doe, and slip the sample in his coat pocket. It would be viable at room temperature for only a few hours, so he had to move fast.

When Mason returned to Annabelle's, he hid the blood behind a yogurt container in the fridge. It would be good there for another twenty-four hours. Despite being in dire need of rest, even a catnap was impossible. Mason's mind was working harder than a steam engine, desperately grappling with cold, hard evidence of the impossible. John Doe's disappearance only left him more mystified. One minute he was there, unconscious as a rock, the next—gone.

Mason began pacing, searching for an avenue through which he could pursue the mystery. He kicked off his clothes and hopped into the shower. There had to be some poor Ph.D. student holed up in a lab at the University of British Columbia who'd be willing to look at the blood for some extra cash. He just needed to make sure they were the right kind of person. *And* that he had it in him to take a day trip back to Vancouver.

It was ironic, he thought, how his attempt to flee the city had led him right back to it.

As a former graduate of UBC, he had no trouble navigating their cluster-cuss of a website. After browsing the graduate student profiles in a fair number of science departments, Mason settled on a candidate he felt might be trustworthy: Sashka Lavović, a tan-skinned foreign exchange student who looked to be about his age, and a doctoral candidate in the field of genetics. Her expression was sombre, tired bags evident under her slate-grey eyes as she peered directly into the camera. She didn't look happy. Then again, graduate students never did.

Composing an email was harder than he'd thought. After scrapping and rewriting several drafts, he finally settled on a vague but only partially dishonest explanation: He was a doctor with a sample of unusual blood from a patient, and he needed more powerful equipment to study it. The matter was time-sensitive and couldn't go through official channels. It was odd, but not convincingly bat-shit. Taking a deep breath, he clicked send, squeezing his eyes shut and praying that Miss Lavović wasn't the sort to be overly concerned with rules.

It only took several nerve-wracking hours of half-hearted web-browsing before Mason heard his inbox ping.

Sashka Lavović was willing to conduct tests—for five hundred dollars and a signed NDA.

He scrambled to write something coherent back to her. It was still morning and the entire day was open for seedy shenanigans. Miss Lavović seemed easygoing enough, inviting him to the lab for lunch. This gave him just enough time to pack his laptop and withdraw the cash before whipping down the highway to Vancouver.

While Mason wasn't the best with spontaneity, it stopped him from thinking too hard. Had Sashka given him more time to consider, he might have panicked at the idea of revisiting the place he lost Amanda. Luckily, the campus was far enough that he could easily avoid the hospital. This was his best chance, he thought. He had to take it. After all, understanding John Doe's blood could hold the key to Mason's redemption. His previous mistakes may have set him on a path that would lead to incredible discoveries—discoveries that could one day save or better thousands of lives.

Mason's world view was shifting back into place. He'd always wanted to be a doctor. When he was twelve, he lost his favourite aunt to breast cancer. She was the reason he was determined to make a difference in the field of oncology. Unlike his parents, who seemed hard-pressed to make sure he spent every waking hour preparing for an elite university education, Aunt Lisa had spoiled her curly-haired, near-sighted nephew with comic books and tales of superheroes.

After Aunt Lisa passed, Mason's parents never again had to make a peep about his idleness. By the start of high school, he was the top of his class, and by the end of it, he had several offers from the best of Ivy League. After his undergraduate degree at Cornell, Mason returned to enrol in UBC's medical school. He was accepted immediately, and his family welcomed him home with proud, open arms. Aunt Lisa may have been gone, but what she left behind became the fuel for Mason to follow his dream of helping people conquer cancer.

Just as Aunt Lisa's death had been the catalyst for his choice of career, perhaps Amanda's death was paving the way to something more than doubt and guilt. It was about the bigger picture, he told himself. He'd forgotten that when he'd slipped into his grief.

Feeling a surge of hope, Mason dressed with renewed vigour and left a note for Annabelle. She'd gone out shopping, leaving him with a spare set of keys while she was gone. Grateful for her thoughtfulness, he jumped into his car and set off on the road. He was beginning to feel like his old self again.

BEING BACK at UBC was bittersweet. Mason still knew his way around like the back of his hand, and it didn't take long to find the chemistry building where Sashka Lavović told him to meet her.

She was waiting for him in one of the labs on the second floor—a plump young woman with long, honey-blonde hair that was tied back in a high ponytail, her bangs swept to the side. She looked as tired in person as she had in her photo, her oval face pale from lack of sleep.

"You must be Dr. Evans," she greeted him with an Eastern European accent, her expression stoic.

"That's right." Mason nodded, trying to sound chirpy for the both of them. He extended a hand to her, and after they exchanged a shake, he sat down on a nearby stool, unsure of where to begin. Before he could say anything, she handed him the non-disclosure contract.

"Did you bring the blood sample?" She cut to the chase after he signed it.

"Yes, yes, I did," he stammered. "But first, I just want to clear up a few... ethical concerns."

She said nothing, waiting for him to continue, so he cleared his throat and pulled out a small icebox housing the vial.

"I've never really done something like this before, but I just want to make sure we're on the same page. I also want to keep this quiet." He paused, thinking about how to continue. "This blood is...atypical. It's from a patient I would like to know more about. I can't quite tell you what's atypical about him though. I'm hoping your tests might offer some clues." He turned the box in his hands, fiddling with the zipper. "I don't normally break the rules like this. I think rules exist to protect people from making bad choices, yet here I am."

Sashka remained quiet, her face revealing nothing of what was going through her mind. When he finished, she crossed her arms over her chest and leaned against the wall. "I understand, Mr. Evans. While I don't share your obsolete idealism, I assure you this test will remain private. I have no intention of jeopardizing my career. And frankly, I don't really care what it is you're doing."

While that certainly wasn't what Mason expected, he figured it was good enough. "That's true. I'm sure you've put a lot of work into your research."

She shrugged, shifting her weight. "To be honest, the only reason I took you up on this is because I'm strapped for cash."

"I'm sorry to hear that," Mason replied.

"It can't be helped." She shook her head, smiling for the first time. "Funding is scarce."

His doubts quelled, Mason handed her the sample, along with half the amount he'd agreed to pay. "I just need to know how this blood is different from ordinary blood," he told her. "The hospital microscope isn't powerful enough to take a closer look."

She frowned, probably perplexed, but nodded. "I take it this is human blood?"

"It should be." Mason nearly choked back the words. He didn't want to reveal too much, yet he already felt dishonest. "But I will say that it didn't present as human blood under our microscopes," he added quickly. "In any case, take a look and let me know what you find."

"An odd request, Dr. Evans." The young woman sighed. "Very well. I'll run some tests. I have some other responsibilities to deal with first, so come back in a few hours."

"Thank you."

With that, she stood up and walked into an adjoining room where he assumed the heavy-duty equipment was waiting for her. Sweat trickled down the back of his neck, tickling him until he rubbed it away. The blood *should* be human. It came from a human body. But the hospital's analysis indicated otherwise.

While waiting for Sashka to run tests, Mason tried visiting some of his former professors' offices but found them locked and dark, so he wandered aimlessly in search of his former self. He realized how much he'd taken for granted, how much safer being on campus had made him feel, and how familiar places, like his favourite sandwich shop, had given him a sense of community. It stood in stark contrast to how unmoored he'd become.

It wasn't until later in the afternoon that Mason returned to the labs and Sashka emerged with a file and a deep-seated scowl. She looked ready to cut into him.

"Dr. Evans, is this some kind of joke?"

"I'm sorry?" Mason asked, puzzled.

"The sample you gave me, from your *patient*," she began, leafing through the sheets. "It's not human blood. No ABO antigens."

"Yes..."

She looked at him quizzically. "But you already knew that."

"Yes." Mason averted his gaze.

"You told me that it didn't present as human, not that it plainly *was not* human! Why not simply ask me to do a species identification test?" She sounded irritated, crossing her arms over her chest.

"It's complicated. But nothing bad. I hope you understand."

Sashka sighed and shook her head. "Did someone mix your samples up with those of a veterinary hospital?"

"What do you mean?" He sat up, shifting around in his chair.

"When I first looked at the sample, I saw markers suggesting the blood was canine."

A cold shudder shook Mason's spine. "Canine? Like, a dog?"

"Yes, like a dog, Dr. Evans." She arched an eyebrow. "But the subject is not a domestic dog. While the blood you gave me has canine antigens, it's from some other species. So I ran some more tests and cross-checked them with a database."

"And...?"

"Well, given our geographic location, I surmised the most likely candidate was a wolf or coyote. I checked first for wolf-specific DNA markers. Your subject is male, and male wolves have particular Y chromosome markers. I analyzed the blood for those and compared your sample to our available databases of wolf haplotypes. I also cross-checked the genotype data and tested for 22 DNA short tandem repeat markers. These have variants specific to wolves."

Mason swallowed several times, trying to dislodge the lump in his throat. "So, he's—"

She tossed the file in his lap. "Canis lupus. More specifically, a Siberian gray wolf. I found genetic markers indicating the wolf's bloodline is from Russia. Most likely."

"Most likely?"

"It's highly probable." She shrugged, dipping her hands into her coat pockets. "Like I said, we have to test for markers and cross-check with genetic databases. One marker alone isn't enough to come to a conclusion, but I've compiled enough evidence to say with confidence that you're looking at wolf's blood."

Mason stared down at the file, unblinking. Air came to a halt in his throat every time he tried to inhale.

"Dr. Evans?" Sashka inquired. "Are you all right?"

He cleared his throat. "Y-yes, I'm fine."

Sashka regarded him with mild interest, then pulled back as if fighting to maintain her aloofness. "There was one anomaly, however."

His eyes shot up. "What is it?"

"I can't quite say," she admitted. "But your wolf seems to have a genetic mutation not yet documented by the Trent University Wolf and Coyote DNA Bank. The mutation may be recorded elsewhere, but currently, this was the only pool of data I could access for analysis."

"I see," Mason mused. He needed to speak with Jazlyn—fast. "Thank you so much for your time." He dug into his back pocket and pulled out his wallet. "And thank you for your discretion with this. I know it all seems bizarre, but you've really helped me out."

He smiled warmly and handed her the rest of the cash. She rubbed the money between her fingers as if to make sure the thickness was about right.

"You're welcome," she said, folding the bills and curling her fingers around them.

Without much else to say, Mason grabbed his coat and nodded curtly, stepping past her and speeding towards the door. When he was finally outside, he took a deep breath, then zigzagged through the parking lot and mashed the buttons on his car remote until he saw the trunk pop and the lights flash. Locking himself in his car and fumbling for his phone, he scrolled through his contacts and nearly missed tapping the right one three times.

"How are you awake right now?" Jazlyn pummelled him after two rings.

"Don't ask," he chuckled. "Lots of coffee and adrenaline."

"Uh-huh, and your OCD."

"Okay, maybe that too. But it's paying off! My mind is blown right now, and I need to tell someone."

"Kay', I'm listening."

"Don't freak out!" he implored. When she went quiet, he relayed the details of his day.

"Christ," Jazlyn hissed. "You're sure?"

"As sure as I've ever been. Unless you've got some sicko switching patient blood with wolf's blood."

"No way," she said immediately. "I know security is pretty lax at the hospital, but even if there was some kind of weirdo doing crap like that, the time frame's way too tight. You checked that blood out barely hours after it was drawn."

"Exactly."

"Well, consider me officially freaked out by this weird-ass town," she huffed after a respectable pause.

"No kidding," Mason mumbled back. "Now I really need to look up Kai Donovan."

"About that," she interjected, "I was feeling a little devious, I guess, so I might have gone and done that already."

"Seriously?" Mason all but jumped up. "Damn, thank you, Jaz. I really wasn't expecting that."

"Don't mention it, Cap. And well, I just told myself it was to find a missing patient."

"That's fair," he conceded. "So, did you find anything?"

"Not a damn thing," Jazlyn sighed. "In fact, we don't even have any Donovans in Black Hollow. There's obviously a bunch in the province, but none with Kai as a first name. Found a Kevin and a Kyle, but they're both middle-aged. I was pretty bored, so I called 'em up and asked if they knew a Kai or a young guy spending time in Black Hollow, but they sounded confused and had no damn clue what I was on about."

The news was dejecting, but unsurprising given the number of strange occurrences. "Empty, huh?"

"Yep." The seconds yawned out before she spoke again, "You know, I think you're right. Kai Donovan is John Doe. Maybe he's not even Canadian. Could be from elsewhere and ran away from the hospital 'cause he didn't want to pay the bill."

Mason's breath halted as he remembered what Sashka said—*Siberian.* "But why would he have his own name written down in his wallet?"

"Who the hell cares?" she chided him lightly. "There could be a million reasons. Maybe he's dissociative. Maybe he's a thirteen-year-old girl doodling in the margins of a notebook. Maybe an old lover wrote it and it's got sentimental value."

"Yeah, you're right." Mason drifted off into thought, realizing just how much there was they didn't know. "We have to find him," he said suddenly. "We have to find this John Doe or Kai Donovan or whoever."

"But...why?"

As Mason contemplated how to answer, his hand clipped a small mass pressed against his thigh. Digging into his pocket, he felt around the three, smooth edges, his heart pounding. How on earth had that gotten there?

The dream stone—he couldn't remember putting it in his pocket. In fact, he had no memory of what he'd done with it since meeting Gavran, but he was sure these were different pants.

Was Gavran calling him back?

"Because I just can't let this go," his voice broke through the silence, and he pushed down the chill that ran up his spine. "I'm holding this file in my hand, and it's telling me that the blood of a man is wolf's blood. The whole night I kept hearing nurses whispering about wolves and the Dreamwalker. I kept rolling my eyes and wanting to school them on psychiatric medicine, but now I feel like the joke's on me. What if he's something else, Jaz? You saw how fast he healed. Whatever he is, maybe he can help people. People who could use some of that freakish healing."

He heard her exhale on the other end. Did she think he was being fool-hardy? "I don't know about that, man. But I'm kind of glad you're the one who looked at his blood. If someone else working at the hospital had done it first, the whole town would be up in arms."

"Shit, Jaz—you're right. Knowing how superstitious they are—"

"Just go get some rest," she interrupted. "We can figure this out after you've slept and had time to let this stuff digest."

"Yeah, you're right." He ran a hand over his face, his eyes burning from lack of sleep. "I've got some explaining to do to my host, too. I've been kind of MIA lately, and I think she's worried about me."

"All right, well, call me when you're lucid, Cap."

Mason smiled to himself, warmed by her support. "Thanks, Jaz."

After saying goodbye and hanging up, Mason sat in his car for a good twenty minutes before driving back to Black Hollow. When he walked through the door of his lodgings, Annabelle was waiting for him in the lounge, her face brightening when she laid eyes on him.

"There you are!" she beamed. "I was starting to worry you'd drowned in your touristic research."

"Nah." He smiled tiredly. "I was catching up with a friend from school. She's been working at the hospital. It's been a while, so we got a little carried away, I guess."

"Oh, well, that's nice!" she said absently as she put her book down. "You do look awfully tired, though. Shall I make you an early dinner?"

He nodded, energized by the prospect of Annabelle's cooking. "That would be really great."

For a moment he caught a flicker of concern in her eyes, though it was gone as quickly as it had come. She headed towards the kitchen, calling back to him as she set some water to boil on the stove. "I know it ain't my business, Mason, but you look real worn out for someone who's just been with a friend. Is everything all right?"

"Everything's fine," he said as he wandered after her. Standing in the kitchen doorway, he watched as she prepared the ingredients, chopping vegetables and sliding them effortlessly into the pot. A question burned on the tip of his tongue.

"Annabelle," he started, shifting his weight. "I'm not sure how to ask this. In fact, I don't really know what I'm asking."

She turned towards him, waiting expectantly for whatever he had to say next. Feeling the pressure, he blurted out in a quiet, mousy voice, "Are there wolves here, in Black Hollow?"

Several moments went by, but Annabelle's expression remained unchanged—impossible to read even as they locked eyes and stared into one another, digging for the right layer of meaning implied in the question.

Then, without warning, she began to laugh. "Well, of course there are!" She flicked her wrist at him before resuming her chopping. "They're everywhere! Why else do you think there's a wolf cull?"

The tension dissipating, he ventured more boldly. "It's got nothing to do with people being afraid of the Dreamwalker coming back? I know Elle Robinson was already murdered because of that fear."

"You really have been looking into the town's history, and through my son's work," Annabelle spoke with her back turned to him, but he could hear the strain in her voice.

"You're also scared to talk about it?"

"No, not me, personally." She placed the last of the ingredients in the pot. "But you have to understand, fear runs deep. This town has a lot of secrets, and if you keep digging for them, you'll end up burying yourself alive."

Mason smiled sympathetically. "It's just a story, Annabelle. It's not real."

"Stories aren't concerned with what's real and what isn't real."

"I'm not sure I understand what you're trying to say," he said, frowning. "Why call anything a story if there's no distinction between reality and fantasy? Fact and fiction?"

It was her turn to smile sympathetically, her expression peeling away the layers of his staunch rationality like a mother reminding her son that he wasn't as wise as he thought.

"Stories aren't told to convey the facts. They're told to convey the truth."

CHAPTER
SEVENTEEN
THE RETURN

MIYA

MIYA WAS BACK under the willow tree, crouching over the dying black wolf. The feathery female presence from earlier had vanished, leaving her alone with her friend. Gently, she placed her hand on his torso, feeling his slow, fading heartbeat. An ear twitched, and a quick breath followed before he exhaled, his body relaxing under her touch. She knew he was relieved to have her near, his fear melting away now that he was no longer alone.

Remarkably, Miya felt his heartbeat strengthen, and when she examined his fur, the traces of darkened blood were gone. His eyes shifted slowly as though he was returning, his nose wiggling to absorb the world around him through scent. Somehow, Miya had healed him. Reassured that he would survive, she fell back on her behind. He raised his head and looked around before his gaze steadied on her hooded form.

"I'm lost," Miya told him as if answering a silent question. "I don't know how to get home."

He cocked his head, eyes shining red with mischief as his lips pulled back to reveal a row of sharp, white teeth. His peeking canines framed a long, smooth tongue that spilled from his mouth. It hung out without a care in the world, hot breath pulsing and fogging the air between them. He was laughing at her, amused that she'd wandered so deep into the woods that she had no inkling of how to get back.

"I'm not afraid," she said with conviction, then pointed at his charcoal nose. "You can't eat me. I saved you."

His pink tongue darted in and out as he licked his chops and swallowed, her asser-

tion putting to rest whatever devious plan he had in mind. How odd, Miya thought, to meet an honourable wolf. She heard a whine before he rolled onto his belly and plunked his head down between his front paws, ears erect as he gazed up at her. Miya wondered if they knew each other. As they sat in silence, she watched the leaves of the surrounding trees turn yellow, then red, then brown, crinkling like burnt paper and falling from their branches. Snow covered the forest, decorating the wispy limbs of the willow and painting the landscape white. She didn't feel cold, but when she looked at her hands, she realized she was shivering while the wolf remained unmoved. His thick, black coat was peppered with snowflakes that caught like silver fireflies, melting into the trap.

As if having made a decision, the wolf jumped up and shook himself out from head to tail, tiny droplets of ice and water erupting from his warm body. He began to walk, swooning a bit at first but managing to find his step. He circled the tree, then slowed as he moved past Miya, deliberately pressing his body to hers in a gesture that spoke.

Follow me, *it said.*

Standing shakily, Miya struggled to put one foot in front of the other as she passed over the snow, gliding on the surface as though weightless. There were no footprints, no disruptions in the perfectly glazed forest floor.

She didn't know where the wolf was leading her, but she could do little but follow. His pace was slow, considerate of her weary body. Every now and again, he turned to glance back at her, stalling to let her catch up before continuing on his way.

Gradually, the forest grew less tranquil. The snow melted, and green life sprung from every crevice. When the commotion passed, the heat of summer pressed down on them with smouldering intensity. Her legs grew heavy, and where her steps were once graceful the earth now crunched beneath her feet like broken glass. This stretch was the longest—the hardest of the four. They found their way only to become more lost until, at last, the heat began to wane, and Miya caught a glimpse of the changing leaves succumbing to the fire of autumn once more. As one full cycle passed, Miya saw the end of their journey drawing near. The edge of the forest was in sight.

The wolf had guided her home—a gesture Miya knew was meant to reciprocate what kindness she first showed him.

She turned to thank the wolf for leading her out of the woods, but he remained in the shelter of the trees, unwilling to cross the threshold into the world of men.

He didn't move, didn't tilt his head or grin. Instead, he waited, something hesitant and sad in the way he watched her. It was as though his repayment brought him no joy, as though despite leading her home, he knew that she was still lost, and he still alone.

As Miya resolved to call out to him, a thunderous gale blew the forest away before her eyes, and she found herself in the village where she first began her journey. The moon rose, and with it came the harrowing call of the wolf. Miya closed her eyes and waited for sunrise, but the night was endless. The dark blanket ebbed, but dawn never broke; the white moon rose again and again in endless reiteration, never questioning the absence of its counterpart. With its ascent, the howls echoed through the village—sorrowful and yearning.

Hearing the wolf's cries wrenched at Miya's heart until she turned and stumbled to the village gates. There, she saw a figure standing by the forest's edge, but it wasn't that of the wolf. It was a woman with a violet-black, iridescent aura that danced around her skin, cloaking her like feathers—wings at rest. Her long, dark hair flowed around her shoulders with the strengthening wind, and her face was hidden behind a mask Miya was unable to make out from a distance. Even from afar, Miya could feel her presence—the same one that had clung to her when she'd first found the wolf under the willow. Miya took a step forward, but the figure turned and walked into the woods.

"Wait!" Miya called out to her, then ran through the field that separated the village from the viridescent sea. She glimpsed something in her periphery—a bar with two dangling vertical chains, its ends fastened to a small wooden board. She turned her head as she heard the squeak of metal, the chains and plank swaying in the wind. But by the time she looked, the image had faded, and she was fast moving into the trees. Miya passed through the threshold a third time, tumbling back into the forest and down into the abyss.

CHAPTER

EIGHTEEN

WHEN MIYA RETURNED from the dream, her eyes were already open, but she was unable to move—paralyzed even though she was wide awake. Her heart crashed against her ribs, and her breath caught in her throat, every tendon and muscle taut with desperation. She couldn't open her mouth, scream, or even gasp for air. All she could do was look right in front of her.

The phantom woman from the dream hovered directly above her, her face inches away as she mirrored Miya's prostrate form. Miya could see the mask clearly now—a hard, bone shell, shaped like a raven's beak. It extended down her face in a sharp V, past her lips and over the edge of her chin. The mask was decorated with gleaming black and purple that swirled together like oil and water, slick against the smooth, flawless ivory. Her lips—quirked at the edges—descended towards Miya's.

Miya squeezed her eyes shut, trying to kick and thrash—whatever she could do to get away. Her skin crawled with spiders, invisible parasites burrowing their way inside her until she was unable to fight the fear any longer. Miya implored the spectre, bargaining with the only thing she felt the woman might want.

I'll go back to the dream, Miya told her. *I'll follow you—wherever you want. I swear. Please, just let me go.*

Air rushed down Miya's throat with such force that her lungs burned when she finally managed to gasp. Her eyes shot open, beads of sweat trickling down her face as she tore over every inch of her room. The apparition was no longer there.

Miya's hand twitched as she flexed her fingers, testing her ability to move. She breathed in again, this time slower, willing herself to stop shaking but with little success. *She's no longer here*, Miya repeated. Her mind was racing, her senses screaming, but she had, somehow, regained control.

Miya sat up, remembering what it was like to be inside her own body. She had the distinct sense of having gone somewhere she shouldn't have—somewhere she risked never coming back from. A bizarre thought to have about a nightmare, but Miya knew in her bones that this was more than a dream. She'd looked into Medusa's eyes and barely evaded turning to stone.

For a brief moment, the fog lifted, and she remembered the events of her first dream—the one that came before last night's. Not only that, her knowledge of the fable had returned. In a frantic tumble, Miya threw herself at the bedside table and reached for her journal. She couldn't afford to forget again; she had to write it down. She needed to know what came next. But the second the tip of her pen connected with the paper, Miya had no idea what to write. She stared down at the lines, her mind as blank as the page in front of her.

The dreams and the fable were gone.

FOR MOST PEOPLE, being held hostage wasn't something they'd ever have to think about. Aside from popular fiction and movies, the experience was far removed—too foreign to even conceive of. Miya never thought about what it might be like to be held against her will either, until now. But her kidnapper wasn't a faceless man asking for ransom, an international crime syndicate, or a serial killer with perverted tastes. No, nothing like that. She was held hostage by her own nightmares. And like any hostage, she couldn't talk about her kidnapper. She was restrained, blindfolded, and gagged by the absurdity of what was happening to her.

A week passed and her insomnia stopped, but she was more exhausted than ever before. Every night she fell into darkness as though not having slept for days, yet she barely noticed time passing. Miya constantly heard howls—inside of her, outside her, around her—everywhere and nowhere all at once. When morning came, she could barely sit up, let alone stand without almost falling over. She'd promised to see Hannah off on her last day in town, but everything from their lunch together to the hug goodbye slipped right past her like a remnant of one of her dreams. Her head was swimming, her vision was blurry, and her mouth was parched. The backs of her eyes felt like thousands of tiny, invisible needles were shooting through them, day after day. She hardly perceived her surroundings, like she was living in an alternate plane—one that was only thinly connected to the world everyone else lived in.

She learned that what happened to her was known as sleep paralysis or Old Hag Syndrome—a not-so-well-understood phenomenon where the mind wakes up, but the muscles remain asleep. The experience was often accompanied by terror, hallucinations, and the sense of an intruder somewhere in the room. But Miya knew she wasn't hallucinating, and nothing from her research explained why she kept hearing things.

She strained to summon back her dreams, but she could only remember one thing clearly: the intruder. Miya documented her appearance, but questions remained. Did the intruder step out of Miya's dream and into her bedroom? Or was she on the outside all along, watching Miya while she dreamt of her? Perhaps the intruder was the one causing the dreams and the howling. Perhaps she was trying to show Miya something.

Miya had entertained that she was hallucinating, that medical science offered a more likely explanation. The intruder could have been an afterimage, a projection resulting from the intensity of the nightmare and from recent stress.

She could have rationalized it all day, but in truth, she didn't buy even the soundest rational explanation for what happened. The phantom wasn't her creation, and she was all too certain of that.

After all, Miya knew who the phantom was.

Even if the details of the fable eluded her, she could never forget the dreaded kidnapper: the Dreamwalker. Now, she was sitting at the foot of Miya's bed.

The question was why. An obvious possibility came to mind—one she'd rather not have contended with. She had no desire to become the next Elle Robinson.

If only Miya could remember her dreams, she'd have some way of knowing what came next—or so she thought. Instead, she was trapped, glimpsing shadows only to spin around and find nothing there. She'd tell herself she was spooked, jumpy and reactive. There were shadows everywhere. They couldn't all be ghosts.

Miya fished through her bedside drawer and pulled out her playing cards. Shuffling the deck, she closed her eyes and took deep breaths, banishing the prickles on her skin and the tightness in her chest. If she was as good a reader as Hannah claimed, maybe she'd see *something* that could help. As the cards slid through her hands, she melted into the darkness behind her eyelids until her finger clipped one of the cards mid-shuffle. The deck scattered to the floor. Sighing, Miya cursed under her breath and picked three cards from the spill in front of her.

Upon glimpsing them, she slapped them face down onto her futon. The six of diamonds—the card of distant lands and journeys—followed by the queen of spades and the dreaded joker. Queens represented truth, and in this case, uncomfortable or unwelcome ones. But just as her king, the queen of spades signalled the presence of a spirit.

And the joker? Well, he didn't know what was going on. The card was as good as the glaring hole in her memory.

As Miya's brain sprinted around the inside of her skull, she felt a vibration against her leg and checked her phone.

Get out of that hole, will you? Go to Hat Ranch Anniversary party, meet some boys, have a damn hot dog.

Miya stared at the words on her screen. It was Patty, no doubt noticing she hadn't left her basement since...she wasn't sure. Miya had no desire to go anywhere, but she had even less desire to agitate her landlady—and a distraction wasn't a bad idea. The excursion would be better than mental gymnastics that tested the limits of her sanity. Besides, the event wasn't too far from her sanctuary; if things got difficult, she could always stop by the swings.

Miya texted Patty that she was on her way out but couldn't promise to charm the pants off any boys. A thorough shampooing later, she pulled on her favourite old jeans and her varsity hoodie. Her concealer was almost dried out, but she managed to salvage a few drops for the dark circles under her eyes.

How she wished Hannah was still here. How she yearned to tell her about what was happening. But Hannah was still settling into Burnaby and shopping for a new telecom deal. It didn't help that UBC had not yet responded to Miya's statement, and none of her job applications were getting bites. Without Hannah, and without a clear path ahead, there was little to look forward to.

Miya gave her face a hearty slap in case she was floating away to that other realm. Grabbing her keys, she shoved her wallet and mini umbrella into her backpack and sneaked out the door. The forecast predicted rain later, but for now, the setting sun was a sight to behold—purplish rays bleeding out of a stunning, orange sphere, then swirling into a darkening backdrop before disappearing into deep blue clouds. For a moment, those waves eclipsed the beauty of the sky; they reminded her of the Dreamwalker's feathery robes and violet aura. Miya wondered if she was still watching.

When she arrived at the ranch, she scanned the area and evaluated the crowd. She saw a middle-aged, balding man with a potbelly and a dangerously undersized t-shirt that read Keep Calm and Drink Beer. Judging by the alienesque protrusion erupting from his midsection, Miya figured he had no difficulty with the "drink beer" part.

She tried to remove herself from the traffic and stand in a corner somewhere, watching people as they passed. It was mostly families with kids; the parents look bushed while their squealing bundles of joy ran around in the most uncoordinated manner possible, smashing into people and knocking things over. Miya spotted a few couples, most of whom were flaunting grossly unnecessary public displays of affection. Then, from the corner of her eye, she caught a familiar face—then two, and finally three: girls from her second-year journalism class. They were in a group project together, and Miya had bailed right before her probation. She hadn't said anything to her classmates, dropping out last minute and leaving them with her share of the workload. They seemed happy—laughing as they held their drinks and walked through the crowd, cheerfully greeting people they recognized. They'd have a few choice words if they spotted her.

Miya ducked away to evade them, but dodging her own feelings wasn't as easy. *You're a piece of shit*, she told herself, the words stinging more than she anticipated. Salty, warm tears spilled over her cheeks and lips. Why was she crying *now*? Miya dug her nails into her arm to try to quell the disappointment, but it only gave way to something else, something far worse. Panic flooded her senses until she was convinced there was no escape.

Her chest tightened. Her stomach seized with pain and nausea. The voices around her began to distort, ordinary chatter morphing into waves of low-frequency white noise. Colours bled into one another, the moving bodies turning into floating blobs until she couldn't differentiate people from objects. The sensation of immobility writhed up her body like a rope— as though someone had tied her up and left her out for spectacle. There were thousands of eyes on her, boring into her skull, tearing through her clothes, burning her flesh—only she didn't know where the eyes were watching from. Each breath drew shallow like her lungs were filling with smoke.

She didn't want to be there. She didn't want to be around the townspeople.

Her mind spun like a wheel, the thoughts cycling faster and louder: *Get me out. Get me out. Get me out.*

CHAPTER
NINETEEN

KAI

LIFE FOR AN INJURED lone wolf was a sack of shit. Toxic shit that had been bagged in a burlap sack and left to air out under someone's window. A few cracked ribs he could deal with. A mangled arm wasn't so bad either. But with injuries from his skull to his ass-crack and beyond, healing was taking far longer than Kai would've liked. He was sore enough that he couldn't even snatch the baby squirrels that routinely got themselves pancaked by cars.

It took Kai nearly ten days to recover enough to walk without needing to sit on a tree stump every ten minutes. On the surface, he looked mostly fine, with only a few nicks and bruises along his torso and left leg. Still, his insides felt like scrambled eggs some mornings. His knee was tender—something between gelatin and baby shit—but his gait was returning to normal.

However, even with his improved condition, he was unable to hunt. That cold bitch Ama hadn't made a peep since her first appearance, yet he felt her watching, and it pissed him off that she didn't at least bring him some road-kill or something. Even the damn raven was less chilly than her, dropping dead rodents and scraps of meat he'd plucked from nearby carcasses through the window. Kai had no idea why the bird had taken to him, but he wasn't about to call him shit-for-brains anytime soon. Then again, pan-seared rat wasn't exactly a delicacy.

The charity helped, but it wasn't enough. Kai knew he'd have to go back into town and scavenge, but the thought of it filled him with pants-wetting

dread. He was debilitated by the prospect of another attack, another accident, another slip-up that might injure him more, or worse, have him found
out. His little trip to the hospital was a close enough call—an excursion he'd
rather have skipped. He knew they'd seen his face; one of them had shot a
laser into his eyeball while he was still unconscious. *That* woke him out of his
coma. He'd been avoiding doctors for over a decade, and now he had to
worry about whether they found anything, whether someone was looking for
him or asking questions. At least the damn hospital wasn't in Black Hollow,
so he'd probably be safe showing his face on this side of the river.

He thought back to the girl on the swing set, trying to do that thing
where people put chocolate icing on a cake made of rhino shit—positive
thinking, was it? It worked, for a little bit, until his heart started to feel
funny, and the pit of his stomach grew even more hollow than usual. He was
hungry, but it wasn't *that* kind of hunger.

Deciding he could still taste the rhino shit under the thin layer of icing,
Kai banished all thoughts of the girl—for now, anyway. He could always
think about her later, but right now, he needed food, not fucking. Struggling
to sit up, he winced at the throbbing in his side, taking a moment to let it
fade before standing and dressing. Splashing water on his face, Kai gripped
the edges of his bathroom sink and looked into the mirror. His breathing
was still a tad laboured, but his heart was strong enough to take the beating.
Running a wet hand through his hair and shaking it out like a dog, he
grabbed his knife and wallet and left the cabin. He didn't look great, but not
bad enough that anyone might stop and ask if he was okay.

It was already sunset when Kai reached town, but something was
different about the human shithole today, and it wasn't just the glowing
backdrop of warm colours. There were banners up in the streets advertising
some event...organized by some historical society...sponsored by some fast-
food chain. He didn't understand why a place that sold heart disease and
fries would care about local history, but he hoped the event was big enough
to have free food.

The event in question—a birthday party for some rotting old farmhouse
—was an opportunity for teens to get drunk and smoke weed behind the
nearest rock while kids zipped around and drove their parents batty. He
didn't understand why people celebrated the fact that an old building was
old. It was like congratulating an eighty-five-year-old for having wrinkles.
Nonetheless, pointless public celebrations meant free food, and free food
meant survival. Perhaps if he'd been cursed with even a fraction of human
pride, he would've rather drowned in kittens than degrade himself by living
off human scraps—pretending to be one of them, lining up like a trained

monkey so he could be rewarded with a cookie and a pat on the head. But Kai wouldn't let his low opinion of humanity flirt with the sweet indignation of self-righteous pride. Sure, he thought humans were parasites scourging the earth, but the idea of kicking the bucket on the point of principle was so...human.

The smoky aroma of a barbeque wafted closer as Kai followed the human hoards to the picnic at the ranch. The great thing about humans was how dull their senses were; they really had no idea who was among them. They never thought twice about who showed up at the watering hole—a predator grazing with the gazelles. Unfamiliar faces were presumed tourists, relatives, or friends from out of town, and most people were too preoccupied with their own business to give a damn. He got a few odd glances as he joined the queue at the barbeque. He could smell their curiosity, and while it prickled his skin and made his lip curl, he knew that if he acted indifferently, no one would bother speaking to him or asking where he was from.

The volunteers were too swamped to pay attention. The girl putting the hot dogs together didn't even bother making eye contact as she shoved the padded beef stick his way, yelling for a new bag of buns.

"Can I have another." It wasn't a question. Kai's voice was completely monotone, devoid of any inflection. The girl looked up and blinked at him through rectangular frames.

"Sorry, only one per guest." She sounded polite enough, but Kai could tell from the subtle movements of her eyebrows, the twitch in her left nostril and the way her chin lifted that she thought he was an idiot.

"It's for my kid sister," he said in the same flat tone, tilting his head towards a group of children sitting on the grass. Two ginger boys and one dark-haired girl.

The volunteer glanced over at them, then turned back to Kai and frowned, the creases around her mouth showing through the layers of foundation she had on.

"Okay," she folded, opening the new bag of buns and preparing another hot dog. Some of the people behind him were glaring, but no one made a sound as he helped himself to seconds. Without thanking her, he wandered off right past the brats.

It took him less than four bites to scarf down each hotdog. Feeling more at ease with a full stomach, Kai took a deep breath and let the multitude of scents wash over him. Something familiar was among them, and he felt it move the thumping mass behind his ribs. Inhaling to relieve the pressure in his chest, he scanned the field for the source of the aroma. Like the remaining bits of sunlight, it was fading fast.

Licking the grease off his fingers, Kai followed the quickly disappearing trail. He was chasing a shadow as it slipped between the cracks, compelled to catch it despite his unease around the townspeople. For once, he was driven by far more than his basic appetites.

It was a hunger to be sure. Just not that kind of hunger.

The whole world melted away as the pursuit became his sole focus. The scent was fleeing, retreating from the crowds in search of a safe and quiet place to hide.

Fine, he thought to himself. *I love a good hunt.*

CHAPTER
TWENTY

MIYA

GET ME OUT. Get me out. Get me out.

Miya repeated the words as she hurried through the tall, slick grass. Her legs barely managed to cut through the greenery as she fled, the chatter growing distant, the smell of soggy, burnt wood and the taste of cinder crumbling away. The playground was almost a kilometre from the ranch, but she ran all the way there even as her heart pounded.

Miya stumbled into the sand and nearly keeled over, heaving for air as she grasped her knees, her hands shaking with adrenaline. She closed her eyes and focused on breathing, dizzy as her lungs gradually opened, and the congestion faded away. Taking a few disoriented steps, she groped around for the swing's chain, pulling herself into the seat as her legs all but liquefied.

Reaching into her rucksack, Miya fished around to check for her keys and discovered a bag of beef jerky—one of the many she'd bought in recent memory. She forgot that she'd sneaked one into her backpack, laughing through her sobs as she stared at it. The sight of the jerky put her at ease, reminding her of the whole reason she always returned to the playground. Tearing the bag open, Miya helped herself to its contents, wiping the tears away with her sleeve as she sniffled.

The crinkle of the bag and her occasional chuckle were the only sounds audible in the quiet of the park. The sky to the east was almost entirely dark, while a few rays of light swam above the horizon to the west. Every now and again, Miya's breath caught in her throat when she failed to restrain her sobs, the hiccup followed by a loud, senseless cackle.

I'm losing my mind, she thought. *I don't even know what I feel.*

The ambivalence was tearing her apart from the inside. She swayed back and forth, the wind against her face and the rhythmic squeak of metal gradually soothing her anxiety. Her eyes were so fixated on her own shadow in the sand that at first she didn't notice someone was there, watching her from a short distance away. It wasn't until she heard the crack of twigs that her instincts stirred from their slumber, warning her that she wasn't alone. She looked up to see a shadow amidst the trees, but it was significantly taller than an animal's. Her heart sank like lead.

"You got any more of that?" a voice called out to her—a man's voice, gruff and brazen.

It took Miya a moment to realize he was talking about the beef jerky. She looked down and blinked at the bag to make sure, half-expecting it to be gone. When she looked back up, someone was standing at the edge of the playground, his toes perfectly lined up with the wooden curb bordering the sand.

Miya wrung the alarm back into her body; he'd moved so soundlessly, so quickly. His face was barely visible in the darkness, but his silhouette revealed that he was tall and well-built—enough to make Miya uncomfortable. His hands were shoved in his pockets as he watched her, waiting for a response.

"I—"

Suddenly, he moved to the left, circling her with slow, even steps. His eyes were still trained on her as he reached a perfect half-circle, then moved back to his original spot. He stalked to the right, repeating the same cycle once, then twice. He was prowling but nervous—a predator unsure of whether he'd chosen weak-enough prey. Unable to speak, Miya extended the bag of jerky, tilting the opening towards him.

At her gesture, he stopped, biding his time before continuing his ritual, moving left and right like a metronome. The circles drew closer, his advance measured and careful, as though he wouldn't dare approach directly. Miya was captivated by the bizarre display, curious to see where it would end. When he was within arm's length, he stopped in front of her, and she could finally see his face.

He looked wild, feral almost. Short, dishevelled black hair, like he'd hacked away at it himself. An angular face. Broad shoulders hidden under loose, tattered clothes—probably second-hand. Even as he tried to keep his face lowered and stay out of reach, he pulled her in like a feather in a maelstrom. She knew him from somewhere—and she was fairly sure he knew her as well. Shaken by the sudden magnetism, Miya's heart hammered faster until she silenced it with a sharp breath.

He looked up, and for a brief moment, she caught his gaze—familiar yet otherworldly. The seconds yawned out until he tore his eyes away, reaching into the bag with a rustle that snapped Miya out of her stupor. His hand emerged with a fist full of jerky. He threw one piece into his mouth and shoved the rest into his pocket, chewing slowly as he watched her like he was trying to excavate something. When he seemed to find it, he turned to leave.

Miya shot to her feet, her own excavation not yet complete. He paused to consider her as her caution gave way to compulsion. She locked onto his eyes—dark, hungry, guarded. But as the shadows passed over his face and the moon made its first appearance, his eyes emitted a bright, eerie shine. Miya caught a flash of colour in the glow—a reddish-brown tint around his pupils, a deep mahogany she had seen only once before. And it wasn't on a human.

Miya's mouth dropped open as horror invaded her—horror, disbelief, and ravenous excitement. As a smile crept over her face, his eyes narrowed, his head canting like he was trying to gauge whether she'd gleaned his secret. Sensing he might flee, Miya took a step forward only for him to step back. He turned and faced her, backpedalling farther away.

"No," he said sternly, his expression hardening.

Undeterred, Miya took another step.

"No." He lifted his finger as though scolding a child who didn't know to keep her fingers from the electrical sockets. While his expression remained severe, Miya could see the subtle changes—a frown that made him look displeased, a slight arch of the brow that suggested he was more confused than put-off.

"You're the one who spoke to me first," Miya retorted, surprised at finally hearing her own voice.

He blinked, appearing amazed that she had the nerve to talk back. She saw the corner of his mouth quirk up, his posture relaxing as he lowered his hand back into his pocket. "You're the one who likes feeding me."

Was that a veiled reference? The hint of playfulness in his tone suggested he knew exactly what he was implying, but Miya could tell he had no intention of staying simply because she'd amused him.

"How about some real food?" she offered, hoping he was as hungry as he looked. The ghost of a smile evaporated from his face, and Miya wondered how deep his mistrust ran.

"Why?"

She shrugged, speaking her mind. "You're hungry."

Unsatisfied, he asked again, "Why?"

"I've never tattled before." She tossed him the bag of jerky, then unzipped her backpack and pulled out her wallet. "There's enough in here for the both of us to eat."

He caught the jerky with one hand, his eyes never leaving hers. "I could just take it from you," he warned, the threat laced with an arrogance that made Miya's lips tug for the first time in days.

She knew he'd say that, her smile widening into a triumphant grin. "Then I really might tattle."

Reluctantly, he nodded, walking towards her and handing the package back. There were so many things Miya wanted to ask, so many questions to bombard him with, but the moment he was in front of her, close enough for her to reach out and touch him, she couldn't think of a damn thing to say. She watched, paralyzed, as he walked past her and into the gathering night mist.

When his silhouette began to fade, he stopped, glancing over his shoulder to make sure she was still there. Not wanting to keep him waiting, Miya threw her backpack over her shoulder and rushed to join him in the field. As they ambled through the grass, she had the sense of being guided, of being led out of a maze, and of being lost and found at the same time. As the fog dissipated and they ventured out of the meadow, there was nothing but road ahead of them.

CHAPTER

TWENTY-ONE

EVERYONE HAD something they hated about themselves. Miya, for one, felt like she never tried hard enough. If she flunked a class, it was because she didn't study hard enough. If she didn't sleep, it was because she didn't count sheep long enough. Anxiety was the product of neglecting to get help fast enough, and when she finally called the helpline—well, she didn't wait on hold long enough. Miya was plagued by the incessant fear that her misfortunes were of her own making, and that every failure was a result of her unwillingness to change—to study harder, to count a few more sheep, to act faster and wait longer.

It was absurd to think the difference between happiness and misery was how long a person was willing to listen to wearisome music on a busy phone line. Still, Miya knew she could have done things differently. She didn't because change was hard. It was easier to stay depressed and angry, pitying and loathing herself. There was a sweet self-indulgence to it that made her feel important. *My feelings, my pain, my losses*; she was caught in them like a bug in a spider's web. *It's all about me.*

But Miya wasn't sure what she truly wanted. Was it magic? Excitement? Adventure? As she stood on the border between the meadow and a river of tarmac, the view wasn't the epic horizon she imagined.

But at long last, she was on a journey...with an irritable, hungry wolf.

"Move it, Lambchop," he grunted when he caught her staring, putting a hand on her shoulder and spinning her around.

Miya found herself facing the opposite way, his hand on her back as he pushed her forward. Had he just referred to her as food?

"Lambchop?" She tried to look over her shoulder at him, but he was nipping at her heels with every stride.

"Don't like it?" he asked with a hint of sarcasm, pushing her along the side of the road.

"My name is Miya," she told him, trying to sound assertive despite being trotted along like a toy.

"I think I prefer Lambchop," he goaded from behind.

"But that's not my name."

"To me, it is."

Miya dug in her heels and thwacked his hand away to keep him from forcing her along. "How would you like it if I called you the first thing that popped into my head?"

"Call me whatever you want."

"How about Beef Jerky?"

He was amused again, giving her that same arrogant smirk from before. He seemed to consider her words, retracting his hand and letting it drop to his side. Taking a step forward, he leaned in by her neck, just close enough to breach personal space. Miya heard his breath draw in, then halt, like he was taking in her scent, testing to see what she was made of.

"Kai," he said, his voice reverberating against her ear. He paused just long enough to feel her hold her breath, then stalked past her. "There's a diner near the highway. A little seedy, but cheap food. Think you can walk it?"

Miya cleared her throat to keep her voice from cracking. "Yeah, I'm good with walking."

They strolled in silence for a good twenty minutes, Miya's mind berating her to say something, anything—but her lips were clamped shut. *I'll interrogate him when we sit down*, she told herself. The diner was a kilometre down a road mostly used by trucks to reach the highway. With nothing else around, the restaurant was easy to spot: a small, yellow-panelled building with an ugly brown roof. The windows were dark and foggy like the grease inside had been caked over the glass in layers. It looked abandoned, save for two pickup trucks and an old Buick with a rusty bumper parked around the side. The name—simply Diner— was half-torn from the top of the building, the E and R completely missing while the N looked like a dinosaur had taken a chunk out of it for breakfast. A half-working neon sign read Open, and the only indication that Miya wasn't amid a zombie apocalypse was the tattooed guy in stained trousers carting garbage out the back door with a cigarette hanging out of his mouth.

Staring up at the sign, Miya ploughed into Kai's back as he stood there, rigid as a goddamn wall. Pulling back, she huffed in irritation while he chuckled to himself, shaking his head and moving towards the entrance. Miya questioned if she really wanted to go in, but Kai looked totally unfazed, like he was walking into his own home.

As if sensing her nerves, he stopped a few feet ahead, waiting for her to catch up. Unsure of herself, Miya stiffly shuffled up to him, all the more aware of his imposing figure as they stood side by side. He was around six foot two and built like a warrior, but it was the don't-fuck-with-me vibe that made her hairs stand on end—like he could turn around and bite her head off without a moment's notice. Shrinking back into her shell, Miya took a tiny step forward, expecting him to snarl and thrust her inside. To her surprise, he didn't. He didn't drive a hand into her back or drag her by the arm. He remained by her side, keeping her pace and a respectable gap between their bodies. Was he actually paying attention?

The swinging double-doors were chipping with blue paint and pin-sized splinters from around the darkened windows. As Miya pushed her way inside, she saw a ratty old playing card wedged in the frame—a king of spades. She eyed the little black spearhead as she entered. Was Kai her king of spades?

The place was dimly lit, with low hanging yellow lamps over grimy off-white plastic tables, burgundy vinyl booths, and faded black-and-white chequered tiles that started to spin if Miya stared at the floor for too long. She stopped in her tracks, her brain seizing from the atrocious decor.

It was half-past nine on a Saturday night, but there was only a handful of people seated around the tiny restaurant—some dude who looked hungover since last week, and a couple whispering angrily from one of the booths. The boyfriend had a mullet—something Miya thought only existed in '80s films —while his girlfriend looked like she'd been electrocuted. Her wiry, bleached hair was sticking out left, right, and centre as she continuously tried to smooth it out with dry, bony fingers.

A waitress approached Miya and Kai, the sound of a nasty cough alerting them to her presence. She was in her fifties, with frizzy brown hair and distracting lipstick that accentuated her scowl. Clearing her throat, she asked if the table was for two in a voice that sounded like it'd been burrowing in rubble since Chernobyl exploded. Kai stared at her, fixated on her tattooed brows—thin and perfectly arched for that permanent look of mild surprise.

"Don't see anyone else with us," he replied coolly, unimpressed by her rote.

"Hah hah," Brenda—according to her nametag—hacked each syllable with no attempt to mask her sarcasm. "This way, please."

She grabbed two menus and led Miya and Kai to a corner booth directly behind the hissing couple. They paused and eyed Brenda with palpable displeasure as she set the menus down and left without waiting for Kai and Miya to sit.

"She didn't sound happy," Miya observed.

Kai opened the menu and scanned his options. "Because her soul is as arid as her lungs."

"Right," Miya snorted, rolling her eyes. "Nothing to do with you being a class act back there."

The corner of his lips quirked up as he continued reading. Miya was about to pounce on him with her first round of questions when Brenda returned, smacking two glasses on the table and a jug of ice water, its contents spilling over as she clunked it down.

"You kids ready?" she asked, pulling a pen out of her hair like it was a magic trick.

Miya had barely looked at the menu, so she blurted out the first thing she laid eyes on. "Uh—chicken and leek pie with mash."

"Cheeseburger, triple up the patty and throw in some bacon."

Miya gawked at Kai, wondering if he was serious. Judging by the total absence of expression on his face, he intended to eat half a cow.

"For your side?" Brenda grunted at him.

"Fries," he grunted back, holding the menu out to her without making eye contact, his focus on Miya.

When Brenda was out of earshot, Miya shuffled to the edge of her seat and folded her torso over the table, staring back at him with equal scrutiny.

"You..." she began, the murmur carrying a hint of accusation.

"Me..." His lips pulled back in a rakish grin.

"Don't play dumb with me," she hissed. "It's you...you're that wolf."

He seemed unsurprised, narrowing his eyes and leaning closer until their noses brushed. "Careful, Little Red Riding Hood, I could eat you all up."

Feeling her face heat up like a kiln, Miya withdrew at viper speed, her back hitting the plastic behind her with a loud thump. He was trying to make her uncomfortable—trying and succeeding with extraordinary ease. "You're not denying it."

"No point." He shrugged and leaned back, resuming his earlier nonchalance while picking at a stain on the table. "You figured it out the second I got close."

At least he was an honest, if volatile, dick.

"More interesting thing is," his eyes locked onto hers, "you're not calling bullshit."

It was Miya's turn to shrug, crossing her arms over her chest. His gaze unnerved her, but she didn't want him to know that. "Sounds like you haven't been in Black Hollow very long. People here believe in weird things."

A chilly smile crept onto his face. "Oh, I've been here a while," he informed her. "Two types of people in this shithole. The ones who believe and stay the fuck away because they're scared; and the ones who believe but pretend not to, so they can go looking for the thing everyone else is scared of." The curve of his mouth widened into a wolfish grin—the kind that convinced Miya he really *was* a wolf. "I think I know which you are."

"You hardly know me. And there *are* people who don't believe."

"Those people don't matter. Either way, you're not one of them." His expression mellowed out as he returned to his fixation on the table. "Just don't know why anyone would have dinner with something most people shit their pants thinking about."

"Only two reasons why people go looking for monsters," Miya mimicked his didactics, and not without a touch of mockery. "Either they're bored, or they want something from the monster."

This gave him pause, his hand going still as he slowly raised his head. "So," he began, "what do you want from me?"

Miya groped for an answer under the weight of his blasé admission, but she was spared further turmoil when her line of sight was broken by Brenda's lumpy arm. She flinched when the ceramic plates dove between them and clanked loudly against the table, followed by ketchup and relish bottles that looked bled dry.

Miya and Kai blinked down at their food, the previous moment's conversation put on hold. As Miya unwrapped her fork and knife from the napkin, Kai picked up his burger—about as tall as a mason jar—and bit into it with alarming zeal. Miya wondered when his last meal was as she absently cut into her pie, swirling the gravy around and taking her time to let the inside cool. She was grateful for the respite.

What do I want from the monster?

The question nibbled at her.

They ate in silence, neither bothering to look at one another as they gorged on every last scrap of food. As she stewed in her own gaucheness, something dawned on her for the first time.

"You said you've been here for a while. How long?" she blurted out as she wiped her mouth with the napkin.

Kai was already done eating, his gaze boring through his companion's skull as though she'd sprouted a third eyeball. "Ten years."

"Oh..." Miya was unprepared for how disappointed she sounded.

"What?" he asked.

"It's nothing. I just thought we may have met once before when I was a kid."

Kai shook his head. "Wasn't in the country before I was sixteen."

Miya did the math while she chewed. Ten years ago, she would've been eleven, which was well after her first encounter with the wolf. "How have you been here that long undetected? I mean, it's not really a big town."

"You mean, where do I live?" he rephrased the question as he broke out into a knowing smile.

"What?" Miya laughed, feeling lighter. "I'm allowed to be curious, aren't I?"

"Maybe I'll show you one day," he teased before the booth suddenly rattled.

"What the hell?" Miya ducked her head as the voices behind her grew louder. The couple was fighting again, their heated argument from earlier escalating until mullet-man slammed a fist down on the table, causing an earthquake to ricochet through the connecting booths. After Kai shot them a seething glare, they resumed their hushed bickering. Miya couldn't make out their words, but it felt like one of those spats right before a pair of Bonnie and Clyde wannabes botched an armed robbery.

"You want to get out of here?" Kai asked.

Miya nodded and reached for her wallet, grateful he was on the same page. Brenda must have been eavesdropping, because she'd already prepared the bill, leaving it on the edge of the table as Miya started pulling out the cash.

"Huh, almost forgot I can see you in colour now." Kai leaned over the table as Miya counted the money.

"Colour?"

"I don't see colours the same when I'm furry." He squinted at her face. "Now it's...green...dark, murky green...like someone shat in a mossy lake."

She blinked at him. "What is?"

"Your eyes."

Miya wrinkled her nose as her brain conjured the image of leaky poop floating through sewage, then burst out laughing.

"That's sweet of you, but I prefer to think of them as a smoky, forest green," she cracked with borderline sincerity, then tucked the money under the receipt along with an excellent tip for poor Brenda.

As they got up, Kai casually swiped the fork off Miya's plate and inspected it like a shiny new toy. She frowned as he passed her, then followed him out of the booth. She stayed a few paces behind as he meandered past the couple, fork in hand.

Before she could blink, Kai thrust his arm downwards with inhuman speed and stabbed the fork right through the edge of mullet-man's sleeve, pinning his arm to the table with a dull twang. Miya flinched, mouth agape, while the girlfriend gasped in horror, her eyes bulging as her head whipped left and right, eyes darting between Kai and the table. The boyfriend took a second, but when he realized there was an eating utensil jammed into the laminate less than half an inch from his hand, he shrieked, yanking his arm away in a desperate attempt to get free. His girlfriend gathered her wits and tried prying the fork out of the table, but it was lodged in there pretty good.

Mortified, Miya peered around the restaurant, but no one bothered giving them a second glance. The lush was still preoccupied with the bottom of his pint, and Brenda's eyebrows were nowhere to be found. Miya sped past the couple and followed Kai outside.

"W-why did you do that!" she stammered as she blasted through the doors after him.

"Guy was pissing me off," he replied as if it was a perfectly legitimate reason to nearly take someone's fingers off in public.

"That's—he was just fighting with his girlfriend! I know it was annoying, but—"

"You were getting freaked out," he interrupted her—like her reaction was somehow the catalyst for his reckless stunt. Grated by the suggestion, Miya sped up and stepped around him, cutting him off.

"Are you saying this is my fault?" she demanded, forgetting their size difference as she planted herself in front of him.

He stopped and looked her up and down, his brows furrowing together as though he was trying to decide how unfair the fight would be. "No." His face twisted like he'd bitten down on something bitter. He placed a hand on her shoulder and shuffled her out of his way. "It's his fault. He made you nervous, so I put him back in his place."

Put him back in his place. Dumbfounded, she mouthed the words to herself. What sort of flabbergasting logic was that? Then again, it sounded primal, which was precisely what one might expect from an animal. Like a dog asserting its dominance over someone it found threatening.

But before Miya could allow herself to feel flattered, her brain smacked her low self-esteem upside the head. *You don't need some guy standing up for you when you didn't even ask for it*, it hollered. *You're no damsel in distress.*

"How did you know I was that nervous?" she challenged.

"Forget it," he muttered, shoving his hands in his pockets and half-turning like he was uncertain if she'd follow. She could see him fiddling with the insides of his jacket, drumming his fingers against the leather. He appeared awkward, a touch self-conscious even.

His ineptness softened Miya's anger even as she wished he'd apologize. "What you did was totally out of line. You don't have to use violence to protect people," she offered. "But, thanks for thinking of my feelings, I guess."

He frowned and narrowed his eyes like he was trying to dissect her. "People are weird," he said. "You want to be understood, but if someone understands too much, you get pissed about it like they're invading your privacy or some shit."

"It's not that," said Miya. "No one wants another person acting on their behalf without asking first. Feels like an imposition, I guess. Especially when you don't want to be seen as weak or helpless."

His expression ironed out as he contemplated this. "Fair," he conceded. "I can understand that."

Miya was relieved they'd managed to make peace without a snarky exchange. "Good," she smiled.

Kai nodded, waiting until she was next to him to start walking. Silence followed, but Miya didn't mind it this time. The need to fill the void was absent as a newfound comfort washed over her. She wasn't sure which of them was leading, but they were headed back the same way they came: down a misty evening road and towards the playground by the forest.

CHAPTER
TWENTY-TWO

MASON

FOR WEEKS after the incident with John Doe, Mason tried to remain on his best behaviour. He heeded Annabelle's warning—curbing his curiosity by helping around the house and sparing no chance to engage his host. But no matter how hard he tried, Mason couldn't stop his thoughts from fixating on the town's beliefs.

Why was this fable buried in the rubble of history and whispered about only when striking fear into disobedient children? The irony was that the adults seemed more frightened of the story than the kids it was meant to scare. So much so, they murdered those kids just to protect that fear.

Mason also couldn't stop thinking about John Doe—or Kai Donovan, as he'd begun to refer to him. The coincidence of a town with an almost mythical relationship to wolves and a mysterious patient with the blood of a wolf was bizarre, to say the least. While he tried to keep the legend, the murder of Elle Robinson, and the case of Kai Donovan schematized in neat, separate compartments, Mason found himself continuously synthesizing them, scrambling to make some kind of connection.

It was hard work fooling himself into thinking he'd gotten over his obsession. That Saturday, Annabelle offered to accompany him to a local event, but he wasn't in the mood, opting instead for a jointly-made meal and some quiet company. They hardly spoke as they ate, but Mason could feel Annabelle's eyes probing him.

"You know, you've been here for a while, and we've hardly talked about why you actually came to Black Hollow," she said after clearing the plates.

Mason fiddled with the hem of the tablecloth. "That's probably because I was trying to run away."

"Run away?" She paused as she scrubbed the dishes. "From the big city?"

"Something like that." He remembered how excited he'd been to leave his worries behind and experience the peaceful rural landscape. "The big city and all the stress that came with it did have something to do with it."

Draining the sink and wiping her hands, Annabelle returned to the table after preparing some chamomile tea.

She placed a mug down in front of him. "Go on."

Mason pulled the mug towards himself and took a breath. He'd never told Annabelle about his profession, despite her sharing Mathias's illness with him.

"I'm an oncologist," he said finally, glancing up to evaluate her reaction.

She looked taken aback, and he wondered if she was upset. It must have stirred some uncomfortable emotions. "Near the end of my residency," he continued when she failed to respond, "I was given charge of my first case. A test of sorts, to see if I could handle the burden of terminal patient care." He plucked at a loose string on the hem. Everything he'd been shoving down crept back up his throat. "I um, I failed."

Annabelle cupped the mug with her palms, tilting it back and forth. "It's not easy," she said quietly. "That's why so many doctors just check out."

"Like my supervisor," Mason sighed. "He's one of those. And I think that's why he gave me this case. He wanted me to learn a hard lesson, and I refused until the bitter end."

"What do you mean?"

Mason swallowed the lump in his throat. He wasn't sure if he was ready, but there was no other way to find out than to simply jump.

"Her name was Amanda." He paused, thinking back to when it happened —when he first held the results in his hand. "I should have told the family their daughter had no chance. That she should spend her last six months doing what made her happy. But I just...I couldn't. They were searching for someone to give them hope..." he trailed off, laughing now as he realized how stupid he'd been. "I wanted to play hero."

Annabelle smiled, but her eyes looked hollow. "You were trying to be kind." She reached over and squeezed his hand.

Mason shook his head, unable to reciprocate. Her words did nothing to console him. He didn't want reassurance; he wanted judgement. "I just—I rationalized. Miracles happen, I told myself. Positive thinking, social support, meditation—all those things that helped miracle patients beat the odds."

"And they do!" Annabelle held his hand tightly, her eyes glossing over. "My Matty lived years past his expiry date." It was the blackest joke he'd ever heard. "What did you tell them?" she asked quietly, reaching for the tissue box as her cheeks grew moist.

"Don't give up."

Annabelle nodded, turning her head to the side as she looked out the window. "That's the only thing people can do."

"You don't understand," Mason hissed, tearfully confessing to the experimental treatment and how it'd ruined her quality of life. "I told them there'd been cases with unexpected results."

He searched her eyes for something other than sadness—anger, regret, hatred even.

Annabelle lowered her gaze. He heard a quiet whimper, though it was quickly silenced with a sharp breath.

"When did she...?"

"Three months in," Mason said. "She died of uterine haemorrhaging, a side effect of aggressive treatment." It was the rawest thing he'd ever experienced and by far the most terrifying. Death happened so quickly, without regard for all the effort put into preventing it. Mason had watched as months of treatment and hope bled out in mere seconds. Amanda's family was devastated, their grief too overwhelming for them to think about who to blame. At the end of it all, they even shook his hand. *Thank you for everything you've done*, they'd said, but all he'd done was kill their daughter. He even received an invitation to the funeral and attended out of obligation.

"Two weeks later," he continued, "I took a leave of absence from the hospital. I needed to get away from it all—the stress, the guilt."

An oppressing silence followed as the two sat across from one another. In front of him, Mason did not see Annabelle, but the mother of a child whose life he'd shortened because of his own unwillingness to accept one simple fact: people die.

"I forgive you." Annabelle's words almost dissipated by the time they reached Mason's ears. It was as though she knew exactly what he needed after having been on the battlefield so long herself. She squeezed his hand to let him know she was still there. "It's what us mothers do."

"Thank you," he breathed out, his shoulders caving in as the weight slid off them. Perhaps this was the moment of healing he had been searching for, and his fractured heart could finally begin to mend. At last, he could look at

Annabelle as Mason Evans would, and not as the guilt-stricken doctor who'd failed. He smiled tentatively, warmth spreading through his chest.

Annabelle too smiled, and the silence stretched on until she finally let go of his hand and pulled back. "You must be tired," she said, though he could see she was equally exhausted.

"I think I'll just go to bed early tonight," he decided, drinking his tea in one gulp and taking the mug back to the sink. He wanted to be alone to process what just occurred. He glanced at Annabelle, still sitting at the table.

"I'll catch you in the morning," he told her, receiving a shaky smile in return.

He paused on his way out and peeked at Annabelle's face, strained with sadness. Their conversation undoubtedly stirred up painful memories. He opened his mouth to ask if she was all right, or if she needed to say her piece —but he stopped. What could he possibly tell her that she hadn't already heard from a dozen other well-meaning doctors and friends? What if his attempts to comfort her only backfired? His heart finally sung with relief; he didn't want to ruin it just yet.

Deciding to cut his losses, Mason retreated upstairs. After a long, hot shower, he crawled under the duvet and sunk into the mattress. It was the first time he really felt how the memory foam melded to his body. Closing his eyes, Mason rolled over to turn off the bedside lamp, the iridescent dream stone resting quietly at its base.

"It's over," he whispered. "All this stuff about the Dreamwalker, wolves, Kai Donovan—I'm done. I don't need it anymore." He broke out into a triumphant smile. "I found my answer."

He reached over the dream stone and switched off the light.

***

When Mason awoke in the middle of the night, a strange man was standing over him. He was pale, sickly, his eyes sunken and his face haggard despite looking about thirty. Something about his coppery hair, the shape of his nose, and the lines of his face struck Mason as familiar. The man stared down at him with a displeased frown, as though he was confronting an intruder.

As Mason struggled to clear the fog, he realized that he couldn't lift his head from the pillow. He tried to wiggle a finger, but he felt nothing in his hands—like his limbs had been severed. But he was too preoccupied with the figure to panic over his lack of mobility. Gradually, the recognition strengthened until he realized who it was, his pulse quickening as he waited for the apparition to disappear. Surely, he was dreaming; surely, he was not looking into the face of a ghost—not after he'd finally earned Annabelle's forgiveness.

Surely, this was not Mathias.

The ailing phantom tilted his head, his features warping monstrously, his eyes and nose melting from his face while his mouth twisted sideways, then upwards into something resembling a smile. Like hot, raw dough, his flesh slewed off, dripping in globs over his shoulders and chest.

Cold sweat ran down Mason's face and neck, his breathing laboured as he grew increasingly aware of his own consciousness—the texture of the pillow, the smoothness of cotton sheets brushing against his legs, the familiar shadows that danced along the four walls he'd grown so accustomed to. But he was unable to tear his eyes away. The creature before him reached up and dug its fingers into its own face, peeling away what remained of the putrid flesh.

Beneath it was something unexpected—another face, a familiar one bearing a cutting smile and two pitch-black eyes that glistened like wet asphalt.

Gavran.

"You never came back," his eerie voice echoed through the vacant space, "so I've come to you."

Leaning over, the old man lowered his head like a vulture, those depthless pools growing larger and larger as his face drew near. When the boundary between them crumbled away, Mason could see nothing else. He fell into the void and onto the other side, to a place beyond what should have been possible.

CHAPTER
TWENTY-THREE
THE FIRST

MASON CAME to standing in the centre of an abandoned village. Many of the buildings were burnt to the ground or charred black. Smoke rose from the trees peppering the town, and the smell of ash smouldered in his nostrils. There were no cars, no lights, no power lines, no pavement, and certainly no signs of life. The buildings appeared to be made of wood and stone, and none were larger than an ordinary cottage. Up ahead, he saw a burning pyre with a post fastened in the middle—but no one was there.

"Where am I?" he wondered aloud, the words swallowed by the open space.

"I told you. I've come to you."

Startled by the youthfulness of the voice, Mason spun around to find a boy no older than twelve standing behind him. His hair was a cold midnight black with a slight iridescent glow, not unlike the plumage of a bird. His skin—white like porcelain but with a touch of sickness—seemed lifeless and waxy smooth. It was like the boy was nothing more than a container. But those eyes—those glistening, inky eyes—told Mason exactly who this boy was.

"Gavran," he all but choked on the name. "Where are we? Why do you look like that?"

The corners of the boy's lips slithered outward, stretching over bloodied teeth. The sound that left him could not have been less human—a throaty cackle echoing into the eerie silence. He chortled with unfettered glee.

"There," Gavran hissed sharply, his eyes widening in delight, the tresses on his head ruffling like feathers. His body jerked awkwardly as he hunched over in a predatory stance, stiffening in anticipation of something in the distance. As Mason whirled around, a shadow passed overhead, mutating the scene.

As if having moved back in time, the village was no longer in ruins. The buildings were intact as smoke rose from the chimneys, and the houses seemed inhabited. Up ahead, Mason saw the orange glow of dozens of torches—a group of men and women congregating around the village gates.

Beyond them he could see the edge of a massive forest—one that struck him as familiar. He was still in Black Hollow. The people in the crowd wore archaic clothing, though Mason couldn't place from what year. They whispered to one another, the air tense as their gazes fixed on someone just beyond the gates. It was a young woman in a cloak. Her face was obscured by a hood, though Mason guessed she was female by her dainty hands and the subtle swell of her hips. She was facing away from the villagers, staring off into the forest, when suddenly a howl erupted from somewhere in the distance—a call both haunting and sorrowful. There was a collective gasp among the villagers before their whispering grew louder, and Mason heard a single word flutter through the crowd:

Dreamwalker.

The villagers battered the hooded girl with mistrusting glares.

"Dreamwalker," they hissed at her again, the name both accusation and revelation.

Was this girl the fabled spirit that haunted Black Hollow?

Was the Dreamwalker just an ordinary young woman, forced to leave her home behind? There appeared to be nothing supernatural about her.

Yet the scene before Mason was anything but mundane. Around the villagers floated a strange, life-like mist. It slithered through the air, approaching each of the townsfolk and swirling around them until they spewed venomous accusations at the alienated young woman. Only then did the dark vapour move on to the next person. A sinister presence was among them, and Mason wondered if it was the source of the villagers' malice.

"He was right," Mason heard someone say, and the dark mist trembled as though laughing. "We should have banished her sooner. No one comes out of those woods alive."

The presence began to shift, gathering into a pool of darkness behind the villagers. The mass was at first formless, its edges flickering like ebony flames. Gradually, it took the shape of a man, his face shrouded save for two sharp, golden eyes—cold like metal gleaming under a florescent light. Whatever it—or he—was, he couldn't have been benign. The malevolent entity appeared to have turned the villagers against the girl— the Dreamwalker. While Mason couldn't fathom what this girl might have done to make him so angry, it was clear that he harboured ill will towards her, that he wanted to punish her.

Mason watched as the young woman began walking towards the forest—towards the howls that echoed from within it. Yet even though everything suggested she was being exiled, Mason sensed a longing in her that matched that of the howling wolf—a yearning to return to something. Was she accepting her fate, or had she chosen it for herself? He couldn't tell which it was. As she moved away, the villagers began shouting, pumping their fists in the air, spitting on the ground she walked on and cursing her name.

Her choice did not matter; the villagers wanted blood, and the malevolent puppeteer stalking the grounds behind them would have nothing less than her damnation. As her figure grew distant, Mason's anxiety mounted. Feeling the need to act, he bolted forward, trying to reach the crowd—yet no matter how hard he pressed his feet into the ground, he didn't get any closer. Frustrated, he called out to them, but his voice was sucked into a vacuum.

The villagers didn't hear him—but he did. The shadowy being turned its attention away from the scene, taking note of the intruder for the first time. His bright eyes lock onto the young doctor.

Mason stumbled back as the dark flames dancing along the creature's form twisted erratically, sweeping outward and rushing closer. He looked towards the village gates and beyond, but the young woman was far out of sight. It was too late to stop her. When he turned back, he was face-to-face with the entity. A low, distorted growl reverberated from the murky depths of the molten black silhouette. The phantom drew nearer with every breath, his gleaming eyes widening with rage as his essence bled out, cloaking the land like a plague.

"It's time to go," Gavran hissed, the boy's breath cold on Mason's cheek before something seized his shoulders. Hands—no, more like talons—plucked him from the ground as sharp, curved nails cut into his flesh.

As he was pulled up, the entity below shrieked with monstrous fury. Colour drained from the landscape as the entity dispersed, swallowing the village—and its inhabitants—until nothing remained but a boundless sea of black miasma.

CHAPTER
TWENTY-FOUR

GASPING FOR AIR, Mason shot upright, his mouth watering as a powerful wave of nausea ripped through him. He could feel the bile rising as he tumbled out of bed and tripped into the bathroom. By the time he keeled over the toilet, he had already thrown up in his mouth, the acidic smell making his insides churn until the rest of dinner came rushing up. When there was nothing left, he rested his elbows against the toilet seat and heaved for air.

What he'd just witnessed—was it part of the legend?

Mason pushed himself away from the toilet and peeled his shirt off, wiping the sweat from his neck. He needed to solve this mystery, and he needed to do it now.

Through his own research and Mathias' fragmented blog critiques, Mason knew about the town's history with murdered girls and wolf culls. The undying belief in the myth, the violence against women, and the mass slaughter of wolves—how were they connected?

Each time they say she steals one, the stolen one burns.

Gavran's words may not have been so crazy, after all.

Mason plopped down on the cool ceramic floor, his mind whirling. The pieces of the puzzle were all there; he just needed to put them together. The girl from the legend—the one they expelled...deep down, the villagers must have known she was just an ordinary woman and not some supernatural creature.

But what about the sinister presence in the dream? Was that embellishment? Metaphor? Why had Gavran forced Mason to see and feel that *thing*?

What on earth was the old man trying to tell him? How had he teleported across space and through consciousness? He seemed to be everywhere and yet nowhere all at once. Mason recalled his experience in the archives—the voice in the shadows, speaking to him in riddles and rhymes.

Then he remembered the testimonials. He'd photocopied every last one.

Scrambling back to the room, Mason swung open his closet door and rummaged around. There were dozens of them to get through, but he was wide awake now, his body shaking with adrenaline.

I thought you were done with this, a tiny voice mocked, but he ignored it and read the date at the top of the first personal account.

October 22, 1868

I feel as though I have survived the coming of the four horsemen. The town lies in ruins, the people frightened, dejected, and hopeless. Even as the alleged evil has perished in flames, the air of suspicion has not lifted. The villagers continue to search for the demonic wolf—a creature they claim is black as night with eyes red as blood. The animal was seen several times, wandering close to the village. Some even say the beast was spotted with our poor angel, God rest her soul.

I, for my part, still cannot believe that such a sweet, delicate lady has been lost to us. Cassia—I dare not speak her name, but I am haunted by her face, her clear blue eyes, her soft pale locks golden like morning sunlight. How could she have been the Dreamwalker's thrall? How could the Dreamwalker ever have taken her?

I am an apothecary by trade—a man of science—and it frightens me that my hand is stayed when I wish to confess here that I do not believe in such fairy tales. I do not believe that our dear girl was possessed or led astray by any Dreamwalker or her demonic wolf.

Yes, Cassia spent her days wandering the woods. Foolish of her, as the villagers always warn of the dangers that lie within—whether they be real or imagined. Yet she did not listen. Her girlish curiosity was her undoing.

What was in those woods that she found so compelling? That she would continue to go back even when I warned her that people would say ominous things? And where was her father? Had he been more vigilant, I do not believe she ever would have gone missing. Cassia had vanished for days before returning. They said she had been spirited away—that her return was a sign of possession and toil undoubtedly the work of the fabled Dreamwalker. One would think that a missing child's return is cause for celebration, not suspicion and fear.

I sometimes catch myself thinking dreadful things. Had Cassia not returned, would I have been spared the sight of her screaming at the pyre?

I want to believe that this was all avoidable, but I am at a loss. The villagers behaved as though they were the ones possessed. Their eyes glazed over like their souls had left their bodies. Jonathan—a kind and gentle friend, a tailor with no more taste for violence than a saint...I'd never seen anyone more crazed than he last night. He pounded his shovel into the earth, cried out like a madman diseased by the full moon, and nearly bit off his own tongue shouting accusations at the poor girl. He and the other villagers would not stop, they would not listen to reason. And those who tried to reason came to fear for their own lives. It was indeed as though something had taken hold of the townsfolk, compelling them to act with incomprehensible bloodlust.

That thing, I have no doubt, is the superstition of old, which casts fear into the hearts of good people.

The remaining paragraphs were scorched, the photocopy black from where the original paper had been burned. The signature was blotted out, and no name had been marked by town officials anywhere on the document. Nevertheless, this apothecary seemed perfectly sane. His testimonial made sense; he was aware of the village's spiral into hysteria. He clearly blamed superstition, much as Mathias had, for the violent crimes committed against the young woman, Cassia.

And he would not be the first. As Mason pored over the legible testimonials, he began to see a distinct pattern. The nameless apothecary was no exception. Each account mentioned good people—friends, acquaintances, and family who got caught up in the alarm and turned violent without any apparent cause. It was a classic case of groupthink, inspired by the same imposter syndrome seen in cases like Gene Robinson's. Someone would believe a loved one had been abducted and replaced, and as they confided in others, the hysteria spread like a plague. Gene's delusions hadn't contaminated anyone because he hadn't shared them; he'd acted quickly, and he'd acted alone.

But there was another theory about what happened to the town in 1868, written by an Agnes Whitener, a midwife. It was...different, to say the least.

November 3, 1868

Twelve days. They still hunt the black wolf. Their desire for the creature's blood has driven them to madness. The forest burns, the flames engulfing everything, and now even the village is in ashes. They don't understand, but there is something else. I can still feel it, seeping into the soil, rotting the land, corrupting our hearts.

I have been so frightened I could not deliver Mrs. Allison's baby this week. The thought of blood makes me all but faint, and I am not one who is permitted to be squeamish by virtue of my profession. I fear that I may be next. I can see the glances—eyes

*filled with malice, searching for someone to blame, someone new to burn. And yet none
seem aware that they are not themselves.*

*I, too, have not been myself. My home is charred, my belongings reduced to dust, but
I cannot bring myself to leave this cabin for fear that I will see that monstrosity again.
Black as death, a voice one could only expect from the devil himself, and two beaming,
golden eyes that pierce even iron. Those eyes saw everything, they controlled everything.
He was speaking in tongues, and though to me, it sounded like grinding bones and flying
locusts, it seduced Mrs. Sibley, Mr. Hawthorne, and so many others. Even the children
were affected, and those who were not soon learned that it was wisest to stay away as
the town sunk into the depths of hell. The creature was there from beginning to end, as
though watching a play unfold, ensuring that the finale was as grand as he'd planned.
He alone had composed this dark tale.*

*I am certain Doctor Edwards would admit me if he knew any of this. I'd be locked
away for melancholia, hysteria, or the town would have me accused a servant of the
Dreamwalker. There are times when even I question my own perceptions when I think
that perhaps I am too feeble-minded and that I simply cannot endure these executions
and hunts. For my own safety, I may very well discard what has been written here.
Even if I am mad, I'd rather not anyone know of it.*

The testimonial ended there, unsigned even though the photocopy indicated the author's name at the top of the page. It was likely added by whatever authority had collected it before poor Agnes had time to burn her diary.
Some of what she wrote fit. Based on the town records Mason had seen,
there was a forest fire in the fall of 1868 that claimed almost the entire
village. Given that it was nearly winter, and the conditions unfavourable, the
fire must have been started by some persistent hunters. If they were trying
to smoke out this mysterious wolf, they must have set the fires repeatedly—
until they didn't have to. Mason wondered if black wolves wandering the
area became the inspiration for the grotesque illustration in the reports.

Even so, Mason wanted desperately to dismiss Agnes's testimonial. It was
utterly insane. But he also couldn't deny it was consistent with rational
narratives of the trial. Moreover, there were other accounts like Agnes's.
Those who claimed a sinister presence was behind the attack were clearly
unaffected by the delirium—just like those who blamed backwardness and
superstition. If Agnes and her lot didn't sink into the quicksand of hysteria,
but on the contrary were aware of it, they couldn't be dismissed as raving
lunatics. They were, in effect, on the same wavelength as the apothecary
who said the rioting villagers only *seemed* possessed. And those villagers were
neither aware of their distorted thinking nor privy to some diabolical presence. They were far more insane than Agnes could have ever been.

Mason was distraught by what was in front of him. The two versions of the story actually complemented one another, and testimonials like Agnes's accounted for what Mason saw in his dream. He was sure they were describing the same monster he'd witnessed—the horror from which Gavran had saved him.

And yet, the clothes worn by the people in his dream hadn't even approached nineteenth-century fashion. If anything, they had appeared much, much older. Had the monster manifested at two different historical moments? His dream may have shown him the origin of it all.

Unable to hold himself back any longer, Mason threw on a sweater and burst out of the bedroom like he was fleeing for his life. He needed to think and to think he needed to pace. After creeping downstairs, he switched on all the lights and stalked from one end of the lounge to the other.

Stopping in front of the fireplace, Mason looked up at the collage of photos. A chill crawled up his spine as he remembered the ghastly face hovering over him earlier that night. It was Mathias—a pale, emaciated Mathias, his eyes sunken, and his expression forlorn. The young doctor had never believed in ghosts before, but the framework of his beliefs was beginning to crack like the windows of a sunken ship. Under enough pressure, they would inevitably shatter.

"Mason?" It was Annabelle, her voice hoarse with sleep as she tied her blue fleece robe around her waist, stopping halfway down the stairs and peeking over the rail. "What are you doing up at this hour? Is everything all right?"

The warmth he always felt in the old farmhouse seemed all too distant now.

"Hey Annabelle," he greeted meekly. She probably needed rest, yet here she was because of him.

Thumping lightly down the stairs, Annabelle padded over to him, her slippers clapping against her heels. Stopping by the massive stone wall, she glanced up at her son. Much of him was obscured by shadows cast by the dim yellow light of antique lamps. "Would you like some company?"

Nodding, Mason moved away from the fireplace and helped himself to the couch.

Annabelle joining him in the adjacent armchair. "What's eating you?" she nudged. "Is it about earlier?"

"No," he shook his head. "But I wanted to talk to you about something."

"What is it?"

Shifting on the sofa, he nervously rubbed his hands together. "The Dreamwalker. The myth about her. And the truth about this town's history."

He saw her shoulders stiffen like she was preparing for the incoming barrage. It was almost cult-like—the way the villagers protected the fable, and with it, the way they protected themselves from their own history.

"The legend—" Mason cleared his throat. He could still smell the charred wood from the pyre, mingling with the odour of burning flesh. "Is it from the year 1868? Around the time of the trial, when the forest was burned?"

The question seemed to surprise her—almost as though it was less complicated than she'd expected. "No, actually. The legend and the trial are two separate events. The legend is much older, though no one's sure where it originates from."

"I suppose that's why it's a legend," he chuckled. "But you know, I've never actually heard the legend."

Annabelle shifted in the armchair and hesitated. "Well," she began, "the story itself doesn't seem like anything special. Basically, a girl from Black Hollow got lost in the woods one day and met an injured wolf under a willow tree. She helped nurse the wolf back to health, and to thank her, he led her back out of the forest. But once she returned to the village, she was haunted by howls echoing from the forest every night afterwards. The villagers referred to her as the Dreamwalker. Eventually, she became this scary figure who kidnaps girls and inspires chaos."

"That's it? That's hardly ominous." Mason huffed and threw himself back against the cushions. "But there's all this stuff about her coming back. The missing girls, the wolves multiplying—I figured out those are the signs," he pondered aloud, bits of the testimonials floating back to him. "I already know the missing girls end up murdered. But the wolf culls. Did they really think hunting wolves en masse would help?"

Annabelle pushed her hair out of her eyes. She seemed frustrated, her eyes pleading with the relentless researcher in him. "The villagers believe that the Dreamwalker uses wolves to carry out the kidnappings. One in particular—a large, black wolf with red eyes. He'd lure the girl away into the forest and take her to his master. If the girl returned to the village after that, it was understood that she was no longer herself. She was...corrupted, I suppose."

She took a deep breath, her grey eyes hardening as she struggled to divulge what had been festering under the wounds of local history for far too long. "To keep girls from being taken, the villagers hunted wolves mercilessly, almost to extinction. They wanted the black one, but, of course, they never found him. The more fruitless the search, the more they killed. It's impossible to kill a living spirit—a god—but you can kill her familiars."

Mason could hardly believe this was the reason wolves were being slaughtered—that this was the archaic cause Gene Robinson took up to murder his own daughter. There was absolutely nothing like this in the grand narrative —nothing in the textbooks that mentioned such madness. From what most sources had to offer, Black Hollow was a quiet town of minor historical significance. So much of what actually happened here had been lost or woven into folklore only known by locals.

And Annabelle—one of those locals—seemed deeply uncomfortable with what she was revealing. The slaughter of an entire species and the murder of innocent girls, riding on the claims of some old fairy tale—he couldn't imagine any of it sat well with her.

But there was something else—something Mason had taken far too long to realize.

"Annabelle." He swallowed her name like a lump of hot coal, sweat clinging to his back as a chilling realization dawned on him. "There's a wolf cull right now."

Annabelle frowned. "Yes, the town is very much in support of it. I'm not, but most folks here still hold onto the whole Big Bad Wolf image, I suppose."

"No—that's not what I mean." He couldn't get it out. The trial of 1868 had coincided with a wolf cull, and now there was another. The only factor that differentiated murders like Elle's from the mass violence of the trial was the wolf cull. "I don't think you understand," he looked up at her, his eyes widening in both exhilaration and panic as the words fell off his lips. "History is repeating itself. The town *will* go on another hunt."

Annabelle's breath halted. "That can't be," she insisted. "Those times are long over. Elle and girls like her are tragic anomalies. Their murderers acted alone."

"Do you really believe that? Was Gene crazy, or is that just an excuse to ignore a larger pattern?" Mason pressed. "When was the last cull?"

Annabelle's grip tightened on the armrest. "There hasn't been one since 1868."

It was apparent to Mason—those times were not long over. The Dreamwalker and her wolf were still here, two cogs in a wheel that turned endlessly. No matter how many times those cogs were knocked out, the good people of Black Hollow would always find replacements. After all, the wheel had to keep turning.

"I think the villagers feel terrible about their own history," Mason speculated. "They're ashamed. All these signs that the Dreamwalker's coming back—it's just their fear and guilt talking. They have to believe the

Dreamwalker is evil to justify all the violence that's happened. And now they're paranoid. They see her everywhere, in everything."

"That might be part of it," Annabelle nodded. "I'm sure they have to believe those girls were killed for a reason."

"If the townspeople really thought they'd done the right thing, or if they could accept that their ancestors murdered innocent girls, they wouldn't still be worried about the Dreamwalker and her wolves. They'd live in the modern world instead of some prehistoric fable." Mason scowled. "How many people in Black Hollow sympathize with Gene Robinson? Too many, I bet."

The villagers were compelled to exorcise their guilt, to purify the demon that haunted them—over and over again. Every story needed its villain.

Mason had learned about the power of collective guilt when he studied social psychology; he knew it was very real. Still, he couldn't believe that something like this could endure in the psyche of an entire town for so long. He'd witnessed the town's fear of the Dreamwalker, first at the market, then at the hospital when Kai Donovan had escaped.

It was a divine act of mercy that Mason had stolen Kai Donovan's blood, but it irked him that there was a kernel of truth to the nurses' superstitious whispers. Could it really be a coincidence that there was a man with wolf's blood walking around a town where demonic wolves allegedly kidnapped girls? He wanted to laugh out loud, tell himself that none of it mattered and that everything would be back to normal in the morning.

Yet he knew that wouldn't happen.

He needed to know there was a rational explanation, and that he wasn't drowning in ink on the pages of a fairy tale.

"Annabelle, there was something else I forgot to ask."

"Yes?" She looked up with a tired smile.

"What you told me can't be all of the story. Of the Dreamwalker, I mean. What happened after the girl started hearing howls every night? You never mentioned how it ended for her, or for the wolf. Everyone's so scared she's coming back, but why?"

He wanted to know if his dream was the answer.

"There are several versions, actually." His host stood up, moving towards the kitchen where he heard the tap, followed by a glass filling with water. She returned and set a cup down in front of him, then sat in her armchair. "In the simple version, the girl came back, but the villagers cast her out because they were afraid of her. That, of course, is where all the Dreamwalker rumours started."

Mason chugged his water then flopped back, turning his gaze to the ceiling. "Shouldn't they have been happy she wasn't dead in the woods somewhere?"

"It's not that simple." He felt Annabelle's gentle voice reaching out to him, "It was a different time. People believed in different things, like spirit worlds that mirror our world. They were taught to fear the realms where spirits lived."

"Spirits?" Mason sat up. "Like, ghosts?"

Annabelle shook her head. "Ghosts are human spirits—the spirits of the dead. These entities are not *dead*, but more like living spirits, gods, and the familiars I mentioned. They aren't human, but they live in other realms just as we live in this one. In Ireland, the Celts called them elementals and faeries. I remember Matty telling me the Japanese have them too—*kami*, I think. Each culture has them in one form or another. And it's not hard to guess where people thought these spirits' realms could be found."

"The forest," Mason guessed.

"That's right." She nodded wearily as he caught on. "Forests have always been places of mystery. Being spirited away—it's a pagan thing. It's how people explained disappearances. When someone went into the forest and didn't come back, they said the spirits seduced them. But of course, every now and again, someone *would* come back."

"And that freaked people out?"

"It sure did," said Annabelle. "They thought maybe the person had changed and wasn't human anymore. That's how she earned her name, the Dreamwalker. It was because they thought she'd gone somewhere else— somewhere she wasn't supposed to go.

"According to the legend, strange things began to happen after she came back. The villagers thought she'd brought something with her from the other side—something bad. To protect themselves, they drove her out, back into the woods. She disappeared for good after that."

"That's it? She just...vanished?" Mason frowned. It certainly validated what he'd seen in his dream, but a plain old disappearance seemed under-whelming. Still, it explained the villagers' obsession with her return; they must have been convinced she was coming back for revenge.

Annabelle nodded. "Sort of. As far as the villagers' side of the story goes, that's the end, yes. But there is another version, hinting at her fate."

Mason squirmed and leaned forward. "What happened to her?"

Annabelle withdrew her smile. "She went looking for the wolf under the willow, following his howls through the woods. But when she found her way back to the willow where the howls were coming from, it wasn't a wolf waiting for her beneath the tree."

"Not a wolf?" Mason parroted. "Then, what was it?"

An excruciating silence followed. As he waited with a painfully clenched jaw, the old grandfather clock clicked and clacked, each second dragging out until the hand struck the hour, the deep, haunting echo jolting Annabelle out of her musings. Drawing a breath, she sat back and looked Mason in the eye.

The words she spoke next would haunt him—not because they were frightening or unbelievable, but because they were precisely what he expected. It meant he'd already looked truth in the eye and didn't recognize it for what it was. Somehow, he would have rather endured Mathias's ghost, looming over his paralyzed form for a thousand nights to come.

CHAPTER
TWENTY-FIVE

MIYA

THE NIGHT WAS as quiet as freshly fallen snow. Only the sound of footsteps and the pitter-patter of rain on pavement trickled into Miya's awareness. She pulled her umbrella from her backpack and offered to share it with Kai, but he shook his head, looking almost offended.

"I'm not a cat," he told her, so she shrugged and raised the umbrella, happy to hog.

She was bothered by how still her heart was, how absent she remained of any transformative emotion. She'd expected her whole sense of reality to crumble, and yet everything remained intact. This was all, somehow, acceptable. Perhaps it was because the wolf was a recurring theme in her life. Perhaps it was fate; the encounter from her childhood might have been a premonition—a sign of what was to come.

"Do you believe in fate?" Miya asked when the crickets got too loud, knocking around the inside of her skull.

Kai's brows slowly knotted together. "Don't care—don't really think about it," he said gruffly.

"Really?" She turned to him. "You never think about whether things were meant to happen? Or if it's all just coincidence?"

"Nope." He shrugged. "Don't see the point. Even if you knew, so what? Fate's just a nice way of saying you're a hamster on a wheel. Nothing you do matters. And if everything's coincidence, that leaves you with about as much control as fate."

This was the most he'd spoken to her without spewing venomous sarcasm. If anything, he actually sounded *earnest*, like he was willing to have a conversation.

"What about freedom, then?" Miya probed.

Kai shut his eyes and leaned his head back, relishing the raindrops. "Nobody wants freedom. They just like the idea of it." He cracked his eyes open and looked at her, demanding her attention. "What people want is to feel safe."

"So, you don't believe in freedom?" she asked.

"You're missing the point, Lambchop." He pulled a hand from his pocket and poked her cheek. "Things like *fate* and *free will* are just ideas. Shit people make up to feel better because they don't want to be honest about how cruel the world is. If there's such a thing as fate, it's nothing more than your beginning."

"Fate is the beginning?"

"Something like that."

"Why did you come with me, then?" Miya challenged. "Wasn't that a choice you made freely?"

His lips curled in a mischievous smile—like he was willing to play along, for now. "I didn't want to, remember?"

Miya pushed back with growing confidence. "You didn't want to, but you did. Why?"

"I can trust you."

"How would you know that?"

His eyes narrowed to a cutting glare, though his tone remained sincere. "Because you're not afraid of the dark. You came looking for it."

"So?" She frowned.

"Well, you found it," he scoffed. "And I bet you aren't willing to share."

He was right—Miya didn't dare tell anyone about him, and not for entirely selfless reasons. Just like the wolf from her childhood, she wanted this secret to be hers. Even now, there was an urgency crawling up her spine. She wanted to slow down, prolong the journey so they could keep talking, but every step was bringing them closer to their starting point.

Miya's brows felt like they'd been stapled together for hours. Suffering from a bad case of thought constipation, she glanced over at Kai. "Are you the only one of your kind?"

It was an obvious question, or so she thought until she heard him breathe in—slowly—then exhale.

"Do you think I popped out of a test tube or some shit?" His eyes bore holes into the side of her skull, probing the squidgy mass inside.

"I don't know! Did you?" Miya imagined something more like genetic mutation, but she didn't dare say so now.

"Nope," he snorted, tapping her between the legs with the back of his hand. "Popped out of one of those."

Miya's jaw went slack. "What the hell!"

"What?" he feigned. "You didn't think a stork dumped my ass next to a tree, did you?"

His act did little to placate her—though she doubted that was his goal. Known for retaliating with the grace of a maddened bull, Miya silently shut her umbrella. Without hesitation or restraint, she walloped the unborn children out of his gonads, striking him square in the crotch with the pointy end.

"Ass!" she yelled as he doubled over, but not before he managed to grab the umbrella and yank it out of her grip.

"Fuck," he grunted as he dropped her weapon to the ground.

Miya expected him to cuss her out the second he could breathe again—hurling insults and profanities that would make the devil blush. But to her amazement, he began to laugh—albeit a little darkly—his shoulders shaking as he rested his elbows on his knees and hung his head in defeat. "You're not as tender as you look, Lambchop."

Miya gave him a half-hearted pat on the back. This time, she was able to appreciate his wit. "Better chew carefully, or you might choke to death, Wolfie."

He grumbled under his breath and carefully straightened up, then shifted around as if testing to see how much pain she'd put him in. "At least you know how to bite back."

Miya raised an eyebrow. "So you *knew* you were being a dick?"

He shifted his gaze to the treetops. "Maybe. Can't always tell."

"Hasn't anyone ever been nice to you?"

He paused, his eyes turning downwards. "A long time ago, yeah," he replied softly as they veered off the road and onto a gravel path leading towards the trees.

Miya's phone was dead, but she hardly felt the pull to go home despite the late hour. Only when she felt Kai brush past her did she snap back to reality. Blinking away the daze, she quickly followed suit. She wasn't sure what to say, let alone what to feel. She didn't want the excursion to end, but there was no excuse to drag it out any longer. Miya imagined inviting him over for dinner, but as the scenario unfolded, she found herself wincing at the aftermath: Kai smashing cockroaches with a closed fist and Patricia coming after him with a spatula.

The silence stretched out like a shadow at sunset.

"Sorry, I wouldn't make a very good house pet." He flashed her a playful smile—a genuine smile—then started walking towards the trees. It was almost as if the bastard knew what she was thinking.

"Who'd want to house train you anyway?" Miya called after him, her heart sinking like a pebble at the bottom of a murky pond.

He lifted his arm and waved without turning.

How did he spend his days in there? Was he often a wolf, or a man? Miya couldn't help but wonder—which side dominated?

And, if he was here, did he know of the Dreamwalker? Would he know what happened to Elle Robinson after she'd disappeared in the woods?

Miya was about to call out to him again, to ask him if they could talk about it, but before she could open her mouth, he stopped, his every muscle frozen when a sound like thunder rolled through the air. Birds flew up from the treetops towards the sky, the forest growing eerily still when the echo faded out.

Time slowed as Miya pushed past her stupor, then took a step towards him. "Was that a gunshot?"

"Go home," he commanded. As if knowing she would protest, he turned to glare at her over his shoulder. His nose and brow creased in a scowl that looked more animal than human. It was a warning.

"But—" Before she could finish, he stalked into the woods, leaving her to wallow in her uncertainty. She didn't trust what she'd seen on his face, but what he did with his anger wasn't her problem.

She *was* curious, though.

Deciding she'd regret not knowing more than she'd regret knowing, Miya rushed after him, running into the woods in hopes of catching up. *You're going to get shot,* the reasonable side of her screamed. Her body started shaking, though she was unsure if it was from adrenaline or fear. She didn't remember the last time she'd been in the forest. It was pitch-black, the thick, crooked branches of ancient trees blotting out most of the starlight.

"Kai?" she hissed, hoping he'd return to save her from her own stupidity. But he didn't respond, and Miya didn't hear anything around her resembling human footsteps. She wandered further in, holding her breath as she traipsed along the forest floor, startled by every crack underfoot. As she stopped to look around again, a man shrieked from somewhere nearby, his voice shrill and laced with fear. Jerking at the sound, Miya tried to locate where it'd come from when another shot rang out—this time closer. Heart pounding, her instincts told her to run before she ended up on the back of a milk carton while her body lay rotting in the woods, but then she remembered she'd have to endure tomorrow not knowing what happened today.

Pathology winning over survival, Miya fumbled through the trees in the direction of the bang. As she approached, she saw two—no, three figures tussling. Leaves shook loose from their branches as Kai slammed a shorter man into a tree then struck him to the ground. He landed with a hard thud and raised his rifle over his head for protection, but Kai pried it from his hands and struck the other, taller man on the side of the head with the butt of the gun. Miya couldn't tear her eyes away as he fell over, blood dripping from his mouth as he hawked out a tooth. Kai snapped the rifle over his knee and whipped half the weapon further into the woods. Leaning over, he grabbed the bloodied man by the throat and held the end of the broken gun against his victim's neck.

"What the hell!" Miya yelled and ran towards them. She had no intention of ending up an accomplice to murder. "Put that thing down!"

Kai turned his torrid gaze on her. She could barely see his face in the shadows, the moonlight illuminating just enough for her to catch a glimpse of the wolf she was trying to talk out of a kill. His expression was bestial— his face contorted in a feral snarl, every pore bleeding with rage. He lifted his head to take her in, the movement slow and measured. His eyes were wild, predatory, and Miya swore that, for a moment, they flashed blood red as the dim lunar glow passed over his face. To say he was displeased with her presence was a grave understatement. He still held the man by the neck while crouching over him, a hunter ready to deliver the finishing blow.

"What the fuck are you?" The battered man gurgled through the blood in his mouth, one of his eyes swollen shut as he fought to keep conscious. To Miya's horror, he wasn't talking to Kai. He was turned to her, gawping as though she was the devil incarnate. "You some kind of witch?" he bellowed. "Go rot in hell, you cunt!"

Miya stumbled to the side and hit a tree, winded by the hatred in his tone. She couldn't fathom why she deserved that, or why she was being attacked at all. A cocktail of fear and revulsion burned in her throat. She looked up at Kai, searching, and saw that his eyes were still trained on her. His expression seemed to soften, albeit briefly, before he returned his attention to the mass of bruises beneath him. He was stone cold again, and in her bones, Miya was sure he meant to kill that man.

Miya opened her mouth to stall him when she heard a click—the safety lock on a gun releasing. She didn't know where from, and she didn't have time to look. Kai kissed his teeth before he dropped the man and lunged the other way, his figure a blur in the darkness. Miya yelped when another firearm went off. She ducked and squeezed her eyes shut, clapping her hands over her ears. As the ringing faded out, she gradually became aware of her own breathing again. She felt no pain, frantically patting over her torso as she warily opened her eyes.

"Shit!" The words came muffled, like her ears were stuffed with cotton. Her limbs hung like icicles, but she willed her legs to move, tripping over a tree root as she struggled to lift her feet. After a few clumsy steps, she could hear the crisp crunch of earth beneath her shoes again, the feedback helping to orient her. She saw something heavy drop into the leaves to her left, followed by the sound of a gut-wrenching snap. The man she presumed to be the shooter howled in pain. Miya moved towards the screams until she could see him, his arm twisted to an impossible angle as he dropped to his knees. Kai emerged from the shadows nearby, ramming the man's skull straight into a tree. He lost consciousness and crumpled to the ground, unmoving. Growling under his breath, Kai stepped over the body and made his way over to her.

"You all right?" he asked, his voice a familiar comfort amid unfamiliar brutality.

Miya's tongue was in a vice, so she nodded, her body still trembling. Now that he was close, she could see his face again; he was back to normal, with little more than a frown of concern to show for the violence he'd just inflicted.

"Come on," he coaxed gently, grabbing her hand and tugging at her to follow him. But the moment she tried to walk, her muscles dissolved into a heap of useless fibres. Her knees buckled, gravity doing its best to topple her before she grabbed onto a tree to keep from falling over.

Kai halted upon feeling her resistance, then sighed as he looked her up and down. "Come here," he murmured, putting an arm around her waist and picking her up. He grumbled as he carried her out of the woods. "This is why I told you to go home, you damn sheep."

Miya clung to him despite repeated attempts to peel herself away. "Y-you would have killed those men," she stuttered.

"Yes," he replied without emotion. "And you would have never known."

She was silent until they were out of the forest and he put her down. She saw blood on his arm, soaking through the grey of his sweatshirt. "Why?" she asked.

Noticing her eyes trailing down his arm, he raised his hand and sucked the blood off the back of his thumb. He didn't appear to have been hurt. "They were hunting somewhere they shouldn't have been hunting."

"That's it?" There was an edge to her voice. She was angry—angry at herself for getting involved when she could have gone home and taken a hot shower. Angry at him for nearly killing two men—innocent or not—for reasons he couldn't properly explain. To make matters worse, he looked annoyed that she was questioning him. If he had no qualms killing trespassing hunters, what else was he capable of?

"Did you have something to do with Elle Robinson?"

The lines on his face deepened. "No," he said tightly.

"You didn't kidnap her?" His violent outburst soaked into her until she spiralled into an abyss of dark possibilities.

"No," Kai repeated, his tone even. "That much, I remember."

"What the *hell* does that mean?" the alarm echoed from her words as she stepped back. His jaw clenched, his eyes like stone as he seemed to bite down on something bitter and hold it in.

"I woke up next to her body. And a few others like her in the past," he confessed. "Always the girls who go missing."

Miya took another step back, preparing for flight.

"I'd never seen any of them before in my life!" Uncertainty broke through his eyes. "I could smell them, calling for help. I'd follow the scent, but I never remember finding them. Next thing I know, I'm waking up next to their corpses. No bite marks, no blood. Always the work of a human."

Miya slowed her retreat, considering his words. There was nothing disingenuous about him; he was crude and unyielding, inconsiderate even, but he never struck her as manipulative. Given Kai's choice of habitat, it wasn't unthinkable that a wolf would sniff out dead bodies.

"The murderer is always someone close to the victim," she told him. "Elle's father confessed to killing her, so it couldn't have been you."

His chest rose and fell with a huff of relief. "I didn't do it."

A lump welled in Miya's throat. She didn't know why she'd suspect him, but after what she'd seen—both from him and the man who'd verbally assaulted her—faith in her own perception had whittled down to a thin, brittle sliver.

Seeing her on the verge of tears, Kai sighed and slumped his shoulders.

"Go home," he said softly, nodding towards the road leading back into town. "You don't belong here."

She wondered if maybe he was right. Maybe she shouldn't have been there. She stared at her feet, considering that she was out of her depth. Gravity was pulling her back to earth, reminding her that this was absurd. When she looked back up again, she half expected Kai to have vanished.

But he was still there, his expression unreadable as he watched her with full attention. Feeling some of her anger melt away, she offered him a weak smile. He didn't react, but as she was about to oblige his wish and leave, she saw a ghost of a smile in return—tired and worn, hesitant, and even a little shattered. It halted her step until he severed his gaze and turned his back to her.

With no reason left to stay, she too turned and headed back to the road that led home. She wondered if those men were alive—if Kai would go back to check, perhaps finish the job when she was no longer around. Miya placed a hand over her belly as her insides churned at the thought, then stopped and glanced over her shoulder. She watched Kai disappear back into the forest, like the phantom from her dreams.

CHAPTER
TWENTY-SIX
THE DESCENT

THE SKY WAS A SHEER WHITE—NO *sun or moon visible through the pale, cloaking tract. It was as though time had stopped in this realm, waiting for Miya to return before oiling its rusty gears. There was no movement or sound, no indication of life.*

Miya stood at the edge of the forest where the Dreamwalker had been waiting. She'd promised to follow her—wherever she went. But for now, Miya sensed she had time to spare. She ventured forward, leaving the village behind her.

The pale, blank sky turned to night, the moon high and the wind crisp. The familiar scent of pine and oak sent a reverberating current through Miya, the sound of rustling leaves and the thrum of the forest's heartbeat quickening her steps. She could hear the wolf howling from somewhere within, waiting for her to find him.

Miya focused on drawing closer to the willow tree where she knew the wolf waited. There was no path to follow; she was lost in the labyrinth, his summon an invisible thread tugging her through wringing wooden walls—walls that had no intention of playing fair. They twisted and coiled, conjuring shadows that hampered her efforts to align herself in their midst.

Miya knew the Dreamwalker was watching, waiting to see if she'd pass her test— if she'd find her way back to the willow. She didn't know what the Dreamwalker wanted with her, what the wolf wanted with her, but she felt compelled. As she moved deeper into the forest, the landscape behind her morphed with sentient expression. The frayed bark flaked from the trees, spirits crawling under their threadbare skin like snakes under sand, trembling and writhing in anticipation of what she would do next. A breeze passed through the branches—music inspiring the leaves to dance. Were they celebrating? She grew more frantic as the howls rung louder, closer, and more imminent.

When Miya reached the small, circular glade, the howls faded into the wind, and all descended into quiet. Only the quivering of the tiny emerald blades gilding the willow's swaying canopy could be heard in the surrounding stillness. There, the willow stood waiting for her, anticipating her return. Overcome with familiarity and relief, Miya felt the grand tree breathing into the earth, welcoming her back. As she approached, the shroud rifted, revealing a shadowy figure nestled against a cleft carved into the tree's impressive trunk. Its form was difficult to discern, masked by careening stems, their movement rhythmic like pendulums. But as the shadow's wistful presence drew Miya in, her perception sharpened, and she became aware of something that rattled her equilibrium.

The shadow was not what she expected.

CHAPTER

TWENTY-SEVEN

THE FIRST THING Miya felt was cold air biting her arms, neck, and face. Her hair whipped past her shoulders as the disorientation hit, and gravity forced her to catch herself before she fell. Her eyes slowly adjusted to the darkness and unfamiliar shadows.

As Miya looked around, she realized she was outside, the streetlight in front of the neighbour's house revealing her location. Gradually, she recognized the shapes of the buildings, the patches of grass, and the poorly lit road running through her street. She was standing on Patricia's driveway just a few paces from the alley leading to her basement. Too shocked to panic, Miya's mind was a white blank as she scanned her memory for clues to how she'd gotten there.

"Miya?" someone called from behind. It was Patricia, peaking out of the garage with her keys in hand. Miya heard the faint clicks from the engine of Patricia's car; it must have been running recently.

"Miya, are you all right?" she asked.

"I..." She felt woozy—swooning and barely managing to find her balance. "I think I was sleepwalking."

"What!" Her landlady gasped and strode over. "You don't remember coming out here?" She frowned, noticing Miya was barefoot in her pyjamas.

"Maybe it's just stress." Miya forced a smile, not wanting to worry her, but deep down she knew it wasn't the stress. Maybe it was time to see a doctor...or a psychiatrist.

"Let's just get you inside." Patricia put an arm around her as she guided her towards the house. "I'll get dressed and take you to the hospital. Something might be wrong."

Miya resisted; she didn't want to owe her any more than she already did. "Patty, I feel just fine. I can get checked out in the morning and—"

Psst.

The quiet hiss stopped Miya mid-sentence. She scanned Patricia's face, but her landlady hadn't heard it. Convinced the sound came from behind her, Miya turned and looked towards the street. There, on the other side of the road, was a figure cloaked in an iridescent, violet-black mantle.

It was the Dreamwalker.

Her long, dark hair flowed around her, but her face remained concealed by the sharp, beak-shaped mask, the tip curling just past her chin. Miya could see most of her mouth, the contours of her cheekbones, and the outline of her jaw, though nothing that would help identify her. Feeling her heart tear against her ribcage like it was trying to escape, Miya sucked in a sharp breath, ready to call attention to the apparition when something seized her entire body. Unable to move, fascination and horror invaded her bones. The Dreamwalker smiled faintly, drawing a finger to her lips before they split open into a wicked grin.

Hush, the gesture spoke. Then, like vapour, she vanished from the physical realm.

"Miya?" Someone was shaking her shoulder. "Are you all right, sweetie?"

Words failed her, so she shook her head, frantic as she stared into the empty space across the road.

"Hang on, sweetheart, I'll get my car."

Miya's chest tightened, her ears deafening as black spots peppered her vision. The panic held her in its clutches as tightly as the Dreamwalker just had.

"I can't see," she whimpered, terror sinking its claws in before vertigo made her crumble.

Patricia grabbed her arm, yanking her to her feet.

"Just breathe, Miya." She stroked the girl's hair. Miya clutched on to Patricia's voice and focused on her breaths—pulling the air into her lungs and pushing it back out. Gradually, the darkness lifted, and she could make out the brick patterns on the side of the house. She saw the fear jump out of Patricia's smoky eyes as she helped her to the wall.

Propping herself up, Miya watched through grainy vision as Patricia rushed into the garage. Minutes later, an old, burgundy Chevy Impala pulled out. Leaving the engine running, Patricia jumped out and circled around the front to help her.

"I'm fine," Miya mumbled, stumbling forward until she reached the back seat. She curled up against the window after Patricia shut the door, the fright and confusion sapping her strength.

As they pulled out of the driveway, the faintly playing radio lulled Miya into a light sleep. She faded in and out of consciousness, though she could feel herself searching for something as she fluttered between realms. Straddling the border, one foot in each world, she knew that she was on the verge of something. It was right there, waiting for her to grasp it from the other side and pull it back with her.

The car came to a stop, tugging Miya from her ethereal wandering, and she sat up just in time to avoid falling out of the car as Patricia swung open the backseat door.

"This is probably a waste of time," Miya told her glumly. "They're going to take a look at my vitals, tell me there's nothing wrong, then send us home."

"They might run some tests."

Miya's heart dropped. She didn't want to be stuck in the hospital until tomorrow, but she tried to look on the bright side: at least she'd get checked out by a medical professional who could tell her if her marbles were rolling away.

At the front desk, Miya realized she didn't have her health card. When told by the nurse that she'd be billed for hospital services, Patricia swore loudly but offered to go back and pick up the card. The nurse accepted this and admitted Miya as she handed her keys over to Patricia.

Miya looked around the waiting room, grateful it wasn't busy. A lady in ripped jeans and a biker jacket slept against her girlfriend, her head teetering as it nearly rolled off the other woman's shoulder. She jerked awake, blinking in momentary confusion before resuming her nap. Miya smiled, thinking they looked cute. Scanning the rows of chairs, she noticed movement from the top left corner of the window above the magazine rack. A dark shape was perched on a swaying branch outside.

"So how can we help you?" A different nurse drew her attention back to the desk, her voice friendlier than her colleague's. She was at least a head shorter than Miya and didn't look much older—mid-to-late twenties, perhaps.

"I woke up standing in the driveway, then nearly blacked out," Miya told her, debating whether to mention what she'd seen. As the nurse looked up at her, Miya noticed she had heterochromia; both her eyes were blue, but the left one had a brown freckle at the bottom of her iris.

Tucking her strawberry blonde locks behind her ear, she sat Miya down and recorded her vitals. "No fever. Blood pressure and heart rate are normal." After taking note, she removed the thermometer. "Has this ever happened before?"

Miya shook her head. "No, but I do struggle with insomnia and anxiety. I think I also—"

The nurse smiled when she broke off. "Yes?"

Miya swallowed, feeling her fingertips tingle. "I think I saw something when I woke up."

The nurse didn't appear concerned, giving her a sympathetic squeeze on the arm. "Hallucinations are not uncommon with sleep disorders. Let's see what the doctor says."

She slipped a wristband over Miya's hand and led her through the double doors to the next room, where she was left behind a set of curtains. A hospital gown awaited on the cot. After changing, she whipped the beige screen open in case Patricia came looking.

The Amazonian woman could be seen from across the ward, marching through the halls with purpose. She eventually found her troublesome tenant and huffed about the nurses up front—preposterously disorganized, she'd called them. She handed Miya her backpack with her wallet, keys, cell phone, and a change of clothes complete with warm socks and her favourite sneakers. After thanking her, Miya urged her to go home and rest.

"You sure?" Patricia raised an eyebrow. "You haven't even seen the doctor yet."

"I'll be okay," Miya reassured her with a smile. "The nurse didn't seem too concerned."

"Honey," Patricia rolled her eyes, "they're trained to downplay everything. Last time I was here, they told me my ovarian torsion was a kidney stone—ended up losing one of my girls because they didn't get me into surgery on time."

"Sorry," Miya winced.

Patricia sighed, leaning into the hall. "Well, you'll probably be here a while. I guess I could go home and take a catnap. If you need anything, my phone's on."

"Honestly, you've done more than enough for me. I can find my way once I'm out of here."

Miya's landlady gave her a once-over. "All right, but don't you hesitate if you need anything," she scolded.

"Thanks, Patty." Miya kicked her feet as she avoided eye contact. "You've really been great to me."

"Oh, hush," Patricia waved her off. She gathered her things along with

Miya's pyjamas. Sentimentality to Patricia was like water to the Wicked Witch of the West.

After she left, the wait dragged on longer than Miya expected. A couple of confused nurses came around, wondering if she was the patient who needed a CT scan or a toe x-ray. It wasn't until three hours later, at six in the morning, that someone resembling a physician graced her with his presence. He had a lab coat and a stethoscope, so she figured he'd do.

"Good morning, I'm Dr. Callahan," he greeted with a noticeable West-Indian accent—a strange contrast to the total lack of inflection in his tone. It was so flat Miya had to refrain from asking how many hours ago his soul died. With puffy, bloodshot eyes, he quickly scanned the chart while scratching through his dense, wiry curls. "No family history of sleep disorders?"

Miya shook her head, and Dr. Callahan frowned. "Says here you experienced a hallucination. Have you been sleep deprived? Taking any kinds of stimulants or recreational drugs? Drinking more than usual?"

"Not much of a party animal, though I haven't been sleeping well." Miya imagined her eyes resembled those of a dead fish as she accidentally mimicked his monotony.

"Any reason for the lack of sleep?" he asked, leaning over to check her breathing and shine a light into her eyes and ears.

She hesitated, unsure of whether to disclose that she'd been hearing wolf howls, hallucinating the Dreamwalker, losing her memories about town lore, waking up with sleep paralysis, and having nightmares she couldn't remember for the life of her. But Miya knew she wasn't hallucinating because of sleep deprivation; no—the sleep deprivation was worsened by the hallucinations.

"Just stressed with school and financial stuff."

"Got it," he said, writing something down again. "If you've been struggling with anxiety and insomnia, I could write you a referral to the psych department."

"Are they going to put me on drugs?" she asked.

He looked up from the chart. "Maybe, but you're always free to refuse."

"Right," she sighed. "Sure, I'll take the referral."

"I'll have it sent in right away. In the meantime, you could probably do with a break." He pulled out his prescription pad and wrote something down, then tore the sheet away and handed it to her. "Herbal supplements, for sleep."

Dr. Callahan clicked his pen and dropped it back into his breast pocket, preparing to leave. "Just one thing," he added, turning back to her. "You should avoid telling people about this. Don't go bragging to your friends. With the rumours going around and the recent tragedy, hearing about another girl your age wandering out of the house in the dead of night might ramp up paranoia. And well—be careful. If it happens again, come back. We can always put you in the sleep clinic for observation."

The prospect of being hooked up to machines was hardly appealing. Like hell she'd be able to sleep in a sea of wires while men and women in lab coats studied her brain waves. And if she really was at risk, wouldn't it be reckless to tell other townspeople? Elle had been killed by her own father. The less people knew about what was happening to her, the less likely she was to end up on the front page of the newspaper. She wondered why he was so concerned, anyway. "Are you saying the Dreamwalker tried to spirit me away tonight?"

A passing woman dressed in a frumpy pink blouse and a green wool skirt slowed just as Miya uttered the D-word. Her face paled, and her eyes bulged before she continued on her way, when Miya cut her with a withering glare.

"That's certainly what some people would say," Callahan replied carefully.

Miya tried to feign indifference. "You don't actually believe that, do you?"

Dr. Callahan shrugged, regarding her with something between nonchalance and the will of a good Samaritan. "I won't say I believe anything. Only been living in the area for a few years and can't say I've ever paid much attention, but I'll tell you this." He stopped, glancing past the curtains to make sure the two of them were safely out of earshot. "Not too long ago, I had a real strange fellow come knocking on my door here in the ER. Strange enough to make the locals working with me lock their daughters away and pull out their rosaries. Now, kid, you don't have to believe any of that, but what you believe doesn't matter much." He threw his thumb over his shoulder, out towards the locals. "It's what they believe that matters. Gene Robinson proved that point well enough."

Miya's gut writhed like she'd swallowed charcoal. A slow burn travelled up her oesophagus until she tasted the ash on her tongue—bitter and astringent. Perfectly comfortable moments ago, she now felt cold. The chill was deep, running straight through the marrow of her bones. Who was more dangerous? The Dreamwalker, or Miya's own neighbours?

Everything she'd experienced up until then suggested she *was* being spirited away. She wondered if it was her fault for entertaining the possibility of finding evidence of the Dreamwalker. Now the Dreamwalker was filling her head with illusions, blocking her memories, drawing her closer, and coercing her to follow. And who knew what she was doing to those around her. Perhaps she'd been responsible for Gene's insanity, too.

Miya felt Callahan's eyes on her. Was her panic obvious? If her struggles were the result of a sleep disorder, it was welcome news. And yet, Miya knew it couldn't be that simple.

Part of her wanted to burst into tears and tell him everything, to bury herself in the safety of adult authority and let him decide what was best. But she was too stubborn. How could she really believe she was the target of a supernatural kidnapping? Where had her skepticism gone?

Yet there was a part of her that wanted it. Was the Dreamwalker coming for her because she *wanted* to disappear? To get away from her life and live in some distant fairy tale? Miya had always yearned for something more. She'd hoped for it since she was a child, since the day she saw the wolf at the playground.

She supposed a better question was: how could she *not* believe? Wasn't meeting Kai proof that there *was* something more?

A light smack on the shoulder jolted her back to the room. "What?" She looked around, bewildered.

Dr. Callahan guffawed, his mood shifting. "Oh, come on," he said, "no need to take it that seriously. I'm just saying, don't put fuel on the fire, okay?"

"Yeah," Miya sighed. "I'll try not to."

With nothing left to be done, he informed her she'd receive a call about her psych appointment, then left her to change back into her clothes. She couldn't wait to leave the hospital, her eagerness forgoing protocol as she walked out the front doors without even checking to see if Callahan had signed her discharge papers. Frankly, she didn't really care. She looked healthy enough, so no one stopped her as she all but slammed through the revolving doors with the restraint of a Soviet tank.

Stopping a few paces past the entranceway, Miya looked up and stretched. It was still dark out, the sun just barely lightening the eastern sky to a dim, blue glow. As she turned to her right, she was startled by a large raven perched in one of the trees by the waiting room windows. He was staring at her, his head lilting to the side as he examined her curiously.

"Yeah, don't ask," she told the raven, not caring if she sounded crazy. "It's been a long night." She watched him tilt his head the other way like he was responding to her. Amused by the unusual gesture, she smiled, her body feeling lighter. "I'll see you around, buddy."

As Miya cut through the parking lot, she swung her backpack over her shoulder and considered where she wanted to go. She needed a detour before heading home. Tugging the hoodie around her shoulders, she zipped it up as a cold wind blasted her head-on. Miya knew she'd be pushing her luck, but she could think of only one place in the world appropriate for a pit stop: her sanctuary. And it wasn't just in hopes of some magical encounter. After all, it had been a week since she and Kai parted ways. This time, she *really* needed to think. Besides, Miya figured if the Dreamwalker intended to kidnap her, she wouldn't do so in broad daylight. That didn't seem like her style. No—she'd want to come for Miya when it was least expected.

It was a long but worthwhile walk; Miya got to watch the sunrise for the first time in ages. She took a seat on the swing and let her body sway. With only the sound of the wind and the creak of metal chains accompanying her, her tension melted away.

She wondered if she was sane to be frightened *and* excited. She could be kidnapped, and yet all she could think about was what might await on the other side. Where did the thrill come from? Was it the prospect of going to a new world? Of learning truths she couldn't otherwise learn? Miya didn't even know if such a journey was possible, but she supposed it didn't matter. It might have been illogical, completely counter to the way reality was supposed to work, but Miya reckoned truth didn't follow the tide of possibility. Whatever tide truth drifted on, it had its own ruler. It just wasn't something anyone would know about.

CHAPTER
TWENTY-EIGHT

KAI

HUMANITY WAS INSUFFERABLE. Up until recently, Kai had been spared its touchy-feely, bleed-your-heart-out and cry-until-your-eyes-turn-to-pudding bullshit. He never had any trouble making decisions, no qualms or second thoughts about turning his back to someone and leaving them behind. Either they left, or he would.

Relationships with people were rare, but they happened, either by accident or out of temporary necessity. He'd once gotten close to a waitress who took her smoke breaks by one of the dumpsters he'd sift through for supplies. He was content to let her bring him leftovers from the kitchen, maybe even share a drink as she complained about her good-for-nothing boyfriend, but when she wanted to get to know him, learn about his baggage —he bailed. Maybe she didn't mind dumpster divers, but he already knew he couldn't be himself with her even if he wanted to. There was no room for sentimentality, let alone the bat-shit crazy that came with it. The dial on people's emotions was more fragile than a frat boy's ego.

And Kai was no stranger to fragility; he had his own wounds to lick. Volatile emotions were the reason he'd almost spent his weekend burying dead bodies had it not been for the girl's timely interference. He didn't need more blood on his hands.

After chasing her off, he left the hunters for dead, hoping they'd be bitten by something poisonous and eaten by maggots. He resisted going back to finish them off, the agitation and restlessness pawing at him with newly sharpened claws. In the following days he tried everything to settle it —hunting, starting fights with drunken men, tree stumps, and walls. He picked women he could sense wanted him and distracted himself with one-night stands—a balm he usually sought when the isolation grew too weighty. Even if Kai wasn't great with people, he understood their bodies far better than their words. People smelled different when they were horny.

He went through the motions—tearing through animal flesh, splitting his knuckles open against bone and concrete, trying to lose himself between a woman's thighs. Yet a bitter taste remained despite all the death, blood, and sex he tried to wash it away with. Something had gotten hold of him, infecting him with a desire he couldn't satiate by indulging his primal urges. He didn't understand it, he didn't like it, he didn't want it.

You don't know what you want.

"Not now," Kai growled under his breath, squeezing his eyes shut as a searing pain shot through his skull, the voice invading him.

You should take her before someone else does. Just don't tear her throat out like that last one.

"What *last one?*" Kai snarled at the air, his head snapping up towards the trees—but as always, there was nothing there. He knew Abaddon was goading him, trying to make him believe he'd done things he'd never do. Thanks to Miya, he was now certain he hadn't hurt any of those girls. His mind couldn't remember, but his body did; he'd followed the smell of their fear, driven by a peculiar impulse to ward off whatever was harming them.

Only he never made it in time. Because of Abaddon, he was always too late. It was a fucking curse.

You know the lamb is next.

The pain grew more intense, his face twisting as a dizzying, high pitched squeal pierced his eardrums, vertigo and nausea rocking his insides. Kai crumpled and tucked his head between his knees, clenching his teeth and refusing to give his nemesis the satisfaction of even a whimper.

He'd hoped for a quiet day in the woods near his cabin—maybe a run if he wound up on all fours. But the migraine was crippling, and he almost wished he could sink into the autumn leaves and disappear into the ground where it was dark and cold.

Kai rolled onto his back and stared up at the sky, flopping an arm over his stomach. Closing his eyes, he waited for the spinning to stop, the dark energy gradually bleeding out of him and into the earth. When he felt stable, he dragged himself to his feet and headed towards town. Kai knew exactly what he was looking for, and his instincts were good enough to lead him there. As he approached the forest's edge, he slowed his pace, prowling the periphery and moving towards the distinct sound of squeaking metal—the swing set at Old Market Playground.

There she was, brooding as usual.

He knew she'd be there, but he didn't want to know why he knew. He just did, and that was enough. He watched from the shelter of the trees, unable to stop himself from smiling in private amusement as she fiddled with the zipper of her hoodie, then sighed longingly. The damn girl was waiting for him.

And like a good puppy, you came running home.

Abaddon was there to piss on the moment. Of course, his antagonist had a point: why'd he sniff her out like a bloodhound? Kai faltered, wondering if he should retreat in case his nemesis plotted to coerce him into murdering a chipmunk in front of his sulking pet girl. He imagined that wouldn't go over too well. But the sinister presence seemed unusually subdued—more irritating than dangerous. Did the lamb do something to declaw the phantom dick? Was she making him bashful?

Before he could change his mind, Kai stalked out of the woods. Predictably, the girl's head shot up as he kicked past the shrubbery. She jumped out of the swing, her arms pressed rigidly to her sides as she took a cautious step forward. He ignored the stupefied look on her face and marched right up to her. Grabbing the zipper on her hoodie, he yanked it up to her chin—annoyed by the repetitive buzzing caused by her fussing. He felt the blood rush to her face and made eye contact for the first time as he glanced up to check how pink her cheeks were.

Neither of them seemed able to speak—her expression unreadable as he stared back at her with a tepid frown.

"Huh, you're ovulating."

Feeling a current of air rush towards his face, Kai stepped back as she swatted at him. He reached forward and whipped the hood up over her head, fighting the smile that threatened to break out on his face.

"Jesus Christ, why would you say that!"

"Because I can smell it." He grinned rakishly. "Guess I can understand why you're back." His mood was improving now that he had an outlet for his frustrations.

"Right." She blasted him with a glare as she peeled the hood back. "Because I need to hang around the playground to think of all the bad, bad things I could do to you." She pursed her lips to keep from laughing. "You could have just said hello!"

"Hello," he echoed blithely, his lips twisting into a smirk as she cast her eyes to the ground and squirmed under his gaze. "Aw, come on Lambchop, I'm sure you've already done plenty to me in that twisted little head of yours," he cracked, watching as she wrapped her arms tightly around her abdomen. He removed his ratty old leather jacket and tossed it to her.

Her arms flailed awkwardly as she struggled to catch his coat, staring at it like he'd just lobbed her a new-born. There would be no future for her in softball, at least.

"You're letting me wear it?" She looked up at him, perplexed like it'd never occurred to her that he was capable of being thoughtful.

Damn, Kai thought. She really must have taken him for a piece of shit. "You look cold," he told her with a shrug. His core body temperature was higher, and his metabolism more efficient at keeping him warm. Cargo pants and a sweater worked just fine. He watched as she silently put his jacket on, zipping it all the way up and throwing on the hood.

"How do I look?" she asked, the sleeves flopping past her fingertips, her face hidden as she lowered her head and stared at the ground.

"Like an armless mugger," he replied, strolling up to her and flicking the hood off. He searched her face for signs of discomfort. "Warm enough?"

She nodded, lightly patting him on the arm. "Thanks."

Something about her made him feel more comfortable in his own skin, which often felt foreign even to him. She seemed to swing between mousy introversion and full-blown aggression, but he kind of liked the latter. Now that she was in front of him and they were alone, he took his time drinking her in. The dark circles under her eyes, presumably from lack of sleep, the fidgeting and flighty glances when she caught him staring too long, as if she was the one who had something to be embarrassed about. The duality of her insecurity and boldness needled him, spurred a desire to rile her up and see what it wrought. At one moment she'd recoil when he loomed over her, and the next she'd burrow in his clothes and greet him with her fists. Was she really a lamb, or a timid lioness?

Kai realized he was attracted to her. He wouldn't have spent so much time picking her apart otherwise. But attraction was easy, commonplace. It was the fact that she'd gleaned his nature that made him stew in consideration. Perhaps he could use a friend—one that wouldn't forget him after a raucous night at a dive bar.

As he inspected her, she grew edgy under his gaze, her brows creasing as she shuffled on her feet. He could taste the snarky remark about to spring from her lips when he heard a rustle coming from the woods. Kai directed his attention to the space behind her, waiting for one—no, two—figures to emerge.

It wasn't until an old man and his beagle came stumbling out onto the grass that the girl noticed they weren't alone. She spun around to face the unwelcome duo. The floppy-eared mutt was on high alert, his stubby little legs twitching with anticipation while he held his head high, nose wriggling. The dumb thing was confounded by Kai; he smelled like a wolf but looked like a man. Whining in confusion, the genetically-befouled fleabag pawed nervously at the ground.

"Come on," Kai mumbled, grabbing the girl's hand and leading her straight into the woods.

"Where are we going?" She squeezed his hand, but he couldn't tell if it was resistance or reassurance.

"Away," he said simply, pulling her into the trees before the canine sausage began barking at him. From the corner of his eye, he saw her glance back towards the playground and halted. "You don't have to come with me."

Her lips pressed together as if to stop the uncomfortable truth from worming out. Eventually, it did. "I don't want to end up as one of those dead girls you wake up to. I know you didn't do it, but—"

"I'm a shit magnet." Kai's lips quirked. "You don't have to explain yourself."

"Thanks," she returned his smile smile, "but I don't feel safe at home either."

Kai adjusted his fingers around her hand. "Why not?"

She took a deep breath and held it until it seemed to hurt. "It's complicated. Where were you going to take me?"

Kai permitted the evasion, for now. "Where I live." He honestly had nothing better to say—no where else to go that didn't require money he didn't have, and he wasn't about to have her feed him a third time.

"Does this mean we're friends?"

He'd entertained the notion moments earlier, but the reciprocation brought the possibility too close for comfort. Kai didn't have friends—didn't know how to have them. He glanced at their joined hands, then let go like he was dropping a thorny rose. "Only if you don't talk about it."

Her expression shifted to one of amusement as she waited for him to continue. When he didn't move, she offered him a balmy smile. "I think I can keep a secret. And I *am* curious about where you live."

Was she now? He narrowed his eyes, caught between grabbing her hand and chasing her off. "Feel free to tag along then."

"Ok," she chirped without hesitation, content to follow him into the man-eating labyrinth of trees and wilderness.

He faltered, about to bark at her for taking candy from strangers in windowless vans, when something warm and soft like chubby hamsters steamrolled over his senses, and he realized he *wanted* her to come back with him.

He dug one heel into the ground while his other foot prepared for flight —a confusing sensation. He should have told her to get lost. But she had his jacket. He couldn't let her go with his jacket. But he'd given it to her barely five minutes ago. How could he ask for it back so soon? It was a predicament he couldn't escape—unless he wanted to act crazy and scare her off for good.

While his mind reeled in ways too human for his liking, the lines on her face creased with concern. "What did you mean when you said you could *smell* them calling for help?"

Kai's face twisted as he tried to remember. "It's hard to explain."

"Did you hear them screaming?"

"It's not like that. I'm just...pulled. An instinct, I guess." He turned and stalked off before he had to relive it again. Of course, the damn sheep followed, but she didn't press him further.

He didn't dare look back for the rest of the journey, though he could hear her uneven footsteps as she struggled to keep up. Every so often he would slow his pace, giving her a chance to catch her breath and regain her footing.

When they were close to the cabin, he circled the perimeter—a precautionary measure in case he had unwanted company. Finding nothing suspicious, he led her to the front, opened the door without a key, and helped himself inside. It was about as messy as usual—clothes scattered about the chairs, his towel on the floor by the table, and several blankets scrunched up on one end of the futon. As he dropped his hunting knife on the table, he looked back to find the girl still standing in the doorway, scanning the room like she was staring into another dimension.

"Relax, the roof isn't going to cave in," he said.

"I would hope not." She ventured inside, then looked down at her shoes. "Should I take these off?"

Kai cast her a dubious glance. "Does it look like you need to take them off?"

"It looks like I need to keep them on."

"I agree."

"So, you're a squatter," she pointed out after a pause, keeping herself glued to the walls as she wandered in. She creaked through the rooms with measured steps, like a cat inspecting new territory.

"Is that blood?" her voice echoed from the bathroom with a hint of alarm.

Kai couldn't help but smile. "Probably."

She poked her head out from the door, blinking at him with a disapproving frown. "Whose blood?"

He shrugged in response. "Recently, mine. Probably some animal blood too. And a drunk I picked a fight with last week."

She wrinkled her nose at him and disappeared back inside. "Your bathroom looks like a kill room. Is the drunk still alive?"

"Yes," came his stony reply as he moved soundlessly into the small space. He smiled when she jumped around and sized him up. "I'm not a psychopath," he told her evenly. "Unless you're thinking of knifing me in the balls when I'm not looking, you're safe."

"And you really had nothing to do with Elle Robinson's disappearance?"

"Well, I could be lying, but," he slapped his hand over his chest and winked, "no girl but you has ever come back to my cabin."

She seemed to relax, her fluttering pulse lulling to a soft, steady beat. "Good." She smiled. "I'd hate to think we bonded over Brenda's eyebrows for nothing."

Pleased that her anxiety had subsided, Kai put his hand out to her. "Good. Now, how about you step out of my kill room?"

She chuckled, accepting the gesture. "Sounds reasonable."

He led her out, then let go of her hand and ambled to the window where he slept, haphazardly spreading the crumpled blankets over the old mattress. He plopped down and thumped his head back against the wall, his eyes drifting shut. All day he'd been resisting the exhaustion.

"Going to sleep?" she asked from across the room.

"So long as you don't jump me, yes."

"Can I?" There was a hint of mischief in her voice.

"Knock yourself out." He yawned. "Might be the only way to keep me conscious." The urge to nap was fast taking over—the stillness numbing his senses—when he felt a sudden rush of exuberance coming from the bloody lamb. His eyes shot open just in time to see her leaping towards him.

"Incoming!" she called out, poking him in the ribs.

He grunted as he felt the jab in his side, then grabbed her wrists and held them firmly, the impulsive gesture turning playful as he dared her to break free with a single look.

Catching on to his game, she tugged against his hold, earning herself a roguish grin when her attempt yielded no result. As her efforts grew more vigorous, his desire to sleep quickly dissipated, and they tumbled into a wrestling match. It may have been painfully one-sided, with the lamb kicking, squealing, and trying to squirm her way out of slaughter, but it was a hell of a lot more gratifying than pummelling wasted deadbeats and going home with faceless women he'd never see again. Feigning boredom, he transferred her wrists to one hand to make his point.

"I could do this all day, Lambchop." He dodged a foot as she wildly swung her limbs in rebellion.

Laughing, he hoisted her up against his chest, his free arm wrapping around her waist and holding her securely as he hooked his ankles over hers —just in case she tried to take his head off again.

Her protests quickly dissolved into giggles, her futile struggle gradually subsiding until she finally settled down and accepted her fate. Heaving from exertion, she flopped back against his chest for a break.

It felt so natural, being close to another person in the midst of play—like it was a fundamental impulse he'd rarely had the chance to explore. For the first time since feeling that gnawing emptiness in the pit of his stomach, the hunger was at least a little bit satiated.

Slumping against the wall and lolling his head back, his eyes began to flutter shut, the sound of her steady breathing washing the tension from his body. But she soon disturbed the peace. She wriggled around to try and face him, so he relaxed his grip and sat up. Her pulse quickened as they came nose to nose, and something inside him stirred.

Her lips grazed his jaw, the sensation disarming. His face hovered a feather's touch away as his arm curled tightly around her midsection. He brushed his nose along her cheek and down the length of her neck, a low growl reverberating from his throat as his teeth kissed the warm skin just under her jaw. The light touch reaped a gasp as she drew closer against him.

But he was only given a brief moment to indulge in the effect he was having on her. A movement outside had him jerk back. He turned to face the door, putting himself between his lamb and whatever was on the other side. The scent was familiar—a thorn in his side that he'd hoped would leave him alone. Without so much as a knock, the door swung open, revealing the dark silhouette of a woman, the details of her form obscured by the gleaming sun behind her.

"I'm sorry, am I interrupting?" she asked sweetly, lingering by the door-frame like a threat.

"Who's that?" Miya whispered, peeking around his arm.

Treating the question as an invitation, the intruder stepped into the wolf's den, the shadows lifting from her face.

"An annoyance," Kai groused under his breath and leaned forward like he was preparing to lunge at her throat.

Ignoring him, the woman's piercing amber eyes fixated on the human girl. "Ama," she said simply.

"Holy shit, she's one of yours!" came the excited hiss from behind him. Miya's heart was racing now, her breath catching in her throat as she pressed herself against his back.

Ama canted her head, no doubt impressed she'd been found out so quickly.

"It's the eyes," the girl explained, touching her cheek to Kai's shoulder. "They reflect light, like an animal's."

Clever. Most wouldn't have noticed. Or they would've told themselves they were on a bad acid trip. Kai counted on people's tendency to bolt past what they couldn't rationally explain. It was a stupid but fortunate practice of the so-called modern folk; they happily ignored the obvious to keep hold of what was comfortable.

Superstitious half-wits, equally delusional in their beliefs, posed a much bigger threat. But it wasn't because they were right; they were simply willing to listen to their fears, and that made them dangerous.

Miya, on the other hand, was enamoured enough with her own fantasy to bypass her fear, but she seemed reluctant to abandon reality all together. Oddly, she was suited to keep one foot in each world.

A wide, elfish grin spread across Ama's face as she was called out. "You sure you can handle this one?" The question was directed at Kai. "She's too smart for you."

"What are you doing here?" he demanded, not in the mood for her riddles.

Undeterred, she took another step forward and circled around the table. "I came to meet your friend," she said as though it were obvious.

"Do we know each other?" Miya interjected, her weight lifting from Kai's back.

"Perhaps." It was as cryptic a response as ever, but Kai sensed a sliver of sincerity. "I was hoping to give some clarity on that. I promise I mean no harm."

Her tone was softer now, coaxing even. Kai straightened and rolled back his shoulders. "Then clarify, if that's what you're here for."

"Your presence isn't ideal." Ama smiled—almost apologetic, but not quite. "Would you mind leaving?"

"I'd rather stick my dick in a pencil sharpener."

"Sadly, I don't have one on hand." She sighed. "I suppose Miya and I will have to go for a walk while you try to acquire one." Her gaze shifted to the girl, questioning and hopeful.

"You don't have to do anything she says." Kai turned to Miya, feeling her anxiety mount under the pressure.

"I know," she said. "I'm curious to see what she wants." She stood up and left his side to address the white-haired beast. "We won't go far. If something happens, he'll know."

"He will," Ama agreed. "As I said, you have nothing to worry about. I'm here to help."

The lamb remained unmoved. "How do you know my name?"

Ama smiled coolly. "A little bird told me."

"A bird?" Miya blinked before her eyes flashed with recognition. "You mean the raven?"

Ama glanced at a seething Kai, brooding in his corner. "Observant little human." She turned back to Miya, stepping to the side and extending an arm towards the door. "Shall we?"

Miya nodded and followed the white wolf away from the haven of the black wolf's den. He watched them step out into the forest, the girl turning and smiling faintly before she shut the door behind her. He listened to their footsteps fade, his eyes searing through the wall as though he could see their figures on the other side. He sat motionless until he knew they'd been swallowed by the maze of trees that no living human could navigate without the sense of an animal. So long as Miya was with one of them, she would be safe. Perhaps even safer with Ama than with him. After all, he had his own demons to fight, and he had no doubt what would happen while she was gone.

Abaddon would soon be making up for lost time.

CHAPTER
TWENTY-NINE

MASON

SINCE CHILDHOOD, Mason had little trouble falling asleep. His mind would sink into darkness, rarely distressing him with the afterimages of his hopes and fears. His dream life was, for better or for worse, not very rich. But that all changed since coming to Black Hollow. As if the incessant, racing thoughts during the day weren't enough, his mind continued its ceaseless prodding while he slept. When he'd close his eyes, he'd see a young woman passing under the branches of the great willow. And every time she did, there'd be a shadow there—its shape indiscernible, though its intention clear; it was waiting for the girl.

Each time the shadow appeared, Mason would fight the dream, trying to slow its progression so he could make out what he was seeing—though he never had enough time. No matter how hard he tried, he always woke up just as he was on the verge of understanding what the shadow belonged to. Even though Annabelle had already told him, his mind simply wouldn't accept it. It didn't make sense.

He was plagued by this vision. The sequence would repeat itself for the entirety of the night until Mason awoke to the bright gold of morning sunlight streaming through his window. The last thing he'd see was the shadow—always lingering in the same place with unwavering patience. And every time it vanished, Mason knew he was too late. If only he could go back for a fraction of a second longer, he'd find his answer—one that was more satisfactory than what he'd already been told.

Mason couldn't understand why he was so troubled by something he didn't buy into. Was superstition finally slipping through the cracks?

The morning after his conversation with Annabelle, he was startled awake by his cell phone vibrating against his hand. The vision was sucked away, disappearing into the black hole of his subconscious. Fighting to open his eyes, Mason groaned sleepily as he groped around the mattress.

"Hello?"

"Hey, you awake Cap?"

Mason sat up, running a hand through his tangled curls. They were knotted together from a rough sleep. "Jaz? Why are you up so early?"

"I'm a nurse, remember?" She snorted on the other end. "Crazy, messed-up hours four times a week. Not even God knows when I'll be awake."

He glanced towards his bedside table—almost seven o'clock. "Wouldn't be so bad if it weren't a Saturday."

"Sorry, but I caught wind of something you might be interested in."

"What is it?"

"There's a town assembly today at ten, at the old church next to the community centre. It's about the Dreamwalker, as bizarre as that might sound."

He rubbed away the sleep keeping his eyelids glued shut. "What? Seriously? The town is actually calling a meeting over this? Who's organizing?"

"A woman named Jenny. She's pretty big on community initiatives." He heard her munching on something—potato chips judging by the crunch. "I overheard some of the gals at the hospital talking. Just thought you'd want to know."

"Wait—Jaz, you have to come with me. This is huge!" Mason swung his legs over the side of the bed.

There was a pause on the other end—hesitation, no doubt. "As much as I'm enjoying this rabbit hole of crazy, I have work, you know?"

"Right..." he trailed off, remembering that she was still responsible for people's lives.

"Sorry, Cap. I'm with you in spirit, though."

"Thanks, Jaz." His voice was quiet, laced with the bitter reminder. "I think I'll go check it out anyway."

"I figured you would," she scoffed. "Just be careful with these nutty bumpkins, yeah?"

"I will."

With neither having anything left to say, Mason offered a goodbye and hung up the phone. He resisted the urge to spiral into self-doubt. He'd come too far to question, too far to consider whether this quest for the truth had morphed into something pathological.

"Better get ready," he mumbled on autopilot. He spent at least forty-five minutes in the shower, killing time he would otherwise have to spend explaining himself to Annabelle. Towelling off, Mason let his hair air dry as he picked out his clothes. But it was only half-past eight, and he wouldn't have to leave for another hour. He stared at his wardrobe; if he wanted to get into this meeting without arousing suspicion, he'd have to look unimpressive. Mason settled for his worn, faded jeans, a long-sleeved t-shirt, and a quilted vest.

When he finally snuck downstairs, he was grateful to find a note on the door from Annabelle, her impeccable cursive informing him that she was out shopping and would be back before lunch. Exhaling with relief, Mason slipped on his shoes and left the house.

Upon arriving at the church, he was surprised by how many people were lining the old wooden benches. No one bothered giving him a second glance as he walked in and took a seat near the back.

"Jenny Raymer will be addressing the gathering today." The announcement came from a middle-aged man with thinning brown hair that peeked out over his ears.

The church was small and cozy, with a burgundy carpet running up the aisle, colourful stained-glass windows, beige walls, and a high wooden ceiling adorned with chandeliers. A microphone had been set up near the altar, and soon enough, a heavy-set woman with broad shoulders marched up to the podium. She looked to be on a mission.

"Thank you," she muttered in a deep voice after clearing her throat. She turned to face her audience, her expression severe. "I am here today to share something with you all, something that happened to me recently. Now, I know everyone here has concerns—concerns that often don't get taken seriously because we are living in the twenty-first century. Most folks are less inclined to believe in certain things."

A few murmurs echoed through the room, followed by nods of agreement as troubled glances were exchanged.

"I'm not sure how many of you are aware," she continued, "but another one of our girls is now missing."

The murmurs grew louder, whispers slithering through the air as people grew restless. "Who is it?" someone called out.

"Emiliya Delathorne. I've known her since she was crawling on the carpets at our community centre daycare. And now she's missing. Her

parents called yesterday after Emiliya's landlady informed them she hadn't returned home from the hospital. According to Dr. Robert Callahan's notes, obtained through a credible source, she was in the ER because of a sleep-walking incident. To make matters worse, her best friend says her phone is off. Her voicemail's full, and she's not responding to texts."

Callahan. He was also Kai Donovan's attending physician. Someone must have illegally leaked his files and implied a connection between the two patients.

"Emiliya's parents are here with us today. They've flown in from Calgary to help in the search for their missing daughter," Jenny continued. "While Andrea is working with authorities, Raymond has decided to join us."

Her eyes wandered to a man sitting in the first row. He stood up and straightened out his navy jacket, then smoothed back his wavy, salt and pepper hair before turning to face the congregation. He was clean-shaven, with a long, thin face and brooding green eyes.

"My daughter, Miya, was always a good kid," he began with a slight shake in his voice. "I'm ashamed to say I haven't been the most present father lately. I trusted she was a responsible young adult, but perhaps I was wrong."

Mason's breath stilled as he took in Raymond Delathorne—the tightness in his voice, the desperation in his eyes, the barely constrained frenzy in his gestures. He was a man on the verge.

"I noticed something was wrong," Raymond continued, throwing his hands out and shaking his head. "She was...different. She stopped calling us. She would never say thank you when we sent her cards and gifts. When my wife would ask if she was all right, if she needed help, she'd dance around the question, never giving us anything to work with, even when we knew some-thing was wrong. She withdrew. She seemed moody, depressed, not at all like the beautiful little girl we raised."

Mason wanted to jump up and protest—to scream that they were all delusional. His fingertips were ice-cold as he gripped the edge of the back-rest in front of him until he got splinters. Raymond Delathorne's words were almost identical to Gene Robinson's, and the people here listening saw nothing wrong with it.

Was there LSD in the water—or worse, poison? There were no tell-tale signs of contamination, no sickness or delirium. And what of Raymond? He'd flown in from another province; he couldn't have been affected by anything local.

"It's just as the legend says," an elderly man wheezed next to Mason, his hand trembling on the hilt of his walking stick. "It's happening again."

Happening again? Mason wondered if these idiots knew their own history, or even read the news.

"This thing is a real threat, folks. This time, our girl won't come back. I'm sure of it." Jenny walked across the altar, her face grim as she looked out at the townspeople. "I know how much everyone hates saying her name—the Dreamwalker—but denying her existence is only making us live in silence and fear. She's taking our girls from right under our noses."

It's not the Dreamwalker, Mason battered internally. *It's you. You're putting them six feet under.*

Yet he couldn't bring himself to speak up; he knew they wouldn't listen. The only thing he could do was find Emiliya before they did.

"Wait a minute—" A man dressed in a logger shirt and a thick hunting vest stood up. There were deep, purple bruises along the side of his face and neck; his lip was split open and his eye swollen half-shut. "We saw a girl in the woods just last week, when we were attacked by some psycho! He beat us up, snapped our guns. Guy looked human, but there was somethin' in his eyes, somethin' not right. Strong as a damn ox too."

"What did he look like?" Raymond called out.

The man looked down at his friend—equally battered by the looks of it. They both shook their heads like they couldn't quite remember. "Tall, dark hair, dressed like a bum."

"Isn't that the same guy who's been attacking people in alleyways, taking their stuff?"

"If he's really that strong, maybe he's not human! The Dreamwalker always sends someone to do her dirty work. He was with a girl in the woods, right?"

"Shit—what if he's with the Dreamwalker? What if he's one of her wolves?"

"He might have taken Emiliya!"

Mason wanted to warn them they weren't cross-checking their facts before jumping to conclusions—but something stopped him. The hunter's description fit Kai Donovan's appearance. It should have sounded ridiculous, but Mason couldn't shake the suggestion that Kai Donovan was a wolf. And if *that* was true, was it a stretch to think he could be one of the Dreamwalker's wolves? It was irresponsible not to consider, given the blood test results. Mason wanted proof that it was all fantasy, but he received the exact opposite, leaving him with no answers, not even a hypothesis. All he could do was remain a witness and see where this journey took him.

"While Andrea and Patricia are at the police station, nothing is stopping us from taking action. I say we organize a search party and go into the woods ourselves." Jenny turned to the bruised hunters. "Gentlemen, if you would be so kind, we would appreciate your assistance. If you could show us where you last saw the young woman with your attacker."

Both men stood up, exuding an almost militant eagerness to follow. "Yes, ma'am. Whatever we can do to help Black Hollow get Emiliya back to her family."

"If she's still a girl," an elderly voice interjected.

Jenny frowned, shaking her head in the direction of the old woman who'd spoken. "The Dreamwalker may be real, but let's not jump the gun." She put a reassuring hand on Raymond's slumped shoulder. He looked half-broken. "If something's wrong with Emiliya when we get her back, there are people who can help. Doctors, priests, psychics. We'll find a way to get the spirit out of her."

"I agree, let's organize," another woman's voice chimed in, the suggestion quickly gaining traction as people got to their feet while Jenny gave out orders.

"Let's get some supplies for the woods. Flashlights, batteries, water bottles, snacks, warm clothes for Emiliya when we find her."

"Those with a hunting license, bring your rifles!" The call was met with cheers. "We don't know what we'll run into while we're in those woods!"

"There's always a hockey stick or a baseball bat if you don't have a gun!"

Mason shot up from the bench and withdrew to the rear. He didn't want someone to notice him—not while tensions were so high. But he had every intention of following the search party into the woods. He had to find Emiliya first—he had to save her. He knew all too well what would happen if the townsfolk found her.

Gene Robinson's face, half-mad and grief-stricken, flickered before Mason's eyes.

He knew what had to be done. Like an undercover spy, he would join their trumpeting cause without absorbing any of its substance. He could already hear Jazlyn and Annabelle protesting—the younger of the two swinging violently at his head as if a concussion would knock sense into him, while the other planted her hands on her hips and sternly told him he was aggravating her crows' feet. No matter. Neither of them was here to stop him.

He felt like a boy again, reading *Sherlock Holmes and the Hound of the Baskervilles*, waiting for the moment the great detective would debunk the unsolvable mystery and explain the science behind the superstition. He needed to know that Kai Donovan wasn't real. He needed proof that the villagers' beliefs were a lie, that they had been led astray by their irrational-

ity. There was no Dreamwalker. There was no wolf. There was no kidnapping. There couldn't be. Because if there were, the ground would no longer
be the ground, and there would be nowhere left for Mason Evans to stand.

But more than all that, Mason had a life to save. He wouldn't let there be
another Amanda or another Elle.

Light the torch of your grief.

Gavran's words, once hollow, were suddenly imbued with meaning.

When night falls, only flames reveal the road ahead.

Mason strove to overpower his grief, but with Gavran's help, he now
understood its place. It would be the flame that guided him to Emiliya, and
it would help him save her life.

"Let's meet back here in two hours," Jenny announced. "There's plenty of
daylight left. We'll break after the sun goes down, but the search will
continue at dawn until Emiliya is found."

With that settled, Mason realized he had to return to Annabelle's. He
was ill-equipped to go into the woods. Annoyed he'd put so much effort into
avoiding his hostess for naught, Mason trudged back to his lodgings,
rehearsing what he'd say. The scent of roast beef wafted through the cracks
of the front door, greeting him as he came up the porch steps.

"That you, Mason?" she called to him once he was inside, the bell on the
door announcing his return.

"It's me," he answered, a little less enthusiastically than he'd intended.
"Smells great in here!" Now that sounded *too* enthusiastic.

"I'm making a pot roast. You okay to stay for lunch?" she asked, turning
the corner as she wiped her hand on a tea towel.

"Of course." He smiled nervously. "But I'll be heading out again after."

He wondered if she'd be suspicious when he didn't elaborate. He avoided
eye contact while examining the lines in the hardwood floor.

"You're going with the search party."

It never ceased to amaze Mason how well-informed Annabelle was for a
woman who spent her days in a farmhouse isolated from the rest of town.
Her interactions with the villagers seemed limited to grocery shopping and
trips to the bank. But perhaps it wasn't the town that was feeding her information. Feeling caught, Mason tore his eyes from the floor, unable to gauge
her intention as she regarded him calmly.

"Oh, don't look so surprised," she chided. "I already knew this was
coming. I hoped you'd let it go, but I knew in my heart you wouldn't. This
town's legends, its mysteries, and its secrets—they make you feel alive, don't
they?"

When he didn't—couldn't—respond, she smiled compassionately, as if to tell him he didn't need to justify himself. "I think I understand. My Matty was the same. And the closer he got to the end, the more engaged he was with these big mysteries. I guess some people are just born detectives."

He huffed and leaned back against the wall. "I think something terrible is going to happen. I can't stop the villagers, but I can maybe get ahead of them, you know?"

"Is that all?" Annabelle questioned. "I don't doubt you, but I think there's more to it."

"There's more," Mason admitted quietly. "I'm not as amazing as your son, Annabelle." He hesitated, searching for the words. "I don't want to believe in any of this. I really don't. But when I see everyone else believing, I feel like I have to prove them wrong. For my own sake. I know that's selfish, but I need to prove them wrong. If I can't, it means I'm the one who's been living a lie."

"But what if you can't prove them wrong?"

"It might destroy me," he confessed, "but it might also mean there's hope. I don't *want* to be wrong, but I have to know the truth. This thing I'm chasing—it might even redeem me."

Annabelle sucked in a shaky breath. "You can't change the past, Mason. And it sounds to me like you want to be right even when you're wrong. But I understand how you feel. You came here to escape. Seems like you can't, though. Not until you put what's haunting you to rest."

"What about you?" Mason asked. "Do you believe?"

Annabelle nodded. "My son believed. And if he did, then I do too."

She padded over to an old wooden desk in the corner of the lounge and forced one of the drawers open with a rough jerk. After rummaging through, she found what she was looking for and came over to Mason.

"Here," she offered, handing him what appeared to be a folded map. "Mathias's old hiking trails. The more he got into the fable, the more time he spent in the woods. Everyone'll tell you the forest's impossible to get through, but no one knows that place like my Matty did. If you get lost, these might help you."

Mason stared down at the ratty old paper in his hand. "Thank you, Annabelle. You don't know how much this means to me. But why are you helping me?"

"I don't want to see anyone else get hurt, Mason." The words were cryptic, but after seeing the meeting in the church, he knew what she meant. She stepped forward and wrapped her arm around him in a tight embrace, her warmth sinking into him.

"I hope whatever you find in those woods brings you peace, Mason."

CHAPTER
THIRTY

MIYA

THERE WAS SOMETHING FAMILIAR, peaceful, yet deeply unsettling about the forest. Like a dream Miya couldn't quite remember, it drowned her in emotions she didn't understand—feelings that had no words to describe them, like an overpowering wave of nostalgia that was warm, pleasant, yet uncanny.

It wasn't as though she'd never stepped foot in the forest. She grew up surrounded by it. But as she floated between the ground and sky, suspended in a living maze, she had no idea where she was. She wasn't even sure how much time had passed since she'd gone with Ama, but the sun was still high. How long ago did she leave the hospital? Part of her screamed it was time to go home—that night was supposed to have fallen hours ago, but she didn't feel hungry, and she didn't need the bathroom. With her perception and her internal clock scrambled, her only anchor was that Kai hadn't come looking for her. If he wasn't panicking, Miya doubted she needed to.

Ama was a few paces ahead, and like Kai, she seemed perfectly oriented. Miya took her in, scrutinizing her idiosyncrasies—the way she moved, how she reacted to sounds and smells. She was like Kai, but there was a sense of cohesion about her that he lacked. Like she already had herself figured out.

"So, you're a wolf?" Miya asked.

"That I am." Ama smiled, weaving through several trees before she stopped in front of Miya. She leaned in, peering into her like she was

172

reaching down into her soul to see what it was made of. "Are you worried I'm one of *her* wolves?"

Her tone was wry like she knew something Miya didn't—something Miya *should* have known.

"I don't know." Miya tilted her chin up in defiance. "But I feel like I know you, or you know me."

Ama pulled back, then circled her again. "We've met before."

Her eyes drew Miya in, the space between the two women melting away. Miya's attention drifted to Ama's hair—beautiful, silvery strands she'd never expect on a young woman. Miya wondered if she was a white wolf, but it was her warm, amber eyes that captivated her most—large, curious, and full of life. She recalled the wolf from long ago, whose eyes remained etched in memory. They too captivated her, filled her with wonder.

"Oh my God—" Miya clamped a hand over her mouth as Ama smiled knowingly. "You're—"

"You were just a peanut then," Ama laughed. "But fearless. You were barely fazed when you saw me."

Miya's heart danced; she finally found her—the wolf from her childhood. "Have you always been watching me?"

Ama nodded but offered nothing further.

"Why?"

"I was told to keep an eye on you."

"By whom?"

"A friend," said Ama. "But that's not what you care about most right now, is it?"

Miya felt the heat rise to her cheeks. "What do you mean?"

A sly smile spread over Ama's face. "It's all right. He's not *all* bad. Kai, that is."

"I have concerns," Miya cleared her throat, "like his connection to missing girls from Black Hollow. He said he's got nothing to do with it. I believe him. But it's too bizarre to just shrug off. I wish I knew why he keeps repeating the same cycle, you know?"

"I think you'll find out soon." Ama canted her head as though listening to something far away. "It's time to go."

A disappointed whimper slipped out. There was so much more she wanted to know. "But you haven't even told me who this friend is, or why they've asked you to watch me! What do you mean I'll find out soon?"

"The one responsible for this mess is on the move."

Miya found herself sinking, disoriented, but before she could steamroll Ama with questions, the white wolf ventured onward.

Wasn't the cabin back the other way?

Miya opened her mouth, but the words wouldn't formulate, so she followed, fearing she'd be left behind. She barely noticed when they ended up back at Kai's cabin.

It looked different now.

There was a strange, mist-like quality to the air—a stillness, heavy like smog as the daylight dimmed, then disappeared altogether. It wasn't dark out—there just wasn't any sun. Everything was dusky, opaque, faded like an oil painting left in the attic too long.

More troubling was the lack of movement inside. She expected Kai to burst out the door, yelling obscenities or at least lunging at Ama's throat and trying to tear it out in a grizzly display of dominance. But there was nothing —not even a rustle or a creak.

Ama walked up to the door, her hand staying on the knob. She looked over her shoulder at Miya. "Something's wrong."

The door slowly chirred open. Miya's eyes followed the sound until they fell on a shadow in the corner of the room. It was Kai, sitting on the floor with his back against the wall, his knees pulled up and his elbows resting on them. His shoulders were slumped, his head hanging as though he was unconscious. The sound of their entry failed to inspire even a twitch.

As Miya stepped past the doorframe, he jolted—his face pale, his eyes bloodshot and wild with a touch of madness. He looked right at her, his gaze digging into her like the barrel of a loaded gun. And yet, he appeared to see neither of the women. He was looking straight through them, at something beyond, from someplace else.

"Kai?" called Miya, but she received no response. Kai remained motionless, unblinking, his expression frozen in agony while the rest of him held like a hollowed shell ready to topple with the breeze.

"He can't hear you," said Ama, her eyes locked on him and her body language guarded. The hair on her arms stood on end, and Miya knew they were in danger.

"What's wrong with him?"

"He's being haunted."

"What?" Miya snapped. "You mean by a ghost?"

Ama smiled sourly. "We typically use the term metaphorically, but yes, in this case, I do mean something supernatural. Not exactly a ghost, though."

A harrowing snarl erupted from the back wall. Kai collapsed to the floor, clawing at the hardwood until his fingernails bled. Miya couldn't see his face, but his every muscle convulsed. His back arched until he began to heave, vomiting something black and tarry onto the floor. The putrid smell reached Miya on the other side of the cabin.

She rushed over and planted a hand on his shoulder. It was like touching a hot stove, her fingertips burning until she snatched her hand back to safety. For a moment, she could feel everything—the pain, the terror, the confusion—the desire to let go and fall into the inferno. As though rebelling against whatever force held him, Kai curled into a fetal position and clutched his knees to his chest. He was barely clinging on. Sooner or later, the dam would break.

"You won't be able to reach him from the outside." It was Ama, approaching her from behind. Their history aside, Miya wanted to blame her, to call her out for backing away the moment there was danger, but she held her tongue. Ama could know how to help.

"You're keeping away," Miya observed. "Why?"

"Angry spirits are not to be trifled with," she replied, maintaining her distance. "I wanted to see how it would react if someone approached."

Miya wondered if Ama had truly been watching *over* her, or just watching. "So you let me be the guinea pig?"

She shrugged. "You volunteered quite eagerly."

"How do we help him?" Miya demanded.

Ama considered her, then looked down at Kai—a mess of tremors and guttural snarls, bile oozing out the side of his mouth as he battled whatever was inside him. "You need to fight it from the inside."

"How!" Miya slapped her palm to the floor, exasperated by her curtness.

"Move from this realm to the next."

Miya shifted her weight, noticing droplets of sweat licking the side of Kai's face. "Which realm is that?"

"The one where you go to when you sleep."

Miya wrinkled her brow. "You mean dreams?"

"Something like that."

What did that mean? "Why do *I* have to do it?"

"Because I can't. And even if I could, I don't care enough for him to put myself at risk." Ama squatted down beside her, dipping her head close and wriggling her nose as though trying to catch a particular scent. "Besides, it's quite easy to get lost wandering the dreamscape."

At these words, Miya's chest tightened. This had happened to her before.

"Are you sure you want to help him?" Ama's snide humour dissipated.

Miya questioned if she really wanted to leap in headfirst. Motivation wasn't her strong suit lately; she was a picture of powerlessness, locking away her fears to avoid confronting them. But there was no time for helplessness now, and she was sick of being at the mercy of things outside her control. Seeing Kai in such unbearable pain shifted something inside her. She realized suffering was a perspective driven by fear. Pain, however, was a reality. If she could uncover the truth Kai couldn't speak, maybe she could change that reality.

It was her fear or his pain. She had to choose one.

"I can't just do nothing."

Ama scrunched up her nose if only to keep from scoffing. "Fine. I'll guide you there—but that's the best I can do. We'll have a weak connection, so if you stray too far it'll be broken, and I will lose you. In that case, you're on your own."

Miya didn't know what she meant by *there* and *straying too far*, but she didn't have time to question her. "Fine by me," she nodded. "I don't know where the hell I'm going, but if you can get me there, I'll figure the rest out myself."

"I'd call you brave, but I think you're leaning more towards stupid." Ama dropped her butt and slid back. She patted the floor between her legs. "Come here."

Miya obliged, and Ama grabbed her hand and pulled her forward, coaxing Miya's head into her lap. The younger woman avoided eye contact as Ama pushed the hair from her face, fingertips resting against her temples. Ama inhaled slowly, then released her breath.

"Don't fight what comes."

Miya nodded, her eyes meeting the white wolf's. She began drifting as her body extended over the ground. Ama cradled her head and pressed a hand against her forehead, the pressure growing heavier with every breath. Miya's body meshed with the earth, and she felt herself slip away.

"Don't fight it," Ama told her softly. "Let yourself descend, as only you can."

Miya didn't know how, but she felt someone watching over her from a tree branch outside, reminding her that she was not alone. She let go, falling into the earth and losing herself to the darkness beneath.

CHAPTER
THIRTY-ONE
THE RECKONING

*M*IYA DISCOVERED HERSELF IN A VAST, *barren desert. She looked up to the sky, grey and colourless, and spotted a raven flying overhead, his shrill voice piercing the air like a knife.*

Was he the one watching her?

The landscape was endless—hills upon hills of brown earth stretching on infinitely. The coppery knolls were littered with bones and rotting corpses, drawing a broad path that guided her line of sight to what she was searching for.

Upon a small mound ahead was a shadowy figure, hovering expectantly. With no one else in sight, Miya walked forward, the air growing thick and heavy as she approached. The presence was sinister, unwelcoming. When she was close enough, she noticed two holes in the dark mass, growing brighter until they appeared distinctly like eyes—blazing and gold, yet colder and greener than the warm honey of Ama's irises.

The eyes locked onto her, then shifted around the entity before vanishing. The shadow distorted grotesquely until the hovering mass took on a discernable human shape.

It was a man, his back turned to her. His hair was jet black and clung to his shoulders, blowing in the wind like a lion's mane. His warrior-like build reminded her of Kai, though his clothes looked out of a different time. He turned to face her, and her heart clenched painfully as she looked upon his face.

Blood-stained from head to toe, he bore a disturbing resemblance to Kai—so much so that Miya wondered if it was him until she saw those same aurous rings from moments ago. But there was a crippling intimacy about him that extended beyond the superficial likeness. Miya knew he was the entity haunting Kai. She watched, horrified, as an appreciative smile spread over face. His voice invaded her.

"It's been a long, long time, little girl. I knew you'd find me."

"You've got the wrong person," Miya said icily. "We've never met before."

His laugh thundered through the desert.

"Once upon a time, when the earth was formless and empty, and darkness stretched over the surface of the deep, we plunged one another into the abyss, and the world has trembled ever since."

His words made Miya's skin crawl, waves of nausea rocking her like a boat in a stormy sea. Was this how Kai felt?

"Your friends, your neighbours—those sheep you call townsfolk —they are all deluded, weaving their own demise through empty tales. And you...you are not ready. You are barely a shadow of your former self."

His voice—deep and rumbling with malice—spun the world on its axis until Miya couldn't feel her feet on the ground. The air was smoggy, polluted, thick with poisonous miasma. Her lungs felt razed as she gasped for air, her vision blurring when the apparition moved towards her, a black mist emanating from his body as he drew near. With every step, the desert ignited in flames that quaked the earth.

"You think he'll save you, but do you truly believe he'll make it in time?"

Miya knew he was referring to Kai and the missing girls whose bodies he'd woken up to. She knew this thing was responsible for Kai's failure to intervene in time, but she could barely breathe, let alone question him. Unable to keep her balance, she stumbled back, her heels nicking an animal's decomposing skull before she fell on her behind, the inhabitant of the wasteland towering over her. His looming face was overcast by shadows, only his eyes gleaming with a pale, yellowish light.

"Do you know my name, girl?"

The question barely registered amidst the feeling of being torn apart from the inside. How the fuck should I know, Miya wanted to say—but before she could spit in his face, a small, black figure swooped down from the sky. It was the raven, his talons latching onto the smooth, ashen flesh as he plunged his beak into the apparition's eyes, pecking them out like crimson yolk from an eggshell. Thrusting his head back, he gobbled down the oozing liquid before releasing an ominous chortle, spreading his impressive midnight wings and disappearing into the sky.

With black, hollowed eyes, the monster gritted his teeth as he straightened from the attack, then smiled wickedly in Miya's direction.

"Meet your King of Spades. Abaddon."

The name was a death rattle, piercing Miya's chest like a jagged blade. She recoiled, but the sand around her collapsed into a bottomless pit, and a stream of tarry, black hellfire bubbled like a witch's cauldron at the bottom of the abyss. The smell of burning wood, flesh, and black smoke seized her lungs. The beast was advancing, and his every step was a terror. She echoed his words in her mind.

My king of spades...

...Abaddon.

"That's not it," Miya hissed under her breath, her thoughts a haze as the assault on her senses triggered something—fragments of memories, images of something long lost. "That's not your real name."

The phantom abruptly retreated, warping like a piece of burning cinder until he appeared farther than ever before. The flames died, the smoke fading as a breeze passed overhead. He looked displeased now, pacing left and right but unable to approach, like he was blocked by a barrier. He unleashed a blood-curdling scream that ripped through the air like a thousand blades. Hatred, resentment, fear, jealousy, anguish, and grief all flooded Miya in one ferocious wave.

Yet his frustration emboldened her. Her lungs clearing, she slowly found her feet. She'd learned something invaluable—something he didn't want her to know. She felt braver, angrier, more willing to bear the burden until a woman's voice stopped her.

Come back.

It was Ama, summoning her to the world of the living.

"Not yet," Miya bickered with the sky. "I'm not finished with him."

You've wandered too far. If you continue, you might not find your way back.

Miya's eyes remained locked on Abaddon, but she felt herself waver. "How?"

Follow the raven.

She looked up and spotted her rescuer flying past her. Trailing him with her eyes, she saw a massive forest floating on the edge of the desert. It was home.

Tracing the raven's path wasn't difficult. Even as he flew overhead, his pace was slow and even. The woods grew familiar, the trees and thickets much like the ones around Kai's home. Miya thought she was close when from the corner of her eye, she caught something white rushing past her. Arrested, she noticed a young woman some ten feet away. She was completely naked, her back turned, but from her figure and the pale lustre of her hair, Miya knew it was Ama. She was younger here—perhaps only a teenager. As Miya contemplated going to her, the raven swooped down from above and landed on Ama's shoulder, cawing his greeting as she, in turn, scratched the feathers on his breast.

Epiphany struck Miya like a freight train as she watched their affectionate exchange: they knew one another more intimately than Miya knew her own family.

How long had Ama been with the raven?

Was she looking into their past?

Don't look that way, *Ama's voice echoed.* **You'll get distracted.**

But it was too late. When Miya turned back, she was in an unfamiliar part of the woods. There was someone up ahead—a girl with slight shoulders and a thin, gold chain around her neck. It was Elle, wandering through the trees with a content smile on her face.

If the dreamscape allowed Miya to see the past, could she somehow warn her?

"Elle!" Miya rushed after her. "Stay away from Black Hollow!"

As if hearing a distant echo, Elle spun around. Her eyes widened as she stared straight through Miya—at something behind her. But before Miya could look, she felt a heavy chill pass through her bones and suck the air from her lungs. Feathery wisps of purple and black lashed out around her. She felt the tip of the bone mask against her earlobe, and a voice hissed over her shoulder—to which of the girls, Miya didn't know.

"Stay away from Black Hollow," said the Dreamwalker.

Miya jerked to the side and stumbled away. Elle faded from sight like a wrinkle in water, and Miya found herself back near the cabin. It had the same hazy quality as when she and Ama had returned from their walk. The door was still open, so Miya let herself in, approaching her own body lying motionless on the floor.

Ama hadn't moved a muscle, her head bowed as her hands rested on Miya's cheeks, her expression intent. When she didn't know anyone was watching, she actually looked quite concerned.

Returning to her body, Miya crouched down and examined her own face, intrigued by how she looked outside the reflection of a mirror. She knew it was time to return to this container, but she didn't know how. As she tried touching her physical form, a strong gust of wind swept her hair back. Lifting a hand to her eyes, Miya peeked through her fingers as another presence made itself known on the other side of her body.

The Dreamwalker was back, her feathery, iridescent cloak billowing around her. She tilted her head to the side as if curious, and while Miya couldn't see her face behind the beaked, shell-like mask, she could feel her speaking.

You've gotten terribly lost, little lamb.

A roar from behind blasted the door right off its hinges. The light outside guttered like a dying lamp and the world began to dim. Abaddon was coming. And with the Dreamwalker in front of her, she was certain she'd never make it back.

The spirit grinned. As she lifted her arms, her cloak spread like the wings of a predatory bird, casting a shadow that crept over the room and swallowed Miya up like a penny in a bottomless well. As the Dreamwalker swooped over her, Miya dove towards her body, shrieking as air rushed past her. She felt fingers against her back, nails digging into her skin and pushing her down. Miya tried to spin around and fight, but it was like being trapped under a thick quilt. Why would the Dreamwalker push her into her body? Did she want her to go back?

Miya squeezed her eyes shut and resisted the fray, focusing instead on returning. She reached down and groped for her physical form. The pressure on her back dissi-

pated, and she sunk into darkness, throwing her arms out and swinging wildly as she pushed her torso off the floor and sat up, her vision still a blur as she gasped for air.

"...Miya?"

She heard Ama's voice before the room came into focus. Miya's breaths drew quick and shallow. "Shit, shit, shit," she muttered over and over as someone gently rubbed her arm.

"It's all right, you're back." Ama slid next to her, dipping her head to take stock of Miya's expression. "You're safe."

Miya nodded as she caught her breath, the adrenaline setting fire to her blood. Then, remembering Kai, she looked frantically around the room and scrambled over to him.

He was still huddled on the floor in a heap of shivers. His eyes shot open when she touched him, his teeth chattering and his face contorted. His canines were longer, the red in his irises more prominent as his lip curled and he growled like a feral animal driven into a corner. He tried getting to his knees, blindly groping around until Miya grabbed his hand. She could see him battling against the remnants of whatever phantom she'd just faced.

"Come on, get a grip," Miya pleaded. "I can't go back there." Her voice cracked, tears prickling her cheeks. "Please don't make me go back there."

Somewhere through her broken mumbles, he looked up at her, his eyes hollow like he'd seen war and returned half broken. But at least he was present—no longer looking through her like she was a ghost. He dropped his head again, biting down until his lip bled. Wracked by tremors, he squeezed Miya's hand and released an anguished cry—tender and grief-stricken. It washed over her like a wave, sweeping away the dread.

Kai's body went limp, and he collapsed onto the floor, breathing heavily as beads of sweat trickled down his neck, his shirt completely soaked through.

"Don't touch me," he growled as Miya reached out to rub his back. She pulled away, stung, and looked over at Ama. But the white wolf remained unfazed, silently watching the interaction.

"That was quite something," she said after a short pause, giving them both a coy smile. "It's almost like you two know each other."

Kai lifted his head and glowered at Ama, then rolled over and sat up. Stripping off his shirt, he whipped it angrily at the wall, refusing to acknowledge Miya's presence as he got to his feet and stalked into the bathroom. Miya heard the water running, followed by several splashes before the tap squeaked shut and he re-emerged, not bothering with another shirt.

Miya gawked at him—she couldn't help that he looked good—but he smelled her attraction faster than a viper and turned his cutting glare on her. Miya averted her gaze and watched his feet as he brushed past her. She heard him pull his hunting knife from his sheath, then snap it back into place.

"Where are you going?" Ama asked casually.

The silence that followed was unbearable. Miya listened to her own heartbeat—the pounding so loud it drew his attention like the scent of blood. His eyes were on her for several painfully drawn out moments before he finally spoke.

"To kill something," he said, then turned and stormed out of the cabin, slamming the door behind him.

"Are you all right?" Ama bore into her human companion.

"Just never seen him like that before."

Ama raised an eyebrow. "You barely know him."

"That's not a side of anyone I'd want to know." She let out a shaky breath and stared at her hands, the tremor still visible. "What now?" she asked. "Are we going to talk about what happened?"

"We should," Ama conceded, "but there's no point if he isn't here to hear it. And by the looks of it, you're in no condition to have this conversation twice."

"I'm fine," said Miya, but the horror was still pulsating down her limbs.

"Fear is never a good starting point," Ama told her. "Why not go for a walk and clear your head."

A walk wasn't a bad idea, Miya thought, so long as she stayed close to the cabin.

"I'll come sniff you out if you're gone too long."

"Thanks." Miya smiled, feeling more stable with her around. Despite being so blasé, Ama knew exactly what was needed.

Miya stared at the door. If she opened it, would she come face-to-face with a pissed-off wolf wielding a hunting knife?

"He's not there," Ama chuckled, reading her mind again.

Miya offered a sheepish grin, scuttling to the door and peeking outside. Surprised by how bright it was, she raised a hand to shield her eyes from the onslaught of sunlight.

Squinting at her surroundings, Miya tried to decide which path to follow. Not that there were any paths. Sighing, she picked a direction instead, taking note of a large, pinkish rock next to a birch tree.

As Miya walked, it occurred to her to call Patty and let her know she was okay. She reached into her pocket for her phone only to realize the battery was dead. It usually lasted two days if she wasn't using the damn thing—and she hadn't touched it since changing her clothes at the hospital. How long had she been gone? Hadn't she been discharged just before dawn today?

Gripped by confusion, Miya turned to go back when something swooped down from the sky, just barely catching her shoulder. She ducked for cover and yelped, clasping her hands over her head and peeking towards the tree-tops. Hearing a familiar caw, Miya batted her head around in search of the raven. Seeing that she was either blind or incompetent, the bird called out to her again, and then once more, until Miya made out a little black blob blotting out the sun on a nearby branch.

"You," she breathed out, straightening up. The raven cocked his head in response like he understood that she was speaking to him.

He dropped from the branch, his wings fluttering as he landed on the leafy ground. He was closer than Miya thought any bird would dare approach, his shining, beady eyes fixed on her.

"You're screwing with me," she told him, then tested him with a step forward. He jumped back but remained easygoing, squawking as though offended by her accusation. Then he turned his tail up at her and began hopping. It was odd that a bird would hop when it had wings to fly with.

If he flies, you won't be able to keep up.

He's doing it for your sake.

Possessed by the conviction that she was *supposed* to follow, Miya ambled after the hopping raven, forgetting all prior resolve to keep track of landmarks and stay close to the cabin. But she was content to be lost if it would untangle some of the knots inside her. Bereft of reason, she wandered after her whim, spurred by a sudden revelation.

Fables unveiled something truly magical at work in the world, persuading Miya she didn't have to despair that life appeared as a series of milestones along a pre-determined path—high school, university, job, marriage, family, retirement. She hadn't achieved many of those milestones, but she *had* stepped into another realm, been touched by spirits, and come face-to-face with a monster. She'd seen first-hand how those spirits and monsters had a footing in a world supposedly ruled by irrefutable laws. Miya finally understood that fables were not merely stories inscribed on the pages of reality. They were a storm that ripped those pages from their binding and re-wrote the world from scratch.

CHAPTER
THIRTY-TWO

KAI

THE ONLY THING worse than a bad hangover was a follow-up visit from hell's most deranged spirit.

Fuck this shit.

Kai stomped through the woods, kicking dead branches as he went.

Fuck everything.

He looked up to see a squirrel in a tree, ignoring his presence as it nibbled contently on an acorn.

And fuck that squirrel in particular.

Kai was annoyed the rodent didn't seem to notice him—or at least didn't care that he was nearby. He felt out of control—disoriented not just by the haunting, but by the presence of others around him when it happened. *Her* presence, specifically.

She saved you.

He could barely admit it to himself, barely register that he was angry about it. And he was angry that he was angry about it. *What's so bad about being saved*, he kept asking himself, trying to beat away the shame he felt for needing help.

The wolf saved by the lamb. What a joke.

Kai never needed saving. After Alice, he took the only thing she'd left him—her surname—and ran away to Black Hollow. He was only sixteen, but that was old enough to get by without help. He didn't have to hide who he truly was any longer. Not that Alice would have ever found out; his ability to change had been repressed since he was ten years old—since that night in the woods when Alice first found him, starving and covered in blood that wasn't his. But the trauma of losing her—well, that seemed to kick things in reverse. All the anger and pain he'd shoved down after she died erupted in one bone-shattering transition that hurt worse than a rusty pole up the ass. It brought him back, forcing him to reconnect with the animal. And since then, he'd been bursting like Old Faithful.

Kai clenched his teeth and growled menacingly at the unsuspecting squirrel. He felt a tingle in his fingertips, moving up his arms and into his back. By the time it reached his neck, it had deepened into a slow burn that crawled over his scalp. He knew it was coming; it always started like this.

He slackened his jaw, aware that it would involuntarily tense a moment later. His canines elongated as his joints locked, throwing him off balance. Every vertebra in his spine broke, muscles seizing and tendons stretching beyond their natural range. His body fought to maintain its human shape— but that didn't last long. Kai clamped his mouth shut so he wouldn't scream and bit into his gums, the iron-taste of blood washing over his tongue. His lower back bulged outward then snapped, forcing him to the ground where his knees broke. They were trying to become ankles for his hind legs.

Every inch of him burned and itched as coarse, black fur sprouted from his flesh. He tried digging his fingers into the dirt to grab hold of something —anything—but his body wouldn't permit even small mercies. His fingers curled in on themselves and fused into stubs. His nails narrowed, thickened, and curved into blunt claws. When the pain became too much, he finally gave in—the wretched cry of a man twisting into a helpless whine.

Sometimes his jaw didn't morph as quickly as his tongue, leaving him choking as it expanded into the back of his throat. His tailbone was always the last to go. It grew pointy, prodding him from the inside before the bones pushed their way out of his body. Several agonizing minutes passed before the flesh grew back and the fur colonized his skin.

Kai lay on the forest floor until breathing grew easier. When he felt steady, he rolled onto his stomach and sat up on his haunches. Whenever he turned into a wolf, the first thing he felt after the vertigo subsided was a deep, ravenous hunger. He wanted to hunt, and he wanted to eat. His every fibre twitched with predatory instinct as sounds and smells invaded him. The squirrel on the tree was no longer of interest, nor was the hare hiding in the bushes several yards to his left. No, he wanted something bigger. He wanted a challenge.

For that, he'd have to go deeper into the woods. Standing on all fours and shaking out his tail, Kai began to stalk, his lips pulling back and his tongue flopping lazily against his jaw. He heard the hare scurry away when he got close but ignored the urge to chase it.

He could smell something far more enticing over the slope ahead.

CHAPTER
THIRTY-THREE

WHEN KAI CAME TO, he was face down in the earth, naked and covered in grime. Nothing felt weirder than mud stuck between the cockles of his balls and cold wind scraping against his ass. As he rolled over and opened his eyes, the first thing he saw were the nimble branches of the towering willow, swaying gently above him. It did little to put him at ease. His whole body felt like it had been mauled by a truck—twice.

Sitting up, he looked himself over, the blood on his arms reminding him he'd been roaming the woods hunting. To the right was a brown mass—a small deer—freshly killed with a grisly trail of blood and entrails tying Kai to the crime scene.

The morning air was colder than usual against his flesh, and, as always, he had no idea where the fuck his clothes were. Feeling like a thousand pounds of lead, he slowly stood to his feet and grimaced. The shame was as stubborn as the bloodstains.

"Get a grip," he growled. Taking a deep breath, he closed his eyes and let the balm of the forest wash over him. He caught the trickle of a familiar scent followed closely by a shrill cry. His stomach twisted.

"No, no, no," he muttered through clenched teeth, stepping around a shrub and making a sharp turn towards the intruder.

Crouching in the leaves was the damn sheep, with the raven creeping from the branches above. No doubt he'd led her to him; she wouldn't have wandered this deep into the woods otherwise. She'd gathered his clothes after following them like a trail of breadcrumbs. His pants and shirt hung over her arm while she held his hunting knife in hand. When she finally noticed him, the colour rose to her cheeks as she tried keeping her gaze above his waistline. Neither of them spoke as they glared at one another in poorly-veiled hostility.

His eyes travelled to the hunting knife, then back to her face. "That's mine."

She stood up and whipped the clothes at him. He made no attempt to catch them, ignoring the heap as it flopped to the ground.

"You're an asshole," she hissed, still holding his knife hostage.

He raised an eyebrow, then bent over to retrieve his clothes. He'd been called far worse for far less.

"Stop that," she ordered.

He glanced up, dusting his pants off. "Stop what?"

"Stop dismissing me."

He snorted. "I don't care if you feel dismissed."

Kai could feel the tension in her body as she marched up to him and shoved him with all her strength. "I care!" she yelled. "You have no idea what kind of hell I just went through—your hell!"

He stumbled back, surprised by how strong she was—and angry. But like an animal under attack, his eyes flashed, and he took a step forward, throwing the clothes to the ground as he roared in her face. "I don't want you in my head!"

For a moment, she recoiled. *Good*, he thought. She should have been more afraid—but his relief was short-lived.

"Don't want me in your head?" she echoed incredulously, gathering her wits. "I was in your head because you needed help!"

Fuck her rational thinking. "I didn't ask for your help, so stay out," he seethed, then pointed towards the carcass. "Or is that what you want?" He threw his hands up for her to see the bloodstains.

She glanced over at the deer, paling at the sight of it. He heard her stomach flip, her throat tightening as she forced down nausea and scanned his bloodied figure.

"Quit chasing me," he warned. "Even if this was a fairy tale, you know exactly what I'd be."

"But *you* came back for me, you dimwit!" she retorted. "*You* pulled me into the woods with you!"

He silenced her by closing the gap between them in one menacing stride. Her heart seized in her chest as he glowered down at her. She clenched her jaw, trying defiantly to hide her fear, but the predator in him could smell the urge to flee rising in her chest like a bird fighting to break free from a cage.

Lifting his hand slowly enough so she wouldn't flinch, he stroked his thumb across her cheek, smearing the blood from his fingertips over her skin. He leaned down and brushed his lips against her ear, whispering darkly, "I'm a wolf in sheep's skin, Miya, and you've mistaken me for part of your flock."

She tried to snatch the air back into her lungs with a sharp gasp. Feeling smug, he was ready to let her run away sobbing—until he realized that she was neither running nor sobbing. To his horror, her shell was cracking, hatching a teething, newborn lioness with a bad temper.

"So what?" she bit back, touching her nose to his. He snarled, baring his teeth, though it failed to deter her. "You want to be the Big Bad Wolf? Fine!" Drawing his hunting knife, she pressed the tip of the blade to his jaw. "Just don't be surprised if the lamb shish-kebobs the wolf in this fairy tale."

Shoving the hilt against his chest and whipping the sheath at his foot, she spun on her heels and stomped off, leaving him to boil like a potato in the stew of his own rage. "And put some damn clothes on. We've got to get back, and you're shaking like a leaf."

"Who's wearing the fucking sheep's skin here?" he cursed under his breath, hopping after her as he pulled his pants on and threw the shirt over his shoulder.

But the wind howled in protest, and the willow rustled as though calling after them. Kai glanced over his shoulder, the hairs on his neck standing on end. Noticing the tree for the first time, Miya too turned and stared up in awe.

"Wait—isn't that—"

Her words were drowned out by a deafening gale. The air felt heavy, the whistling breeze a call to something long forgotten. Kai's gaze remained fixed, his body fraught. He was overcome with a sudden, inexplicable fear of dying, right there beneath that damn willow. He couldn't explain it, and he didn't understand it. All he knew was that his terror ran bone-deep and that he wanted to run straight to the woman he'd been trying to chase away.

Slowly, he turned to Miya and offered her his hand.

CHAPTER
THIRTY-FOUR

MIYA

MIYA WASN'T sure if this was the past, the present, or the future. It was like being suspended in time—locked in a liminal space. It might have been a premonition or a memory, a dream or reality.

She stared at Kai's hand, wondering if he'd pull her towards the tree. The willow's wispy canopy seemed like shelter, gathering her up in its embrace and telling her not to be afraid.

She reached out and took Kai's hand. It was warm, his grip firm as he curled his fingers around hers. Without a word, he tugged her from the glade.

They retraced their steps hand-in-hand. Exhausted after their sparring match, Miya didn't protest as he led the way. Ama was waiting inside the cabin when they returned, drumming her fingers against the table she was seated at. She raised both her eyebrows as they dragged themselves in.

"Have you two made up?"

"Piss off," barked Kai, dropping Miya's hand.

Miya couldn't remember when she last ate or slept, and she still didn't know how much time had passed. It was unsettling—being unaware of her own bodily needs.

"Are we going to talk about what happened, or am I no longer needed here?" Ama asked while Miya stared after Kai. He moved towards the table and placed his hands on the backrest of the chair opposite Ama.

"Lambchop?" His eyes were still fixed on Ama as he spoke. Cuing into the invitation, Miya shuffled over and sat down. His fingertips brushed her shoulders—a quiet reassurance.

"Tell me what you saw," said Ama.

Miya swallowed, willing herself back to the desert, the corpses, and finally—

"A shadow." It was the first thing out of her mouth. "He was standing on top of a hill, covered in blood. I remember when he turned, he had yellow eyes," she directed the statement at Ama, "but not like yours. They were different. Colder."

Ama laughed, the sound sweet and light like the chime of a beckoning bell. "Did you think it was me?"

Miya shook her head. "I knew it wasn't you. Eventually, it changed form. It looked human." She hesitated, repainting the face in her mind. "The eyes stayed the same, but—"

"Did he look like me?" Kai's voice dipped, quiet and guilt-ridden. He squeezed her shoulder, drawing her attention to him.

She leaned her head back and gazed up at him. "How'd you know that?"

"I've seen him before," he admitted.

"Maybe he's messing with you?" Miya reached up and poked his jaw when his eyes began to wander. "He can obviously shape-shift."

"But he's been consistent with his appearance," Ama interrupted. "A shadow, and a man who looks like Kai. Both with the same eyes."

Kai squinted suspiciously at Ama. "I never saw a shadow. Where else did you get that from?"

She looked between Kai and Miya. "You two aren't the only ones who've encountered this entity. But that's not important right now. Was there anything else?"

Miya was irked by her evasions, but she wracked her brain nevertheless. "He knows me." She tiredly rubbed her face. The memories were already fading. "He told me that we've met before. And he seemed to want to hurt me."

"How can he know you?" Kai let go of the chair and paced the room. He looked an eye-twitch away from murder, stalking back and forth at a dizzying pace. "He's been with me since I was a kid. He can't know *you*."

"He called himself my king of spades," Miya recalled. "Not too long ago, that card fell out of my playing deck. I saw it again at the diner. Maybe it's no coincidence. Maybe he does know me."

"Perhaps not from this life," Ama said, her eyes downcast as she traced a circular pattern on the surface of the table. "What you're dealing with is no ordinary spirit, from what I can tell. This Abaddon—I don't think he's just some ghost who's lingering because he has a few petty regrets. Besides," she quirked an eyebrow at Kai, "you may be a menace, but you're still young. I doubt you've done anything bad enough to deserve this. At least not in this lifetime."

Kai growled as she scrutinized him. "Why do you keep talking about lifetimes? I've only been here for one—"

"Wait!" Miya slammed her hand down on the table, jolting them both. "He calls himself Abaddon, right? That's the name of a biblical demon. So that can't be his real name—" She stopped mid-sentence, eyes widening as fragments of the journey flitted back to her. "But I already knew that. I called him out, and it weakened him, I think."

"Perhaps he doesn't have a single name," Ama suggested, her finger halting on the table.

Kai too paused, then resumed pacing. "Who cares what he calls himself?"

Ama sighed and rolled her eyes. "I've studied spirits for a long time. Ghosts usually aren't intelligent enough to give themselves names. If a spirit is intelligent, it's because it belongs to an old soul—one that's lived many lives. I wonder if Abaddon goes by a biblical name *because* he is ancient. What if he's more than just the malicious remnant of one unhappy life, but the amalgamation of countless unhappy lives—all lived by the same spirit?"

"Amalga—" Kai whirled around. "A what."

"A collection," explained Miya. "A spirit that's lived a bunch of crappy lives, right?"

Ama nodded. "And these lives must have ended in tragedy. Despite the constant effort to right past wrongs, this spirit likely repeated the same heartbreaking cycles over and over again throughout his many lives, until he became a monster."

"But if there is such a thing as reincarnation, why wasn't he reborn?" Miya challenged. "How does a spirit just stop the cycle?"

"Something fuelled only by the desire to destroy inevitably loses its desire to live," she explained. "If wilful enough, a spirit can become a force capable of resisting reincarnation. It sustains itself by haunting the person it blames most for its misery." She peered up at Kai, her amber eyes glowing as a shadow passed over from outside. "You."

Kai halted his patrol, the words percolating between his ears as his face twisted through an entire range of emotions. Shifting his weight, he leaned against the wall and crossed his arms over his chest. "So...he's a cocktail of shit?"

Ama chuckled. "Sounds about right."

"And here I thought I'd pissed off enough people in this lifetime." Kai dropped his arms, looking skyward like he was mentally combing through a list of individuals he'd wronged.

"Whatever this grudge is, it runs deep," Ama told him. "It's probably something that's been repeating for several lifetimes, if not more."

Kai squeezed his eyes shut and took a deep breath. "All right, fuck all of this for now." He spun around and headed to the bathroom. "I need a shower."

Miya watched him leave, then turned to Ama, who appeared lost in her own world. She didn't want to interrupt, but her tailbone was sore from sitting on the edge of her seat, so she got up and helped herself to the futon.

Her mind was preoccupied with the last thing she saw before she found herself back in her own body: the Dreamwalker. She glanced at Ama, wondering what the white wolf knew that she didn't.

"Do you find it difficult to accept the notion of reincarnation?" Ama asked.

Miya propped herself up on her elbow. "I guess not after all this. I wonder, though—do you think it's possible that I knew Kai as well? In another life?"

"That would be my guess, especially if Abaddon claims he knows you."

"Do you think this was meant to happen? Like destiny?"

"You sound doubtful," Ama laughed, "but reincarnation isn't so straight-forward. Things don't happen just so you fulfill some arbitrary destiny. A person can have many past lives." She pushed the chair back and stood up, then leaned over the table and stretched like a cat. "Kai's past life with Abaddon may or may not be entirely separate from his past life with you. Perhaps the two of them have lived multiple lives together—some with you, some without you."

"You said that Abaddon might be a spirit who's been repeating the same cycles until it turned him into a monster," Miya recalled. "Can someone really mess up so many times and never learn?"

"Sure, they can. It's no secret that we're drawn to what's familiar, even if it's something bad—like abusive relationships. No one wants to be in an abusive relationship, but if it's what they're used to, they'll continue seeking out abusive people." Ama whisked to the side as if prowling. "Sometimes, it takes multiple lives to learn one life lesson. You may not be conscious of it, but it's all inside of you—the culmination of your soul's experiences. It's what you were born with; it's your fate. And fate is always the beginning."

Fate is the beginning. Kai too had said those words. His past life with Miya and his past life with Abaddon may have been two separate paths at some point, but they were now coalescing—here, in the present. Miya realized that the past, long-thought forgotten, had been right there with her all along. It was alive, and it was breathing down her neck.

"So why bother being so cautious?" Miya asked. "You watch your own skin. You don't like danger. But if you get infinite chances, doesn't life lose meaning? Isn't dying irrelevant?"

Ama shook her head. "Life is precious. Every little thing we do leaves an imprint and affects who we become in the next life. If you're careless because you think you'll get another chance, it'll come back to bite you. Besides, it's instinct to preserve one's own life. And instinct can be far more powerful than what we think we know."

"Where did you learn all this?" Miya flopped on her belly. "You're like a spirit encyclopedia."

Ama shrugged. "I've lived with an old kook most of my life. He taught me a lot, but I learned some on my own, too."

A light flapping noise caught Miya's attention, and she looked over to see a raven perched on the window sill. "Hey! It's you!"

Ama followed her gaze to the window. "Kai's new friend. He seems to like it here."

"Kai has a bird-friend?" Miya laughed as she imagined him sitting at the table and whipping scraps of food at the raven. "I've been seeing this guy everywhere. He was in the dreamscape, too. He helped me." She turned to Ama. "I saw you with him while I was there."

Ama smiled—a smile different from all the others. It was warm, laced with affection and nostalgia. "He raised me."

"The bird raised you?"

Ama shook her head. "The master of the bird—and the bird." Her lips pulled back further, the warmth giving way to mischief. "Who's to say who is who? He's very old, after all."

Miya was flooded by an image from her dreams, of a small figure standing in front of a giant redwood tree, then erupting into a conspiracy of ravens. She recalled the yearning that welled up inside her when she first saw him and wondered if he was the one Ama referred to.

"Is that why you're here? Why you know so much? Because you're helping your caretaker?"

Ama's eyes shifted to the raven. "Aside from my own curiosity, yes."

"Why does *he* want to help?"

"The only thing that shithead helps with is crapping on my roof." It was Kai, emerging from the bathroom with damp hair and a clean t-shirt and jeans.

Ama paid him no mind, ignoring his reappearance. "He's a living spirit, a god with a mortal form. He's been watching the cycles of time far longer than any of us can know, and this is a vital moment in those cycles."

Kai took pause, his posture stiffening. "Living spirit? Like Abaddon?"

Ama shrugged. "Minus the malevolence. His existence isn't rooted in a focused cause the way Abaddon's is. And he's sacrificed quite a bit to remain in this realm."

Again, Miya envisioned the small figure by the redwood. "Is he going to interfere?" she wondered aloud. "If this is an important moment in the cycles, is there a chance to break them and get rid of Abaddon?"

Ama glanced between her companions, then sighed. "Honestly, I don't know if he's going to interfere. I can't say my master is a force for good or evil. His alignment is more...chaotic. All I know is that he's interested in what Abaddon might be up to. Perhaps he knew Abaddon, and others, once upon a time."

"Others? Like the Dreamwalker?" Miya offered.

"He mentions her from time to time."

"So are we just collateral damage?" Miya continued as Kai muttered under his breath. "Is he watching us through the raven because we'll lead him to the Dreamwalker or Abaddon?"

"We're bait," Kai concluded, his voice dipping.

Ama leaned back in her chair, frowning. "I wouldn't say that. He wouldn't have sent me here if he only considered you slabs of meat to lure out the goblins."

"Great," Miya sighed, then noticed the orange-red glow of sunset gleaming over the horizon.

"You've been here quite a while." Ama stood and headed for the door. "But you should probably stay the night. Once the sun goes down, it's not safe out in the woods."

Miya's mouth popped open. "Why can't Kai take me home? I'm pretty sure there's nothing out in the woods scarier than him."

Ama glanced back from the threshold, her bright, brassy eyes glistening. "Nothing of this world, no."

Miya stared after her as the door creaked shut, and she was left alone with the Big Bad Wolf.

"Kai?"

"Hm?"

"Is Abaddon the reason you blacked out before finding Elle?"

"Yeah." He sighed. "I think so."

She turned to the window to see that the raven hadn't left with Ama. "So, does the bird have a name?"

Kai grabbed a pear from his kitchen counter and threw himself down into a chair, clunking his head against the top of the backrest. "He's not my pet bird."

Miya raised an eyebrow. "Oh? But you named me after your favourite food even though I already have a name."

He lifted his head to look at her. "Sorry, but you're not my favourite food, Lambchop. I prefer bunnies. The cute, fluffy kind. Meat's way more tender."

"You're evading the question, Big Bad Wolf."

It was his turn to raise an eyebrow. "The bird is not a pet." He crunched into his pear, then smiled balefully. "But you are."

Miya narrowed her eyes, then turned to the raven, grinning defiantly while Kai glared. "Maybe I'll give you a name."

"Don't do it," Kai warned.

"Kafka!"

Kai blinked. "What?"

"The raven." Miya spread her arms. "I hereby christen him Kafka."

"The bat-shit Czech guy who wrote the cockroach story? That's—" His sentence was cut short as the pear vanished from his hand. Kafka, now a safe distance away, pecked contently at his juicy prize, having plucked himself a meal straight from the wolf's jaws.

Miya laughed triumphantly and fell back on the futon. "You deserved that."

Kai jumped to his feet and came at her with ungodly speed, grabbing her by the waist and yanking her towards him. She squealed as he darted onto the mattress and trapped her legs between his knees. He tickled her mercilessly while she tried to kick him off, but he evaded her attacks, then dove forward and nipped her neck.

Miya shrieked and choked on her own spit, coughing as she latched onto a pillow and curled into a fetal position, waiting for the assault to subside. Her eyes stung with tears as she dissolved into a fit of intermittent giggles and hacks. All the while, Kai grinned ear-to-ear as he rubbed her back to soothe her angry lungs, then crawled off her and helped her sit up.

She smacked him with the pillow she'd been clutching. "I like you better when you're playful."

"Playful?" He raised an eyebrow. "I heard tickling was a popular torture method."

"Sadist."

He leaned forward and bit the tip of her nose. "You love it."

Miya squeaked and scrunched her face from the sting. "Maybe sometimes."

Kafka finished his pear and watched them as though they were a spectacle. Noticing the attention shift his way, he sank his beak into his plush blue-black feathers, then dove from the window and flew away.

As soon as they were alone, Miya's stomach growled. Loudly.

"...I'm hungry," she said sheepishly.

Kai reached for his hunting knife. "I'll go stab you a rabbit."

"What!"

He flashed her a wolfish grin, his eyes filling with glee. "You know, those adorable, floppy-eared fluff balls that hump a lot."

Miya whacked him on the arm. "*You* can go hump a tree!"

"Don't worry," he reassured her with mock sincerity. "You won't even recognize the mangled bastard when I'm done with him. And there are softer, fleshier things I'd prefer to—"

"Not helping!" she protested.

He snorted. "Would you feel better if I said I was going to stab a wild hare? They're kind of big and ugly, so sticking pointy objects in them is cool, yeah?"

Well shit, she thought, *he got me there*. Defeated, she hugged her knees and pouted. "It's okay. I won't starve."

He hesitated, then strapped the knife back to his belt. "Sorry."

"Huh?" Had she hallucinated an apology?

"For not having more jerky. I've got whisky, though?"

A smile spread past her cheeks, but she didn't dare ruin the moment with a quip. "I probably shouldn't drink on an empty stomach."

He shrugged, then said after a pause, "I guess you are staying the night."

Miya shuffled back against the wall. "Hope you wash your sheets."

"Never."

"Ugh!" She hugged herself and cringed.

He laughed, then got up and yanked the blankets out from under her before tossing them over her head. Miya felt him drop down beside her, his arm wrapping around her blanketed form and pulling her against his side.

"You get the wall," he said as she finally dug her way out.

"Why do I get pinned to the wall?" she whined.

"Because you're twitchy. If you roll off in the middle of the night and hit the floor, I'll kill you."

"Okay," she squeaked.

"Good." His lips quirked up, and he whipped the blanket into the air, letting it float down over their bodies.

"You know, you haven't told me anything about your past." She felt him turn onto his back. "Seems kind of weird lying next to a guy I know nothing about."

"I don't really talk about it," he said curtly, then put an arm around her shoulders, his fingers absently running through her hair.

Miya took this as a good sign to venture forward. "Were you always alone?"

He shook his head. "Not always."

Of course not. He probably wouldn't have survived. "Did your parents teach you about human society?"

"They did," he recalled. "But it was mostly an old woman, Alice Donovan. She took care of me for a few years."

"But before that—your parents..."

"Shot dead by hunters when I was ten," he answered bluntly. "Saw a kid roaming around with two wolves, assumed the worst and panicked. We just happened to be in different bodies that day."

Miya swallowed down her discomfort. His tone was cold—too cold for someone talking about the death of his family. Like he'd sealed the grief away long ago, and the key to that vault was likely lost at sea. "I'm really sorry."

"I don't remember it in detail," he told her like it didn't matter. "Just bits and pieces. I know I attacked the hunters afterwards, and they hit me pretty hard on the noggin with their rifles. Made me lose my memories for a while. When Alice found me, I couldn't remember a thing."

"I mean, your parents were killed. That would mess anyone up. Maybe you pushed it down and repressed it?"

He took a deep breath, his fingers going still in her hair. "Probably. I recovered from the concussion. Some of the memories trickled back. But the change—that took a while to come back."

"When?" she asked quietly.

"Six years later, when Alice died."

"Shit..." Miya trailed off. "Did something happen?"

"Lung cancer. Her death hit me hard, and I got a little unhinged," he confessed. "Ended up having to run away."

She shuffled next to him, burrowing in the blankets. "How come?"

There was a pause before he answered, his tone the same as when he spoke about his parents. "I nearly killed someone, and not even for a good reason." His voice sank to a whisper. "He was just a dumb teenager, like me."

He stopped, like he was waiting for her to jump out of bed and run, or perhaps rain holy judgment down on him. When she did neither, he continued. "The kid got me pissed. When the fight started, I couldn't stop. By the end of it, I could barely hear his pulse. Blood was everywhere. The sounds, the smells, the rush—it unlocked the animal in me."

Miya watched his cavalier persona thaw away. She couldn't judge him, but she was approaching some kind of understanding as the pieces fell into place. His poor socialization, his anger and disgust towards humanity, his seclusion from society; they were products of his experiences growing up, not merely his conflicted nature. Everyone he'd loved was taken from him too soon. Kai's Hobbesian outlook—his belief that the world was cruel and barbaric—wasn't just because he was a wolf.

Miya pushed herself up on her elbow. "Where did all this happen?"

"Granite Falls. A small town in Washington." He adjusted his arm as she moved closer. "I fled to Black Hollow when I introduced Shit to Fan. And I've been living like this ever since."

"You're an American wolf?"

He reached over with his other arm and tapped her on the nose. "Siberian," he told her. "My family's from Siberia."

"Russian?"

"Russian-Tatar," he corrected. "Mom was Tatar, dad was Russian. You could say I'm a bit of a mutt."

With her eyes finally adjusted to the dark, Miya drank him in as best she could. It was true—he didn't strike her as someone with North American ancestry. "Did Alice know you're a wolf?"

He shook his head. "Nope. I told her a few times, but she thought I was just being a typical kid, making stuff up. After a while, I stopped mentioning it. Didn't matter, anyway, since I was stuck." He raised an eyebrow, watching her curiously as the wheels turned in her head. "What about you?"

"Oh...I grew up in a house."

"No one died, huh?"

Miya shrugged. "Only the goldfish."

"That must have been rough, Lambchop."

"The worst."

"All right, let's sleep," said Kai as the conversation came to a close.

"Wait—why are we sleeping so soon after sundown?" she questioned.

"Because I'm tired."

Despite suffering from insomnia, Miya's eyes were peeled wide open. "But I'm not."

"Don't care."

"But how am I supposed to sleep?" she griped.

"Count sheep. Masturbate quietly. Whisper sweet nothings to Abaddon so he leaves me the fuck alone."

Miya's head reeled at the prospect of staring at the wall *trying* to sleep. It was part of the futile cycle that resulted in *not* sleeping, and she hated it more than her basement cockroaches. So much so, that she was willing to stoop to new lows.

"All right." She sighed. "You asked for it. One...Two...Three...Four...Five—" she counted in a monotonous voice while Kai remained motionless. She was almost certain he was holding his breath, trying to keep himself from throttling her. "This isn't working," she mumbled, so she threw her arms up and pretended to speak to the invisible presence she knew was lurking nearby. "Abaddon, baby, don't be like this. I know you're not as well-endowed as your marginally less evil punching bag here, but we all learn to love ourselves the way God—"

She was cut off by a low growl in her ear. "I think I smell a hungry grizzly outside."

"Hey, I'm just following your suggestions."

"You skipped one," he cracked dryly.

"Then, don't mind me." Feeling facetious, Miya shuffled under the covers and slipped her hand into her jeans. But she hesitated, peeking over at her audience.

Even through the darkness, she could see the white of his teeth betraying that roguish grin. "Need my help with that?"

Miya's hand shot out from under the blanket faster than an arrow. The thumping mass in her chest twisted and thrashed, but she smiled despite herself. Maybe Ama was right—maybe she did know this vulgar ass from a past life. She hardly knew anything about him, but she didn't remember the last time she felt so at ease with someone.

Kai clicked his tongue as though disappointed. "All talk."

"Sorry, I'm not bold like you."

He stifled a snicker. "What makes you think I'm bold?"

"You seem like you don't care for pretence," she reasoned, then grinned coquettishly. "I could see you losing your virginity in an alleyway behind some seedy diner."

He didn't respond, a smirk crawling up the side of his face as he eased himself back down.

"Oh my God!" Miya sat up and shoved a finger in his face. "You totally lost your virginity next to a garbage dumpster! Or in a bathroom stall!"

"Maybe." He playfully snapped his teeth at her finger, then grabbed her arm and yanked her down next to him. "And when are you going to lose yours?"

Miya yelped as she was toppled over, her mouth dropping like a fly trap. "You can tell?"

"Oops," he simpered. "I guessed right, huh?"

She went off like a thunderstorm and whipped the pillow at his face. He turned away, laughing as she battered him with a bag of feathers.

"What are you so embarrassed about?" He snatched her weapon away.

"I don't know," she said, fumbling for an explanation. "People get weird about it. You're either too young to have sex or too old to be a virgin."

"Relax," he snorted. "It's not a real thing—just a way to let men fuck and judge women for it."

Miya stared at him like he'd grown another head.

"I don't care what you put between your legs." He rolled towards her and threw his leg over her thigh. "Unless it's mine. Then I might."

She choked through her giggles as she kicked him off. "I have no intention of putting anything of yours between my legs."

"Oh, really?" Kai grinned. "You were considering it a few minutes ago."

"I don't know yet," Miya shot back coyly. "Might need to give you a test run before committing."

He erupted into laughter, then pulled her into his side. "I'm a quick learner," he whispered in her ear, sending a current of electricity through her body.

The hunger had moved lower. Miya wasn't yet ready to bare herself entirely—literally and figuratively—but she had never been a person of extremes. Wedging her leg between his, she pushed him onto his back.

"I'll be the judge of that." There was challenge in her voice as she pressed her lips to his. He eagerly accepted and tangled his fingers in her hair, deepening the kiss as his free hand wandered down her body.

He was no longer interested in sleep, and that was fine by Miya. The Dreamwalker could hunt her in her dreams, but she wouldn't be there tonight. Temptation lay on this side, and although she wasn't prepared to fully indulge, it was where she intended to stay.

CHAPTER
THIRTY-FIVE
THE UNVEILING

"S*WEETIE, CAN YOU HEAR ME?*"

The voice sounded muffled but familiar. Perhaps someone she'd met before—someone who'd left a strong impression.

"*Miya, please, wake up!*"

The call was clearer now, more desperate.

"*Miya!*"

Her eyes shot open. Someone was holding her hand; cold, clammy sweat tickled her palm as she flexed her fingers and looked around.

"*Thank goodness, you're all right.*"

Miya recognized her mother's voice. She tried absorbing her surroundings, but everything looked like grey silhouettes on a dark background.

"*Mom?*" she tried to sit up, only to feel hands on her shoulders.

"*Don't move too fast. You're still weak.*"

Miya didn't feel weak. "*Why do you think that?*"

Silence followed, the blobs in front of her only marginally discernible. She could make out another figure—a man—standing in the back of the room.

"*You were missing.*" Her mother's voice cracked. "*You were kidnapped.*"

"*How did I—*"

"*You don't remember anything.*"

Why was she being told rather than asked? "*I don't think I was...*"

"*Don't strain yourself,*" her mother hushed. "*There's no use in thinking about it. All that matters is that you're back.*"

Back from where, Miya wondered.

"Andrea." It was her father—the man at the back of the room. "May I have a moment alone with Emiliya?"

Emiliya. He never called her that.

She heard shuffling, felt a weight lifting from the bed as her mother retreated. Why was she leaving? Before the abandonment could sink in, her father's heavy footsteps echoed closer.

"So," Miya chuckled, trying to break the tension, "took a kidnapping for you guys to visit me."

He didn't respond, but his hands fell on her shoulders and yanked her up. She winced and pulled back, trying to break free of her father's hold.

"You're hurting me!" She yelped in pain, but his grip only tightened.

"Don't lie to me!" His voice shook with rage, his fingertips digging into her skin until she felt bruised. "You're not my daughter!"

Miya grabbed his wrists. "Dad! What are you talking about? It's me!"

"Liar!" he spat, ripping his hands away. Before she could speak, fingers curled around her throat. "You must be banished. You're a curse on this place, and you must be exorcised!"

Miya clawed at her father's arm, fighting for every waning breath. Her heart shrivelled as she realized she couldn't convince him of her identity; what he saw in his daughter's place—an imposter—was all that mattered.

What would it take for her to be seen?

Tears welled in her eyes. I don't want to die. *She couldn't gather the breath to form the words. She had no voice, no power, no means to actualize her will.*

I don't want to die.

I can't.

I won't.

I won't let them hurt me anymore.

Anger and spite crept into her, pooling like liquid fire in the pit of her stomach and imbuing her with inhuman strength as she thrashed, flailed, and finally kicked herself free. A raw, war-like scream ripped from her throat as she struck her attacker and shoved him away. Salty tears spilled over her face and washed out the grey filter that blinded her.

She saw her father slumped against the wall, his eyes wide open, blank as paper. Disoriented, Miya surveyed the room—a hospital room—then looked at her hands. They were emaciated, her fingernails broken and bloodied, dirt caught in the calluses on her palms. Then she saw the black and violet feathers cascading over her shoulders. Miya shakily felt around her head. Her hair was tangled in plumage that sprouted from her scalp like it had taken root and infected her. She squeezed one of the stems and plucked out a feather, gasping when a sharp pain shot through her spine.

"Unpleasant, isn't it?"

Miya jolted at the intruding voice, her eyes darting up to find Kai—no, Abaddon —standing next to her father's limp form.

"What do you want?" She crouched on the cot and inched away only to find her back against the wall.

Abaddon's mouth twisted, his resemblance to Kai unsettling. He took a single step forward, then stopped.

"You know what happens to the girls when they return, yes?"

Miya swallowed, her neck still burning at the memory of her father choking her.

"You're just like the rest of them." *The words were accusatory, vicious.*

Miya gripped the sheets on the bed and clenched her jaw. "I won't be a victim!" She squeezed her eyes shut, banishing the malevolent presence. She knew this was a dream, a haunting. Eventually, she'd wake up.

"And then what?" *Abaddon's voice echoed as he read her mind.* **"You'll be back in the woods and only closer to your death."**

Miya straightened and caught Abaddon's gaze with a fearsome glare.

The lull in their exchange yawned out until he looked down at her father's lifeless body. **"You'll only hurt them,"** *he said in a tone that bordered on compassionate.*

"What does that mean?" asked Miya, but it was too late. Thorny vines sprouted from the floor and coiled around her limbs, biting into her flesh. As though commanded by Abaddon's laugh, they ignited into black flames.

Miya screamed and writhed against her bonds, but her blood and fear only strengthened them. The vines drew tighter, the blaze intensifying until the pain grew unbearable, and she withered and sank deeper into the dreamscape.

THIRTY-SIX

MASON

When Mason joined the town's search for Emiliya Delathorne, he hoped she'd be found quickly; but three days went by, and there was no sign of her anywhere. This, of course, only served to cement the conviction that she'd been kidnapped. The villagers tore through every inch of the forest they could map out, and yet they always missed something. No matter how many times they thought they knew where they were going, they discovered new places—groves and valleys that simply hadn't been there before.

The twists and turns that sprung with every expedition inspired more and more paranoia. The deeper the search party went, the more shadowy everything became. The air grew foggy and dense; trees cast ghoulish shadows that appeared alive in the white vapour, moving like creatures from storybooks. Some gave up, going home and wanting nothing more to do with the forest. Others grew more militant in their efforts, stocking up on rifles and all manner of hunting equipment. The most radical enthusiasts even brought ghost hunting paraphernalia—night vision accessories, EVP recorders, spirit boxes, EMF readers and the like. They were convinced that if they could somehow contact the spirits of the Dreamwalker's previous victims, they might find clues regarding Emiliya's whereabouts.

Throughout the chaos, Mason was a fly on the wall, eavesdropping on conversations while refusing to engage. Even though he'd awoken the following two mornings exhausted and sore, he couldn't pull himself away.

He feared he'd miss some integral piece of information—or worse, the search would end without him bearing witness to its resolution.

On the third day, the party broke up into groups of five or six, hoping to cover more ground. They set out in the morning and continued well after dark. Fatigue had worn down Mason's mental faculties enough that he'd forgotten—or perhaps simply given up—on recharging his phone. He had trouble focusing, losing himself to the fleeting sounds and sights of the forest. He'd broken away from the others, opting instead to use the maps that Annabelle gave him. Up until that point, he hadn't bothered checking Mathias' trails. Jenny had continued to take the lead; her family had a long history in Black Hollow, giving her access to old documents, maps, reports, and journals. Even then, the information was fragmented.

Mason had grown weary of walking in circles. He pulled the dream stone from his pocket—something he now kept close at all times. Placing it on the map in the palm of his hand, he muttered a haphazard little prayer, not expecting it would actually do him any good. But it couldn't hurt. He asked the forest to be merciful—to keep him from getting lost.

Much of his path was dictated by the height of undergrowth. He passed through a thicket of towering pine trees interspersed with firs, sugar maples, and aspens, then came across a small glen with a gorgeous white oak, densely surrounded by paper birch trees and a shallow stream. But the deeper Mason ventured into the woods, the less he noticed time pass until night fell and he was unsure of where he'd wandered and how to get back. Everything looked the same—the trees, the rocks, the spaces between them. Occasionally he'd hear whispers—or were they the cries of birds and animals? He swore they were telling him, *This way!* But whenever he turned in their direction, there'd be nothing there.

Something in his periphery grabbed his attention—the way the breeze sounded, gently nudging the leaves and branches. The stone in his hand began to hum, the song growing louder as Mason trailed the wind until he found himself drawn into the glade where the grand willow resided. He knew by the size and shape of its great mane that it was the same tree from Mathias' photo. Had he found it, or had it found him?

Mason felt compelled to touch this magnificent beast, to feel with his own senses what was behind the town's madness.

"What are you?" His fingertips hovered near the bark before he finally laid his hand on the massive trunk.

Drawn into a vacuum, the tree took hold of him. Sensations, perceptions, and emotions Mason knew weren't his own penetrated his body in disorienting waves. It was like they belonged to a multitude of people who had come to this place before him.

Then he saw the girl, the same one from his dreams. He recognized her even without the cloak—her long, dark locks swaying in time with the willow's limbs. A torrent swept through him—one he'd only felt twice before: in the dream with Gavran, and when Amanda died. Was this girl Amanda? It was torture—to recognize a person he was unable to place. When would his failures cease haunting him? He couldn't seem to bury them, no matter how deep he dug the grave.

"Why me?" He asked, meekly. "Why was I chosen for this?"

From somewhere within, the response echoed loud and clear.

Who says you were chosen?

When it became too much, Mason tore his hand from the tree. The girl disappeared like vapour, severing their moment of contact.

Mason quickly shook his head. "No, no, no, no," he whimpered. "This isn't real. You're not really here. I've heard the story—I don't want to hear it again."

From the forest behind him, Mason heard thrashing wings approach, and although he couldn't see him, Mason could feel his familiar, uncanny presence pressed against his neck.

He heard two voices—the boy's and the old man's—their every syllable in perfect synchronicity, enunciated by the same, chilling entity.

"Everything beats in cycles."

The words sucked the breath from Mason's lungs and pulled the strength from his body. Before he could utter his watcher's name, Mason released the singing dream stone and crumpled to the forest floor, his consciousness extinguished like a candle flame.

CHAPTER
THIRTY-SEVEN

KAI

EVEN WHILE HE SLEPT, there wasn't a scrap of sensory information that eluded Kai. He knew something was wrong when in the middle of the night, he was awoken by the girl's heart hammering hard enough to feel against his chest. Her arms were like ice, but her face was scorching.

Kai tore the blankets off and sat up, his gut sinking when he realized she was still asleep. He'd hoped the threat would be some intruder he could rip to pieces—another hunter or a bear.

No such luck.

He looked Miya over, but she was physically unharmed, which meant only one thing.

Abaddon was diversifying.

He cursed under his breath and pulled her into his lap, trying to rouse her with a gentle shake. "Lambchop."

She shuddered and tried to scramble away, flailing her arms. He caught her wrists, but she yanked them back with surprising vigour.

"No!" she shrieked, still unconscious. Her heels slid against the mattress as she fought against an invisible foe and thrashed violently until she nearly tumbled to the floor.

Kai tried to grab her, but she slipped through his grasp like water. His urgency mounted with her terror, adrenaline and cortisol an acrid odour in his nose. Her fear needled him beneath his skin like ants crawling in his veins, tramping his nerves.

"Please wake up," he pleaded, fumbling to keep her close, his mind paralyzed as he grappled with what to do. Ama wasn't there to help, but why should she be? He should've been able to deal with this himself.

Helplessness ensnared him like a bear trap. He hadn't felt this way in years—not since Alice died, not since his body first bent and broke and left him at the mercy of his surroundings. Miya was harbouring his demon because he'd let her take a step towards him when he should've turned her away. She'd known his secret before they'd even spoken—was the first to ever know—and that'd been enough to crack the lock on his defensive cage.

A whimper crawled from the hollow pit in his chest, morphing into a wrathful shout that echoed through the cabin before drowning in the rot of the old wooden walls. He hated feeling powerless, hated that he wanted to curl into a ball, hide his face in a tail he didn't have, and sleep until the next snow.

She saved your fucking life, he reminded himself.

Little Red Riding Hood had more teeth than the Big Bad Wolf.

She grasped weakly for his arm as though unsure if she wanted to stay put or pull away, but Kai only wanted her to wake up. A heaviness pressed against his lungs, leaving him straining for each breath.

"What do you need?" he whispered, desperate for guidance. Even the raven's squawking would've been welcome. He wove his fingers with hers, a gesture he thought useless as he watched her struggle against the malice he'd been battling all his life. Every second that passed was sheer torment, a winding downward spiral of self-loathing and shame. But Kai couldn't tease apart his myriad of emotions; he only felt the subsequent anger, and the desire to act.

Do something.

He squeezed her hand, wishing the pressure was uncomfortable enough to penetrate her nightmare.

Just. Fucking. Do. Something.

Mired in panic, Kai sunk his teeth into the underside of Miya's forearm, sparing no tenderness as blood filled his mouth. He continued clutching her hand as his jaws locked tighter. When she didn't react, he only bit deeper, harder. Crimson spilled over his lips and down her arm, soaking into her clothes and staining the sheets.

Kai heard Abaddon's wicked laughter, an echo from another realm. He was no doubt pleased. He'd succeeded in making Kai hurt the first person he'd grown attached to since Alice.

Succumbing to the futility, Kai released Miya's arm and wrapped his hand around the wound to quell the bleeding. He rocked forward and released a guttural roar. Blood smeared his face, dripping from his teeth as he squeezed his eyes shut.

The laughter came closer, rumbling from outside. When Kai looked up, *he was no longer in the cabin. A dark hallway framing a single door stretched out in front of him. Standing on four paws with his centre of gravity low to the ground, he could smell what was on the other side of that door. He had to reach it.*

"You'll never make it in time," *rumbled the voice of Abaddon.* **"You're always too late."**

From the corner of his eye, Kai glimpsed Elle standing at his side, her face blank as she wrapped a hand around her own neck, fingers grazing the bruises left by her necklace. He'd failed her, but he wouldn't fail Miya.

Kai bolted down the shadowy tunnel and slammed his body against the door until the knob shook loose, and he pawed his way inside. A hospital room. He saw Miya's toes on the cot, digging into the mattress as she shrunk away from flaming, thorny vines that coiled around her body like snakes.

Kai didn't need to look for the attacker; he knew Abaddon was right next to him. With a feral snarl, he lunged at his doppelganger, knocking him to the ground and ripping into his throat. Even as blood spewed from the phantom's neck and flooded from his mouth, he laughed maniacally, gurgling when he could no longer cackle. Immune to the carnage, Abaddon spread his arms and stared at the ceiling as he melted into the vinyl—a stain on what was once a pristine floor.

Kai leapt onto the bed and gnawed at the thorns until they snapped. When Miya's bonds loosened, she looked up from her huddled form, and relief caressed her lips into a smile.

Abaddon had been wrong. This time, Kai made it in time.

Miya threw her arms around the wolf, and he leaned into her embrace, willing his paws into hands that he could actually use.

He knew it'd worked when he felt her skin against his, now warm to the touch as she emerged from the haunting. They were back in the cabin.

Miya heaved for air as she withdrew, her face bewildered and glistening with sweat. Her eyes darted around the dim space before settling on Kai.

"You're welcome." He smirked—albeit weakly—and gently thumped his forehead to hers.

She sucked in a sharp breath and twisted her wounded arm around to find the source of her pain, gaping at the splatters of red everywhere. "What the hell happened to me?"

Kai fought the urge to sink into his mortification. "I...didn't know how to wake you."

"So you bit me?" Miya inspected the lacerations, a blend of fascination, disbelief, and ire crossing her face. "What if it gets infected?"

Kai sheepishly passed her his whisky. "This'll kill just about anything."

"If I'm lucky." She groaned, pulled out the cork, and poured the liquor over the wound, sucking on her teeth as it burned.

"Cat bites are worse," he mumbled and took back the bottle. "You'll probably be fine."

She cast him a withering look, everything from anger to mistrust working through her expression until she slumped her shoulders and sighed. "I know you were just trying to help. And you did get me out of there."

Kai chuckled and wiped a speck of blood from her neck with his thumb. "Could've done it without the horror aesthetic."

Miya tugged on her shirt and stared down at the bloody tie-dye. "Well, this is ruined." Shuffling to a clean spot on the bed, she stripped off the soiled garment, all sense of propriety abandoned with Abaddon's phantom corpse.

Not that Kai minded. He had no qualms enjoying the show even if every inch of her was sticky with blood and sweat. His eyes trailed over her modest breasts, down the length of her torso, and over the curve of her hips as she peeled off her jeans. A playing card fell from the back pocket—a momentary distraction from the view.

Miya picked up the card mottled in red and turned it over. "King of spades," she murmured, then showed Kai. "It's not just Abaddon. I think it also represents you."

He smiled wryly. "Maybe that's how I got to the other side. Blood. And your card sorcery."

Miya fixated on the card. "You may be right."

Kai wasn't in the mood for sobering discussions about blood magic. He crawled onto the bed, plucked the card from her fingers, and tossed it aside. The fear had drained from his body, but the adrenaline hadn't—at least not yet—and his patience was ground to dust. Placing his hands on either side of her, Kai pushed Miya to the wall, desire overpowering restraint as he caught her lips in a hungry kiss. He was done being playful and tired of acting aloof. The moment he smelled her arousal, felt her reciprocity, he pushed away the sullied sheets and dragged her under him. Miya slinked her arms around his neck, wrapped her legs around his thighs, and pushed her hips into his, her breath hot against his ear.

They were both exhausted and bloodied, their inhibitions stripped away by their savage brush with peril.

Words were not needed, but they both knew the test run was over.

CHAPTER
THIRTY-EIGHT

MIYA

Miya had never seen Kai look so raw. He was rattled, the nightmare whittling away the last of his defences. He didn't seem like someone who feared loss, but perhaps Miya was naïve to think that. No one was invincible.

His mouth was on hers so fast that she barely had time to think. There was a feral hunger to him, and for the first time, she saw how deep it ran. It was more than just appetite, more than a taste for vices like alcohol and sex; it was a gnawing emptiness—a loneliness that cut to the bone. Perhaps he'd gotten a glimpse of what it would mean to have his solitude salved, and the prospect of returning to that void ignited a fervent need to slake his hunger.

Miya's limbs wrapped around him without her say-so, her body commanding her to meet the weight of his hips on hers. Her breath caught when she felt his arousal against her naked thigh, but he was completely unabashed, a low groan rolling through his chest as he took her bottom lip between his teeth. They'd haphazardly fooled around earlier, their touches playful, exploratory, absent of any investment. Now they were both scalding, and neither of them seemed keen on tempering the heat.

Suddenly aware of her own blood pumping furiously through every vein, Miya fisted Kai's shirt with both hands, equal parts nerves and excitement as she swallowed the lump in her throat. The pain in her arm had subsided. Despite the haunting that'd nearly bested them mere moments ago, Kai's expression was calm as he took her in with those molten eyes—waiting, appraising. His hands rested against her thighs, thumbs smearing some of the blood that'd soaked through her clothes. She gave a small nod—permission—and he reached for her bra clasp.

"Wait," Miya stopped him, realizing how close she was to complete vulnerability. "You first."

His composure suffered a hairline fracture as he broke into a smile, his nose nudging her cheek. He rolled back onto his knees and stripped off his clothes, tossing his t-shirt, jeans, and boxers to the floor next to the mattress.

Miya sat up and pressed her back to the wall. She thought getting him naked would even the playing field—make her feel less exposed—but alas, she was a fool. Her eyes travelled over his torso, lingering on every line, then stopped at the inevitable. She'd already seen him unclothed—bloody and enraged under the willow—but she'd avoided looking below his waist in the name of some brittle veneer of propriety. Now, she couldn't stop staring, a cocktail of anxiety and anticipation swirling violently through her gut.

Kai, for his part, seemed completely nonchalant. He canted his head, eyes never leaving her as he evaluated her state. "You going to be all right, Lambchop?" There was teasing in his voice, a balmy smile ghosting his lips.

"Yeah," she croaked. "I just don't really know what I'm doing...comparatively speaking." She figured honesty was the best policy. He was clearly more experienced, and even though he already knew her history—or lack thereof—she had no intention of fibbing her way through a sexual encounter with him.

She half expected him to decide it wasn't worth the effort, but he showed no sign of giving a shit. He closed the distance between them and placed his hands on either side of her hips. Nipping along her jaw, he hooked his thumbs over the band of her panties and tugged them down, lifting her just enough to yank off the garment.

"Do you know what you like?" he asked without ceremony as he cast her underwear aside, then removed her bra.

Miya was sure her heart was straining to get blood to every part of her that needed it. Her face went hot as a kiln as she realized his meaning, her lack of clothing suddenly the last thing on her mind. She may have been green with other people, but that didn't mean she was clueless about her own body. Her mouth went dry, but the answer bubbled up regardless.

"Yes," she said when she finally recovered.

His lips curved into a smirk. "Let's stick with that then." His eyes dragged up her naked form before seizing her gaze. She saw that hunger there again, laced with the shameless certainty that she would listen when he said, "Show me."

Miya froze as the words crept into her, years of feminine socialization sending her reeling at his demand for candidness. "You want me to—" she nearly choked on each syllable, "show you...like, show you...what I do?"

Kai's brow arched, his eyes lighting up with something between smugness and amusement. "If it'll make you feel better, I can go first," he offered blithely, then ran his hand up the length of his cock, his thumb skimming across the head as though it were the most casual gesture in the world.

Miya wanted to throw a brick at him, but his confidence was intoxicating, calling to the side of her that yearned for the same reckless abandon that'd landed her there.

He wants you, she reassured herself. *Otherwise, he wouldn't be kneeling there on display.*

Drunk on his brazenness, Miya succumbed and did as she was told. She pressed her back into the cool cabin wall as her hand wandered down to the apex of her thighs. She watched as he languidly stroked himself, the reciprocation motivating.

Kai braced an arm against the wall by Miya's head and encouraged her with a ravenous kiss, his knuckles grazing her skin as he positioned himself between her legs, spreading them wider. He was so painfully close, yet she didn't dare touch him as she let her fingertips press against the small bud of nerves at her centre. Desire seared through the pit of her stomach, sinking lower, urging her to grind her hips towards him as her pleasure swelled.

Every now and again, a jostle in her chest—that persistent prickle of anxiety—wrenched her out of the moment, but Kai was there to distract her, his lips keeping her occupied, coaxing her to enjoy herself. Their bodies touched—just barely—his warmth and bare skin hovering like a wild temptation to which she was too afraid to surrender. But as she slipped a finger into her cleft and felt how wet she was, some of the trepidation finally abated, hurtling into the abyss beyond Kai's cabin. She pushed back against his kiss, deepening it until a low growl reverberated in his throat. His arm slid from the wall, and he tangled his fingers in her hair.

Remembering that she too had another hand, she ventured over his abdomen and chest, allowing herself to feel every groove sculpted by adversity. Then, she meandered lower, trailing the sharp angle of his hip bone before their hands brushed. Kai twined his fingers with hers, then let her take him in her grasp. Her fingers closed around him, hard as hell but somehow still soft to the touch. The weight of him in her hand felt good, and the way his breath caught as his teeth snagged her lower lip emboldened her to savour having some power over him. Her anxiety faded as she slipped another finger into her wetness.

Miya's pulse quickened, desire overrunning inhibition as her arousal mounted. She felt Kai smile against her lips, knowing, before his head dipped to her neck, and he peeled her from the wall. He left a trail of fire over her skin, pausing at her breasts to run his tongue over the erect peaks. His hands smoothed over her back as he dragged her under him, and her hips rose when he kissed lower, fixing himself between her thighs. Relieving her of the task he'd given her, he took her wrist and sucked off each of her fingers, then plunged his tongue inside her with an appreciative moan.

The sensation sent her writhing, and she instinctively reached down to touch herself, but he swatted her hand away without looking—damn his freakish senses. When he glanced up, his red-tinged eyes gleamed with something predatory yet playful.

"Capitalizing on my hard work?" she quipped, and his laugh rumbled against her pelvis, sending a satisfying shudder through her spine.

"I'm *learning*," Kai said emphatically, reminding her of his earlier comment.

I'm a fast learner.

His tongue flicked over her most sensitive point as he replaced the vacant space where her fingers had been with his own, and that alone nearly sent her cascading over the edge.

He definitely noticed, his grip on her thighs tightening as he drew a slow circle with his tongue, teasing around the very spot she needed to finish.

"You're an ass," she hissed, fingers knotting in his hair as her frustration intensified.

"Since you think I'm a freeloader," he murmured, "I wouldn't want you to feel cheated."

Being touched by another person was nerve-wracking, but thrilling when it was welcome, and it dawned on her that his two fingers didn't even approach what *he* would feel like. His tongue rived her from the thought, swooping lower. Increasingly feverish, Miya ground her hips against him— his hand, his mouth—aching for release.

Finally, Kai obliged. No longer teasing her with fleeting touches, his mouth descended on her where she most wanted it, his tongue sweeping over her clit. Her breaths grew wild, her pulse thundering in her ears as the crescendo surged over her, one hand lost in Kai's dark hair while the other raked up his arm. Her legs squeezed around him, but he pressed his palms to the undersides of her thighs and pushed her legs up, spreading them wider. Pleasure erupted from her core and rippled across every limb, the aftershocks leaving her in a state of rapture.

"Holy shit," she breathed out as the tremors slowly faded, her eyes fixed on the crumbling ceiling.

Kai released her legs, and she stretched them out as he half climbed on top of her, his hardness greeting her shin. Wiping his mouth, he sucked off the side of his thumb and ran his tongue over his lips. Miya's heart leapt into her throat at the bald-faced display, all insecurities about how she might've tasted soundly put to rest. The fact that it'd taken twenty-one years for her to get this far with anyone had been such an uncalled-for source of shame.

Make sure you give it away to someone special, everyone had said. But as her friends' first loves crumbled into wasted time and painful regrets, it became clear there was nothing all that special about *the first time*. What was there to give away, really? While her classmates stumbled through bad teenage sex and pregnancy scares, Miya stayed at home, hidden beneath her bedsheets as she quietly explored her body, learning every crevice and wondering if she still counted as a virgin. She figured her time would come eventually. Someone would sweep her off her feet, and she'd have a sweet but awkward first encounter. She imagined it would be some steady suburban boy who liked comic books and indie rock concerts.

But it never happened, and by the time she was halfway through college, she'd discovered that virginity was no longer an appealing trait. The men she met found it a bother. According to them, virgins were clingy or too much responsibility, and they didn't want to have to coddle someone through sex. One guy had even told her that he wanted a confident but classy slut—whatever that meant. As if Miya was some sexless, wilting flower because she'd never had a dick inside her.

So, she withdrew altogether, having lost her appetite for relationships. In the end, she grew to resent the very men whose affection she'd longed for.

Still, she never expected *this*. Not a house party with a childhood friend or a college dorm with a drunk frat boy, but a cabin in the woods with a man who looked like he'd take gunshot wounds on a dare and use the bullet casing as a shot glass. He'd probably seen and done more than any of the shitheads who'd rejected her for being too innocent.

Miya felt his arousal as he shifted his weight, his lips grazing her stomach. Now that she'd had a taste of Kai, she burned to know what the rest of him was like.

"I still want to have sex," she blurted out before the words died in her mouth.

He lifted his head, his expression unnervingly mild. "Wasn't sure you'd be up for it."

"What would *you* do if I wasn't?" She wiggled her ankle to prod him between the legs.

"I'd jerk off," he shrugged, then added with a roguish grin, "and give you a show."

Miya choked on a laugh. "I think my head would explode like a tomato in a microwave." She propped herself up on her elbow, a storm of unpleasant memories still percolating under her skin. "I want to know what it's like. With you, I mean."

The corner of his mouth quirked up. "I've never fucked me, so I'll let you be the judge."

His crassness and lack of pretence had grown on her, and while it may have caused trouble in some contexts, it now made her simmer with want. Apparently, romance was overrated.

Kai pushed himself up, reached over the side of the mattress, and rifled through his jeans until he found what he was looking for. As he turned back towards her, the sight of a condom dizzied her with relief. She'd been about to ask, her brain kicking itself for her lack of forethought.

Kai tore the package open with his teeth and rolled the condom on like he'd done it a thousand times before. Miya's stomach tightened with apprehension as she watched.

He glanced at her, catching whatever bewildered look she was giving him. "Don't worry, I'm clean," he said quietly, like her stare had hit a sore spot.

Guilt crawled up her chest. She was thinking about how many people he'd been with—how many detached, impersonal encounters had led to this moment. And he'd sensed it.

"How do you know?" she asked carefully.

He shuffled over to ease himself down next to her, his brow knitting as he struggled to get the words out. "I can smell when someone's sick," he said at last, "but I don't fuck with anything that needs a prescription, whether it's antibiotics or an abortion. I just break the condom dispensers in public bathrooms and take what I need." His eyes trailed down her body, stopping at her stomach. "In your case..." He patted her beneath her belly button, then gave her a weighty look.

"Right..." Earlier that day, he'd rudely declared that she was ovulating. "Not a bad ability to have—that nose of yours."

He shrugged. "It can be distracting, smelling everything from the clap to a bad diet."

Miya wrinkled her nose. "That sounds...unfortunate. And not very sexy."

"Trust me. Bodies smell pretty rancid when they're infected with something." His arm snaked around her midsection, reeling her in as he rolled onto his side. "I can tell you eat the occasional vegetable."

She snickered and turned to face him, her palm finding his chest. "I try to eat something green at least once a week—like kale or whatever."

Kai made a face. "Fuck kale."

"What did kale ever do to you?" she asked, tracing lines over his torso.

"Kale's just a weed skinny rich people decided to turn into a fad. I'd rather eat asphalt."

Miya's eyes widened as she sucked in a breath and pressed a hand over her mouth, her face lighting up.

"What?" Kai asked flatly.

"I just thought of a dirty joke," she mumbled through her fingers.

He raised a hand and gestured for her to hurry along. "Don't leave me hanging, Lambchop."

Her cheeks began to hurt from beaming behind her little shield. "I was going to say," she nearly squeaked, "that you'd rather eat pussy."

Kai blinked. His lips pursed, and his brows shot up in disbelief before he erupted into laughter. He spun onto his back and slapped her thigh, the light sting jostling her into a yelp as she grabbed his hand, her face scorching with embarrassment and mirth.

He pounded a fist to his chest, hacking, and took a deep breath to calm himself. "I'm so proud of you," he feigned admiration, caressing the inside of her leg in approval.

"How's uh...how's that boner doing?" she asked meekly, unable to stop grinning from ear to ear.

He lifted his head and looked down the length of his body. "Still kicking," he reassured, then sat up and flipped himself on top of her in one smooth motion. "I guess we should probably do this in missionary," he mused aloud as he leaned on an elbow to keep his weight off her.

Miya balked at him, and he asked slowly, "Unless you...have a preference?"

She quickly shook her head, and he shrugged, his fingers casually stroking over her opening. His lips tugged into a half-smile as he looked down at her. "Still wet for me, huh?"

Miya's heart somersaulted as a pleasant tingle ravelled down her spine and swirled in the pit of her stomach. She didn't have the courage to tell him how much she loved his brazen honesty, his utter shamelessness with her body. At least, not yet.

"Guess you don't need my confirmation," was all she could muster, and his smile widened into a grin, like he knew she was withholding. His fingers curled inside her in a teasing motion, and she rolled her hips up with a slight gasp before he pulled out.

Kai spat in his hand and reached between his legs. Miya grimaced, her face flinching back.

"What?" he chuckled. "Did *you* bring lube?"

She tried to lock down the laugh, but it only resulted in a hiccuping snort. "N-no," she said through a snicker.

"Well, I sure as fuck hope you've got more juice left in you then." He grabbed her thighs and yanked her lower so their hips were aligned.

"And I sure as fuck hope you have enough nerve endings on your dick to know if there's chafing," she hissed back.

His shoulders shook as he tried to suppress a laugh. "I'll let you know. But feel free to jump in if there's, you know, pain or something."

She whacked his arm, but it only served to propel him into full-blown glee. He pulled her into a hungry kiss as his tip nudged her opening. She tried to relax, sighing against his lips as she let her muscles sink into the mattress. As if feeling her slacken, he pushed in, pausing when she tensed. His thumb caressed the side of her neck, and his tongue coaxed a soft whimper from her.

As her body gradually loosened again, he slid his free hand beneath her. Pulling her hips up, he gently rocked forward, burying the rest of his cock inside her. The sensation was foreign but pleasant, accompanied by a dull ache that radiated through her abdomen.

"You good?" he asked, his hips flush with hers as he let her adjust.

She nodded. "Not the first time I've had something up there, though it was...admittedly smaller."

His eyebrow arched as he smirked. "Sex toy?"

"Bought one on a whim when I moved out to live on my own," she confessed.

"Such a rebel," he said dryly, sending her skittering into laughter.

Miya grasped his forearms and tugged him forward, yearning for the warmth of his skin. She crashed her mouth to his when their bodies met, her previously idle hands now running over his arms, his shoulders, his back. Kai growled against her lips, the vibration sending a euphoric shudder through her. His hips pulled back—mercifully, not too far back—before he thrust into her slowly, though less tenderly than before. The ache subsided, and she coiled her legs around him, offering an encouraging squeeze. His mahogany eyes flitted to hers, ensnaring her before he thrust in again, harder this time. Miya's breath caught, the fullness below her belly gradually morphing from something unfamiliar into something welcome. Every time he withdrew, she found herself craving the feel of him inside her.

Kai buried his face in her neck, stifling a groan as his fingers pressed into her thigh, his grip tightening. His breath was fire on her skin, and she snaked her arms around him, fingers knotting in his hair as she pulled him closer, her back arching. His teeth scraped along her shoulder and neck, nipping and kissing in ways she was certain would leave a mark—testament to what'd happened between them. Her gasps only made him wilder, and she briefly wondered what he was like when he wasn't holding back or being gentle.

Kai pushed himself up, his breaths heavy. He peered down at her with unrestrained hunger, eyes roaming over her body. His lips pulled back into a rakish smile, and his calloused hands smoothed along her every curve. "It's too bad my furniture's shit."

"Why's that?" Miya asked between the thuds in her chest.

Kai dropped to his elbows, his mouth on her ear as he whispered, "Because I'd break the table fucking you on it."

Miya's heart hammered up her throat as the image flashed through her mind, and for a fleeting moment, she wondered if she'd ever wanted anything more in her life. *Screw the journalism degree.*

"A new table might be a good investment," she said quickly, earning herself a breathy chuckle as Kai took her chin between his thumb and forefinger and turned her face towards him.

Sex on a sturdy enough table would mean doing this again. And doing this again would require something that resembled constancy. Whatever snarky quip Kai had planned, he'd clamped down on it as if realizing the commitment was premature. Instead, he crushed his mouth to hers, devouring her lips when he couldn't say whatever he'd originally intended. He tugged on her hips, his fervour mounting, and a low, feral sound rumbled in his throat as Miya's legs encircled him. Feeling coy, she locked her hips and pushed him back for sport, constricting his movements.

Her playful resistance only spurred his intensity. Kai tangled his fingers in her hair, firmly gripping at the roots as he lightly jerked her head back— tit for tat. Her lips parted in surprise before she cursed at him, the choice words reaping a devilish smile as he relished their game.

Miya had no idea what possessed her then—perhaps his boldness was contagious—but in that moment, all inhibition melted away as she dragged her nails down his back and said, "God, you're so fucking hard."

She saw his throat bob as he suddenly swallowed, his eyes widening a fraction before his breath caught.

"Fuck," Kai rasped, the word strangled as his control slipped. He released her hair, fisting the edge of the mattress as he slammed into her one final time.

Kai bit back a snarl, muffling his climax into Miya's neck. His shoulders went taut, and he released a long breath, his limbs slackening as his weight slowly pressed down on her. After a moment, he raised his hips just enough to remove the condom and fling it aside.

"Sorry, I couldn't finish," she said sheepishly after a protracted silence, their limbs still entwined and their bodies lying flush.

Kai lifted his head like it was made of bricks and squinted at her. "I wasn't expecting you to."

"Really?" she squirmed under him, shifting to examine his face.

He reached down and stroked her clit, the sensation jolting her out of her skin. "Still out of commission," he remarked, then flopped on his back.

"It's a little oversensitive, yeah," she said through a laugh.

His head lolled to the side as he studied her. "Did you enjoy it?"

She nodded, still reeling from the novel sensations.

"That's all that really matters then. Besides," he nudged her with his foot, "you already came on my tongue. Don't be greedy, Lambchop."

"I just thought *you'd* be upset if I didn't finish during sex."

Kai snorted. "I've fucked enough women to know not to place my bets on this guy." He pointed below his hips.

Miya wondered how many women qualified as *enough women*. "So, you always wear condoms then?" she asked evasively, his history still a burning question in her mind.

"With strangers, yes. With you..." He paused, his eyes drifting to the ceiling. "I guess that depends on how often you want to do this."

His declaration about the table flitted through her mind, and not without the accompanying image—one she was sure would occupy her fantasies for days to come. He'd stopped short when she'd suggested getting a new one, but something told her it wasn't the financial expense. She suspected that his sexual encounters up to then had been largely casual, free of any entanglements.

"Wouldn't it also depend on whether anyone else is involved?" she asked, dodging the question.

Despite her caginess, he caught on, cracking a smile as he repeated his earlier sentiment. "And wouldn't *that* depend on how often you want to do this?"

She supposed he was right. If they were only hooking up occasionally, then it would be strange to demand commitment. "Not...infrequently..." Miya stuttered, the acknowledgement snagging on its way out. "I mean, I'd like to be friends..."

He turned onto his side to face her. "Are you asking me to be your special friend?" he asked wryly.

"Yes." Her gut twisted with trepidation the moment the admission left her.

He scrutinized her as she squirmed, evaluating something only he was privy to. "Okay," he said finally, his tone revealing nothing.

Taken aback by his nonchalance, Miya blinked away her stupor. "So... does that mean I get you to myself?"

He settled on his back as she gingerly tucked her head in the crook of his arm. "If that's what you want."

"It is," she mumbled warily, though she sensed no resistance in him.

"I assume I get the same," he said after a short lull.

Miya huffed dramatically, some of the stiffness leaving her. "No way. I'm starting a reverse harem."

Kai's breath halted before he barked out a raucous laugh. "Please, you'd come crawling right back."

"What makes you so sure?" Miya sputtered at his blatant arrogance.

He snatched her wrist and hauled her high enough to press his lips to her neck, tracing a path to her ear. She felt a momentary prickle as his mouth passed over what she knew was a raging hickey. "I'm sure," he murmured, "because you're still thinking about that table."

Her eyes widened, and she felt his lips tug open against her skin, teeth grazing with feather-like softness.

"Don't think I can't hear your heart trying to pull a prison break on your ribcage," he chided.

"Okay," she squirmed against him, "but that was really hot."

"Mhm," he hummed like the compliment meant nothing—or like he already knew and was simply agreeing.

Miya wedged a leg between his knees and plastered herself against him, melting into his warmth. She'd never been naked with anyone—had never known the comfort of feeling exposed skin against her own. For all of Kai's edges, she was grateful he didn't mind a little affection and pillow talk.

The tumult inside her finally quieted. The earth hadn't shattered even though everyone kept telling her it would. She was still the same person, and if anything, she felt good for the first time in a long while.

"Have I worn you out yet?" Kai asked with a light squeeze.

"Plenty..." She'd been so reluctant to sleep, but her body felt almost liquid now. Her eyes drifted shut as fatigue overcame her, and everything faded to black.

CHAPTER
THIRTY-NINE

MIYA STIRRED when the warmth enveloping her peeled away, and Kai's weight lifted from the mattress. Stretching her limbs, she banished the dregs of sleep and squinted into the darkness. She caught Kai's silhouette as he straightened, buckled his belt, and threw on a shirt. He paused and turned towards her, his animal senses no doubt alerting him to her wakefulness.

"Where are you going?" she asked groggily. The cabin walls were threadbare, the chilly autumn air seeping in and leaving goosebumps over her skin.

"Hunting," his voice cut through the blackness.

"Aren't you tired?"

He picked up his hunting knife and strapped it to his belt. "I only sleep a few hours at a time. Four at the most."

Miya curled into a tight ball. The prospect of being alone in the forest at night left her uneasy. She wracked her brain for an excuse to make him stay —anything.

Why do you need an excuse? Just say you don't want to be left alone, she badgered herself, but her mind wouldn't stop spinning. There had to be a better reason than that—something he couldn't say no to.

Yet no matter how much she tried to eschew the truth, she couldn't think of anything convincing. Realizing she had no pretence to fall back on, Miya braced herself for a rebuff—or worse, mockery. Without any time to rehearse, she choked out, "I don't want you to go. Your cabin is creepy as hell."

She thought insulting his cabin would make the whole thing seem more

224

casual, but instead, she felt like a wimp. She'd never made such blatant demands on anyone. She couldn't even ask her parents for help or talk to her best friend about how afraid she was, how lost and alone she felt.

Kai laughed sharply as she insulted his home, the sound shredding the stillness. "I'm not going far."

"Please," she insisted. "I'm...really not used to being in a lightless ramshackle in the middle of the woods—with a demonic spirit lurking around to boot. And frankly...it's *freezing*. I hadn't noticed earlier because you're a damn space heater."

He hesitated then, shifting his weight as though considering her words. "Aren't you hungry?"

"Yes," she said, "but I'd rather have you than food. I'll eat in the morning."

At that, he unstrapped his hunting knife and came over to her. The mattress dipped with his weight, and the moment he was within reach, Miya wrapped both arms around him and hauled him down. Mercifully, he cooperated, chuckling as he stripped off his clothes.

"What?" he asked when he caught her staring. "Skin on skin feels better."

Her heart flopped hopelessly against her ribs, but she wasn't about to protest as his arms encircled her. He maneuvered her until she found her backside pressed snuggly against his hips. His warm breath fell on her nape, and she craned her neck as his lips roamed over her skin.

"Thanks for staying." Her eyes drifted shut, though she began to wonder if he'd been itching to leave. "How long have you been awake?"

He shrugged, shifting his arm. "Not sure. A few hours maybe?"

"And you've just been lying there, staring into space?"

"Dozing mostly," he said, shifting onto his back.

He didn't even blink when she plunked her head down by his shoulder. After a moment, she found the courage to roll into him, sneak a leg over his thigh, and splay her hand over his abdomen. He didn't react. No awkward shuffling. No sudden tension. The only perceptible movement was the steady rise and fall of his chest. His fingers found her hair, gently combing through the long wavy strands.

Unnerved by his calm, Miya asked, "What are you thinking about?"

"Absolutely nothing," he said blandly, no hint of sarcasm.

It wasn't until she grew restless and her limbs scraped over him that the night's earlier activities cascaded through her mind in a delicious flurry. Her gaze trailed the lines of his naked form.

Miya was sure he heard her pulse quicken. He smiled knowingly, making no effort to move away.

"Get used to it," Kai advised with a yawn.

Try as she might, Miya found herself unable to move past those words. Did that mean they'd be waking up together more often? She supposed they'd agreed to...*something*. They hadn't really given it a name, and truthfully, Miya wasn't sure what *special friends* meant. Hannah would have stared at her and declared, *So, you're fuck buddies?*

Which would've been fine had Miya wanted that, but she'd explicitly avoided semantics that would've given him permission to be cavalier.

Not that Kai had given her reason to think he'd be callous towards her. Still, there were a million shades of grey between friendship and romantic love, and Kai was somewhere on that gamut. Where, exactly, was a mystery. Miya decided the important part was that he'd agreed to exclusivity, but she kept tripping over the prospect of it going smoothly. When did relationships ever go smoothly?

As her mind battled itself, Kai idly stroked her abdomen, drawing slow circles that wound lower, then lower still.

Was he being coy? Trying to hint at what he wanted? Or was he just messing with her, knowing full well the effect he was having?

When Miya finally glanced up, he was grinning, the mischief in his eyes answering her question. As if a wolf would practice subtlety in anything, let alone seduction. He'd simply wanted to make her squirm.

"Ass!" She smacked the arm responsible for caressing her.

Kai laughed raucously, her flustered flailing clearly a source of entertainment.

"Screw you," she chuckled, then lightly whacked him below the waist. "And this thing too."

His laughter only intensified, echoing through the cabin like a riot. "You did screw me—"

She groaned loudly before he could finish. When her embarrassment passed, she risked a gander.

"What?" he probed.

"Just...getting to know you," she said carefully, and he snorted in response.

"Did you need measuring tape?" he asked, his fingers trailing lightly down her shoulder and over her arm.

She rolled her eyes. "It's not like I've got a point of comparison."

He raised an eyebrow, a smirk playing on his lips. "Just enjoying the view?"

She smiled back. "Something like that."

He looked more relaxed than she'd ever seen him, allowing her the space to act at her leisure. He didn't care that she was studying him like a specimen under a microscope, or that her mind was wild with confusion about how, exactly, she was supposed to behave. He just lay there, entirely unbothered, skimming over every inch of her with a lazy, featherlight touch.

Wait three days before texting. Act casual. Make him think he wants you more than you want him.

She was afraid that being honest would incite his ire, or worse, his revulsion. Miya knew it made no sense to feel that way, yet years of poor outcomes with other men had taught her to expect the nonsensical.

I thought you were chill, one college freshman had said when Miya asked him why his tongue had found its way down a classmate's throat. He knew Miya was interested in him.

It's not like I'm dating you, he'd sneered in non-response, then promptly blocked her on social media.

As if they had to be dating for him to treat her with common courtesy.

She couldn't stop mulling over how it continued to affect her—how hard it'd been to ask Kai to stay. Some part of her was still petrified that he felt smothered or annoyed.

How trivial, to be scared of the dark.

She'd gone through life never making demands on people because she was afraid her demands weren't worth anyone's time. And that included the trifling ones—something as small as a hug or as banal as an honest conversation.

She hated it. She didn't want to live in fear of being denied, but she couldn't stop herself from wondering what he thought of her—if he regretted giving her the opportunity to ask for his commitment.

"Hey—" she ventured.

He slanted his head. "Hm?"

"This thing we're doing...we're not just exclusive fuck buddies, are we?"

His mouth tugged into a frown. "Is that what you're freaking out about?"

How did he know? Could he smell *that* too?

"It's just...I don't really know what a *special friend* is," she admitted. "Maybe I should have asked—I'm sorry. There's a lot of terminology that gets thrown around and I don't know what any of it means and—"

His hand clamped down on her forearm. "Slow the fuck down," he interrupted, then sighed heavily. "Did you think I was going to fuck off because you wanted to touch my dick?"

Her mouth opened and closed. "I—maybe...And because I made you stay with me when you wanted to leave. I thought you'd decide I'm more trouble than I'm worth."

Kai grumbled under his breath and dropped his head on the mattress. "How gaping of an asshole do you think I am?"

Miya wrinkled her nose at the idiom. "I don't think—"

"All right, listen," he interjected. "First off, I didn't *want* to leave. I got up to hunt because I was done sleeping and you haven't eaten in a week—"

"It's been, like, a day..."

"Whatever. Practically a week. Second, you didn't force me to do shit, *Lambchop*," he emphasized her nickname. "You said you'd rather have me than food, so I gave you what you wanted."

"I guess..." It never occurred to her that he'd actually *want* to oblige her wishes.

"Third..." He rolled his neck out, then glanced at her. "You've seen me drooling on the floor half dead and looking like a goddamn potato. I puked up what tasted like literal shit right in front of you, murdered Bambi, and bit your arm like some rabid dog trying to wake you from a nightmare, but you're worried I'll *fuck buddy* my way out of this?"

"I don't know," Miya stammered. She turned onto her back and rubbed her hands over her face, her voice muffled behind her palms. "It's not the first time I've felt like I've bonded with someone only to have them ghost me."

"I thought we agreed you could have me to yourself," he reminded her.

"We did, and I'm happy you're okay with it." She hesitated, fighting the lump that kept crawling up her esophagus. She dropped her hands to her sides and looked at him. "But that's just sex."

He let out a hefty sigh. "You also told me you wanted to be friends."

"In my experience," she began, "friendship means a lot less to people once they start sleeping with you. Hence the fuck buddies."

Kai scoffed. "I think we're well past the point of being *buddies*, fucking aside." His jaw clenched as he considered her, and for a moment, she thought she saw him tamp down a grimace. "Do you know why I don't have any friends?"

"Because you live out in the woods and hate people?"

He rolled his eyes. "Besides that."

"Not really, no."

"Because I take that shit seriously," he said, his voice low. "It takes a lot out of me, and after Alice died, I couldn't be bothered to give that much of myself to anyone. And what's the point if I can't be myself? Besides, most people don't have friends. They have...bodies they kill time with."

Miya's mind ceased its crazed spinning as she mulled over this. He was a wolf—an impossible truth to disclose, but a necessary one for a genuine bond. Had Kai avoided commitments precisely because he took them seriously? "Other than Alice, have you had any friends?"

He thought about it for a moment. "No."

Miya took a deep breath, her heart heavy. "No love to spare, huh?"

"No love, no trust, no loyalty," he said. "So, when I told you we could be friends, I meant it. The fucking doesn't change that."

Miya rolled onto her stomach, her arm pressed to his side. "If you really take friendship that seriously, you'd make a better boyfriend than most guys who say they're looking for their soulmate."

Kai winced at the b-word, and Miya snorted. "Sorry, do you prefer *friends with benefits* then?"

He gestured up and down his body. "I wouldn't call this a benefit."

"Oh? What is it then?"

He angled his head, struggling to keep a straight face. "The core package."

Miya blinked, then snorted back a laugh. She supposed that was true; *friends with benefits* made it sound like the *benefits* were somehow external to the relationship—something tacked on. Suddenly, the phrase *special friend* didn't sound so foreboding. It hadn't been an evasion or an understatement; it actually meant quite a lot.

"And you're okay with our...difference in experience?" she asked, quieting the last of her fears.

He flashed her a roguish grin. "Don't worry. By the end of the month, you'll be as filthy as I am."

There it was again—that unnerving confidence of his, seeping into her bones and stirring her senses like a drug. "So, we're stuck together?"

"We are," he confirmed, no hint of regret in his tone.

Uncertainties salved, Miya lowered her head onto his chest. Her eyes drifted shut, and the pull of sleep dragged her down until she sank into its welcoming embrace.

CHAPTER

FORTY

MASON

Mason slipped in and out of consciousness. A woman's voice echoed through his mind, incomprehensible but comforting. He knew this woman; he knew they'd met before. It wasn't Annabelle or any of the villagers he'd come across. No, this voice belonged to an outsider. At one point, he heard her arguing with someone—a man.

She leaned close and whispered something in Mason's ear. He didn't understand what she was saying; he only understood that it was soothing.

Mason heard the man storm out, followed by another presence.

The woman's voice grew murky. It was like sinking underwater. Everything from the surface grew dimmer until finally, it all went black.

When Mason awoke, his eyesight was blurry. He could tell from the size and shape of the room and the grimy wooden panelling that he was neither at Annabelle's farm nor at the church. A pillow was tucked behind his head, and a scratchy wool blanket covered his legs and stomach. Taking a deep breath, the smell of wet lumber, dust, and wildlife filled his nostrils. Mason surmised he was in the woods, and this cabin must've been used by the villagers while they were on their search. He remembered blacking out—the reasons for which were unclear to him—but he figured someone found him and brought him here.

Mason rubbed his eyes, his surroundings coming into focus when he opened them again. The cabin was barren, save for the futon under him, a small nightstand, and a wooden table accompanied by two chairs. There was a small kitchenette with no appliances—just a few cupboards and a countertop with a portable element.

Sitting up slowly, Mason took his time adjusting. His legs were wobbly, but after giving them a good shake, he was able to stand and move around. The sun was setting. How long had he been out?

His memories of the previous night were like a dream—a vague, evanescent memory—but they'd felt far too real. There was the willow, the image of a girl, and then Gavran.

He'd also dropped the dream stone during the ordeal. After frantically patting down his pockets—all of which were now empty—Mason spun around to find the purple labradorite resting on the nightstand.

He didn't remember it being there when he first woke up.

Scooting over, he picked up the rock and held it up to the light as if to authenticate it. All the patterns were there, and he could feel the faint but familiar scratch marks with his thumb. Sighing heavily, Mason slipped the stone back into his pocket, wondering why he'd grown so attached to it. Perhaps it *did* help anchor him.

He could hear murmurs outside—voices speaking to each other around the periphery of the cabin. They sounded completely human, and in that moment, nothing could have made Mason happier. He figured they were volunteers who'd stayed behind to care for him. It was embarrassing, and he would likely have to explain himself—who he was and what he was doing there—but he was too grateful to feel bashful about it now.

There was still a shred of humanity left in this forsaken labyrinth, and it was waiting for him outside.

FORTY-ONE

KAI

KAI TUGGED on the knot to make sure it was secure. A slow grin spread over his face; he'd been rewarded with a new toy after his little adventure, and he was eager to test it out.

"Seriously, where did you get that?" Miya eyed the hammock suspiciously. She'd conked out pretty hard after their fun the previous night, though Kai reckoned her exhaustion also had something to do with the otherworldly shenanigans. Now well into the following day, she seemed intent to stick around even as the sky darkened. Time flew by when they were together, and he had to admit...it was nice.

"Stole it from some campers while you drooled on my pillow." He flashed her a devilish grin, tying another knot. He'd gone to scavenge for food and came upon a campsite complete with stale burgers, beer, and the hammock.

Kai leapt into the canvas net, tensing up just in case it collapsed. "Safe."

"I'm not sleeping in that," she told him, taking a step back as he pouted.

"Why not?" He snatched her wrist and tugged her towards him. "It's not like we're going to have sex in it."

"Oh, you've considered it."

"Crossed my mind." He smirked. "But then I realized you'd bitch about the rope burn."

"Wow, I'm such a buzzkill," she laughed, then crawled onto the hammock next to him.

"So," Kai prodded her with his elbow, "how was it?" He'd already asked last night, but he would've appreciated a bit more ego stroking.

"How was what?" She batted her eyelashes, feigning innocence.

Kai arched a brow, scantly amused by the fib. "Did you already forget about us fucking?"

"Oh, that!" She smiled sheepishly. "It was fine."

His mouth dropped open, every muscle taut as her words sunk in. "*Fine?*"

Miya shrugged. "Can't say I feel any different. The world is still the world, and the earth hasn't shattered beneath my feet or anything."

Kai eased back and chuckled. "I did say it wasn't a big deal." His eyes narrowed at a passing cloud. "Really, though, just *fine?*"

He could hear her pulse thundering under her skin like a war drum. She was grinning when he glanced over, her cheeks ablaze as she reached over and patted him on the crotch. "You were magnificent," she patronized.

Kai hacked on a snort and burst into maniacal laughter. "Say whatever you want, Lambchop. That tomato you call a face doesn't lie."

"Well, I guess you don't need my validation, then," she shot back, her eyes sparkling with glee.

"Touché," he grumbled his resignation.

She shuddered against his arm, sucking in a breath through clenched teeth. "I'm going to freeze out here."

Kai reached under the hammock and grabbed the wool blanket Ama had left them. She'd flown in like a homing missile after sensing Miya's distress—though she arrived pretty late to the party and well after the fireworks. Of course, that didn't stop her from casting judgemental glares after seeing the literal bloody mess Kai made. Fearing his incompetence, she supplied them with blankets and an ointment for Miya's wound.

Kai spread the quilt. "If you want someone to blame, blame that shit-nugget inside."

"The unconscious guy you found while you were robbing that campsite? I've seen him before at the market." Pulling the quilt up to her chin, she curled up against his side like a cat. "He's a tourist."

"I remember his scent from the hospital." Kai lifted his arm so she could get comfortable. "Would have left him to the coyotes, but I want to know why he's following me. Ama thinks he'll wake up soon, so she fucked off and left him with us."

"Wait—you were in the hospital?"

"Long story," he said. "Got hit by a bus."

"What! How are you—" She gestured over his body.

"I heal freakishly fast. Consider it one of my perks." He winked.

"And you never thought to tell me!" She threw an arm up and let it fall limply at her side. "Fine then. Can I just stab you when you're evasive and insufferable?"

Kai leaned close and scrutinized her. "Between the two of us, I thought *you* would have healthier conflict resolution skills."

"Not under your influence," she puffed.

Kai opened his mouth to respond when the cabin door swung open, and out came the shit-nugget. He looked hungover, squinting at the sky like he'd just seen Jesus. Kafka circled overhead, squawking like a personal alarm system. Kai was aware this fool had been in his hospital room, rummaging through his things while he pretended to be unconscious. Survival instincts told him this man was dangerous; not because he meant to be, but because he was a moron. He considered snapping his neck at the first opportunity, but something told him his teething baby lioness wouldn't be pleased. Kai begrudgingly accepted that he wanted to see more of her, and murder wouldn't help his chances. He watched as their intruder stumbled out in search of salvation.

"Should we get his attention?" Miya whispered.

"Naw," Kai grinned. "Let him find his own way." He dropped his head back against the hammock, closing his eyes and enjoying the cool breeze while his ears remained attuned to the nearby irritant.

The stranger wandered up to them and cleared his throat. "Excuse me, could you tell me where—" he stopped mid-sentence, his heart pounding like a greyhound's feet on tarmac.

When Kai opened his eyes, the man's mouth was agape, his bloodshot eyes like saucers as he gawked at the pair in the hammock. The colour was fast draining from his face, his expression stupefied.

"It's you!" He pointed an accusatory finger at Kai. "The man with wolf's blood."

Miya pushed herself up on her elbows and peered at him. Feeling protective, Kai too sat up, his nonchalance falling away.

"Are you Kai Donovan?" the intruder asked pointedly, his shock morphing into something sharper. Something aggressive.

"Who's asking?" Kai regarded him through slit eyes.

A relieved smile spread over the man's face, and he extended a hand. "Mason Evans."

Kai ignored the gesture. Handshakes always came from people who wanted something. He fixed a cold stare on Evans's face. "Your name doesn't mean anything to me."

"Of course," the man withdrew his hand with a tepid smile. "I've been looking for you. Your blood has to be the stuff of miracles."

"Did you stalk me into the woods?" Kai pinched the bridge of his nose and muttered, "You're worse than that fucking tree."

Evans shook his head. "I'm not a stalker. I just didn't expect to run into you here." He paused when he noticed Miya shackling Kai to the hammock, his face exploding into a mural of squirrelly emotions.

"I remember you from the market." He sounded sure of himself, turning his finger at her like a laser-pointer. "You're the girl they're looking for. The girl from the village."

She loosened her grip on Kai's arm. "They?"

"The villagers," he began, "They've been looking for you. You've been gone for almost five days."

Kai heard her heart pattering against her ribs. She was gripping hard again, squeezing the blood right out of his wrist.

"F-five days? That's not possible—it's only been a day and a half! Two at most!" She threw the blankets off her legs. "There's no way—"

"Time works differently here," Kai broke in, placing a hand on her knee. "It's happened to me, too."

"Listen," Evans raised both hands as if he were calming a child. "The villagers are looking for you. They're on some witch hunt. They think you've been kidnapped and they're ready to burn down the whole forest to find you. You know what happened to Elle Robinson, right?"

"Why would you go with them?" Miya asked. "You're not from here, so why would you go along with it? Couldn't you stop them?"

"No way!" he exclaimed. "They would have lynched me. I came here to warn you!"

Kai felt his blood boil. He knew they were referring to the legend. Every time one of the girls went missing, the villagers blamed their bedtime stories. Now they were trampling through his home, hunting their boogeyman.

Evans sighed. "It sounded insane—everything people here believe. But I had to know if it was true," he admitted. "There must be a reason for this."

He spoke like a man with blinders on. Whatever his goal, Kai could smell he was trouble.

"That's cute, but what exactly do you want from me?" He grunted.

"Your blood." Mason Evans didn't hesitate as he looked Kai straight in the eye. "I want to study it."

"Why?" Kai growled.

"You survived what should have been a fatal accident—without any treatment. If there's something in your DNA that helps you heal, you could save countless lives."

"What are you? Some kind of mad scientist?"

"I'm an oncologist," he replied. "I know you probably don't care, but I've been through too much to mince words."

Miya frowned, eyeing him suspiciously. "If you're a doctor, why are you here? Shouldn't you be in some big research hospital at a university or something?"

He turned to her, the lines in his smile bleeding a sickening nostalgia. Kai hated sentimentality, and this guy was constipated with it. "I came here to get away from something. A patient of mine. She died before her time, and it was my fault. I came here to forget about it. But then I heard about the Dreamwalker, the willow," he returned to Kai, "and then you."

"Wait, back up," the little lioness interjected. "You've been running around with these lunatics to stalk Kai because you want his blood?"

Evans's mouth popped open, his face scrunching in displeasure. "As I said, I came here to save you."

Kai snorted. Was he expecting thanks?

"Save me?" Miya raised a brow. "And is that for *my* sake, or for *yours*?"

"Does that matter!" Evans threw his arms out. "The point is you're in danger and—"

"Someone's coming," Kai hushed them, jumping out of the hammock. "Two of them."

Evans opened his mouth, but he was quickly shushed by Miya. Barely a moment later flashlights could be seen, and two men emerged from the trees. One of them had a rifle, while the other carried an axe over his shoulder.

"Oh no," said the onco-whatever. "You two should get out of here before they start trouble."

"They've already started trouble," replied Kai. He knew what bloodlust smelled like. From the corner of his eye, he saw Miya take a step back and move closer to him. She seemed to trust his instincts.

"Who's there?" The man with the axe called out as they approached. He was the more confident of the two—tall with bulging biceps and shoulders. Hopefully, the shorter one with the gun wasn't nervous *and* trigger-happy.

"Who the hell are you?" Axe-man demanded as he puffed his chest out at Kai. He gave the scrawny doctor a suspicious glance but seemed less threatened by him.

Seeing the snarl creeping onto Kai's face, Miya quickly cut in. "He's just—"

"Wow, not so fast, miss," the other one warned, cocking his rifle. "We've been instructed to be real cautious with strangers out here."

"But I'm the—"

"No one asked you anything!" the burly one hollered. He shone his flashlight in her face before addressing Kai again. "Now identify yourself. I haven't seen you with any of the search parties."

"You wouldn't know me," Kai glowered. As the light passed over his face, crimson reflected from his mahogany eyes.

"Shit!" the lumberjack wannabe jumped back, dropping the flashlight to the ground and swinging the axe off his shoulder.

The other one raised his rifle, pointing it straight at Kai. "What's wrong?" His voice wobbled as he glanced wildly between his target and his friend.

"His eyes, man! He's not human!"

Before the bullets came blazing at him, Kai kicked the flashlight straight at axe-man's face. The gym rat managed to turn away just enough to avoid a concussion, so Kai lunged at him to draw attention away from Miya.

It worked. The gunman shakily followed while his friend roared in a fit of rage, swinging his weapon like a berserker. With Kai's nimble body and quick reflexes, those heavy swings were easy to evade. Yet as the man turned to face him, something else caught the wolf off guard; his attacker's face was warped beyond recognition. His eyes were pitch-black, his mouth twisted open and disjointed while his flesh cracked and split like a chasm. Dark blood oozed from the cavity slithering up the side of his face. It was enough to break Kai's focus, though he managed to pull himself together for the second flurry of attacks.

Kai could hear Abaddon's laughter emanating from a shadow lurking somewhere behind the logger. He knew the phantom was the puppeteer pulling the strings, and the human nothing more than a faceless puppet wearing a grotesque mask.

"Kai!"

Miya's voice snapped him back just as the blade came down towards his shoulder. Sidestepping the swing, faded iron passed heavily through the space beside him, pulling the man forward with unchecked momentum. Kai quickly closed the gap between them and grabbed the axe arm. Twisting viciously, he forced the logger to release his weapon. Kai snatched it up and smoothly flipped the haft to turn the blade, striking the man on the back of the head with the butt and knocking him out cold.

Just as he turned towards the second attacker, the deafening sound of a gunshot rattled through the air. The ringing silence that followed was dizzying; he heard Miya cry out as a sharp pain cut through his left arm. Kai flinched but quickly regained composure before the gun was aimed at him a second time.

"What's wrong with you!" It was Miya, throwing herself at the gunman. She grabbed the rifle, yanking it from his grip. The hunter quickly tugged back and shoved her—but not before she kicked him in the nuts.

Seeing her tumble back, urgency wrenched at Kai's heart. He rushed at them with superhuman speed, locking the length of the barrel under his arm and landing a punishing elbow against the hunter's face. His jaw snapped out of place, the crack followed by a satisfying wail. Fuelled by blind rage, Kai grabbed him by the back of the head and snarled in his face, then clamped his teeth around the man's ear. Ignoring the muffled plea, he viciously jerked away, ripping the appendage clean off.

An agonized scream followed as the villager fell to the ground, thrashing as he clutched the side of his face. Kai spat out the ear like it was rotten fruit, then brought his heel down on the villager's head to knock him unconscious.

He could smell the fear and adrenaline as he stalked up to Miya and took her by the shoulders.

"Are you all right?" he asked evenly, though he knew his eyes were still ablaze, blood dribbling down his lips and chin.

She nodded quickly, her body trembling under his touch. He wondered if part of her was repulsed by him.

"He shot you." Her voice quivered as she clutched his arm. "You're bleeding."

"It's fine," he sighed, glancing down where the bullet had grazed him. He gently pulled her by the elbow. "Let's get back inside."

"Kai—you're shaking."

Stopping, he looked at his hand—still balled up in a fist. The tremor was noticeable, but it wasn't from the fight.

"It's Abaddon," he seethed. "He's doing this."

"If he's possessing people, we need to get out of here," Miya urged. "Ama will be back soon. She might have some ideas."

For once, he didn't feel like badmouthing the white-haired she-wolf.

"Hang on!" It was the Golden Turd, finally emerging from his paralysis. He rushed over to them. "We can't just leave them here! You seriously hurt them!"

Kai turned his wrath onto the doctor. "I will fuck the sun out of your sky if you don't get out of my way," he threatened, his eyes flashing with poorly controlled anger.

The girl quickly turned to Mason—his face pale as he recoiled. "Not a good time," she warned. "Just come inside with us."

"But we need to put his ear on ice!"

"Screw his ear! He tried to shoot us!" she yelled.

"But—"

She threw her arms out in disbelief. "They're clearly not here to save me. They're out for blood, just like you said! So you either come with us, or you stay here to sew Van Gogh's ear back on and risk becoming target practice for the next trigger-happy psycho that strolls by."

Kai was grateful she took the reins in light of his dwindling restraint. He watched as Evans descended into a moral crisis.

"I'm a doctor," he insisted. "It's my sworn duty to help people."

"And what about us?" Miya's temper flared as she jabbed him in the chest. "What about your duty to the people who had guns pointed at them for no reason?"

His face twisted like someone had gutted him. "I still don't think they deserved this."

"It's not about what they deserve," said Kai. "It's just survival."

The doctor turned to him, their eyes meeting properly for the first time. Kai knew he was running. The coward didn't want to make a choice; he didn't want to dirty his hands.

"If you try to save everyone, you'll end up killing them all." Kai glanced at Miya, then back at Evans.

"I destroyed one thing to save another," he said, wiping the blood from his mouth. "It's the only thing I've ever been able to do right."

CHAPTER
FORTY-TWO

MASON

MASON EVANS WAS at odds with himself. The final pieces of the puzzle were dangling in front of him, but to pursue them, he'd have to abandon the wounded villagers that had been shredded by Kai Donovan. He wanted to flip a coin, but he had nothing on him. All he had was the dream stone, and he already knew where its vote would be cast.

Mason turned around and followed the pair towards the cabin. Who knew what possibilities were in Kai Donovan's blood? Who knew *what* Kai Donovan was? A man? A wolf? Mason couldn't abandon that—not now.

"I think we broke him," Mason heard the girl whisper.

"He's fine," Kai dismissed her concern, then turned to frown at Mason. "Hey, unpucker your asshole. Makes everything run smoother."

Mason's mouth popped open, but he was at a loss for words. *My asshole is just fine, thank you*, he wanted to retort, but decided against it. He saw what happened to those men; he didn't want to get on Kai Donovan's bad side.

When they stepped into the cabin, Mason's eyes fell on the woman he'd met at Gavran's treehouse—Ama. Was she the one speaking before he awoke? She was sitting at the table, her face serene like she'd been expecting them.

"Did Gavran bring me here?" He couldn't stop the words from leaving his mouth. His mind was still on the two men outside—that one ear lying in the grass as its cells slowly died, making it impossible to reattach.

"Who's Gavran?" asked Kai, raising an eyebrow at Ama. She smiled but said nothing.

"You don't know him?" Mason's stomach churned as he re-imagined Kai spitting out the ear like it was gristle off a lousy steak.

"Never heard the name," Kai shrugged, then turned to Ama and motioned his head in Mason's direction. "You know this guy?"

"We've met once," Ama acknowledged.

"You said we'd meet again," Mason recalled.

"And we did." She seemed undaunted. "What was the commotion outside?"

"You attacked those men," Mason accused Kai. "I know they were armed, but you attacked first. Maybe they wouldn't have used their gun if you'd been less confrontational."

"I don't need to stick my dick in a tiger's mouth to know it'll get bitten off."

"Mason," Ama drew him back, "you might find this hard to believe, but I trust Kai's instincts. I don't think he would have attacked unless he already knew those men posed a serious threat. You might have all ended up getting hurt if he didn't."

"Or butchered like a cheerleader in a '90s slasher film," Kai added, stripping his shirt off and examining the wound on his arm.

It was a deep nick—possibly in need of stitches—but Kai didn't even flinch as he cleaned the blood off with a rag and some whisky. Mason watched, suspended in medical horror, as Kai took a swig of the liquor after pressing the cloth to his arm, then tossed it to the end of the bed. The bleeding had already stopped, further convincing him there was something special about this man's genetic makeup. Kai Donovan was built like a rock. And given the way he fought those men, Mason couldn't help but wonder if this rogue had once been part of the military. Perhaps some experimental program? But that didn't explain the markers of wolf's blood Sashka found. Nothing could explain that.

"I'm sorry, Ama, but that's illogical," Mason argued when his thoughts grew too loud. "We can't speculate what those men might have done. There was still time to talk things through."

"What about this whole situation even approaches logic?" Miya interjected. "They had guns. They obviously *wanted* to hurt someone."

Emiliya Delathorne wasn't the sweet, demure Amanda he remembered—and yet she still tormented him with a familiarity he couldn't place. He peeked at Kai—an oppressive presence in the corner. Even though he said nothing, he also let nothing slip.

"Why are you looking at me like I fucked a horse?" he grunted when he caught Mason side-eyeing him.

Mason wasn't sure what he'd gotten himself into, but he'd wanted the truth, and no one said the truth would be pretty. He didn't know how deep this rabbit hole ran, but even with Kai threatening to defile the sun from his sky, Mason was determined to follow it to the bottom.

"Just never seen anything like you before," he replied.

Kai smirked and tipped the whisky bottle Mason's way, his dark eyes mocking him. "And you were never meant to, golden boy."

CHAPTER
FORTY-THREE

MIYA

ALL THE FEAR had drained from Miya's body. Her heart was still, her hands steady. Was she tougher now, or had she grown desensitized to things that should've unsettled her?

As she looked over at Kai, poking at the bullet wound in his arm, she realized how much easier it was getting through that last ordeal. She had a comrade in him—someone she knew had her back. That alone made the fight worthwhile.

He'd wound up being more than a few firsts for Miya. She'd always been standoffish, and yet here she was, sharing every inch of herself with a wolf in the woods.

But where would that take them? They'd agreed to more than a tryst, but what did that mean for Kai? Was he capable of love? Did he understand romantic partnership? He'd pledged his friendship and loyalty, quelling some of her trepidation, but how deep did those sentiments run? It was true that entangled bodies were nothing earth-shattering, but entangled hearts and lives—that left her pulsing with both excitement and terror.

Miya wished Hannah was still with her. Her best friend had always faired so much better in relationships, but she was out of reach when Miya finally needed her for one.

Yet Kai was hardly flippant the way many humans were. On the contrary, his intensity could bite through steel. And while this was welcome in their more intimate moments, Miya wondered if the wolf could be pacified when necessary. It was impossible to know, but she was struck by a jarring revelation.

She wanted to stay with him, terror be damned.

Miya could have walked into a fistfight blindfolded, and she would have felt safe with Kai by her side. Hell, she might have even taken a swing.

She trusted him.

It was more than she could say for most people, especially the new guy, Mason. She didn't know him, but she knew she didn't like him. The judgment was accompanied by a pang of creeping guilt; didn't he deserve a chance?

Sure, he was a bit pretentious, but he wasn't mean-spirited or stupid. Maybe it was his obvious naivety or the way he drooled after Kai, treating him like a rare specimen under a microscope. Maybe it was both. Or maybe, Miya thought, it was that he was a coward, just like her. Neither of them seemed favourable to facing reality, and this led her to an uncomfortable conclusion.

You're projecting, she scolded.

She could tell Mason Evans was everything she loathed to become: preoccupied with appearances, disoriented by a puritanical morality, trapped by a religious commitment to some veil of logic. He was a slave to the insecurities driving him. If all Miya wanted was to be self-aware, becoming Mason Evans would have been her ultimate punishment. Yet she feared they weren't all that different.

"He was there. Pulling the strings," said Kai. He sat on the bed with his back against the wall, one knee drawn up as he glared into empty space.

"Abaddon?" Ama's question was met with a nod.

"Who's Abaddon?" Mason asked.

"The thing you saw out there, making the villagers rabid," Miya explained. "Ama—" she walked over to the table and sat down. "I think I'm onto something."

"What is it?" Ama asked, leaning forward on her elbows.

Miya took a deep breath, glancing at Kai, then at Mason. Hopefully, Sherlock's brain wouldn't shatter. "I can't shake what I saw in the dreamscape. The first time I tried to get back to this side, the Dreamwalker was there, hovering over my body while Abaddon was nipping at my heels. It can't be a coincidence they were both there."

Ama smiled like she'd anticipated this. "Go on."

"Then I find out Abaddon knows exactly what happens to the girls who disappear. He told me so himself. Now the villagers are out looking for me.

They think I've been kidnapped by the Dreamwalker. It's always about the Dreamwalker. And yet here's Abaddon in the middle of it. These two *must* know each other."

Before Ama could respond, Mason cut in. "So there's another spirit involved? I didn't hear or read anything about an Abaddon in the legend."

"But you did see him." Ama glanced up at Mason, refusing to break eye-contact until the light bulb went off.

"The shadow from my dreams," he realized, his back hitting the wall as he ran a shaky hand through his curls.

Kai swung his legs over the bed and eyed the new member of their cabin, then glared at Ama. "You knew about Abaddon's consistent appearance because of this guy."

"Gavran showed me in a dream," Mason continued. "While she was alive, the Dreamwalker was driven out of the village by this shadow. The shadow was responsible for turning the villagers against her."

"Seriously, who the fuck is Gavran?" Kai grumbled.

"From what the three of you have seen, I suppose we can string the pieces together," said Ama. "Obviously, Abaddon and the Dreamwalker are linked somehow. Mason," she looked at him, "according to you, Abaddon— or one of his incarnations—was responsible for the Dreamwalker's original exile. Presumably, this exile is what prompted the town's paranoia and collective guilt."

Mason nodded. "They're afraid of her retribution. That's why they keep inventing these stories about her coming back to kidnap girls. It's some kind of sick repetition of the same event. They drove her out, so now they imagine her returning every now and again. And whenever she supposedly comes back, the village turns on their own girls."

"Are they being driven mad?" Miya suggested. "Sure, they're paranoid that she's coming back for revenge, but every time they think someone's been kidnapped—"

"They end up killing the girl they were trying to protect," Mason finished her thought. "Just like Elle Robinson."

"That doesn't sound good for you, Lambchop." Miya met Kai's gaze, his expression forlorn.

"If the town is manipulated into hurting its own girls over and over again, the Dreamwalker's revenge is always complete," Miya offered, her eyes still on Kai. He was on his feet now, pacing like a nervous animal. "The villagers always think her revenge is on the horizon—but it's already happened. And it keeps happening because they keep repressing the memory of their own history."

"What if it isn't her?" Kai stopped in his tracks, drawing all eyes to him. "What if all of this is Abaddon, and he just wants people to blame her?"

"It's possible this is his doing," Ama agreed. "You saw him out there influencing the villagers. It's very likely he's contributing to this mess."

"But he and the Dreamwalker are enemies according to Golden Boy, here." Miya pointed her thumb at Mason, the nickname catching on. "It's like they're still at war, and the village's sanity is a casualty. What happens in this world is just collateral damage."

"And what if it's none of that?" Mason cut in. "What if the legend is just a legend? What if it doesn't matter whether it really happened or not? What if people's belief in the story is powerful enough, and all of this is just the result of a tragic case of mass hysteria? Nothing spiritual, nothing ghostly. What if the haunting is purely metaphorical?"

It was the smartest thing he'd said all night. Miya dropped her gaze to the floor. She knew her life was in danger, and over what? "I don't believe there's nothing spiritual in this. I've seen too much to think it's all in our heads. But I also think you're right that it doesn't really matter whether it's a real haunting or a metaphorical one. It's still a haunting. It's been going on for centuries." She remembered what Kai went through—what she went through. "And I think you're right too, Kai. Abaddon is definitely involved. If he and the Dreamwalker are enemies, then he's also to blame."

Miya pushed the chair back and stood up, flattening her hands on the table and hanging her head. She was drained of everything she had, and yet she felt more alive than ever before. She was teetering on the edge of a cliff with nothing to catch her at the bottom. "I feel like the Dreamwalker is trying to communicate with me. Whether it's by kidnapping me or haunting me—she's obviously trying to say something. I just don't know what, and I don't know how to find out, either."

Ama's fingernails drummed against the wooden table, then abruptly stopped. "Maybe she wants you to do what she does."

"What do you mean?" Miya looked up. "Do what?"

The white wolf's lips pulled back. "Walk dreams."

Miya recalled the feeling of descending into another world—gravity disappearing beneath her feet, her body weightless and free. "We need to go back there," she gasped. "We need to go back into the dreamscape and find out what happened."

"The dream-what? But we already know what happened," Mason protested. "We've been talking about it this whole time, haven't we?"

"That's just historical information," Miya argued. "We need to know what *really* happened, and why—what motivated them, what the events meant on a personal level. Ghosts won't be put to rest by a history lesson."

This was it. This was the kind of investigation that called to her, made her feel whole—not some half-baked fluff piece on the new poutinerie on Main Street. Her encounters with Abaddon were taxing, painful even, and yet she felt more like herself than ever before, unencumbered by anxiety and guilt.

Ama gave Mason a come-hither gesture with her finger. He obliged, unable to break her spell until he was standing in front of her.

"In your pocket," she said and, on command, he reached into his jeans. He pulled out a crumpled piece of paper and placed it on the table. After smoothing it out, recognition and wonder crept into his eyes. It was a drawing of some kind; there was a grotesque black wolf with crimson eyes and blood dripping from its teeth, the background of the picture decorated with screaming women strapped to burning crucifixes.

"You've been touched by the other side," Ama told him. "The dream stone made sure of that."

Mason fumbled around his pocket again, fishing for the stone in question. "Where is it?" he asked frantically.

"In the room," Ama said in a sing-song voice, then looked at Miya. "We're sending you back."

"How?" Miya asked. "I can't get there at will. It's not like Kai—"

"We will need Kai, too," Ama interrupted as she spun her chair around to face the wolf in question. He narrowed his eyes as she smiled mischievously. "You will need him as an anchor to Abaddon's memories."

"Do you think I'll find the Dreamwalker there?" Miya asked.

"Maybe," she shrugged. "Maybe not."

Ama pulled out a shimmering, fang-shaped stone about the size of her palm—the one Mason had asked about, no doubt.

"How did you—" Mason began.

"Don't worry about it." She winked at him playfully. "The three of you—come lie down on the floor."

To Miya's shock, Kai was the first to listen. "Fuck it," he mumbled. "I'll do whatever it takes to purge this flaming asshole from existence." He walked over and plunked down in front of Ama, lifting his hand and gesturing for Miya to take it. It was enough to convince her, so she slipped her hand in his and sank down next to him.

"I-I don't understand," Mason stuttered. "What are we doing?"

Ama stood from the table and placed a hand on his shoulder. "It's hard to explain. Just know you're needed."

"Why the hell do we need him?" Kai groused as he and Miya lay on their backs, still holding hands.

Ama chuckled and shook her head. "Miya is the one who will travel to the dreamscape." She lightly tapped Kai on the shoulder with her foot. "You are the anchor to that world." She then tapped Mason on the chest with her fingertips. "And you are the anchor to this world."

"We didn't have so many anchors last time," Miya pointed out.

"You didn't go as deep last time," Ama replied sternly. "I was your anchor. But this time, you'll need a stronger one—someone who is more rooted in the physical plane. And even then, you might still become lost."

Kai's grip on Miya's hand tightened. "Why does she have to do this? Why not me?"

He was frightened, and yet he was still willing to take her place.

"You don't have the ability." Ama gave him a cutting look. "Only some have an affinity with the other realms."

"Wait," Mason interjected. "Are we going to die?"

Ama's lips tugged downward. "To think that traversing realms is the same as death," she sighed. "You'd make a poor detective."

Mason balked at the suggestion. "That's not true."

"You believe that only what you see while you're awake is living," said Ama. "I guarantee it's not so."

Kai huffed and glared at Mason. "Just get over here. We're losing time."

Miya thumped her head against the floor and looked up at a frowning, upside down Mason. He shuffled over and eased himself down next to her. "I'm sorry I was mean to you," she apologized.

Mason sighed, shaking his head and smiling. "It's all right." He lay down and extended his hand to her. "I'm sorry I didn't listen."

Perhaps he wasn't so bad.

"Truce?" he asked, and she nodded, reaching out and taking his hand.

"Truce."

Miya turned back to Kai and squeezed his hand. "It'll be okay."

He inhaled and flexed his fingers. "I don't know what you're going to see over there, or if any of us will make it back, but..."

She held her breath, waiting for him to finish. "But what?"

Something wet trickled on her forehead, and she craned her neck to see what was dribbling on her face. "Ama, did you just cut your hand?"

"I did," Ama said without elaboration, then smeared the blood above Miya's brow with her finger.

Kai grumbled as she did the same to him. "You sure this isn't some satanic ritual?"

"I don't believe in Satan," Ama advised. "Consider my blood a kind of unifier. To keep the three of you spiritually connected." She snickered. "The hand-holding helps too."

Kai tugged at Miya's hand, drawing her attention back to him. "If you don't come back, I won't either. I'll find you, and I'll stay. That's a promise."

For a brief moment, everything fell away—all the uncertainty about her future and finances, all the problems she thought spelled the end of the world. Kai meant what he said, and Miya believed him wholeheartedly. His tone was sincere, his eyes gentler than she remembered them ever being. "Don't worry," she whispered back. "I'll be the one finding you, pup."

Ama sat behind them and breathed deeply. Just as last time, her hands rested against Miya's temples, coaxing her to close her eyes in preparation for what she knew was coming. Heat emanated from Ama's fingertips, sending currents of warmth through Miya's body. Each pulse thrummed deeper until her eyes grew heavy, and the blood on her forehead sizzled from otherworldly energy. The veil between worlds was so close she could feel the breeze from the other side, but she fought it, wanting to stay with Kai a moment longer.

The pull was magnetic, the air fragrant, and Miya found herself unable to resist any longer. Kai's face was the last thing she saw as Ama repeated the same words from before.

"Let yourself descend, as only you can."

FORTY-FOUR

THE DARKEST NIGHT

MIYA

When Miya opened her eyes, there was only darkness. Her physical form was absent, yet she knew she was there—a distinct, unified core, invisible but present. She wondered if this was what the afterlife was like and if there was any god that ruled the plane where spirits resided.

"If there is a god, he is cruel. He has condemned us to a fate we cannot escape. We are born to die, then reborn again—doomed to repeat the same mistakes, to suffer the same loss. We are no different than the machines we ourselves have made. Like clocks, we spin around the same axis without alternative, infinitely, as though to turn in circles is the very purpose for which we were made. And all the while the world passes us by. We erode, and yet we continue to tick and tick and tick until the axis itself grows weary of our burdens, unhinges, and finally, we break."

The voice was impossible to locate; it was directionless, everywhere and yet nowhere all at once. She wondered if the entity could read her mind—if thinking and speaking were the same in this realm.

"Are you the thing that calls itself Abaddon?" her words echoed through the dark vacuum. He sounded weak, worn down.

"Abaddon." *He repeated the name as though it was vaguely familiar.* **"Yes...and no."**

"Are you a piece of him?"

"Yes..." *The voice sounded closer.* "Mirek...I was...Mirek."

He sounded breathless, wounded. "Mirek. And before that?"

"And before that...something else. That is why we are Abaddon."

There was a brush of dry, icy air like he'd moved beside her. He too had no physical form, but she was aware of being in his territory. He was surprisingly mellow, unlike the spirit she'd encountered earlier. Perhaps he was willing to talk. Even a monster would seize the opportunity to be understood.

"Who were the others?"

"The First was before...the beginning...the last...Mirek."

"Will you tell me about the First?"

"You will meet him if you can find your way. But I am not here to tell his story."

"Then whose story are you here to tell?"

"The story of...Mirek."

The name burned like a hot coal on flesh. Miya felt herself inside his mind—searching, digging, grasping for something to hold on to. A moment, a memory —anything.

"Mirek."

This spirit—Kai's tormenter—she was compelled to become one with him, to understand him. The boundaries of flesh and spirit, dark and light, blurred, until Miya and Mirek were no longer separate. Whether it was his voice or her own—she couldn't tell.

CHAPTER
FORTY-FIVE

MIREK

MIREK COULD HEAR his brother calling him, tugging at the edges of his mind. He turned to see the large black wolf emerge from the trees. His little brother—always so brazen.

"You shouldn't come so close to the forest's edge looking like that," Mirek told him sternly. "They're not like us. They'll shoot us dead and skin us for our pelts if they catch us."

The wolf snorted, unconcerned, and disappeared back into the darkness of the woods. His favourite companion—a mischievous raven—followed closely at his heels.

Although Mirek and his brother Vuk were both wolves and men, it was as though one brother had taken all the wolf, and the other all the man. Mirek had his reason; his brother had his instincts. Mirek tried to keep them safe, but Vuk wanted to live unfettered.

That would've been fine if it weren't for the settlers and their village nestled in the nook of their forest. Mirek didn't know why they chose this place. They didn't like it. They feared the forest and told absurd tales of its malevolence.

They rarely ventured in. Sometimes they came with their guns to hunt game, but they preferred their cattle—an easier kill. Mirek knew his little brother was responsible for at least a few missing chickens.

The villagers flew into a panic with every vanished hen. They scurried about with their pitchforks in search of some sinister monster they were convinced was lurking behind their sheds and devouring their flock—feathers and all. They couldn't fathom that a hungry animal had simply found easy prey. When they ventured beyond what they knew, they found evil stalking in every dark corner. Mirek couldn't believe he and Vuk were the wolves and they the men. The younger wolf found them amusing, fearful, and pathetic. Mirek supposed they were, but any wise hunter knew that a fearful animal was at its most dangerous.

Wolves especially were the stuff of nightmares for these settlers. The howls frightened them, and their fables were filled with wild beasts and witches that gobbled children whole. Then there was the Dreamwalker—a living, malevolent spirit that struck more fear into those fools than anyone, though Mirek never saw any sign of her.

He resolved to keep his distance. Concealment was wisest.

MIREK FOUND his brother on his knees one day, clutching the dirt and gasping for air as his ribs snapped back into place to make room for his lungs. Between the two of them, Vuk changed more frequently, but for that Mirek was thankful. They were deep in the woods this time, far from any danger of being caught—or so Mirek thought—when he heard the snap of twigs nearby.

It was a young woman. Her clear blue eyes pierced right through him, freezing him to the ground where he stood. She was one of them—those villagers. Her golden hair fell past her shoulders, her face whiter than snow. Vuk struggled to stand, using Mirek's shoulder as a crutch. Mirek could see his brother was intrigued even as he fought to gather his bearings.

"Did I scare you, girl?" Vuk laughed in his usual wry humour. She looked at them both as though they were ghosts.

"Are you Indians?"

Vuk looked her up and down. "Indians?"

"I've heard that Indians can turn into animals at will."

"Indians are human."

"And you are not?"

"No." He smiled. "Not always."

AT FIRST, Mirek was mistrustful, fearing she would run back to the village and declare there were demons in the forest—wolves wearing the flesh of men. Vuk dismissed his concern, claiming the girl was not of that sort. This time, he may have been right.

She—Cassia—often went into the woods to gather herbs and mushrooms, against the wishes of her father and the other villagers. Over time, it became clear that her reasons for returning were more than medicinal.

Cassia was with them almost every day. Rather than fearing them, she was curious—though her fascination was directed more at Mirek's brother. He, in turn, seemed to take pleasure in divulging their secrets and playing tricks on her, but Mirek was weary of these indiscretions. They didn't need more attention.

MIREK WAS grateful his fur was the colour of bark. It was good camouflage and distinguished him from his notorious brother—especially when rumours spread of a demonic black wolf roaming the forest, attacking unsuspecting hunters. The Dreamwalker's familiar, they kept saying, though Mirek suspected it was only Vuk. The black wolf didn't need the Dreamwalker to motivate his recklessness. He was putting them in danger. He was putting Cassia in danger. Mirek urged her to stay away from Vuk, but she wouldn't listen. She had made her choice.

CASSIA WAS CLEANING Vuk's wound when Mirek walked into the grove.

"What happened?" Mirek asked.

"A hunter shot at me."

"And?"

Vuk's mahogany eyes were still bright from the violent encounter.

"I tore the rifle right out of his hands."

"You shouldn't have done that," Cassia chastised him, though it sounded more like a plea.

"They'll come back with more men to hunt you down. These villagers are not just fearful, they're proud." Mirek paused. "Did you hurt him?"

His brother's lips twisted into a smirk. "He may have lost his trigger finger."

THE HUNTS BECAME MORE FREQUENT, more persistent. Almost daily, they came into the woods in search of Vuk—the demonic black wolf they believed was a spawn of Satan. Mirek remembered their parents teaching them of the battle between God and Satan—a battle the villagers enjoyed re-enacting. In the end, their parents were killed in God's name, hunted down by men who believed them to be the devil's messengers. Now they brought priests who called out to the spirit of the Dreamwalker, demanding she expose herself and her familiar.

It didn't help that Vuk put every effort into driving them off when he caught them poaching. Men who hunted simply to mount an animal's head on the wall were not worthy of the right to kill, he said.

Yet Mirek couldn't help but think him foolish. How could he be so brazen? So bold and unafraid?

And Cassia—seeing them together sickened him. Her warm smiles, the brightness of her eyes, the melody of her laughter—it haunted Mirek. Why had she chosen his brother? What made him worthy of her?

"THEY'RE WARNING me not to come back here," she told Mirek one night. "They say I'll be taken by the Dreamwalker. Some even think I am the Dreamwalker."

"Nonsense."

"It's what they believe."

It was Vuk's fault the rumours had spread. The black wolf had become the great evil of the forest. He abided by the whims of the Dreamwalker and did her bidding. Now they were offering a reward for anyone who brought in his brother's head.

"I would keep you safe," Mirek told her. "I'm more careful than he is."

He searched her eyes for any sign of acceptance but found nothing resembling the warmth she radiated towards his brother. She did not speak, and in doing so spoke what Mirek most dreaded to hear.

He disappeared further into the woods, running from those clear blue eyes.

THE VILLAGERS WERE FALLING ILL—THOUGH it was a disease of the mind that consumed them. It spread like wildfire from one person to the next until dozens were afflicted. The Dreamwalker had taken her next victim, they said, and the name of this victim was one Mirek couldn't bear to hear.

Cassia.

He knew she hadn't been spirited away by any Dreamwalker, but only by the black wolf.

And yet they continued to whisper of her curse, this spirit whose thirst for vengeance was insatiable, eternal.

Mirek wondered, was the Dreamwalker even real? When had her story begun? How could he believe a story about an exiled girl when there was no record of her having existed?

For Mirek, there was no Dreamwalker.

There was only the black wolf.

CHAPTER
FORTY-SIX

MIYA

THE BLACK WOLF.

His haunting, mahogany eyes struck Miya as they always did. She knew him. She knew his presence.

He called her out of his tormenter's memory, leading her back into the forest. And there he lay—wounded as when they first met. Miya watched him, crumpled on the ground, blood pooling around his limp form.

She heard cheering from somewhere beyond the trees, somewhere close to the village. She could feel their fear as she was blinded by the burning light of torches.

Burning.

Something was burning.

Miya looked up and saw flames, red as the sunset.

Miya was being burned alive. Only it wasn't her—it was the girl with clear blue eyes.

Gazing through them, she saw a harrowed Mirek. His sorrow tore her from the fire, and she merged with him once more.

CHAPTER

FORTY-SEVEN

MIREK

Cassia was gone.

The smell of burnt wood and human flesh polluted the air, and Mirek was disgusted by the thought of even breathing. He would have rather suffocated than filled his lungs with even a particle of her remains.

He kept thinking that if he ran far enough, called her name loud enough, she would have eventually appeared.

But he knew that wouldn't happen. He saw the smoke rising to the sky; he heard her screams, smelled her blood, tasted her fear like ash on his lips. Her cries rattled inside his skull, trapped there until his heart began to break and he wanted nothing more than to stop the pain. Yet there was nothing he could do but bear it until it was over—and after it was, he was all too aware that his burden had only begun.

"It was him...It was him...him...HIM..."

"It was his fault."

He did this.

"If only she'd chosen to stay with me." **Not him.**

If that hunter had killed him.

"She'd be alive."

VUK FELL TO THE GROUND, clutching his side, the bleeding from his wound profuse. The villagers had nearly killed him, but it wasn't enough.

"Get up," Mirek hissed.

Vuk did as he was told, knowing he was to blame.

"You did this."

"The villagers did this." His voice was barely a whisper.

"You did this!"

Vuk's face twisted, and Mirek knew something in him had broken. He loathed that his brother even dared to grieve. He didn't deserve it.

Mirek struck Vuk's broken ribs. He stumbled, jaw clenched, but Mirek hadn't finished. He drove his fist into the side of his brother's face. Once, twice, three times. He saw blood, but it didn't stop him. Mirek wanted to bring him to an inch of his life and let him crawl back from hell's gates. Then he wanted to do it again.

Before Mirek could resume pummelling him, Vuk shoved him away with inhuman strength. His eyes were wild; sharp, canine fangs protruded from beneath his lip. Mirek could see the animal fighting to survive, but he knew the man wanted to die.

"Stop it," Vuk snarled.

Mirek didn't listen—not to him, and not to his own instincts. Like a madman hurling himself off a cliff, he lost himself to the grief and rage. His vision was blurred by tears, his screams laced with hatred. He blamed his brother, battered him, cut him with his words—all the while, Vuk held the wolf inside himself at bay. Until he couldn't any longer.

The animal struggled to live more than the man yearned to die. He lunged at Mirek, teeth bared and eyes ablaze.

MIREK'S BLOOD soaked the ground, and he knew he was a dead man. He could see his brother hovering over him, his expression fraught with recognition. Vuk's hands, painted red with Mirek's life, hoisted him up. He screamed with violent desperation, but Mirek couldn't hear any of it. He was slipping away.

The sun was bleeding into dusk—a fitting metaphor for Mirek's own demise. He mustered all his strength to reach up and cup his brother's face. The black wolf looked down at him, silenced, and Mirek realized just how much he hated him. It felt like a poisonous snake had hatched in the pit of his stomach. It slithered around, eating away his insides. The venom spread, turning everything rotten.

"Monster."

It was the last thing Mirek said before the light left his eyes...

"...And I joined my brethren in the darkest night..."

FORTY-EIGHT

MIYA

MIYA WAS BACK in the void, wraithlike as she floated through time and space. She searched for her feet, trying to force herself lower until she touched a pathway with nothing but darkness around it. The stones were weathered, cracked, and crumbling. She sensed him nearby, waiting for her to speak.

"You were there when it happened," she said. "When they burned the girl—your girl."

"She was his girl, too."

The voice remained disembodied. "You blamed your brother for what happened. But you also blamed the Dreamwalker."

"I didn't know this Dreamwalker while I lived. But the First knew her. I joined the First when I died."

"You and the First share the same soul."

"We do."

"But the First hates the Dreamwalker," Miya insisted. "Joining him only continues this vicious cycle. You're just creating the same destruction that destroyed you."

"Creation...destruction...we think of them as opposites, and yet they are like brothers—two sides of the same coin."

"Like you and your brother? You seem to think he's the destructive one."

"He is. He ended me." *His words betrayed a lingering wound.* **"But I wished for him to lose the girl as penance for his destruction, and this desire created fertile soil for fear to grow among the villagers.**

My thoughts were in one place, but my heart—my soul—was in another."

"You think your soul created this fear? But you didn't do anything wrong," Miya called into the void. "I was in your head; I heard your thoughts. You were jealous of your brother, but you didn't want anyone to get killed."

"But did I truly, in my heart of hearts?" *the voice of Mirek confessed.* **"I always looked down on my brother. Something in me wanted to see him punished. It was justice."**

Miya wondered: could the darkness hidden in a person's heart—passed down from histories they didn't even understand—be so contrary to what they believed in their mind?

"Do you think those desires were inherited from the First?"

"Was it not the First who began it all?" *He laughed—a bitter, humourless sound.* **"If I share the same soul as the First, am I not responsible for birthing such fear?"**

"You weren't able to cope with the guilt," she observed, "so you blamed your brother. You convinced yourself it was his fault for being destructive, but deep down, you believed you created this. You thought she died because of you."

"I did it. I wished it, and it happened. It was my will. It was the First's will."

"You overestimate your importance," she hissed, repulsed by his narcissism. "History is bigger than you and your feelings."

"Feelings are all I had. Even after so many lifetimes, I could not best them."

Miya never imagined one of Abaddon's incarnations to be so self-deprecating. Yet what was it worth when the self-loathing became an excuse to loathe others? His guilt was meaningless.

"What happened after you died?" she asked.

"I returned, unified with the First," *he told her.* **"We awoke as Abaddon. And together, we created madness. The villagers set fire to the forest—burned it all to the ground just so they could find the black wolf."**

It was crippling; to think an emotion could be so overpowering, that it could birth a collective driven by a singular purpose. "And did they?"

"My brother and I always find each other."

"But it brought you no peace."

"I have forsaken peace. The First and I—and all those between —will remain here forever. Our axis is long broken."

Miya whirled around, trying to find the source of the voice. "So the First is the author of all this? The one who set the village against the Dreamwalker?"

"We are her enemies, yes."

"But that's insane!" Her voice echoed through the hollow chasm. "Can't you see that the woman you loved was burned to death because of the choices you made in a past life? Your first incarnation set this in motion. You've merely lived the consequences of that. Now you're wilfully choosing to continue doing the same thing?"

"Do you think reason matters to the cursed, girl? I only came here to tell you of what I lived. As for the First—his story is his own."

"Why does the First hate the Dreamwalker so much?" she interrogated him, but he only dwelled on his own loss.

"My brother took her from me. And she took my brother from me." *There was a pause before he continued.* **"In the end, I was alone. The First understood this. He lived it."**

"I want to meet the First."

"For that," *the voice rumbled,* **"you will need to go deeper."**

The stone path beneath Miya's feet crumbled. In the distance, she saw a speck of light, like a firefly, floating amidst the darkness. Gradually, it grew larger, ascending like the sun as she fell into the abyss beneath her. As her body tilted with the pull of gravity, Miya found herself upside down, the sunrise turning to sunset. The great orb disappeared, and her feet found the ground.

Up ahead there was a hill covered in dozens of scattered lumps, but Miya couldn't make out what they were.

As she approached, she realized the protrusions were comatose bodies, lined up in perfectly symmetrical rows that stretched to the horizon's edge. They were unmoving, lifeless as gravestones. And like gravestones, they all looked the same—similar in size and build with blurry faces and plain, grey garments. Still, Miya knew them; her soul reverberated with recognition. They were her previous incarnations—the victims of the spirit she sought: the First.

He was sitting on a large rock at the top of the hill, staring down at the women as though he was their king. His face was obscured in shadow, but his presence was distinct; it was the same as the king of spades who referred to himself as Abaddon.

"Come here," he crooned, his voice inviting.

Miya wanted to meet him, but she remained guarded in her approach. At first, the climb seemed endless, like no matter how far she walked up the hill, she couldn't get any closer. She heard him laugh before he extended an arm, pulling her to him as though he was a magnet.

As soon as Miya was in front of him, she realized he was the one who looked like Kai—the man with cold, yellow eyes. She could see him clearly now—the lines of his face identical to those of the man she'd grown close to.

"Are you—"

"I am the First," he answered, his voice smoother and less gruff than Kai's.

"Does the First have a name?"

"You don't remember my name, girl?" He seemed disappointed.

"Like I said before, we've never met."

"Ah—that again," he chuckled, then spread his arms out towards the mass of bodies before them. "Why not lie down and rest?"

His offer was surprisingly tempting. He must have known how exhausted Miya was, how badly she wanted to sleep. She reckoned he was the one draining her.

"Is that what you told these other people?" she challenged. "I already know that if I fall asleep here, I'll never wake up."

"You will," he smiled, "if you know where to stop."

The words meant nothing to Miya. He was trying to seduce her, to distract her from her purpose. "You're the reason Kai's in so much pain. You're also the reason this village hasn't been able to move on from its bloody past. You keep bringing it back. You're the reason Elle's dead."

"I don't make the villagers kill their women." He sounded offended by her insinuation. "They do it themselves. Sometimes alone, sometimes as a community. Even when warned by the Dreamwalker, your Elle fell prey to Black Hollow's madness."

"You push them to it." Miya swallowed, something tart and astringent oozing down her throat. "I'm not trying to absolve them of their sins by blaming you. They're accountable for their actions. But you're also accountable for your intentions."

"You would judge someone for their intent alone?"

"You're a spirit," she told him. "Intent is all you have."

"Do you believe that intent has power, girl?"

"You've already proven it does," she said. "But what's the point of this? Endlessly repeating this miserable cycle? You've condemned your soul to an eternity here just so you can carry out some vindictive scheme a million times over. What does any of this prove?"

He pulled back and looked at her with eyes that bled pure malevolence. "It proves that I have control."

"Who the fuck do you think you are? God?" Miya glared down the phantom. He was so unlike the man lying next to her back in the physical world. "Having control over someone else doesn't make you free."

He said nothing, but smiled bitterly, his cold eyes faltering in the brief second it took her to blink.

"You would say that, wouldn't you?" he mocked as though he knew her, then sighed once the irritation had washed over him and passed. "But it has always been you I despise most."

"What did I ever do to you?" Miya demanded. "Why'd you turn so bitter?"

"There is no pleasure in exiling someone who wants to be exiled," he spat. "And *there is no sense in talking about reasons. They're like quicksand. The past is the past, and it cannot change the present."*

Miya didn't understand his meaning. Had he confused her with someone else? "But it has changed the present," she insisted. "And it continues to. Haunting changes things."

A hint of a smile coloured his sinister lips before he asked, "Why are you here? How did you get so far in?"

He didn't need to know the truth.

"I had help."

The First threw his head back and laughed—the sound vacant. "Or you are not who you think you are."

His words rattled her until she lost awareness of her feet. Looking down, Miya saw thorny roots coiling around her ankles.

"Sleep with these people," he tempted her again. "Dream with them. If you wake up, I will show you what you wish to know."

"There is no waking up from this," she rebuked, certain he was trying to trick her.

Again, he smiled, his teeth shining like pearls as he repeated his earlier condition. "You will wake up if you know where to stop."

"You'll have to do better than that if you want me to risk my life," Miya challenged. This monster had chipped away at Kai for years—a dark taint that followed him wherever he went. The First had a singular goal: to create misery no one could escape, least of all Miya and her black wolf. Even if Miya didn't care for the townspeople, she cared for Kai deeply enough to risk everything to free them both. "Giving me information won't be enough. If I win this wager, you have to break the cycle. Leave Kai, and Black Hollow, forever. Promise me that, and I'll take you up on your offer."

At first, he appeared stunned she'd bargain with him, but his expression quickly soured. "Greedy woman," he accused, his mouth twisting into a grimace. "Your death is not worth that risk."

"Fine," she held her ground. "What would make it worth the risk? If I lose, what do you want from me?"

He took pause and weighed her words. It was like he'd never considered it because no one had ever asked him. For a moment, Miya felt something other than disdain towards him—pity, perhaps—but it vanished when she saw that cold smile spread over his face.

"You," said the First. "I want you. Here. Forever. Willing and aware—a living spirit in my own personal hell."

"You...don't want to be alone?" Miya staggered, amazed that an entity who kept the company of corpses would desire the companionship of his enemy. "Why would you want that?"

"A living trophy is far more appealing than a dead one."

"Didn't realize you were in the market for a new toy." Miya wondered—if she

failed, if she ended up trapped with him forever, would she ever be reincarnated in the physical plane again?

"Accept my challenge," he cooed, "and you may be the first to survive the flames. You may even break this wretched cycle. I will bring you home, and this will all come to an end."

"And if I don't?"

His lips pulled back. "We both know you are well beyond the white wolf's reach. You will never find your way out, little lamb. And if you do, death by fire awaits you." He waved his hand through the air as if sweeping aside a partition to the next world.

Smoke filled Miya's lungs; she could smell the char. She heard Mason's cries as he ducked into cover while Ama fought off a man twice her size. She saw Kai, blood-soaked and backed into a corner. He was clutching his arm—limp from a wound to the shoulder. And behind him, she saw her own body lying unconscious, helpless, useless.

"You could be lying," Miya refuted, but she could still feel the flames licking her skin. She knew the villagers were on their heels. There was no reason to doubt they'd burn everything in their path. If she didn't stop this, they'd keep coming until she, Kai, Ama, and Mason were dead.

"That is your risk to take," he replied with a mild shrug, the vision dissipating with another wave of his hand. "Even if you die, there will always be another. And another. And another."

He had a point.

Battered by doubt, Miya lay down on the hill with the rest of the bodies. "I don't trust you," she said to the figure looming over her.

"A fair prerogative," he chuckled.

Just as Miya was about to close her eyes, she remembered a burning question. Mirek and the black wolf were brothers, so what of the First and Kai? She looked up and asked him, "Who is the black wolf?"

Still sitting on his throne, the king of corpses leaned over, shadows enveloping his face as those two golden eyes gleamed at her—drawing closer until his lips pressed against her forehead and he whispered, "My brother."

The reiteration of this bond and the violence it inspired—reincarnated through the ages—sucked the air from Miya's lungs. She was all at once pulled into the earth and buried into darkness—sinking deeper into the dreamscape until she was certain that she was lost.

CHAPTER
FORTY-NINE

MASON

Mason awoke, gasping for air, his heart crashing against his ribcage and his body covered in sweat. His skin felt like it was on fire—like he was being burned alive. A strangled cry escaped from somewhere inside of him as he began to thrash. Someone held him down, but he only fought harder. There was a voice, deep and indistinct—the words impossible to make out. But gradually it became louder, clearer, higher in pitch—until finally, he recognized it as Ama's.

"Mason. Calm down."

He closed his eyes and tried to tune out the internal chaos, focusing on the rhythm of his breathing. The fire fizzled out, leaving an unpleasant tingling over every inch of him. There was a twitch over to his right—Kai stirring with a groan, though the girl was still unconscious. Kai's eyes shot open, and he sat up, his hand unlocking from Miya's just as Mason let go as well. They looked at each other, then doubled over, lurching to the side and vomiting violently. Both men were shaking, their fingers digging into the cracks of the floorboards.

"What the hell?" Mason hacked as he spat out the acrid taste in his mouth.

"It's all right," Ama said, rubbing his back. "When you let go of her hand, the connection between the three of you was severed a little too quickly. Your bodies are just catching up."

Mason took a deep breath and nodded, staring at the adjacent wall as he recuperated.

Kai also finished emptying the contents of his stomach, plunking back and breathing heavily. Only then did they notice that Miya wasn't moving.

"What's wrong with her?" Kai asked as he cast Ama an accusatory glare.

The woman with white hair knelt next to the comatose girl and placed a hand on her forehead. Mason joined her, checking her vitals to ensure she was at least physically unharmed.

"She's stable," he told them. "I don't know why she's not waking up."

"She's lost," said Ama, standing up again. "Don't move her," she warned as Kai stepped forward to pick her up. "Her body needs to remain undisturbed if she is to find her way back."

"Why did we wake up then?" Kai demanded. "Aren't we anchoring her?"

"She's gone far deeper than I expected," Ama replied. "At this point, she has no anchor. She's doing this all on her own."

For the first time, Mason saw concern crack through Kai's stony facade.

"And what if she can't get back?" Kai asked tightly.

"We have bigger things to worry about right now," Ama replied, her head snapping towards the window.

Kai kissed his teeth and strode over to her, keeping flush with the wall as he peeked outside.

"Fuck, they're back."

"It's because you left those bodies outside," Ama sighed, her callousness unnerving Mason.

"I wasn't going to bury them," Kai barked. "It's not like they're dead."

Their argument was cut short by a knock on the door.

"Open up, or we'll burn the whole place down!" a man shouted. The threat seemed disproportionately severe, sinking Mason's heart as the worst-case scenario unfolded in his mind. Mob mentality was in full effect.

Mason looked at Ama and Kai, both of whom were glaring at each other unflinchingly. After several moments of complete stillness, Ama moved towards the door and opened it. Outside were about half a dozen villagers, all sporting guns, crowbars, axes, and baseball bats.

"Whose property is this?" demanded the leader. He was at least six feet tall and built like a grizzly bear, his arms crossed over his chest as he peered down at Ama. She was no taller than five foot six, yet she glowered at him like a brewing thunderstorm.

"You're not wearing a badge, nor do you have a warrant," she replied coolly. "I'm not obligated to entertain your vigilantism."

The man faltered, clearly not having expected her to defy him. "We're looking for—"

"Jesus Christ! Jake! That's him!" It was the axe-wielding logger whose friend lost an ear.

The leader, Jake, quickly glanced around the room, his eyes first landing on Mason. "This guy, Ryan?"

"No!" Ryan shouted, squeezing himself next to Jake so he could see inside the cabin. "The one in the corner!"

He was referring to Kai, who was standing protectively in front of Miya.

Jake quickly unstrapped the rifle from his back and pushed past Ama, roaring at Kai, "So you're the freak who's been messing up our town!"

"He's the Dreamwalker's!" Ryan pleaded. "I saw his eyes flash red, man! He's not human!"

"You piece of shit," Jake muttered as Mason froze, watching with bated breath as the bear-like man raised his rifle. But before he could aim, Ama grabbed hold of the gun with an iron-like grip and pushed the butt of the weapon straight into the man's chest. He tried shaking her off only to find himself overpowered, the rifle's stock digging deeper into his torso.

"You're not welcome here," she spoke in a low growl and bared her teeth at the intruder.

"She's one of them too!" a woman shouted from the crowd outside. "They're all wolves!"

Panic seized Mason as the villagers stormed through the door. They flooded into the cabin like a black swarm, their eyes wild. Without rhyme or reason, they raised their weapons and began swinging at anything that came up in front of them. They smashed the table, threw the chairs at the walls, and pounded at the cupboards with their crowbars and axes. Even the men with guns appeared to have forgotten how to use them, batting them around like cavemen with sticks.

Mason ducked, a glaring light alerting him to a flashlight being thrown at his head. He fell to the ground as someone struck him hard on the back, nearly knocking the wind from his lungs. Concerned Miya would get caught in the crossfire, he turned towards her prostrate form, only to find Kai locking one of the villagers in a vicious chokehold.

"Behind you!" Mason yelled as someone jumped on Kai.

But the man with wolf's blood was a force of nature. He stood with his attacker dangling from his back, lifting him off the ground and flipping him over his shoulder with little effort. The villager leapt up again, but Kai was quicker. A flash of silver emerged from the back of Kai's belt—a hunting knife—pristine for only a split second before it was plunged into his attacker's leg. Kai tore the blade through the man's thigh, bringing him to his knees. His eyes glowed with an eerie red hue as he stared his victim down, the murderous aura around him almost palpable.

Mason was transfixed until something whirled right by his face again. Ama had thrown one of the crowbars right past Mason's nose to take out one of the nearby rioters. He felt utterly incompetent, useless as he scrambled about. If not for Ama, he would have been attacked.

The madness was louder than the screaming. Ama had levelled several people, but more kept trickling in—reinforcements who'd heard the commotion. There was no end to them, and the more Kai and Ama fought to protect Miya's unconscious body, the more chaotic the townspeople became.

Only then did Mason notice it was hard to breathe; the smell of smoke assaulted him, his lungs filling with noxious fumes. He looked around, but everything was swirling in fog. He felt sick to his stomach, the burning odour overpowering as he searched for its source. Mason gasped as he struggled to get back to his feet. He focused his attention on Miya, wanting desperately for her to wake from her otherworldly coma. But what he saw when he looked her way had him stumble back and trip over one of the concussed villagers. He fell onto his behind, his breaths quick and raspy as he tried to make sense of what he was perceiving.

There, in front of him, was a girl in the midst of flames.

CHAPTER
FIFTY

MIYA

EVERYTHING WAS A HAZE. Miya strained to make out the silhouettes of towering tree trunks as dim, foggy light peaked through their crooked boughs. She was in the forest from all her dreams. Urgency and longing welled up inside her—locked up memories thrashing to get out. She now understood that her dreams had been taking her back to the same place, each and every time.

Feeling more at home than ever before, Miya began to walk, knowing she was supposed to go somewhere. She knew her intended destination; she just didn't know how to get there or what it looked like. No matter, *she thought.* She'd recognize it when she saw it.

Just as Miya drew close to the place she thought she was supposed to find, she grew unsure of what she was seeing.

"Is this it?" she wondered aloud.

She fixated on a white oak nestled in a bundle of birch trees. Its leaves looked as though on fire, their edges blurred and flickering like flames. Miya thought this must have been it, so she stopped and turned to move towards the tiny grove.

"Not yet," a voice whispered—so close that she felt breath tickling her ear. Dark violet and black shadows crept around from behind her, licking the backs of her legs and sending a chill up her spine.

It was the Dreamwalker.

"Keep walking," the spirit hissed, and Miya chose to obey.

The Dreamwalker followed, tracing her every step. Miya didn't dare turn to look for fear the phantom might possess her. Instead, she traipsed silently through the woods, ignoring the eerie presence hovering behind her until once more, something caught her eye, and she thought she may have reached her destination.

Again, the Dreamwalker whispered, "Not yet."

Miya's breath caught, her body feeling suspended, like some force was holding her in place. She stumbled forward, disoriented as the forest warped around her. Objects and colours bled into one another until they were unrecognizable. Miya's senses were muted, rendered useless by the onslaught.

But her destination didn't change, no matter what happened, no matter how different everything around may have appeared. With the world spinning, Miya pushed onward, focused on a point in the distance until finally, she found herself at the willow tree—the only constant in this illusory maze.

In front of it stood a boy—no older than twelve—with short, midnight black hair that had a peculiar, feather-like sheen. His irises were inky black—so large they monopolized the entirety of his eyes. He was wearing a feathered cloak, not unlike the Dreamwalker's, and there was something painfully nostalgic about his presence. Miya realized he was the tiny figure from her first dream.

"Welcome," he said, the cloak resembling raven wings as he spread his arms.

Taking a step forward, Miya called out to the boy.

"Kafka?"

A sharp smile cut across his face—a frightening smile that looked like someone had taken a knife to his lips. Without answering, he turned and walked straight through the willow, disappearing from sight.

Miya chased after him, the Dreamwalker—now strangely tranquil—still at her heels. As Miya reached up to touch the willow, her hand moved directly through the trunk. The air stilled as time and space halted, and the forest fell away, dissipating like dew being wiped from a window. The willow dispelled before her.

Once through to the other side, she stood on a lake of still, clear water that seemed to stretch out infinitely with no land in sight. In the willow's place was a colossal, door- less red gate in the shape of a pi symbol, ornate carvings swirling around the massive, round wooden posts. Miya craned her neck to gauge the gate's size as she wondered how it could possibly stand on water—and how she could too.

She looked down, expecting to see her reflection, but the water was now murky and clouded. Nothing down there resembled her. In fact, she couldn't see anything at all.

"The mirrors of this world are different from the ones you make in yours," the gate told her in a serene, androgynous voice. The water around it rippled out with every word. "These mirrors show you exactly what you are. Your reflection is as it should be. At least for now."

Miya looked down again and discovered that the water was now a bottomless, white void. Nothing in this place made sense. The rational part of her wanted to escape —to return to a place where the rules of collective knowledge still applied. And yet, there was something here that felt like home. Should she have denied it merely because it didn't make sense?

And that, of course, was the trick. The First capitalized on the human desire for simple truths, for answers to questions that were all wrong to begin with. Miya had been so overwhelmed trying to orient herself in a world she assumed foreign, she didn't allow herself a moment to sink into the familiarity of it. This was no maze or prison; it was a sanctuary.

Miya's reveries triggered a tidal wave—a realization that would forever elude the corpses under the tyrannical king's watch: this place was the deepest part of her. Nestled in the darkest corners of the dreamscape, Miya had fallen asleep on a hill and found her own soul.

This was where she stopped.

"He promised me answers." She suddenly remembered their deal. "He promised to end this. To take me home."

"He will tell you nothing," said the gate. "But he doesn't have to. You can find the truth right here, reflecting from within you. All you have to do is look."

Miya turned her gaze towards the water a third time but again saw no reflection.

"Closer," the gate urged, so Miya got on her knees, placed her hands on the cool, wet sheet, and leaned in.

As she did, something fell from the sky, breaking the perfectly still surface. She gasped and pulled back as the water swelled. She could feel the tiny crescendo rolling beneath her feet until gradually, the ripples calmed, and an image began to form.

It was the Dreamwalker; she was staring back at Miya through her bone mask. On either side of her stood a man—their faces not yet clear. They were both the same height, the outline of their bodies revealing unruly, mane-like hair and a warrior's build. Miya focused on the image, but all that became clear were two distinct pairs of eyes: one red, and the other gold.

"This is it," she spoke to the reflection, then looked at the shadow with golden eyes. "There's nothing to wake up from." The Dreamwalker's lips moved in time with Miya's. "I'm not dreaming."

The shadow's lemony eyes narrowed, and Miya knew she'd won their wager.

"You just didn't want me to know who I really am, where I really belong." Her mind flashed back to the unconscious women littering the hills. "You made them think they were lost, that they needed your help getting back. But they were already home," she realized. "I'm home."

Miya reached out towards the perfectly still reflection in the water. As her fingers grazed the surface, she caught the red eyes flash with recognition, coming alive as they focused on her. A dark, spectral hand burst from the mirage and grabbed her wrist.

Miya cried out and fought to tear her arm back, but its grip was too powerful. Bits of shadow flaked away from the phantom's limb, passing through her like vapour. A deep, rumbling voice reverberated from all directions.

"As promised."

It was the last thing Miya heard before she was dragged under the water.

CHAPTER
FIFTY-ONE

MASON

MIYA WAS ENGULFED in violet and black flames. She remained unburnt as the fire flickered around her sleeping form. It licked her skin and haloed her hair, caressing her body in a loving embrace. Above her, a woman floated through the air—her face hidden behind a mask and her body cloaked in shining, iridescent feathers.

The Dreamwalker.

She was humming quietly to herself as she peered down at the comatose girl, then reached out to stroke her face.

Mason recognized her from his dream, and from the vision at the willow tree. She was the girl who had been driven out of the village by that shadow. She was different now—her face and figure obscured by her unusual garments, but he could still see the flow of her dark brown hair, identical to that of both previous apparitions.

She hovered over Miya, then leaned her face close to the unconscious girl and tilted her head like a curious magpie. She seemed at peace—yet the flames surrounding both women grew more ferocious with every passing moment.

Unable to tolerate the vision any longer, Mason turned away, scanning the room to see the bloody state of the battle. Kai too was enveloped by a dark mist. His eyes were red, his movements blurred as though he were amid a dream-like fog. In front of him were several of the townspeople, their faces distorted and their eyes blank as dark shadows sprang from their spines like tentacles, each one attached to something malevolent drifting around the entrance of the cabin. The villagers were all being controlled by the same entity.

Most of the guns were lost in the scuffle, broken or damaged by Kai and Ama. But there always seemed to be a weapon nearby. Jake, the man who Ama first confronted at the door, stumbled to his feet, his face swollen and bruised from the fight as he grabbed the last remaining rifle and swooned forward, pointing it straight at Kai.

"I'll kill you!" he raged in a voice that didn't sound human.

Mason felt like he was in a nightmare, the faces around him grotesque, twisted and misshapen—completely unrecognizable from the citizens of Black Hollow who had gathered in the church only days prior. Black, tarry blood oozed from their orifices as strangled, beast-like moans emanated from their throats. These were not ordinary people any longer. On the contrary, they looked like the monsters they believed themselves to be hunting.

And they weren't alone.

Dark shapes flickered across the wall—shadows cast by no object. They were frighteningly lifelike, undulating and rippling over the villagers' heads. It was as though they'd gathered from the other realm to spectate the battle with gratified sneers and thunderous laughter.

Mason squeezed his eyes shut. *This can't be real*, he thought. *It just can't be.*

From somewhere deep within, the little boy who stood by Aunt Lisa's bed as she took her last breath spoke up for the first time in decades.

But it is real, he whispered, at first meekly, then with urgency. *This is all real.*

You're just going to have to find your place in it.

When Mason opened his eyes again, the shadows were still there. Perhaps they'd always been there, and he'd only failed to notice.

Ama and a snarling Kai barricaded Miya's unconscious form.

"I won't huff, or fucking puff," Kai muttered through clenched teeth as he took a threatening step towards the throng of villagers. "I'll just burn you all to the ground."

The question of whether Kai Donovan was a man or a wolf struck Mason as foolish then. It was clearer than anything happening in the cabin; Kai was neither one nor the other. He was both man and wolf.

But Kai's advance was cut short by the deafening sound of a gunshot and the smell of burnt powder smoking from the barrel of Jake's rifle. Mason expected Kai to fall, but he gave them nothing but a throaty growl as he clutched his arm. The bullet had struck his shoulder, the force of the blow pushing him back as blood trickled down his arm and dripped from his fingers.

The villagers froze, the ringing from the gunshot fading into deafening silence. The wind outside howled until the walls sheltering them began to creak, the entire structure teetering.

Kai looked up with a menacing, blood-stained grin. "Who's afraid of the Big Bad Wolf?"

Mason's heart seized in his chest. Kai wasn't bluffing. The phantoms and the villagers, the wolf and the man—these were not two realities colliding; they were already a coherent whole.

Mason heard a sharp, disembodied laugh from behind him. It sounded like Miya—but when he spun around, he came face-to-face with the Dreamwalker, still hovering over the girl's body. Her lips stretched back as she brought a finger to her lips and silenced the young doctor with a single hush.

Everything grew calm and still before the storm struck. The door of the cabin tore open from outside, the Dreamwalker's laugh answered by a high-pitched caw that Mason recognized as a raven's. Was it the old man? Or the boy? He could only imagine that it was Gavran—and Gavran appeared to be many things. Mason swore he could hear the rustle of the willow tree's branches, its tiny emerald blades blowing inside with an ethereal glow. The villagers watched, hypnotized. Their arms went limp, and their weapons hit the ground in a series of hollow thuds. One of them gasped, about to release a blood-curdling scream when a black mass darted into the cabin. It was indeed a raven, slicing past the crowd towards Miya. The bird slowed before the Dreamwalker, beating its wings and landing on the phantom's outstretched arm.

Mason was dumbfounded. How could this animal perch on a spirit? The raven had always appeared so life-like, but perhaps it too was from another realm. Or at least, someplace in between. The raven's beak yawned open as its wings spread wide, and it chortled joyously, as though happy to be reunited with an old friend.

When one of the villagers regained his bearings and stepped towards them, the raven thrust out its head and released a low, threatening death rattle. It seemed to be protecting Miya, challenging anyone who dared approach.

Mason's eyes drifted back to the Dreamwalker. As though feeling his gaze, she turned to him and smiled like she was passing a secret. Her mischief had given way to something else—something gentle, perhaps even compassionate.

Mason's heart filled with grief. He finally understood. All this time he'd spent trying to prove the stories false only further cemented them in reality. If he was so confident they were fiction, why did he need proof? He had undertaken his own witch hunt; he was no different from the villagers he'd accused of destroying what they tried to protect. He wanted to shield his simple world, and in his efforts, he'd smashed it to pieces, leaving a vacuum for everything he thought impossible to take its place.

How had he not seen it? The truth was in front of him all along. It was the same as with any cancer treatment.

The poison was the cure.

Yet Mason had no time to dwell; the battle was not yet over. Shaking off their stupor, the villagers turned their attention back to Kai. As though smelling the blood from his wounds, they lunged like starved animals.

Kai brushed off their careless swings with ease, tearing his knife through bone and flesh alike. As he did, the shadows lifted from the villagers, erupting into murals of blood that licked the walls. The townsfolk went limp and fell to the floor as the remaining darkness bled out and whisked towards the Dreamwalker. Mason followed it with his eyes, watching as the rapidly dissipating blackness lashed out at her in what appeared to be one final attack. Yet having lost its substance, the shadow struck her like mist on a rock. It shattered into a thousand tiny particles, vanishing into the air.

Who are you, Mason found himself thinking, his lips barely moving to form the words.

With her free hand, the Dreamwalker reached up and traced the outline of her bone mask. Gripping the tip of the beak, she slowly pulled it aside.

Mason's vision clouded over, and the woman's face faded into darkness as he fell towards the ground.

"Did I not tell you..." echoed the voice of the old man and the boy in unison.

"...that everything beats in cycles."

CHAPTER

FIFTY-TWO

EVEN WITH HIS CLOSED EYES, Mason could see the hot glare of florescent lights as they blasted through his eyelids. He tried to speak, his voice hoarse and muffled as he realized something was cupping his mouth.

"Dr. Evans?"

It was a man's voice, calling to him from a distance.

"Dr. Evans? Can you hear me?"

The voice was close now. Someone pried his eye open, another white flash darting left and right across his visual field. He was able to focus in on the beeps, consistent like a metronome. Was he hooked up to a heart monitor?

"He's awake," the man said as Mason stirred. "Stop the oxygen."

He felt cool air against his face, the string that had been cutting into his cheeks finally giving way as the mask was removed. Slowly the room came into focus—white ceiling, white walls. It wasn't Annabelle's. It wasn't home.

"You're at the hospital," a gentle voice told him. It was familiar—young and sweet. "You sucked up a lot of smoke."

"Looks like he's stable." It was the man again. He recognized the name on the tag: Dr. Callahan. "I'll leave him to you."

As the figure in the white lab coat retreated from the room, another face came into view. "Damn it, Mason, I should have kept you home."

It was Annabelle, the lines of her face stricken with worry as she peered down at him.

"I'm sorry," he croaked. He tried to swallow, but his mouth was parched.

He looked past Annabelle to see Jazlyn marking something off on his chart, realizing she must have been the woman who spoke first.

Annabelle sighed shakily. "You had me worried sick. You were gone for days without a word."

Days? How many days? He was afraid to ask, afraid to even think about it. He looked around the room, taking in the brown bulletin board and the poster advocating for a medication he didn't recognize. "How'd I get here?"

Jazlyn put the chart down and came over to stand by the bed. "There was a forest fire. It was contained, but you were there when it happened. Firefighters found you unconscious on the ground."

The mention of fire sent a splitting jolt through Mason's skull. The Dreamwalker's face invaded him—the pandemonium he had been in the midst of.

"What happened to the search party?" he asked, squeezing his eyes shut to banish the memory.

The two women looked at one other, their expressions wary. "You were the only one they found," Jazlyn swallowed, "alive."

Mason's lethargy dissipated as he stared at them, searching for a hint that there was something more to be said, but neither of them so much as parted their lips. They simply stared back, concern written on their faces as they waited for him to react. Mason forced down the bile.

"I see."

He mentally thumbed through the people he'd met. They were all gone now, casualties in a war between gods. But why had he been spared? And what of Kai, Miya, and Ama? Were they safe?

Mason had never been so close to the edge, so intimate with Lady Death that he could feel her breath on his face. It was like honey laced with arsenic. He opened his mouth to speak only to find that some invisible force had him locked in a chokehold. His throat constricted, and his eyes stung like someone had poured lemon juice into them. Tears streamed down his face as the acid ate away his mask. His chest heaved as all the confusion that had taken root over the duration of his journey blossomed into something terrifying and exquisite—a hopeless reverence for feelings with no words to describe them, and a crushing awareness of the unknowability, the sheer futility, of his quest for credence.

The poison was the cure.

"I saw her...I saw her," he sobbed quietly as Annabelle rushed to comfort him, throwing her arms around his shoulders and stroking his hair.

And the wolf. Mason had always known the shadow under the willow was the wolf. Annabelle had told him as much; he just couldn't bear to accept it. The prospect of a magical world terrified him.

Jazlyn remained frozen. She likely never dreamed of seeing such a display from him.

"I'm sorry." He pulled back after the tears ran dry. "I'm all right, honestly."

When neither of them responded, he forced a smile. "Would you mind leaving me alone for a bit? I know you're worried, but I'm fine, I promise. I just can't believe I put you both through this."

"Don't you worry about us," Annabelle reassured him. "We're just glad to see you breathing." She smiled at Jazlyn, who nodded back as she gathered her shoulder bag under her arm.

"You know where to find us," she chirped.

Mason kept his eyes fixed on the ceiling. His mouth wouldn't form words, even as he tried to give her an inkling of acknowledgement. There was a pause before he heard them shuffling around, whispering something to one another as they left the room.

He was grateful for the silence, the quiet helping to calm some of the horror that still lingered in his bones. He tried to retrace his footsteps and recollect every instance in those woods, every decision that led to this moment. But it was all a jumble of madness and incoherence, and there was nothing he could do to fix that. He felt stranded on a plank of wood left floating in the middle of the ocean.

Had he been selfish? Had his idealism been wrong? He remembered Kai, crushing those men to protect Miya. And there was his superior—the tired old doctor he'd sneered at for being too afraid to care.

But maybe Kai and Dr. Lindman were right. They disowned idealism, forsook moral perfectionism, but at the end of the day, they accomplished what Mason couldn't: they saved lives.

Amanda might have lived twice as long had she been in the care of a jaded man more committed to grim truths than his own ego.

As for Mason's vacation—he was no closer to overcoming his grief than when he'd left home. He could still see Amanda's face; he could still feel the painful squeeze of loss deep in his chest.

But there was something besides the grief and the desperate scramble to be rid of it. Finally, he allowed himself to surrender to the humility grief demanded. He was done with Kai Donovan's blood, and he was done with the Dreamwalker.

Sitting up, Mason unhooked himself from the equipment and tested his limbs. He could still taste the smoke, but he ignored it. There was a world full of air he could breathe. He didn't have to remain in the haze just to check if he was suffocating.

Grabbing his clothes, he took his time dressing, then folded the hospital gown and left it on the edge of the bed. Glancing down at the admittance bracelet, he caught the name of the hospital curving around his wrist.

Ashgrove & District Hospital.

He tugged on the edge and tore it off.

"I think it's time to go home."

As he opened the door, he patted himself down to check for his wallet. It was exactly where he'd left it, though there was something else bulging from his coat pocket. Reaching in, Mason felt around for the triangular object, his fingers running over the familiar cracks. It was different now, smaller, one of the three sides more jagged than he remembered. It was broken, half of it missing.

He couldn't just banish Kai Donovan and the Dreamwalker. He'd tried with Amanda, and he'd failed. He wouldn't make the same mistake again. Pulling out the fractured stone, Mason sucked in a shaky breath. The Dreamwalker had taken off her mask and shown him her face. She had given him the truth he so desperately wanted. At last, Mason knew who she was: Miya, the girl from the village.

"Guess you're here to stay," he mumbled, then placed half of her favourite stone back in his pocket for safe-keeping.

As he stepped out of the room, there was a group of people passing in the adjacent hallway. Among the many bodies, he caught a glimpse of something familiar—a lock of white hair, stark against a dark leather jacket. Time went still. Amber eyes twinkled with mischief and plump, pink lips quirked in a knowing smile.

The jaws of the white wolf seized Mason by the throat. Her presence reminded him of the only truth he could ever be sure of—a truth that survived the question of whether wolves walked among men, of whether fairy tales leapt from storybooks and crept among alleyway shadows. It came at him like the plague from Pandora's Box, the final words spoken to him by a phantom living in the dark crevice of a fable.

Everything beats in cycles.

FIFTY-THREE

THE WOLF UNDER THE WILLOW

KAI

THE LAST THING Kai remembered was Miya's laugh—or at least, it was a woman who looked, smelled, and sounded like Miya. She was dancing over his lamb's body, devoured by flames. What happened afterwards was a blur.

As he raised his head from the leafy forest floor, he felt entirely at peace. Perhaps it was that the voice of Abaddon had finally quieted—and not in a manner that left Kai with the stink of foreboding. Perhaps it was the comfortable feeling of thick, black fur covering every inch of his flesh, or that he had a tail he could whip over his nose when it was cold. Or perhaps it was that the villagers were gone. He was in the forest, alone, and neither his wriggling nose nor his twitching ears detected danger for miles.

Jumping up on all four paws, Kai dropped his nose to the ground and took in the multitude of scents. He knew which one he was looking for. It was sweet as honey, but with a touch of tartness, like spiced apples. It was Miya's scent, and he knew he'd find it if he was patient. The forest was a living maze, especially here, in this foreign realm, and yet it was one that felt frighteningly close to home. He remembered crossing the threshold every now and again, often upon waking or falling asleep, often beneath the willow tree where he found himself without explanation. The willow always found him, and he always returned to its protective embrace.

The caw of a raven alerted Kai to its nearby presence, and he huffed in turn, hot air blowing out of his nostrils as he swished his tail in greeting. Shit-for-brains still knew where to find him, no matter how far he travelled. The raven, he had to admit, if nothing else, was a loyal nuisance. He canted his head and chortled, then rushed into the air with a beat of his wings.

Kafka. That was what she'd named the bird, at least in this life.

Kai began to wander, having no use of his eyes. His body and its long, slumbering memory knew where to take him.

Before long, he found himself in the glade with the willow tree. The soft breeze rustled the tiny emerald blades—a warm welcome as the tree's wispy limbs danced at seeing their old friend.

Kai stepped into the shade, his body transitioning seamlessly from one form to the other. He sat beneath the giant willow's canopy and looked towards the sky—an expanse of shimmering blues, violets, and pinks. For the first time, he loved that these eyes saw colour. Where the light was warmest, with shades of honey and azalea, a large, white sphere—both sun and moon—hung near the horizon.

Kai knew he'd have to wait. The hanging star would traverse the endless sky many times before the girl from the village would return. Even though he'd promised to find her, he knew seeking her out was not his place. Returning would be her decision alone.

But he would wait, nonetheless. And if she found her way back to him, he would fulfill the rest of his vow, and remain with her, as promised.

CHAPTER
FIFTY-FOUR
THE GIRL FROM THE VILLAGE

MIYA

When Miya opened her eyes, she was standing alone in front of the willow. The Dreamwalker was nowhere to be seen.

Miya almost missed her presence in the eerie silence of the dreamscape.

She looked up at the majestic tree, wondering just how ancient it was. She heard the red gate's voice whisper to her from somewhere within:

"Cut the seams of reality, and chaos is bound to spill out."

And Miya had spilled out along with it. She'd fallen into the part of the dreamscape where the willow tree resided—where its memories overflowed to all those who encountered it.

It wanted to tell her something.

After having stood guard in the forest for so long, watching the ebb and flow of time in complete silence, the willow's memories spanned centuries and realms far outside the framework of even the most unhinged mind. But there was one memory the willow was particularly fond of, one that it wanted to share with Miya: a memory of the distant past—her past. It was a fable drawn from the hearts of ancient spirits:

Long ago, there was a girl from a village who one day wandered into the woods. After becoming lost, she stumbled upon a majestic willow tree nestled deep in the labyrinth of the forest.

There, resting under its long, protective limbs, she found a black wolf. He lay injured and dying, his will to live having long left him. Taking pity on the poor beast, she fed him what little food she had and

nursed him back to health as best she could. With this small kindness, the wolf recovered. He thanked the girl by helping her find her way out of the forest so that she could return to her village. Then he disappeared back into the woods from whence he came.

Time went by, and every day, the wolf would sit under the willow, waiting to see if the girl would return. And every night when the moon would rise, he would howl as if calling to her, hoping that it would somehow guide her back. But autumn soon passed, and as snow blanketed the land, no humans entered the forest. It wasn't until the warmth of spring had thawed away the bitter winter ice that the girl wandered back into the woods in search of her old friend.

After circling through the maze many times, she finally came across the familiar glade. Only this time, there was no wolf.

There, sitting under the willow in place of the black wolf, was a man.

This memory, the willow told Miya, was its most cherished, but Miya could no longer tell if the story was being told to her, or if she was living the story herself. Gradually, she was pulled into the fable.

Miya was standing in the girl's place. Or perhaps, she was the girl. She and the girl were one and the same—the original spirit—united as Miya walked in her own footsteps at long last. And as she did, she finally began to understand: a Dreamwalker was someone who could walk through other realms. But not every girl murdered by her family and community was a Dreamwalker, nor were any of them spirited away by her. They were just innocent women who happened to wander too far from home.

The only person who was ever spirited away by the Dreamwalker was the Dreamwalker herself, fighting to awaken.

Rousing from an eternal slumber, Miya finally remembered...

She chose to leave; she wanted to be lost in these woods, and now she was finally home.

She won the devil's wager. She beat the First at his own game, and she'd finally broken the cycle.

She looked up and saw a raven perched on the crooked limb of a white oak.

"Am I dead, Kafka?"

The raven swooped towards the ground and erupted into dark, effervescent swirls that gradually dissipated to reveal a boy with hair like crows' feathers and eyes black as ink—the boy from her dreams.

"No," said Kafka-the-boy as he plucked a stray feather from his cloak. "Dreams are not death." He reached into the shroud, fishing around before placing in her hand a bright, iridescent stone that shimmered with deep purples, meadow greens, and sunset golds. It appeared to be broken, but beautiful nonetheless. "You are simply home."

Miya smiled at her feathered friend—a silent thanks. She could feel the stone's familiar power humming against her hand as she clutched it tightly.

Kafka moved out of the way, bowing as he cleared her path towards the willow. Miya continued on her way, confident they would see more of each other soon.

As she approached the willow, a gentle wind parted the swaying branches, revealing a man's figure. He was sitting still as stone, leaning back against the imposing trunk. Miya knew he was waiting for her.

As she passed under the willow's canopy, she was finally able to meet his gaze. He smiled at her, the moonlight catching his mahogany eyes and illuminating that haunting red tint she knew so well. Slowly, he reached out to her, and this time, she reached back without hesitation, taking his hand and allowing him to pull her in. Miya fell as she'd never fallen before—without caution or restraint. She was exactly where she wanted to be, cocooned in familiar warmth as he buried his nose in her hair and inhaled. He began to speak—a language she'd never heard before—and yet she understood every word.

"You've strayed too far from the flock again, Lambchop."

Triumph tugged at Miya's lips, and she smiled as the words echoed through her spirit, and far into the ages. People are, after all, creatures of habit.

ACKNOWLEDGMENTS

First and foremost, this book would not have been possible without the amazing guidance of two outstanding people: Jaimee and Malorie. Jaimee— you took my dumpster-fire of a first draft and taught me how to turn it into something truly great. Thank you for believing in my work and for always giving me the extra push I need. And to my cheer- leader, Malorie, who suffered through three drafts of my monster-baby and kept me sane when I was at the end of my rope. Thank you for re-tweeting me through all those nerve-wracking pitch contests, for supporting me, and for tolerating my every minute update.

Thank you, Hannah, for years of caffeine-fueled rage-fests in McDonald's parking lots. You've been my partner in crime since my fledgling days as a writer and have helped me iron out countless plot holes. I think Navi and Suki would be pleased with the quantity of chicken nuggets we've devoured over the last decade.

Von—I owe you decades of sleep. I will never forget the nights we spent brainstorming ideas—some of them absurd

and some of them brilliant. The depth of your imagination remains truly terrifying. You've done Gavran proud.

Thank you, Brenton, for being my closest confidant, for reading my drafts, for listening to my infernal ramblings, for always lending an ear through all the rejections and dashed hopes, and for celebrating my every success with more jubilance than my black heart could muster over a lifetime.

Laura, thank you for being my yes-man, for giving me much needed insight, and for helping me fix the opening pages of my book. Your keen eye has been invaluable, and you knew what was bothering me better than I did.

Thank you, Julie, for opening my eyes to a whole new way of knowing. Your wisdom has submerged me in an ocean of inspiration and gifted me a new lens through which to see the world.

To my beta readers: Stu, Stephanie, Bethany, and Jack- son. Your feedback and affirmations have been lifesavers. Thank you for being thorough, thoughtful, and for helping me improve my work. You are all gems!

And last but certainly not least, thank you to the Parliament House team —Amanda, for choosing this book among the many in your slush pile; Shayne, for designing the most stunning cover I never could have conjured; Chantal, for managing the entire editorial process; and to the editors, for putting up with my tome-length emails and poring over this beast multiple times. Thank you for making dreams come true.

Finally, to my readers, remember: Stories aren't told to convey the facts. They're told to convey the truth.

MIYA AND KAI'S JOURNEY CONTINUES IN...
THE ECHOED REALM

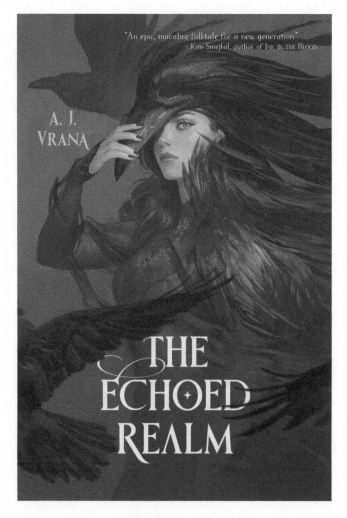

TURN THE PAGE FOR A SNEAK PEEK OF BOOK TWO IN THE CHAOS CYCLE
DUOLOGY.

CHAPTER
ONE

MIYA

THE STREET WAS as empty as the eye of a storm. Save for the wind scattering autumn leaves over cracked asphalt, a lone young woman stood in the middle of the road. Her long, dark brown hair whipped around her face, and her muddy green eyes prickled from the sharp cold that howled at her to go home.

Home, however, was a long way from here.

She canted her head at the sound of a shrill cry echoing through the vacant night. A mass of black feathers and a sharp, curved beak entered her periphery. Talons dug into her shoulder, but the animal trilled contentedly.

"Hey, Kafka." Miya scratched the raven's breast, enjoying his silky plumage.

He squawked back, beating his wings as he clung to her.

Miya trained her gaze on the house up ahead. Lily-white paint chipped from the rickety panelling, and the bumpy driveway, with its patchy interlocking and overgrown weeds, reminded her of a world she longed to forget. But Summersville, West Virginia was no Black Hollow. A faded, grey sign was splayed on the lawn, the text barely discernable: *As seen on—*

Ghostventures.

America loved its ghosts. Amateurs armed with EVPs and electromagnetic readers went barging into people's homes, yelling taunts and expecting answers. Did they think proof of the supernatural would keep the demons at bay?

Truth was never an antidote—only a drug too short in supply to meet the demand.

Taking a deep breath, Miya clutched the pendant that hung around her neck—a copper raven with its talons contoured over the top of an iridescent stone. The dream stone—a piece of it, anyway.

As she started up the porch steps, her companion flew away and perched on the blackened compass atop the roof. Kafka-the-boy—the one who'd gifted her the labradorite—had been absent from the dreamscape for three long years, but she suspected he was watching through Kafka-the-raven. He always stayed close.

"It'll be ok," she whispered to herself. "You've dealt with much worse."

Refusing to use the ghastly colonial doorknocker—a brass lion's head clutching an ornate hoop between its jaws—she rapped on the door three times before it swung open.

The woman who answered looked like she'd stumbled back from the afterlife or was on her way there. The only sign of animation was the bare look of surprise on her face as she took in her visitor.

"Are you the..."

"I'm the witch," Miya cut to the chase. She didn't have the patience for dishonest terms like *medium*, *psychic*, or *empath*. Strictly speaking, she wasn't a *witch* either, but it was the closest thing to her true nature that people understood. Outside of Black Hollow, no one knew who the Dreamwalker was.

"R-Right," the woman stammered. "I'm Dawn. We spoke earlier?"

Miya strained a smile, and the corners of her lips felt like they were chapping. "I remember. I take it the *Ghostventures* crew didn't help?"

"No, they didn't." The door whined as she opened it further. "Please, come inside."

Dawn's slouched shoulders obscured her otherwise robust figure. Miya wondered if she was having trouble eating; her clothes hung loose, and her cheeks sagged. Her light brown hair was parched, peppered with silver strands that almost looked gold against the dim orange light of the hall.

"I'm sorry it's so cold in here." She wrung her knobby hands as she led Miya towards the kitchen. "The heat's technically working, but it's just... always so cold."

"Asshole spirits will do that," Miya mumbled. She clutched her dark mauve leather jacket around her sides and lifted the hood over her head. It helped her stay focused when she knew she was surrounded by malevolence. Dawn took a seat at the table and rubbed her arms with a sigh.

"It started a year ago, when my husband got his new job. We were struggling, and this house was such a steal. We figured it was because the town was small, too far from any major cities, but strange things began to happen almost right away."

Miya helped herself to the chair across from her client. "Weird noises? Bad dreams?"

"The noises didn't bother me." Dawn fiddled with a wine bottle that'd been left on the table, then poured herself a glass. She'd obviously been finding ways to cope. "But the dreams...My husband, Greg, didn't think they were a big deal. He thought I was being dramatic, or that I had a sleep disorder."

Miya snorted; the narrative was almost cliché. "It's always the husband who won't believe."

Dawn hesitated, then nodded slowly. "I suppose so." She offered a tepid smile. "So, are you really a witch?"

Miya curled her fingers under her palm. "Sort of. I don't worship the devil or eat kids if that's what you're asking."

Dawn's voice grew quieter. "Do you believe in the devil?"

Miya caught her client's gaze. "I believe in far worse."

Dawn bowed her head and clutched the cross around her neck. "Anyway, the dreams kept getting worse—more vivid. Most nights, it felt like I hadn't slept at all. A few times, I woke up elsewhere, in the basement or the backyard. I did what Greg asked and went to see a doctor, but my test results came back normal. Nothing was wrong with me, so I figured it must be the house."

"Why not move?" Miya asked.

"Greg refuses." Dawn's voice fractured, frustration bubbling to the surface like boiling water licking the lid of a pot. "It's like he's waging war against this *thing*, only he doesn't even believe in the thing he's fighting!"

"And what do you think this *thing* is?"

"I-I don't know. Our church preaches that spirits aren't real. There's heaven and hell. Nothing in between." Dawn covered her face with her hands, her shoulders trembling. "But I know it's real, no matter what my faith says."

Miya's heart clenched. She could feel this woman's pain, and it sundered whatever distance she'd worked to keep. "I believe you," she whispered. "Even if you moved, there's no guarantee *it* wouldn't follow."

Dawn's breath drew in. "Is it a ghost?"

Miya shook her head, scanning the room. Claw marks were etched into the wall, revealing the entity's path. "Ghosts are human spirits. This one's not, and it isn't friendly, either. To tell you the truth," she stood and reached into her back pocket, "I've been hunting this one for a while."

This was her life now—not out of choice but out of necessity. Miya never could have imagined just how many malicious spirits preyed on people in their dreams, and as the Dreamwalker, she was in a unique position to help them. She enjoyed it, but it wasn't altruistic. The monsters haunted her too.

A crack, jagged like lightning, splintered the drywall, oozing something black and tarry. A low, wet gargle reverberated through the kitchen.

"It's happening!" Dawn yelped, knocking over her chair as she jumped up.

Miya's hand steadied on her back pocket. She glared down the fissure in the wall—or rather, a fissure in the seam of reality.

"Dawn," Miya said evenly. "Get behind me and stay in cover."

The older woman scrambled to the other side of the kitchen and ducked behind a cabinet. Grateful Dawn didn't peek, Miya pulled a single playing card from her jeans.

It was the king of spades, copper stains marring him from a nightmare long ago.

She threw it down, face-up, and unsheathed a hunting knife strapped to her belt. "I didn't think we'd do this here," she called to the spirit, and it answered with a ferocious roar that ruptured the drywall around the blackened rift.

Miya winced as she dragged the blade across her palm. Clenching her fist, blood ribboned around her fingers and speckled the card on the floor.

She grinned into the oncoming void. "Long live the king."

Wisps of black mist slithered upward and coalesced into the shape of a man.

The house rumbled in dissent, and the border between Dawn's world and the dreamscape pulled taught. Something sinister was lurking.

Normally, Miya had to lie down and let her spirit descend into the dreamscape, but the demon spared her the effort and shunted her wholly across realms. The quaint kitchen, decorated in canary yellows and smelling of fresh casserole, stilled like a film on pause. The lemony hues melted to muddy browns. Tables and chairs fused into ghoulish shapes. A vase levitated from the crumbling windowsill, then hurtled towards her.

The man made of smoke extended an arm, clipping the vase just enough to slow it down. Miya stepped aside, watching, unfazed, as it drifted past her nose and dissipated.

The house was gone. Miya found herself in a sea of black fog, the laminate counter and spring-coloured backsplash sinking like sand through an hourglass. The plywood chimera, fused from fragments of domestic life, roiled in the dark. Its misshapen wooden joints screeched painfully as it tottered away. The stench of sulfur wafted with the haze, and Miya clamped her jaw to keep from retching. The spirit's true form glinted up ahead. With the dream stone glowing against her chest, the darkness parted around its lavender light. She could see a silhouette: an imposing figure with long, slender limbs and fingers that dangled like knives.

"Are you the dream demon that calls itself Drekalo?" Miya stopped several feet from the grotesque creature, spindle-like with a head too large for its elongated neck. Its dappled skin was a chalky grey, scaly and splintered like a stone gargoyle.

The phantom's jaw unhinged, and it released a bone-shattering shriek, its sharp teeth bound only by strings of thick, red saliva.

"How did you come here, witch?" its reptilian voice quivered.

"It doesn't matter how. I needed more time."

"You can't kill me," Drekalo slavered. "This is the dreamscape, where all is timeless. Death doesn't exist here."

Miya regarded the demon, then shrugged. She was waiting for the man made of smoke to become flesh and blood. Slipping off her leather jacket, she watched as it evaporated into the fog. When the last specs of mauve disappeared, she turned to the demon.

Throwing her arms back, she cut across the expanse. Her hand shot out to wrap around Drekalo's throat. His gangling body careened to the side, but he couldn't escape. Violet swirls enveloped Miya, then erupted into a billowing cloak of spectral feathers. A raven beak made of bone drew over her face, black and purple bleeding onto the ivory like oil mixing with water. The bottom edge of the mask cut over her lips in a sharp V, and she flashed the demon a wicked smile.

"Let's take you somewhere death exists."

Drekalo gasped—the start of a protest that never came. Miya hauled Dawn's tormenter into the in-between—a sliver away from either realm. She could see the faint outline of the kitchen—all blurry lines and morphing shapes floating behind an ethereal curtain. The in-between was neither here nor there; it was a cell, trapping the demon where he couldn't roam.

The bars to this cell were open to the blade, and the executioner always struck from the earthly plane.

The demon shrieked and flailed as Miya released him. "Y-You're no witch!" His voice sounded garbled. "You're—"

Drekalo's accusation died in his mouth when a knife was thrust through his throat, then twisted for good measure. The man, it seemed, had finally arrived, and he'd reclaimed his beloved weapon.

The fissure in the wall sutured shut, and Miya returned to Dawn's kitchen. She snatched up the half-full wine glass from the table and raised it in a toast.

Wiping his hunting knife, slick with black viscera, Kai turned to the Dreamwalker. He took the glass from her and spilled its contents onto the floor, then tossed the delicate crystal aside. Tilting Miya's chin up, he swooped down and stole a kiss before she could say the words. He pulled back, grinning rakishly, and said them in her stead.

"Long live the fucking king."

MIYA STILL NEEDS YOU

Did you enjoy The Hollow Gods? *Reviews keep books alive!*

*Help Miya by leaving your review on
Goodreads or the digital storefront of your choosing. She thanks you!*

ABOUT THE AUTHOR

A. J. Vrana is a Serbian-Canadian academic and writer from Toronto, Canada. She lives with her two rescue cats, Moon- stone and Peanut Butter, who nest in her window-side bookshelf and cast judgmental stares at nearby pigeons. Her doctoral research examines the supernatural in modern Japanese and former-Yugoslavian literature and its relationship to violence. When not toiling away at caffeine-fuelled, scholarly pursuits, she enjoys jewelry-making, cupcakes, and concocting dark tales to unleash upon the world.

WWW.THECHAOSCYCLE.COM

facebook.com/AJVranaAuthor
twitter.com/AJVrana
instagram.com/a.j.vrana